Jess,

Always fight fascism

Thanks for the follow, and

I hope you enjoy!

THE CLOCKWORK EMPIRE

LUCAS J.W. JOHNSON

Fireside
FICTION COMPANY

Boston, Mass.

Published by Fireside Fiction Company
Boston, Mass.

Fireside
FICTION COMPANY

Firesidefiction.com
ISBN: 978-1-7341549-6-2

To Ken
You make my heart tick

Remaker, Remaker

Day 1

I've remade things before, but I never thought I'd get the opportunity to do *this*.

My name is Martin Fullius. I received my PhD in Engineering and Thaumaturgy at the Imperial Londinium College at Oxford. I am a certified free-lance remaker. This is a journal of my latest work—for my own records, and for the historical record should I be successful.

It began this morning. I returned to my lab after an uneasy night to continue my private research. The sky was grey, as usual, making it difficult to see the Imperial Skystation that's been docked over the city for two weeks now, doing Jupiter-only-knows-what. I'm grateful for the clouds.

There were children playing outside in the rain, singing.

Remaker, Remaker, make me a hand...

They play at remaking often, a game they call "Remaker and Remade." Being the remade is always the preferable role.

When I entered the lab, he was waiting for me. A pristine black suit, a high-collared cloak, hair so blonde it's almost white, slicked back with oil. His features pointed, a stark intelligence in his eyes. His accent told me he was from Rome. He'd come a long way.

I asked him how he got in, but his only response was to offer me a job. He knew my work—finesse with clockwork, hands with exceptional manual dexterity, legs with exceptional strength. The veteran soldiers whose missing limbs I replaced with weaponized prosthetics, the entire contubernium of new recruits I outfitted with grafted crossbows last year, the athletes who competed for the privilege of my designs so they could take part in the upper echelons of competition. But he also knew my other work, my personal research, my secret projects. He knew that my grants were running out. He offered to sponsor me, patronize me.

He offered me anything and everything I needed to focus entirely on my research with no need for outside commissions.

I gave him the only answer I could.

Day 2

His name was Servius. I realize in my excitement that I neglected to mention it, despite the fact that I found it odd he only gave a praenomen.

He came again today to deliver his starting funds. It's enough denarii to keep me working for a month.

I can only assume he works for the Imperial Philosopher's Council. Where else would he get that kind of money?

The children are playing outside again. They distract me from my work.

Remaker, Remaker, make me an arm...

Such a trifle. Attach basic clockwork to existing muscles. Add an engine for extra power, if desired. I've made dozens.

It's nothing to what he wants.

Day 4

I want to get right into the application, but of course that's impossible. There's so much preliminary research to be done, and I've barely scratched the surface in my sparse free time.

Servius said he can get me resources; he has access to books I could never get on my own. It must be the Council. I gave him a shopping list of famous texts—P. Serrelius Cato's *On the Application of Clockwork*; C. Cornelius Wyrfyr's *Thaumaturgy: Technology, Biology, and the Forces of Nature*; Jean Claudius's *Philosophy of Steam*; William Pound's *Difference Engine*. I doubt he'll be able to get half of them.

Day 5

He returned already. He brought every book on the list.

Day 15

I have become engrossed in my research. My laboratory looks like Alexandria after it was sacked—codices and rolls strewn everywhere, held open to certain pages and stuffed with bookmarks; notes and diagrams pinned to every available surface, layers of them scattered over tables and floor; pens and ink stains everywhere. I haven't even touched a gear yet—the theory must be sound before I even attempt application.

Remaker, Remaker, make me a leg...

I cannot. I am too busy.

Day 31

Servius returned today to check on my progress. He seemed impressed, though I detected impatience in his eyes. He will have to wait.

Day 37

I've done as much as I can. I have a starting point, but now it requires testing. I've ordered a vast number of supplies—tiny gears, engines and tubes and valves, springs and wires and pumps.

My difference engine broke yesterday, and I had to complete my final calculations by hand. The numbers have become so familiar that it hardly mattered. But I've ordered a new one. What's a few hundred denarii when you're on the government's bill?

Day 41

After struggling with my designs, I've realised the flaw in my plans. I have little hands-on experience with anatomy other than bones and muscle. I need to learn more, and more textbooks are not enough. I've asked Servius for bodies—he must have connections with the morgue, and corpses are used by the Council for research all the time. I need to study the organs, how they connect and interact.

Remaker, Remaker, make me a heart...

I am trying.

Day 53

My work has advanced in leaps and bounds. Servius provided me with several cadavers, and the autopsies I performed have given me so much better understanding—I've studied anatomy before, of course, but never so intimately, never with my purpose so clearly in mind.

The way in which everything is connected astounds me. Nothing works independently, each system feeding and being fed by each other system. If I am to replicate an organ, I must have this same interconnectivity or the whole body will fail.

Day 61

If only I could see the organs at work, then perhaps I could understand their connections—I could see not just that they feed each other, but exactly *how* one feeds another.

I can't design a system I don't fully understand.

Day 63

I voiced my concerns to Servius.

He told me to pack my laboratory, that he could better serve my needs in Rome itself.

I think he smiled when he said it.

Day 66

We're flying across the Channel right now. I can see the continent looming over the grey water. The hum of the engine fills my mind, and I cannot concentrate. It's worse than the singing children.

My entire life fits in this airship. And it's mostly research.

Servius promises me that I'm getting somewhere. I want to believe him.

Day 85

I've finally been set up in Rome. The city is cleaner than Londinium, to my surprise—at least in this quarter. I can see the blue sky through the smog. I can see the Colosseum from my laboratory, too. Servius tells me they hold bouts of remade fighters on the day before kalends each month, that the sound of the crowds can be heard even from here.

I can imagine the competing remakers, designing more powerful arms, large engines to be carried by the gladiators, more sophisticated mounted weaponry.

But each one is restricted—the grafted limbs, the steam engines and clockwork parts are only as strong as the gladiator's body can handle. But what if the body itself is remade? Their capacity for power increased?

A remade heart is not just steam and gears. It's not just a philosophical breakthrough. It's power.

Day 89

Servius brought me the first subject today.

His name is Proculus. He's a soldier from the 43rd Legion. His lung was badly damaged in a battle against the Ottomans. He will die within the month.

And so, he has offered himself to my cause.

Day 92

I have done what I can non-invasively. Proculus has insisted that I go further. He wants me to cut him open, observe the organs first-hand. He insists that he will die anyway, and he'd rather help me with my research than die without a cause.

I'm not sure I can do it. The procedure will likely kill him. Does Dis care if he would die anyway?

Day 97

I have accomplished nothing since I performed the procedure on Proculus. It was the most informative study I have ever performed—I could see how the blood travelled from system to system, how the heart pumps it through its chambers and around the body so efficiently, so quickly before returning.

He did not live long. The heart is so necessary; the blood gives life to everything else.

There was so much blood.

Day 98

Servius brought me another subject.

Claudius is another dying soldier. A foul growth has attached onto his liver and is quickly destroying it—he is unfit for battle, and will soon be unfit for anything but the gods.

I told Servius I wasn't sure I could do it. He reminded me that

Claudius would die anyway, and that if I succeeded, I could prevent the deaths of hundreds.

What choice do I have? Proculus gave me so much. I'm forming theories, crafting models. I think it will be possible.

Day 114

I have examined and tested ten soldiers now, each dying from a different condition. I stopped asking their names.

I have enough research now. I can begin a working model.

Day 143

It has taken me some time, but I believe it will work. It's only a test model, of course—certainly refinements will have to be made.

My work was assisted greatly when Servius brought me an apprentice, some time ago. He is a young nobleman, Greek, working off indentured servitude. He is a brilliant philosopher, and has a real knack for thaumaturgy, though he is physically weak.

My model must be tested now. I have asked Servius for another soldier.

Day 147

What a catastrophic failure. My device could not sustain the body's systems. It must be refined.

Day 156

The refined model fared much better, though the soldier still died. I fear that a dying system is not the best testing ground.

Day 158

Servius bought me an old slave. He lacks the flaws of the dying soldiers.

Day 163

I am close. Three slaves have died by my hands, but I am close. Their bodies were too weak.

Day 165

I no longer believe Servius works for the Council. I sent a clock-work spy after him yesterday, after he delivered another slave. I wasn't able to learn much, but he seemed to avoid government buildings like the Plague. His money certainly doesn't come from there.

Day 167

The slave screamed as he died. The steam engine burned his insides.

Something that he screamed concerned me. I'm not sure he was really a slave.

Day 173

My apprentice has been avoiding me when I run tests. I believe I now know why—his heart is weak. I think Servius wants me to remake him—make him my project, my success.

But I'm not ready yet.

There are children outside my window. How interesting that the same children's rhymes of Londinium exist in Rome.

Remaker, Remaker...

Day 179

The children were outside again yesterday.

My tests have not been working. I needed someone young, someone without the flawed systems of the adults Servius has brought me.

But the clockwork couldn't sustain his small body.

Day 204

I don't know where he gets the people. I don't care anymore. They are young and strong. They all die screaming.

I am on the verge.

Day 217

I am ready. Ready to remake my apprentice.

Day 220

I never knew such success could be wrapped in such failure.

His heart and left lung have been replaced by clockwork and steam pumps. The systems interact, the blood flows, and he lives.

I assume he lives. As soon as he rose, he struck out at me. I think he cracked a rib. Such strength from that new heart.

He disappeared.

When Servius returned, he was furious. I tried to explain that it had been a success, but he was concerned only with the apprentice. I do not understand it.

Now he has forsaken me. He, too, has disappeared, and I assume with him my funding. I will not be able to pay for the lab. Soon, I won't be able to afford food.

I look around my ruined laboratory. Machinery is strewn everywhere, broken or only half-completed. The boy destroyed much when he left. Steam billows from my generator, impotent. The difference engine won't calculate. Books are ruined. Blood stains every surface.

I sit here in near-silence, and I wonder what I have done.
Children sing outside my window.
Remaker, Remaker, make me a soul...
That I cannot do.

PART 1

Chapter 1: Blood

JULIAN

*R*emaker, Remaker, make me a key to these chains…
And in a way, he had.

Julian had woken to a faint *tick, tick* that he felt more than heard, and a pain that radiated from his chest throughout his body. And he'd woken to blood.

The doctor had stood over him, pensive, when he stirred. His smile, slowly breaking as he realized his success, was short-lived. Julian had lashed out instinctively, like a caged animal.

Now Julian stumbled through the streets of Rome. He was still addled by the poppy juice that had been slipped into his drink. He couldn't remember where he was, which direction to run.

His mind may have still been addled, but the pain wasn't being held back. His chest burned. Felt heavy.

He knew what was there, though he hadn't yet let himself look. He'd wrapped a coat around himself when he ran out of the workshop. He'd run so far already.

And he wasn't tired.

He'd run for blocks, past warehouses and tiny shops and people going about their business—had they stared at his passing? He didn't know—and yet he wasn't tired.

He finally stopped, down an alleyway. Dropped a bag on the ground—he'd grabbed it on his way out, stuffed it with papers and whatever was on the desk, some part of his mind needing supplies or evidence or something. He sank back against a wall.

But his breathing came slowly, calmly. No panting. No wheezing and rasping. No racing pulse from the run.

His hand moved instinctively to check his heartbeat, to feel for the telltale signs of a problem.

He recoiled when it touched warm metal.

When Julian was born, the only son of a family of landed nobles in the Southern Greek Province, one of the slave girls was also birthing a boy. The good timing, attributed by Matron Maria to the kindness of Juno, allowed the slave girl to be Julian's wet nurse. Moreover, the family decided that her son would be Julian's own servant. Soon after their births, though, Julian sickened, barely surviving a wracking pneumonia that left his body weak and his heart damaged.

He never fully recovered. He never grew strong, as he grew up.

So the slave boy Gaius became his guardian as well.

There was a window nearby, facing into the alley. Julian approached it slowly, his footsteps unsteady even as his blood pumped with such calm regularity.

The face in the reflection was sweaty, haunted. His hair ragged. A smear of blood on his cheek.

He didn't care about that. Slowly, he opened the coat he'd thrown over himself.

His chest glinted brass back at him in the reflection. A finely hammered sheet of metal embedded in his thin body, fused with his flesh, covering his entire left side. A pressure gauge sat in place of his pectoral. A translucent window showed gears ticking methodically within, regulating the pumps and the release of steam that now powered him.

Thaumaturgy moving through the fine systems.

A dribble of blood seeped from a seam where the metal met flesh. The edges were searing pain, the dulling of poppy wearing off.

Julian stared at it, the line of blood falling slowly down across his belly. He couldn't look away.

Then he saw another face in the window. Inside. Staring.

Julian jumped, pulled the coat back over his chest, grabbed the bag off the ground, and ran.

What had they done to him?

He hadn't wanted the doctor's hands on him. Not after what he'd seen the doctor do. It had started innocently enough—but even then, there was always so much blood. Then the soldier. Then the children— Martin had tried to hide those. Julian had known.

But he'd had no escape.

Until now. Until the doctor had turned his attention to him.

Julian had known it was coming. He'd figured out what the goal was. What Servius wanted for him.

But the doctor's hands were stained with blood that would never come out.

So Martin Fullius had slipped the poppy into his drink. And with it, the key to Julian's cage.

He ran, and his heart did not tire.

The remaker had made Julian strong.

When they were children, they were always together. Gaius was a strong, active boy, but when Julian was forced to stay indoors for his health, Gaius stayed with him. They read, or played games together. They spent hours and days exploring the old tunnels beneath the villa, hiding from angry parents—or, more likely, servants and maids. They became friends immediately, never strayed from that friendship. To them, it didn't matter that Gaius was a slave. Julian never ordered him around. He was a friend, and Julian treated him that way. He was part of the family.

To their parents, however, things were different. Julian's mother would never let Julian forget who he was.

"You are the son of the Praefectus Meridianus Graecus, Julian. You are destined for great things. You have people who will do anything you ask because it is your right." Then she'd turn to Gaius, sitting nearby. "Boy! It's getting damp. Fetch Julian a blanket."

Gaius had to obey.

But for Julian, he would have done it anyway.

The two boys schooled together along with the other noble children of the town. A tutor was hired from Italy to instruct them in the usuals: history, Latin, rhetoric, geography, mathematics, law. Julian was smart, taking quickly to philosophy, politics, and language, while Gaius more easily grasped the less theoretical subjects like geography and history. They each helped where the other lagged.

The boys helped each other in different ways as well.

"Hey, Julian! Come and play in the rain! Or won't your slave boy let you?"

"He can't. He'll get sick and die if he gets wet."

"Splash him, splash him!"

"I hear he even needs his little slave boy to wash him!"

Gaius had heard enough. "Bugger off!"

"Yeah? What're you gonna do, slave boy? You hurt us, we'll have you flogged!"

Gaius made a move to attack anyway, but Julian stopped him. "Gaius, don't. They're right. They'll hurt you." His breath rattled in his throat; his chest was starting to hurt.

Gaius stopped, but hurled words right back at the schoolboys. "Yeah, well, at least he has the help. Or do you like your little cloud of flies, Alex? And Helephes, I hear the Delphic Oracle predicted your birth—told your mother she'd have a new pig on the property!"

"Gaius—" Julian wheezed. The pain was increasing, like a vise around his small chest.

"No, they can't say that and get away with it. Hey Quintus, how's your dad? I hear he spends more time at the stables than his own bedchamber, but the boys there said it wasn't for them. He buggering the horses, then?"

"Gaius—"

"I'll show them," Gaius began, then turned and saw Julian. He'd fallen to the ground, hand on his chest. He felt cold. He tried speaking again, but nothing came out.

Gaius's eyes widened and he ran to Julian's side. "Jules, you okay?" Julian tried to respond, but couldn't. "Help! Someone get help!"

He felt a hand on his chest—Gaius feeling for a heartbeat.

As Julian began to slip into blackness, he felt Gaius begin to pound on his chest. "Beat, damnit!" Tears were in Gaius's eyes. He leaned over, put his mouth to Julian's, forced air into his lungs, pumped harder at his heart. "Come on, Jules! Come back to me!"

When the doctor arrived, running, Julian gave a gasp and began to breathe again. Gaius sank to the ground beside him, exhausted, held him close in relief. "I'm so sorry," he whispered.

They were eleven.

But Julian was alone now. He had been for over a year. Since he was taken from his family, his home. Since Servius took him in.

He wondered what had become of Gaius. The boy who'd been with him his whole life. Disappeared into the aether when it all came crashing down.

Julian had been so powerless to stop it. He hoped he'd at least saved Gaius.

He continued to run through the alleyways of Rome, though his pace slowed now. He didn't feel tired, wasn't gasping for breath as even a long walk would have left him before. But his legs had started to hurt. They couldn't keep up with the heart. Not yet.

He'd watched the doctor work on limbs. Helped, even. Learned the basics of thaumaturgical theory. He wondered what it would be like to replace his legs. He'd already replaced his heart. He could replace his whole body, become a machine.

Maybe then he'd forget the blood.

He almost ran right into a legionary.

"Whoa there, friend. What're you running from?"

Julian froze. Were they looking for him? Had the doctor called the guard already? Had Servius found out what had happened?

He turned away, tried to keep moving. But the legionary grabbed his shoulder.

Julian panicked. Spun around. Lashed out at the soldier.

The man, twice Julian's size with steel grafted to one arm, was pushed back hard, tripped over his own feet, and landed on his rear with a grunt.

Julian looked at his hands.

He was strong now. The thaumaturgical lacings that bound this heart to his flesh—it couldn't work in a body that couldn't keep up.

He looked at the stunned legionary.

And he ran.

The man called after him, but he didn't stop, clutching his bag to his chest like it would hide the brass and steam from the world. He took turns at random, running carelessly through Rome.

He was strong in a way he'd never been before. He was alone, but he could protect himself now. Maybe he could survive, alone.

Then he emerged from an alley into bright sunlight. Crowds and voices and buildings towering over him.

He'd run into the Forum.

They were fifteen. Julian had harboured secret thoughts for months—thoughts he was "entitled" to but shrank from, unsure, unwilling to risk alienating his only friend.

"Jules?" A knock on his door. Gaius's voice.

"Come in," Julian called. He lay in bed still, naked under the covers, the curtains closed against the bright day. Shivers and sweats had been trading places through the night; he was finally feeling better, but he had no desire to leave bed yet, not if it meant facing other people.

He did want to get outside, though, and go to the shooting range his family had set up on the property. It was where he'd been when the bout of illness had hit, where he went when he felt most helpless. He abhorred the idea of violence, would never consider using a gun against anything but a target—but holding the pistol, practising at this one physical skill, gave him a sense of control. It was something he could do, something he was good at.

Gaius carried a tray into the room, glancing at Julian's half-covered form before lowering his eyes. "The senator is here, visiting your parents," he said. "He wishes you could join them."

"Caesar's shit," Julian replied, slowly sitting up as Gaius approached. Gaius always knew when he was just prolonging his apparent recovery—not that he would tell anyone. "You know what they're doing?"

"He's here to discuss the local taxation policies with the praefectus, to talk about some new initiatives." Gaius set the tray down on the bed, and finally looked at Julian. His eyes were soft, beautiful in his strong face.

"No," Julian stated, ignoring the soup and cheese. "He's extorting them. He's making them pay *him* off so he can keep funding his little side projects. You know what he does? He researches perverse kinds of remaking, and tests it on slaves. He's trying to make a personal army of steam-powered people, Gaius, and when he fails, he just throws the latest body in the junk heap and tries again."

Gaius frowned, sat at the foot of the bed. "Why don't your parents do something about it?"

"Like what? As soon as they try, he'll punish them for it. He'll dig up some obscure legislation and nail them with it. He has the power. They're all corrupt in Rome."

The two fell silent for a moment. Julian's hand clenched reflexively, yearning for the familiar feeling of the pistol grip, before relaxing.

"Anyway," Julian said, softening. "Thanks for not telling them I'm feeling better. I couldn't face him."

Gaius nodded. "Of course."

"I don't know what I'd do without you, Gaius," Julian continued, almost to himself. "I couldn't handle it all. You keep me... grounded." He looked towards the windows, though the curtains were pulled shut. He wanted to say something else, something more... But he couldn't ask for what he wanted. His words would always be a command. He suddenly felt very conscious of his nakedness.

He turned to look back at Gaius, saw Gaius looking at him, though he quickly turned away. He moved to stand up, but Julian grabbed his wrist.

"Wait."

Gaius turned. Julian was looking at him intently. Had he imagined that look?

"I don't know what I'm going to do," Julian said.

Gaius frowned. "About what?"

"Something has to be done to stop them. He can't be allowed to keep on doing this. But I don't know what I can do." He felt empty all of a sudden, defeated, emotions flying between two extremes. "I pretend I'm better, I do my studies, I try to lead a normal life, but I can't. I don't have the strength. I can't *fix* it!"

Gaius moved closer, put his hand on Julian's arm. "We're still young, Jules. You may not have the strength physically, but you have it deep down. You can make a difference in your life."

Julian had looked away, and when he looked up at Gaius again, there were tears in his eyes. "I just don't know how. I feel like I can't do anything with this damned body!"

Gaius gathered Julian close, held him. "You can. You will. You have all the strength you need in that body."

Julian's heart pounded, and he looked up at Gaius.

Gaius looked down, then back into his eyes. "...I can show you."

Julian wrapped his arms tighter around Gaius, and nodded into his shoulder.

As he learned, he had not been alone in his secret thoughts.

Someone touched his arm as they passed, and Julian recoiled.

Voices assaulted him from all sides as soapbox orators shouted their uninformed political opinions or tourist scams. The walls of the grand government buildings seemed to loom over him. The garishly painted marble statues of Emperor Geminius rose authoritatively over the proceedings, hand pointed into the sky where airships floated like lead clouds. The monorail screamed with steam and power, passing overhead towards the Colosseum. At the opposite end of the Forum, the Curia Julia, seat of the Senate, sat like a patriarch at the head of a table.

Julian backed away from it all, overwhelmed. His back hit a wall— he heard a soft *clunk* of metal against brick when it did.

The seat of power of Rome for so long, the place Julian had associated with everything wrong in the Empire. He'd only ever seen it once before Servius had brought him to Rome. That image had burned itself into his memory.

He remembered feeling powerless.

How could anyone do something against the sheer inertia represented by this grand scene?

Servius's voice came to him. They'd been in Martin's lab, watching the doctor at work.

"It's always fascinated me, how remaking can take something so... imperfect as the human body, and make it... better," Servius had said. "Take out what is weak or rotten, replace it with something infallible."

Julian hated Servius's views on remaking. The focus on trying to "fix" people. People weren't "broken"—society was. But all he'd responded with was, "Even clockwork needs maintenance."

"Yet so much easier to deal with than people. It follows rules. *People are so subject to the whims of the gods...*"

"It can't fix everything," Julian said. He'd said it bitterly. He'd thought of the corruption, of his parents. Of Gaius.

"Can't it?" Servius asked. Then, "The Senate meets this month to determine new legislation for remaking. To discuss dropping some of their old regulations. Perhaps we shall see what clockwork can yet fix."

Now Julian looked towards the Senate building. They'd be in session soon. Senators coming from all over the Empire. To discuss war and industry and power. Probably thinking of all sorts of ways to exploit the technology.

What could one person do against such power?

But Julian was strong now. Maybe he *could* make a difference somehow.

A clockwork walker pulling an empty pallet turned its lensed head towards him.

Julian turned suddenly, stumbling back towards the alley.

He couldn't do something here, not now. He was being watched. Searched for. He'd escaped with Servius's greatest work—

His mind stopped mid-thought.

He'd been the success the doctor had been working towards.

And now—he was a fugitive.

He had to get out of Rome.

If he was near the Forum, the train station wouldn't be far away. Not with his newfound stamina. He broke into a run once more.

His legs were burning again by the time he got there. And his mind had started to burn with questions, problems, barriers. How would he get a ticket? He was surrounded by crowds again, but these people couldn't care less about a bedraggled youth clutching a single bag. Julian found a small alcove, crouched to tear through the things he'd taken from Martin's lab.

Papers, mostly. Notes he'd taken for Martin—and now taken *from* Martin. His clothes, taken off his poppy-unconscious body.

And then, a small bag that jingled lightly. Denarii.

He sighed in relief. He'd already started concocting ideas, plans to mug someone or steal what he needed. After all, he was strong now, physically. Part of him could have done anything to get out of here.

The other part was glad he wouldn't have to.

He pulled out a shirt, wriggled out of the coat while trying to shield his body from the view of the crowds. Blood still oozed thickly from around the metal. His running was not helping the healing process.

He could rest soon. Once he got out of Rome. Once he got away from prying eyes...

The clicking of metal drew his attention. A clockwork crawler. A spy. Had it seen him? He threw the shirt on, pulled the coat back over to hide the bloodstains already seeping through cloth.

He had to get out of here.

He tried to compose himself. He didn't know how successful he'd be. At least his heart didn't race with nerves or exertion. He felt strangely calm, physically.

Mentally—well, he wasn't sure he'd ever be calm.

He walked towards the ticket counter.

The soldiers arrived at the villa early, that morning. They knocked, demanding to be let in on order of Senator Vivarius. His parents began to scramble, gathering the slaves and servants, arming them, hiding them in case there was a fight.

Julian and Gaius heard the commotion from upstairs, where they clung to each other in bed. They were eighteen now.

"They did it," Julian said. His voice trembled. "They finally struck back against him."

A crash downstairs as the door burst open announced the entry of the soldiers. They heard yells, couldn't make out what was said.

Julian and Gaius stumbled out of bed, grabbed clothes. "I told them it wouldn't work," Julian said, throwing on a tunic. "They'll seize our assets, take everything from us."

"What about you?" Gaius asked.

Julian went to the door, put his ear to it. "They'll arrest my parents—probably execute them." He tried to speak matter-of-factly, but his heart was pounding, tears springing to his eyes. "Any of the slaves who survive will be sold. They'll likely insist our assets don't cover everything, and anyone left will be put into indentured servitude. I've seen it before."

Gaius looked horrified. "They can't do that!"

"They can, and they will," Julian said. In a sudden anger, he threw a lantern across the room with a clatter. "Damnit! Why can't I stop them? Why do I have to be so useless?" It wasn't even his heart holding him back now. What could he even do against the power of the Empire?

"You have to get out of here," Gaius said.

Julian shook his head. "They'll just chase us down, and then execute me when they catch us." He turned, paused, looked at Gaius, and became thoughtful. "But *you* can get out. You don't have to be a part of this."

"What? I'm part of this family, too. I'll stay with you. We'll get through it together."

"You're my slave, Gaius!" Julian said. "You'll be seized like the rest of the assets and sold!"

"Well, I can't just leave. I'll be killed! I'll be a runaway—"

"No," Julian interrupted. "You won't be. I free you."

"What?"

"I'm freeing you! As of right now, I no longer own you. This family doesn't own you. You're free. You don't have to go through this."

"I can't just leave you, Jules!"

"You have to. Or you'll die. Just—please, promise me you'll come back to me, someday."

"I—" Gaius hesitated.

Julian didn't want him to leave. To be left alone. But he had to save Gaius. There was no choice.

"I promise."

Julian smiled a bit, wryly, though tears were in his eyes. "I'll *make* you come back if I have to."

The train shook as it came to life. Julian huddled in a cabin, blessedly alone.

Alone. He was truly alone now. His parents had been taken away. He'd sent Gaius away. He'd run from Servius and Martin.

Everyone had left him.

All he had left was himself. And the endless ticking of his heart.

Chapter 2: Wages and Waiting

GAIUS

The last time Gaius had seen Julian was when he was set free. They'd been in bed together when Senator Vivarius's men had arrived. He'd held Julian closer than ever before in those final moments. Now they were farther apart than ever before.

It had been over a year ago, and yet Gaius still saw glimpses of Julian's face in the reflection of the welder's torch in the rough metal of the factory line, out of the corner of his eye at the crowded bars where the workers gathered after hours.

The last time Gaius had touched Julian—a moment he desperately tried to hold onto as memories of their love merged into a morass of indistinguishable feelings, like alloys smelted together—his hands had been soft against Julian's body. More used to doting on nobles than working on machinery. Now, they were rough, calloused. Gaius often worried that Julian would recoil from them when they found each other again.

Whenever that might be.

"Watch what you're welding, bricon!" the supervisor yelled, directly behind Gaius.

He jumped, snapping back to the moment. It had gotten so easy to slip away into memory rather than endure being present in this place.

But he'd almost welded a hinge shut on the mobile artillery platform.

"The army needs these cannons on the front lines," the supervisor yelled at the workers across the factory floor. "No one's leaving tonight until they're done."

Gaius swore under his breath as the supervisor moved on.

"I can't believe they're keeping us late again," Frederic said from his left. "I got kids to go home to."

"What are we going to do?" Marin said to Gaius's right. "I need the money."

"What little there is."

Gaius had been a slave all his life—working for the East India Company was pretty much the same.

Frederic put down his blowtorch to stretch with a groan and massage his knee where flesh met remade iron. "I dunno. If we all just stopped working—what could they do? Like what happened in India, you hear about that? The Company had a full revolution on their hands!"

Gaius grunted. "Sure. Then they killed everyone. Revolution over."

Frederic shrugged. "Come on, they couldn't do that *here*." He picked up his torch again.

"Why not?" Marin said. "Anyway, I can't afford to just stop working. I need these denarii, every one of them."

"But we could get more! Remember what Alesse used to talk about?"

"Yeah, well, Alesse is in Rome now."

"Making a difference. Fighting for us!"

"Yeah? You hear from her recently? I think she's just working for the politicians now instead of the Company."

Gaius *had* heard from Alesse, but he didn't say anything. Alesse had been a mentor to him when he first got this job. Trying to save up enough money to go to Rome himself to find where Julian had been taken.

He sighed. Julian would have some idea how to fix all this. Some revolutionary speech about changing how things worked in the Empire. Gaius had always admired Julian's optimistic fire—even as he saw how futile it was.

Nothing would change, not while the powerful had power.

The world slowly grew dark outside the tiny windows of the factory until at last the workers were allowed to leave. Gaius checked the clock on the wall—it was late. He hoped not too late.

"Join us for a beer?" Marin asked him.

He shook his head as he quickly rummaged through his locker. "No time tonight. Gotta get home, sorry."

Marin grinned. "Got a lady waiting, eh?"

Gaius grimaced.

The night air was warm, humid, as Gaius jogged down the street. The street lamps were lit already, warm gas flames dotting the cobblestones, though only a few carriages rolled past at this time.

He had to get home before tenth bell. Before the clockwork messenger would turn around, message failed to deliver. If there was a messenger. But he couldn't risk the chance.

Couldn't risk missing news of Julian.

All he'd been able to learn of what had happened to Julian after he'd fled the villa was that Julian had been taken to Rome by Senator Vivarius's men. And he couldn't afford to travel to Rome, not yet.

But when Alesse had left Parisium for the Italian peninsula—her promotion within the East India Company unintentionally giving her access to the political structures that could help her change how business was done and protect working people—Gaius had approached her with his request.

"I'd think you'd be happy to be rid of a former master," she'd said.

"It's not like that. He was never—his parents never let me forget it of course, but Jules—Julian—" He'd trailed off, not sure how to express... everything.

Alesse had just smiled. "Ah. Yes, I can keep an eye out. Sounds like he might be in a bad place, though..."

Gaius had nodded. "I need to find him."

"I'll send messengers if I learn anything. I can build them easy enough once I get my workshop. Best not use the postal service—who knows what the Agentes might think of someone sending mail to a former slave about a boy whose family was extorted by a rising senator."

Gaius had nodded. He'd not even thought of that—the Agentes in Rebus, who took post across the Empire, were well known to be agents of the state.

"Just be careful. They'll be set to return to me if they can't deliver their message. You can't miss it if I send one."

Gaius had nodded again. "Thank you."

"No promises, Gaius. But you need someone to take care of you."

He'd smiled.

He'd always been the one told to take care of Julian.

The clock tower that loomed over the district began to chime. Gaius swore and broke into a run.

It seemed fruitless. He hadn't heard anything from Alesse in a month, hadn't heard much of substance at all. Just that Julian was alive and maybe working as an indentured servant somewhere. But he couldn't risk missing something, no matter how small. He needed news. Needed something to hold onto.

His apartment, such as it was, was shoved between two larger buildings down a small street, a tiny tenement easily missed. It barely had room for a bed and sink, but Gaius hardly spent any time here anyway—work tended to take up twelve or more hours every day.

He rounded the dark corner, panting.

No messenger.

He sighed, and leaned back against the wall.

No news was good news, they said. But he yearned for *something*. Anything.

No, not anything. There was news he would not be able to bear.

He sighed again, trying to jog his thoughts back to the present, and rooted through his bag for his keys.

That's when he heard the faint *click clack* and the whir of a tiny engine starting up.

He looked up and around in a panic. There, above him, the clockwork messenger was climbing spider-like up the bricks of the building, getting to open air as its dragonfly-like wings began to whir.

"No!" Gaius shouted, as if it would stop and listen. It was too high up, out of reach. Not thinking, he flung his bag into the air towards it.

The bag hit the wall, short of its target, and the clockwork thing skittered farther away in self-preservation.

"Shit, no, no, shit—"

Gaius wasn't thinking rationally any more. He needed that messenger, even as it skittered out of sight onto the roof. He looked around, black edging into the corners of his vision.

A pipe across the alley—a storm drain. He leapt at it, scrambled for purchase, and pulled himself up the wall, hand over hand. Rolled onto the roof, two stories up, across the alley from his building where the messenger was getting ready to take flight.

His mind was racing against itself, trying to decide if he could make the jump across the alley—unlikely—while also screaming about keeping himself alive.

He was about to risk it when the drone began to lift off—and turned towards him.

Of course—heading southeast back to Rome.

He had one chance at this. He backed up along the roof—stumbling a little up the slope of it. The messenger began to fly towards him, gaining some height as it did. As it cleared the alley, Gaius sprang into a run, leaping just as the thing was going overhead.

His fingers found metal. A gear ground against his left palm, burning—forcing him to let go—but his right hand had found one of the metal insect legs. Its wings had no hope of supporting his weight, and he landed heavily on the roof, pulling the drone towards him as he tumbled.

His momentum stopped at the edge of the roof. The messenger buzzed weakly against him.

With sweaty, aching hands, he pulled the scroll tube from its underbelly, then let it go. It took off haphazardly into the night sky as he popped the end off the tube and unfurled the paper within.

Julian last seen fleeing Rome, alone on train towards Frankfurt.
Good luck.

Gaius's heart pounded, and not from the climb and leap.
Julian seen. Leaving Rome.
His mind raced. He couldn't afford the trip to Rome.
He might be able to afford a trip to Frankfurt.

Chapter 3: The Praetorian Guard

LIA

The tavern was dark and cramped, like everything on the Imperial Skystation. Space had to be preserved when you were trying to keep thousands of tons hovering in the air, but there was always room for ale and wine. The whole place hummed, the walls and floors vibrating constantly with the force of the engines far below.

Praetorian Marshal Lia Song strode through the door into the claustrophobic room, hailed by a gust of icy wind from outside. Her heavy grey overcoat flapped as the door closed behind her. She pushed her goggles onto her forehead and glanced around in the gloom, poorly lit with gas lamps.

An Ethiopian woman sat in one corner, a cup of something in her hand, her feet on a chair. She caught Lia's eye, then set her cup down. Her finger extended from the handle to the other side of the room. Lia acknowledged her only by turning to where she pointed.

A man huddled at a table, looking like a worried rabbit, nursing a honeyed wine. A typically Roman drink. Lia pulled out a chair and sat on it backwards, her arms resting on its back, confronting the man. The rifle slung over her shoulder settled nicely. He looked up, startled.

"Septus Duronius?" Lia said. "You're a tough one to track down given that you're supposed to be in jail."

His eyes widened almost imperceptibly. "Who are you?"

"Praetorian Marshal Lia Song." She held up a badge, smiling. "Let's skip the part where you pretend not to understand what I'm talking about. You're the captain of the pirate ship *Red Raven*, recently captured, and yet here you sit. You want to tell me why Legate McAvoy let you go?"

"The authorities were told to leave me alone," Septus said. There was a hint of contempt in his voice—alongside a hint of worry.

"My authority is broader," Lia responded.

Septus didn't even glance towards the door before leaping from his chair and bolting for it.

Lia watched him go.

He pushed open the door—and was clocked upside the head by a burly arm. A muscular man with an eyepatch and a green-dyed mohawk bent down and hauled Septus back to his feet. One brass and steel leg clunked heavily against the floor as he marched Septus back inside.

Lia finally stood, as did the woman in the corner, converging on the pirate.

"Thank you, Brendan," Lia said to the green-haired man.

He smiled back jovially.

"I was trying to make this easy for you," Lia said to Septus. "Answer my questions and you can go, just like the legate said. The cargo in the *Raven*'s hold is gone. You were hired to steal it from the East India Company, and to get caught. What did you steal, Septus? What was the cargo?"

Septus looked up at her, and she detected a sudden resigned look in his eyes. "Why don't you ask Vivarius yourself?" he said. And then there was a click, and he gasped, his whole body jerking before falling limp in Brendan's grasp.

"Jupiter's ass-crack," Lia said.

Brendan lowered him to the floor and turned him over. "Some kind of clockwork thing stuck on the back of his neck," he said. "Shoved a needle into his jugular."

"Death collar," the Ethiopian woman said quietly, looking around the bar. "Someone was watching."

Lia nodded. "Turner, see if you can find them. Walk soft. Brendan, get rid of the body. We have a banquet to attend."

She pulled her goggles down over her eyes, and walked outside into the icy wind, thousands of feet above Londinium.

Senator Vivarius. All her investigations kept coming back to him. It seemed only appropriate. It was his involvement in the Imperial East India Company decades ago that destroyed the Chinese Empire's ability to regulate the opium trade; her parents had relayed stories to her from the friends they had left behind in China of how even now it was destroying the lives of millions. Now that he was a senator, his influence and his greed had only spread.

She wrapped her overcoat around herself. The sky was grey all around them; the Imperial Skystation *Munimentum* hovered near the clouds, imposing its presence over all Londinium below. Its massive engines rumbled far beneath her feet, powering the six giant propellers that kept the station aloft. It wasn't a particularly efficient use of energy, but it was a demonstration of the Empire's power. Several skystations were used in the southeast as flying fortresses, patrolling the Ottoman border, each holding a legion of soldiers and all the services they required.

She wondered if it was just greed that drove Vivarius. The more she saw, the more she thought there might be something else going on. But without more information, she had no way of knowing what.

Of course, as Fortuna's luck would have it, he was aboard the *Munimentum* for the special Ides banquet in honour of the recent appointment of Legate McAvoy, the new commander of the skystation.

She frowned. No, probably not luck.

The skystation was constructed like some cross between an airship and a castra. A single road ran up the centre from bow to stern, the via principalis, just as it would in a military camp or fortress. At the end was the aftcastle, the Praetorium, where the legate lived and worked. On either side of the via, more buildings offered housing and entertainment for the legionaries; each extended below deck as well, and their roofs formed the upper deck where the main fortifications were.

Brendan rejoined Lia as she walked down the via principalis towards the Praetorium.

"Handed off to the vigilia to deal with," he said. "They didn't seem to want any trouble from the Praetorian Guard."

"Good," Lia said. "It's looking like we'll have enough trouble."

Brendan nodded. "I'm looking forward to a break after this. A nice evening at the baths, maybe a night or two with some young nobleman or something. You know, someone who's not constantly involved in Imperial security."

Lia grinned. "A visit to Bath does sound nice. Don't know that we'll have much time for a break, though. Let's see how this plays out."

"Just a chance to get clean and look at naked men, that's all I ask."

"Maybe I'll put in a requisition for you. 'To the requisitions officer: For my current mission, I require three naked men. It's a matter of Imperial security.'"

"Think they'd buy it?" Brendan asked.

Lia smirked. "I'd love to find out."

By then, they'd reached the entrance to the Praetorium. The building rose above them, an imposing edifice of authoritarian architecture. Statues of Augustus and Emperor Geminius flanked the large black doors; above them, an eagle extended its wings, meant to make those below feel small, powerless, defensive.

Brendan pushed open the heavy door, and Lia swept inside, her overcoat billowing behind her in the rush of warm air.

"Ah, Officer Song," a steward said, bowing. "Welcome. The ceremonies are to begin shortly. Agent Turner Lane is already seated."

Lia nodded, and the steward led them onward and into a banquet hall. It was small for such a hall—space on a flying fortress had to be preserved, after all—but still impressive. Three oaken tables ran the length of the room, one raised slightly for the legate and the other officials. Lia, Brendan, and Turner were at one of the side tables; Lia had been invited when Legate McAvoy learned that a Praetorian Guard would be aboard. It was likely politeness only—the Guard was officially the arm of the emperor, so keeping on their good side was a priority. And though no one spoke of it, the Guard also wielded power beyond the emperor. After all, whoever guards the emperor's sleeping quarters has the power to change who sleeps there.

Lia was not a huge fan of the current emperor, Geminius, who allowed his senators and provincial governors far too much freedom, but her dislike came mostly from his ineffectualness rather than from actual corruption. Corruption was Lia's focus.

She scanned the room as she entered, doing a quick analysis of the guests. There at the head of the central table was Legate McAvoy, an imperious woman who had proven herself as an airship captain on campaign against the Ottomans. Immediately to her right sat Senator Vivarius, giving an air of being in control of the situation, as he always did. He was in his fifties, and had been a senator for a decade. He still looked hale and strong. Held himself tall.

The tribunes sat nearby along with a collection of centurions. The rest of the room was filled with minor noblemen from Londinium, visiting captains, and anyone who wanted some extra social credit by showing up to such an event.

Turner sat in a far corner with two empty seats beside her. Lia and Brendan joined her. Brendan drew a few looks as they passed—his size, green mohawk, eyepatch, remade leg, and pretty Irish face were all attention grabbers. Still, it meant the Ethiopian woman and Chinese woman with him drew less notice than they might otherwise.

They took their seats as Senator Vivarius rose.

"Welcome, everyone, to the Imperial Skystation *Munimentum*. We are here to celebrate the appointment of Fiona McAvoy to Legate of this fortress."

He went on for some length on McAvoy's military exploits against the Ottomans and her political affiliations. Lia tuned out and gazed about the room; not too many people she recognized. Doors in the back of the hall led to the kitchens and on to the private living quarters of the skystation's commanders.

She tuned back in as Vivarius was finishing. "The lamb slaughtered for this feast went without a sound or protest. This is an auspicious appointment. May Legate McAvoy serve the Empire for many a year."

There was a smattering of applause, mostly from the military attendees. McAvoy stood.

"Thank you, Senator," she said. Where the senator had spoken in Latin—a common language across the Empire still—McAvoy spoke English in a thick Irish accent. "As commander of this skystation, it is my honour and privilege to welcome you all to the feast. Imperator Geminius diu vivat."

The assembled people toasted the emperor's health. Then McAvoy continued, her voice rising with rhetoric. "The problems of the Empire are many. For centuries, the Ottomans have clamoured at our gate with ever-improving technology. We are forced to trade with other nations for the bare necessities of life, and to deal with 'corporations' like the East India Company. Some, like the Aztecs, continue to refuse trade, and threaten our western colonies. And here at home, provinces shout for ever more power and resources. Even below our very feet, rumblings of protest and revolt creep through Britannia against Roman rule.

"The plight of the colonized, they say. Has Rome not brought us prosperity? Health and technology the likes of which the world has never seen? For a thousand years and more we have been part of the glorious Empire and benefited. And yet those who have not raised themselves up with us blame Rome for their misfortune. It is a sad delusion, but it threatens all we stand for. Therefore, I am pleased that my friend Senator Vivarius is here, and would invite him to announce our new initiative."

There was a slight murmur through the room. No one had been expecting any official announcements. McAvoy sat as Vivarius stood again.

"Thank you," he said, adopting McAvoy's English preference, presumably for the benefit of the local crowd. "The Senate considers the problems of Britannia to be of the utmost importance. Here in the seat of industrialization, you are the heart of the Empire. Therefore, we have pledged to prioritize the health of the province. And it is my honour to announce that the Senate has decided to station the *Munimentum...*" He paused for effect, arms sweeping wide. "...*here*, above Londinium. Here, your legions will best be able to provide the safety and security that Britannia needs. Here you will guard not the borders against the barbarians who fling themselves helplessly against our walls, but the very heart of the Empire. This is an honour of the highest degree."

Lia frowned and glanced at Turner and Brendan.

"If you have to say it's an honour, it may not be," Turner muttered to her.

She nodded. This felt like an insult to the legionaries, but, more so, it felt like a disproportionate response to Britannia's problems. There hadn't been any kind of rebellion or anything. Lia didn't like it.

But the speeches had come to an end, and with a final toast to the Empire, the gathered guests drank and began to feast.

Brendan dug into the food with gusto; Lia and Turner ate more sparingly, and they didn't touch the honeyed wine or British beer.

"I didn't catch your names," someone across from them said, helping themselves to some meat pie.

"Lia Song, Praetorian Guard," Lia said. "This is Brendan Kansky, my lieutenant, and Turner Lane." She didn't mention Turner's official position since it was best to keep that quiet—she was a member of the Agentes in Rebus, the Empire's intelligence web.

The woman raised her eyebrows. "We're honoured by your presence. I'm Elizabeth Ryan, just the captain of a merchant ship currently docked for a supply run."

Lia smiled amicably. "Upon the wings of the merchants does the Empire float."

Elizabeth chuckled. "The helium merchants, perhaps. With the East India Company declaring their independence from Rome, likely only the Americans are doing decent trade these days."

"I'm sure you heard of the capture of the *Red Raven*," Lia said. "What's the scuttlebutt among the merchants?"

"Faked, of course," Elizabeth said, leaning in. "Likely a ploy to make the new legate look good."

"Anything about the cargo that was confiscated?"

She shook her head. "Plunder from some caravan, I suppose."

Lia nodded, smiled, and raised her cup.

Turner glanced at Brendan as he forked sausage into his mouth before returning her gaze to keeping an eye on the room at large. "Hungry?" she asked.

"Always. Anyway, the British know how to *cook*."

"I don't think I've seen a green vegetable all evening."

"I know!" He took another bite of a shepherd's pie. "But you know how I like my meat." He winked at her.

Turner just shook her head, trying not to smile.

There was a short break after the first course as plates were collected and drinks refilled. Several people took the opportunity to stand and mingle, chatter filling the room. Lia stood to casually make her way towards the back of the building. Turner touched her arm—under the table she held a key ring.

"Found these. Might find them handy."

Lia smirked and took them. "Thanks. I'll be back."

"Take your time."

She walked towards the back, passed a servant—a slave—with a confident smile that said of course she could go back there, and pushed through the door. Cramped hallways led to the kitchen, meeting rooms, and then stairs to a second floor. She took them two at a time.

Her hope, as she rounded a corner, was to find Senator Vivarius's room before anyone noticed her absence. She was unsuccessful.

"Officer Lia Song, what a surprise."

She'd almost run into a man standing in the hallway, arms crossed, a coy smile on his lips. He was young and lithely handsome, and wore the red sash of a centurion with a star on the breast that indicated he wasn't assigned to the *Munimentum* but here on special duty.

"Destin Stormcloud," Lia said, unimpressed. "I would have expected you to be at the feast, with the alcohol and the pretty women."

"That would be *Centurion* Stormcloud," the man said. "What are you doing here, Praetorian?"

"My job," Lia responded.

"Snooping into other people's business?" Stormcloud said. "Such an honourable job it is."

"Careful," Lia said. "I can arrest you."

"I'd like to see you try." He said it with a hint of lascivity. "But I'm not here to get arrested. I should warn you, though. Drop this investigation."

"Why would I do that?"

"Trust me. You'll be better off."

"I'll take my chances."

Stormcloud leaned a shoulder against the wall. "I'm serious, Lia. You don't want to touch this one. Of course, you could just forget all about it. Touch something else instead."

Lia snorted. "Not with a ten-foot pole. Anyway, that line won't work with me."

"Ah, of course," Stormcloud said. "Officer Lia Song, Ace Praetorian." It was likely meant as a barb, but Lia just smiled a little. She'd always appreciated the apt double-entendre. "Your loss."

"Hardly," she said.

Stormcloud frowned. "Tell me, who gives you your authority, Song? 'The Empire,' as if it's a thing with will? You supersede the Senate, who are elected officials. You ignore the will of the people!"

"We haven't been a republic in almost two thousand years, Destin," Lia said. "Besides, who gets to elect those senators?"

"All citizens of the Empire."

"Citizens. Do you understand that I was not a citizen until after my military service? Less than ten percent of the Empire's inhabitants are 'citizens.' The Senate is *not* the will of the people."

"At least they have someone to check their power. Even the emperor does in the form of the Praetorian Guard. Isn't that your stated purpose these days? But answer me this, Song: who guards the Guard? Who makes sure you do not overstep yourself?"

"And right now, you imagine that's you?"

"No. I'm just here to give you a message. I can't stop you, Song. But you should stop. It'll be better for your health."

"Is that a threat?"

"Not from me."

With that, Destin Stormcloud swept past her, and took the stairs down.

Lia frowned when he had gone. What was his warning supposed to mean? She had full authority to investigate corruption in the government—that was her job. The Praetorian Guard had long been protectors of the emperor—but they were also protectors of the *Empire*. For the good of the nation, they had been responsible for "removing" dangerous and ineffectual emperors in the past.

Their powers weren't limitless, though. And it would be entirely possible for an "unfortunate accident" to befall her if she stepped on the wrong toes. Which she was sure she was doing. But such were the risks.

She moved on.

It didn't take long to locate the room Vivarius was staying in. It was the only one with a guard standing in front of the door, in a red jacket uniform, plumed ceremonial helmet under one arm.

Lia walked up and showed her badge. "You're needed downstairs."

"Yes, ma'am," the guard said. He rushed off without question.

Lia waited until his footsteps had faded, then withdrew the keys

Turner had handed her. She flipped through them until one fit the lock on the door and entered the senator's room.

It was well-appointed for a military fort—opulent even. After all, it wouldn't do for a senator to sleep in anything less than luxury. A large bed covered with pillows sat against a wall, Chinese silk sheets draped over it. A mahogany desk took up much of the rest of the room underneath an elaborate clock, along with a plush chair covered in Egyptian linen—quite the commodity since the Ottomans had taken Egypt centuries earlier.

Lia went straight for the desk. A few papers sat neatly on it, waiting for the senator's attention—minor notices and orders awaiting signatures. A quick glance told Lia they held nothing interesting. She opened the desk drawer, but it just contained spare paper and ink, wax and a seal.

She scanned the room. A trunk by the bed would hold the senator's clothes and effects, not likely anything of note. She bent down to look under the bed—aha. She pulled out a fine leather satchel. His personal possessions. She opened the flap. Inside were mostly papers, a book, a scroll, some minor clockwork knickknacks. Quickly, she started scanning through the papers.

One caught her eye, a letter addressed to the senator, the seal already broken. She pulled it out to read.

Vivarius,

The cargo has been secured and is on the way to its destination. I trust all is arranged on your end. I'm sorry to hear you won't be attending the senatorial summit in Rome, but I understand you have duties elsewhere. I hear the sittings promise to be quite fiery.

Hopefully you have my shipment secured by now. Inform me when you are ready for the next step. You know how to reach me.

— Servius

The cargo, the shipment—was it referring to the *Red Raven*? So Vivarius likely did have something to do with it. What was it, though? And who was Servius? Lia wracked her brain for someone of any import with that praenomen, but only minor officials and soldiers came to mind.

She read over the letter again to commit it to memory, then slid it back in the satchel. The meal would be resuming soon—she had to get back to the banquet hall.

She carefully replaced the satchel under the bed, took a quick look to make sure the room was as she had found it, then quietly slipped back into the hallway.

...where a half-dozen legionaries stood waiting for her.

"Lia Song?" the centurion at the front said. "You are under arrest."

Lia narrowed her eyes and pulled her badge from her coat. "I'm afraid there's been a mistake. I'm a Praetorian Guard, and I have full authority here."

"A missive arrived an hour ago," the centurion said. "There is no Praetorian Guard named Lia Song. You have been impersonating a guard, harassing citizens, and now breaking into a senator's quarters. Come with us quietly, or we will take you by force."

Lia blinked. "What?"

The centurion laid his hand on the pistol in his belt. "I said, come with us quietly—"

"I am a member of the Praetorian Guard," Lia repeated. "I have been given authority to investigate—"

"You are a fraud and a criminal," the centurion interrupted. "Please put your hands on the wall."

What in Dis was going on?

You should stop. It'll be better for your health.

Lia turned and placed her hands on the wall while her mind raced. Clearly Vivarius was involved. She had stepped over some line, and it wouldn't be hard to convince people she was a fraud; unless she could get access to Praetorian records in Londinium or Rome, it was the senator's word against that of a foreigner, and a woman at that.

But if the senator was pulling this big of a move, it could mean nothing good for Lia. It was unlikely she'd ever get the chance to access the Praetorian records or contact her friends in the Guard—not that she had many. She'd always pursued her missions with more fervour than was usually deemed appropriate. After all, there could be just as much corruption in the Guard as the Senate.

In the middle of the Praetorium, her only option was to go quietly. She cursed the fact that they were on an Imperial Skystation—without a ship, she was stuck here, at Vivarius's mercy. And he didn't have much of that.

One of the legionaries took her rifle while another briefly searched her, removing her knife and the badge she had shown. Then her hands were bound behind her back, and she was forced to turn and march back down the hall towards the banquet room.

A hush fell over the guests as she emerged with the guards. She looked around the room. Vivarius was looking at her intently, his face radiating exultation, though he refrained from smiling. Brendan was being pulled from his seat by another pair of legionaries, protesting until he saw Lia. His face fell, and he acquiesced quietly. Turner Lane was nowhere to be seen.

The guards marched Lia towards the exit. When she came abreast of Brendan, she murmured, "Where's Turner?"

"Disappeared shortly after you left."

"Good. Don't do anything rash, okay, Brendan?"

Brendan cast her a glance, a half-smile on his face. "I just follow your lead, my dear."

The guards poked them in the back with guns to get them to hush. As they approached the Praetorium exit, they passed Stormcloud, standing with his shoulder against the wall, watching them. His look said *I warned you*, but there was something else mixed in there. Lia frowned, unable to put her finger on it.

The biting cold of the outside air hit them like a fist. The via principalis was wide, the wind rushing along it between buildings. There were eight soldiers around them.

There would be no trial, she thought. She'd either be let go after some indeterminate time, with the whole thing passed off as a misunderstanding, but the warning clear—or she'd simply be made to disappear. She thought the latter was more likely.

She sighed. Brendan glanced at her. She didn't know yet how she would get off the *Munimentum*. But she knew she couldn't let Vivarius get away with this.

She glanced back at Brendan.

Then she dropped to the ground, shooting her foot out at the guard with the gun pointed at her back. He tripped, and the gun fired into the sky. Brendan whirled, clocking the guard behind him upside the head with his bound fists.

The guards rallied, pulling guns and swords, but Lia was on her feet and running, ducking into an alley. Brendan ran in the opposite direction.

A pistol fired, and a shower of splinters rained over Lia. She ducked, weaved, and turned down another alleyway.

The skystation was big, but not big enough to lose herself in. Guards were chasing her, and before long a grid search would be organized to flush her out, even if she could hide. But she knew one place where she might not be found—at least long enough to come up with a plan.

She made for the edge of the skystation, around wooden buildings that housed the legions and supported the upper deck. The alleys between them were like a warren, the main ones wide enough for two soldiers walking abreast, others barely big enough for one. Above her head, planks served as bridges for guards and deckhands. Above those, ropes and masts supported the giant helium balloons that helped keep the station aloft.

But the majority of the power that kept the skystation in the sky came from six huge propellers on either side of the massive fortress. And the force that kept them spinning boiled away in the gigantic engine beneath their feet, sending vibrations throughout the station.

Lia reached the edge of the station, where metal-reinforced walls encased the whole thing. There was a door here—INGENIUM written across it.

She had only moments before guards caught up to her. She sat with her back to the wall, keeping an eye on the entrance to the little access alleyway while she maneuvered her bound hands past her feet and in front of her. Then she awkwardly pulled the keyring from her pocket and slid to her feet.

It took four tries to find the right key, but the door opened, and she slipped into the echoing darkness beyond.

She stood at the top of a tight staircase. As soon as the door closed behind her, it was almost pitch dark. She took a few slow breaths to calm her heart rate and allow her eyes to adjust. She could barely make out the outline of the railing. She placed her bound hands on it, and carefully made her way down into the vibrating, rumbling depths of the skystation.

Through another door at the bottom and Lia emerged into the Complex, the labyrinthine maze of pipes, catwalks, access hatches, and storage rooms that made up the greater part of the bowels of the station, dimly lit by tiny portholes looking onto the greyness of the sky beyond. This was the beating heart of the skystation, the gigantic steam engines that drove the propellers. After the cold of the outside air, the heat from the engines was stifling. She was sweating in seconds.

The soldiers might suspect that she came down here when they couldn't find her above. Luckily, it was easy to get lost in the passageways of the Complex, formed more from the space between huge pipes than any architectural intention to make a hallway. They were access points meant only for engineers; Lia wasn't sure how they stood the heat. There were many reasons Lia had never become an engineer—not the least of which was her general incompetency with mechanics. She had only the vaguest understanding of how the huge fortress even remained airborne.

She jogged forward, entering the maze, and started taking turns at random. She tried to remember the turns she took, but it soon became impossible. It was entirely likely she wouldn't be able to find her way back out again, but evading recapture was top priority right now.

After ten minutes, she finally grew too tired, sweat pouring down her face. She sank to the floor, back against a cooler pipe, and closed her eyes while she caught her breath—and her thoughts.

What had even happened? One moment she was investigating the senator, and the next she was being arrested by people who didn't have the authority.

Who guards the Guard?

She was being framed for something, that was for sure. She had stepped over some invisible line, and now the senator needed to make her disappear.

That meant she had been on to something. Something big enough to warrant her disappearance. They could have just killed her and passed it off as an accident, but that might get too much attention. If they tried to make it so she was never a Praetorian Guard to begin with, they became the good guys.

Something big. But what? Who was Servius? And what was the cargo in the hold of the *Red Raven*?

It had been a long day. Amid the warmth of the engines, she felt suddenly exhausted. She'd just rest for a few more minutes...

She hoped Brendan was okay as she nodded off.

Chapter 4: The Power to Change

JULIAN

Julian woke to feedback over the speaker system as a voice clicked in. "Next stop will be Frankfurt, Germanic Province, arriving in one hour. Next stop, Frankfurt."

He uncurled himself from the bench where he'd slept. No one else was in the cabin with him, which he thanked Apollo for. His body ached all over—mixes of pain unlike he'd ever felt. Kinks from the poor sleeping position, aching in his limbs from yesterday's exertion, and still the burning around his chest.

He checked his shirt. It was stained brown with dried blood, but at least it wasn't fresh. If he didn't move too much, maybe it would eventually heal.

But he'd have to move.

He looked out the window at the German countryside. The train followed the path of the Rhine; to the right, mountains rose covered in the thick primeval Black Forest. He tried to remember his dreams. Running, pain, exhaustion. Something chasing him. A moment of peace—Gaius's embrace before he'd woken.

Above all else, he felt... tired. Overwhelmed, even. He'd... run. Run from what had become of his life. Run from legal indentured servitude—however illegally arranged. Remade. Strong.

But so tired.

All his life, he hadn't had control of his own destiny. First the responsibilities, the conditions growing up in a family of nobles, politicians. Helpless to his parents' inactions, the whims of the more powerful. Then taken away, forced into servitude, working in Martin's lab, taking notes for the man called Servius.

Now he'd taken control, and all he wanted was to rest. But the world wouldn't let him. Servius would be looking for him—maybe already knew he'd left Rome.

Anger began to roil in him. Anger at Servius and the doctor, anger at his situation, anger at Senator Vivarius and at the whole damned Empire.

He thought of the Senate meeting Servius had told him about. Those men coming together to decide the fate of the world. Mostly for their own interests, too. How many of them had investments in remaking, in the military complex, in the East India Company? War raged against the Ottoman Empire because war made them money. Helped them keep control when there was a common enemy out there.

He'd wanted to do something about it. Wanted to change the world. But he'd always believed that his heart would hold him back. That he wouldn't have the strength.

Now he did, though, didn't he? But now he was a fugitive. And even with this new strength...

What could he actually do?

His clockwork heart beat away with its soft ticking. He still tried not to think about it.

"Jupiter's fucking cockwarts," he said aloud.

He hated everything. He had no idea what he was doing, where he was going. How he'd survive.

He threw his bag onto the bench beside him, dumping its contents. Coins spilled out over dozens of pieces of paper, a half-eaten calzone, a set of bandages and medical detritus from the doctor's desk. Julian suddenly realized how hungry he was and stuffed the calzone into his mouth, chewing furiously as he flipped through the papers.

Mostly notes in his own hand, which he'd taken during Martin's previous experiments. Observations on human biology, clockwork devices, thaumaturgical necessities. There was some business paper-work, too—requisitions from Martin to Servius for materials. And some of Servius's papers that he must have left behind. Half-finished correspondence, instructions for the doctor, and what looked like manifests.

One caught his eye—an airship shipment departing from Frank-furt. He held up the page as he swallowed the last of the calzone—he'd definitely eaten it too quickly.

A huge shipment of parts, maybe for remaking. It was hard to tell. But they weren't for Martin—these were weapons-grade.

It included an obscene amount of gunpowder. It was set to depart from Frankfurt tomorrow.

No—today. It was a new day.

So much military strength: the fruits of the Empire. Holding their power over everyone else, fighting their wars and lining their pockets. Ignoring or stepping on everyone else. Him, his parents. Folks like Gaius. The people who died at Martin's hands.

Abusive. Selfish. Corrupt, every one of them.

He snorted. The Empire would be better off to wipe them away, start with a clean slate. Start all over again.

His eyes locked on the manifest.

The entire Senate would be convening in a day.

Enough time to fly an airship across the Alps.

He was strong now. Maybe he *could* do something.

Wipe the slate clean.

He repacked his bag.

Frankfurt was the transportation hub of Europe. The train station was huge—split into multiple stations, even, for personal and commercial and private steam engines. Towering overhead as the train pulled into the city were massive airship docks. Sprawling from this centre of ac-tivity were warehouses and businesses and bars to cater to the workers and travellers. This was industry; this was the Empire's own clockwork heart, pumping out goods and people all around the continent and beyond. For all that, though, it wasn't even a real centre of trade—just the waystation, the junction between stops, Janus's threshold to whatever came next.

A worthy threshold for Julian to cross now as he disembarked—the liminal space, the transition to something different. Janus, god of beginnings—and endings. Julian's coat was wrapped tightly around his thin frame and blood-stained shirt, his eyes on the airship docks, mind already over Rome once more.

This may be the working heart of the Empire, but the brain was rotten. The clockwork rusty, the spring needing to be wound once more. Or, more likely, replaced.

Julian emerged from the train station, blinking in the sunlight. It was cooler here than Rome, but his chest was kept warm. Pumping away.

He'd come up with something of a plan in the last hour—a wild, desperate thing, fuelled by anger. He knew it. He could feel it burn in him like a welcome old friend. He hadn't been truly angry like this since Greece. He'd been too tired, too defeated. Now it raged in him anew.

He wanted suddenly to see how far he could push his new heart.

Crowds moved around him, a river of people heading to and from the station. For a moment he was disoriented, looking up at the airship skydock and getting pushed around by the moving people. He refocused on his immediate surroundings, holding his bag against his chest, trying to hide or protect himself—he wasn't sure which. He was so used to being small, to being pushed around or controlled, and now he'd been feeling like he had this secret to conceal.

Someone shoved into him, and he stumbled—and then angrily snarled at himself. He planted his feet, stared at the next person coming his way, forced them to go around him. Then he began to walk with purpose, with anger in his eyes.

People moved out of his way. If they didn't, he walked through them.

Once he got away from the entrance to the station, the crowds thinned a bit. He stopped to look up at the towers again—there were three of them, each with a handful of ships docked—and someone ran into him.

He didn't move this time. The person seemed to bounce off him.

He pulled out the manifest and glanced over it. It listed the tower and dock the ship would be at for delivery. He looked up again, and spotted it high above—a medium-sized airship with a hard-sided balloon anchored in place above it. Black and green, probably an independent trader of some kind. This wasn't an official shipment. Servius was trying to keep it quiet, maybe.

He started walking towards the right tower, again moving through the crowds with purpose.

The area around the docking tower was clearer. Two large men stood at the entrance, wearing all black with pistols strapped to their hips. East India Company guards. Maybe more inside.

Julian stopped a ways away to observe and think. He'd have a hard time getting past them. If he could manufacture a distraction of some kind—maybe trip up some of the crowd, start a commotion...

One of the guards turned as if hearing something from the tower, then disappeared inside. Julian watched tensely. After a moment, the guard emerged again and said something to his partner, who shrugged.

Then they both walked away.

Julian frowned. Strange. But convenient.

He quickly walked to the entrance, acting for all the world like he belonged, and went inside.

The room at the base of the tower was empty. There was a desk and some radio equipment and lots of paperwork, as if someone should be manning this station, but no one was here. An elevator led up the tower to the docks.

Julian didn't give it a second thought. It was an opportunity, and he took it. He moved quickly across the room towards the elevator door before someone came back—but stopped as something on the desk caught his eye.

A revolver, presumably left behind by the guards.

He'd need some leverage, some show of power if he was going to be able to do this. And a pistol was so familiar in his hands. Gave him a sense of control—something he sorely needed right now.

He heard voices outside, presumably the EIC guards returning. He didn't have time to think anymore. He moved quickly, grabbed the gun, and then slipped into the elevator.

The doors closed just as he heard the guards enter. He let out a breath he hadn't known he was holding. He could feel the adrenaline of the moment, but his heart pumped as steadily as it had before he'd entered the tower.

He checked the revolver—loaded, clean. He'd use it for show, for intimidation. He abhorred the idea of violence, had never considered it...

...Not until now. He steeled himself, and prepared to force his way onto the airship.

Chapter 5: Heart

GAIUS

The steam engines hummed, the only sound on the bridge. The small control crew, bound and gagged, huddled against the walls, fear in their eyes. The cargo ship flew south. It crossed the Alps far more easily than Hannibal ever could, and it carried military gear and explosives towards Rome. It carried destruction.

Gaius didn't dare move closer than he already had. He stood stock still at the bottom of the steps leading up to the helm. Beads of sweat trickled down his back as he watched Julian, their eyes locked like so many times before—but this time in opposition, in fear.

"Talk to me, Julian," Gaius said, trying to stop his voice from trembling. "You don't have to do this. Just tell me what's wrong."

Julian stood tall. His face was serene, but anger smouldered in his eyes. "You wouldn't understand. You never understand."

Gaius shook his head. "I always understand *you*, Jules."

Gaius had arrived in Frankfurt without much of a plan. He'd had no idea how to find Julian in such a big city—no idea if Julian would still be there. His only hope would be to ask around. Based on the timing of his train and how long it took the clockwork messenger to fly from Rome, he'd hoped he would arrive shortly after Julian. Close enough that he could keep an eye on the train station, ask the ticketers and engineers, hope he caught Julian before the boy left again.

He'd asked around as soon as he'd arrived. Described Julian as best he could—it had been so long. But based on Alesse's letter, he could make some assumptions.

Alone. Scared.

He hadn't been wrong. But he hadn't expected this.

Someone had finally pointed him towards the airship towers. Julian had just been by. A boy clutching a bag to his chest like a tourist worried about pickpockets. A tired, hunted look in his eyes. But anger, too.

Then he'd seen him. Seen him enter the tower. Gaius had called, but Julian couldn't hear over the crowds. He followed, saw the guards slowly making their way back, found the empty room at the base of the tower.

Gaius had been confused. Worried. What was Julian doing? Had someone lured him here?

But then he'd seen him again. Gun in hand, forcing the crew to let him onto the ship. Gaius had hidden, then, not calling out this time. Confused and scared himself now. He'd slipped aboard just as the gangplank was being drawn in.

They'd flown past the fields and forests of Europe. Now Gaius could hear the engines straining as they fought to keep the ship in the thin air above the mountains. Rome would be mere hours away.

More imminent was the danger the pilot was in, chained up beside the helm. Julian held a revolver to the woman's head.

"What do you hope to do, Jules?" Gaius's voice was soft, non-threatening. He tried to take a step forward, mount the stairs, but Julian's hand tightened on the pistol, and Gaius backed off.

"Show them." Julian glanced to the control crew, who were too scared to move as he adjusted his grip on the weapon. "Show them all."

"Show them what?" *Keep him talking*, Gaius thought. *Just keep him talking*. He was bewildered. What had happened to Julian in Rome? What had happened to make him like... this?

Julian practically snarled. "Show them that I can do what needs to be done."

The hot steam that powered the ship's propellers did nothing to warm the control room, not this high up. A shiver ran through Gaius, but he ignored it.

He looked at Julian, eyes running across his body. He was different. No coughs wracked him, no wheezing accompanied his impassioned breathing.

"Why do you need to show them, Jules? Why does it have to be you?"

"Because I'm strong now, Gaius! I don't need anyone to protect me." Julian grabbed his shirt, and ripped it open.

The left side of his torso had been replaced. Where once Gaius had seen soft flesh, now he saw hard brass. Where once a lung, now a mechanized valve, a little gauge tracking the interior pressure. Where once a heart—damaged as it may have been, but so large, so good—now only cold clockwork, pumping away.

"See?" Julian was yelling now. "They thought to break me, but they made me strong, and they paid. I don't need your protection, Gaius. I don't need you. I can do it alone now."

Gaius had only pity in his eyes as he saw what Julian had done to himself. "But you don't have to."

Julian's metal heart pumped, and he seemed to tower over the room.

"I can fight them now. I can do what we always talked about. I can fix the world!"

The mountains were slowly being left behind. Gaius could see the glittering Tyrrhenian out the window, the hills and highlands of Italy stretching before them.

"And what is it you're going to do, Jules?" Gaius asked. He gestured to the bound pilot, the rest of the crew. "How is killing these people going to fix the world?"

"It's not just them, Gaius. It's bigger than them."

"What are you going to do when we get to Rome?"

Julian stared straight at Gaius, unblinking. "When we arrive, the Senate will be in session. All the senators from across the Empire. And I'm going to destroy them."

"What?" Gaius said, aghast. "Gods, Jules, why? What will that do?"

"That's where it all starts. That's where the power is, the corruption. It all stems from Rome. But I can fix it. Wipe it clean. Let the world start itself anew."

Gaius shook his head. "That's ridiculous. You won't save the world, you'll doom it! War is at the Empire's borders already, conflict's brewing in our own provinces. You can't fix the world like this, Jules!"

"*Stop calling me that!*"

The outburst was sudden, unexpected. Gaius stepped backward. "What?"

"No one calls me that!"

Gaius frowned; his face hardened. "*I* call you that, Jules. I always have."

Julian abruptly turned away to look out the window of the bridge. He was away from the pilot now. The gun lowered a bit. The ship moved inexorably forward on its own towards Rome. Gaius mounted the first of the stairs, tried to get closer.

Julian had changed. Gaius didn't understand him anymore, after all this time—he didn't understand *this*. He didn't know how to react. The Julian he knew always talked about change, about the corruption all over the Empire—but *this*? He could never believe Julian would do this. What had changed? Did he truly want this?

Gaius watched him. Breathing, standing tall. But trembling softly. Gaius shook his head.

He didn't believe, deep down, Julian could change this drastically. No matter what had happened this past year. No matter how... angry he was. No matter how mechanical his heart.

"Look at yourself, Jules," Gaius said. "Maybe they changed your heart. But that doesn't change *who you are*. You have other choices! Killing everyone won't do it—corruption will rise elsewhere. Fighting will break out into civil war. Millions of people will be killed if you go through with this."

"And what do you expect me to do?" Julian asked, whirling. "Just let it continue?"

"Of course not," Gaius said, taking another step forward, climbing a little closer. "There are other ways to fix the world. Ways that don't require killing innocent people."

"There are no other ways. They don't work! They never work. My parents tried, Gaius. My family tried to fix things, and they were *taken from me*!" He was shouting now.

"I know," Gaius said. "I know, Jules, I was there."

"You *weren't* there!" Julian screamed. "You *left* me, Gaius. I had no one left! I was left alone to face them, Gaius. I had no one."

"You freed me so I could be safe from them."

"And you disappeared!" He raised the pistol, pointed it this time at Gaius. "It would all have been okay if I had you. I could have survived. But you disappeared."

"I promised I'd come back. I promised I'd come back to help you."

"And you never did! You know what they did to me? I was forced to work, then thrown into his facility, made to watch, listen to the screams of the remade slaves, and take *notes*. They destroyed me, Gaius! Because you never came back!"

Gaius stepped up the last two stairs, came face to face with Julian so that the pistol touched his chest. He looked into Julian's eyes.

"I came back, Jules. I came back when you needed me the most."

"When?" Julian spat.

"Right now."

Silence reigned over the control room. The crew had stopped struggling; even the engines seemed subdued. Gaius and Julian looked at each other for long moments without a word.

"I couldn't stop them," Julian finally whispered. He choked on the words. "They took my parents. They took me away, Gaius, and I had no one left."

Gaius swallowed. "I know. I'm sorry. I know."

With a sob, Julian dropped the gun, collapsed into Gaius's arms. He was heavier with the prosthesis, but Gaius didn't notice. All he knew was that Julian was in his arms again.

"Come on," he whispered. "Let's get out of here."

Julian nodded. They made their way slowly down the stairs. As they passed the pilot, Gaius stopped and cut her bonds. "Let us out somewhere before Rome," he said. "You'll never see us again."

Chapter 6: De Facto, De Jure

LIA

She was thirsty. That was Lia's first conscious thought upon waking. Sweat drenched her body, and her tongue was parched. Years of training brought her mind to focus quickly with regained consciousness, and she started thinking of ways to gather water—condensation, leaks perhaps—before she even opened her eyes. Then she heard a *clang* and remembered what had woken her up.

Her eyes shot open. It was dark among the pipes, but light filtered through from unknown sources—portholes or gas lamps that were spread throughout the Complex for the engineers. A pair of forms was moving through the pipes towards her.

She scrambled to her feet. Had the guards found her already? How long had she been asleep?

Another *clang*. But it wasn't the sound of swords. Metal on metal, reverberating through the area despite the constant loud humming. Then voices, indiscernible in the noise.

Engineers, probably. She couldn't let even them find her, though she thought she could convince them not to give her up if it came to that. Lia made ready to run again.

Then one of the forms passed through a stray shaft of light. A form

Lia recognized—like out of a dream.

The two figures rounded a corner and into Lia's passageway. She simply stood still, watching them.

The figure in the lead started.

"Lia Song?"

"Sydney Irons."

Sydney was thin, though muscular, wearing loose linens and a leather work belt. Their dark hair was cropped short, their eyes a very pale blue, now staring widely at Lia.

"What in the name of Vulcan are you doing in my engine?" Sydney asked, aghast.

"*Your* engine?" Lia said. "You *work* here?"

"What does it look like? I'm on vacation? After that thing in Parisium, I needed a job, I'll remind you."

"But an Imperial Skystation, Syd? Really? I never took you for a government worker."

"These things are masters of engineering!" They grinned. "Anyway, the money's good. But what are you doing here?"

Lia glanced at the man behind Sydney. He was muscular, dressed in protective leathers, and carrying a large crate. A badge on his shoulder marked him as a slave.

Sydney glanced back at him, following Lia's gaze. "Joey's harmless," they said.

"I could use some water."

Sydney nodded. "Fair enough. Let's go back to my office."

"You have an office?" Lia asked, walking forward as Sydney motioned down the passageway.

"Of course I do. I'm the head engineer." They moved through the maze of pipes like they had a map in their head.

"*Head* engineer? Wow."

"Don't sound so surprised. I flew *your* ship through that storm in the Austrian Province, and it badly needed repairs at the time."

"I remember. You saved our lives."

Sydney glanced at her. "Like that was the only time."

Lia snorted. "Well, it's just been Brendan, Turner, and me for a while. We still get in our share of trouble."

Sydney nodded quietly, then said, "How is Tur—how is everyone?"

"Turner's good," Lia said.

Sydney nodded, then changed the subject. "I can only imagine why you're in the underbelly of a skystation."

"Seemed like the place to be."

They'd emerged from the pipes and valves, past an enclosed chamber that must have held one of the massive steam engines, and stood at a door. Sydney waved the slave off somewhere and brought Lia through it into an office protected from the worst of the engine noise by heavy insulation. A number of instruments of various kinds—compasses, clocks, sextants, clockwork abaci, an elevation meter—sat strewn across a desk, all rendered useless by the incessant vibrations of the engines and propellers.

"Something's happened," Lia said. "Something big."

"Is this going to be a conflict of interest for me?" Sydney asked. They poured some water from a jug and handed it to Lia, who took it gratefully.

"Most probably."

"Go on."

Lia explained what she had been doing on the skystation—and the events leading to her being asleep in the Complex. Sydney raised their eyebrows.

"Where's Brendan?"

"I don't know. Safe, I hope."

"Shit. All right, we have to get you off the station."

Lia nodded. "If I can get away, maybe I can figure out what in Jupiter's ass-crack is really going on. But as long as I'm stuck here, I'll be too busy trying to stay alive."

Sydney absently tried to steady the sextant on their desk to no avail. "And they'll find you eventually. If it's as bad as you make it sound, they'll chase you a long time."

"I'll deal with that when I get there. And I *will* deal with this. There's something big going on, Syd, bigger than I thought. Senator Vivarius is making some kind of play. I would say he's aiming to be emperor, but I don't know. My gut tells me there's something else. You ever heard of someone named Servius?"

"Servius what?"

Lia shook her head. "I don't know. Just Servius."

"Sure. It's a common enough praenomen."

"Yeah." Lia frowned, thinking. She needed to get to safety, but she also needed clues. And she needed them before she escaped—after all, the evidence was on this skystation and would be unreachable once she left. "Where would they take captured cargo?" she asked.

Syd frowned. "Here? Probably just to storage, beneath the Praetorium."

"Not to a secure vault or anything?"

"It's a giant flying fortress, Lia. How much more secure could it be?"

"Fair point. Is storage accessible from down here?"

"Sure."

"Can you take me there?"

Sydney hesitated. "You need to get out of here, Lia. I can't hide you forever—and if they find out I'm helping you..."

Lia turned to look at them. "Sydney, I need to figure out what's going on. I was just arrested, told I was a fraud. This isn't some petty senatorial corruption. Something is happening, and it's happening—to some extent—right here. I need to find out as much as I can. The Empire could be at stake, here."

"It sounds like that isn't your job anymore, Lia," Syd responded, unsure.

"They've taken my title, not my duty. I can still do the job. I can still root out corruption without their resources. Can you help me or not?"

Sydney sighed. "You always were driven. All right, let's go."

Sydney grabbed a small oil lantern on their way out of the office, and they re-entered the twisting pathways of pipes and steam. Sydney moved assuredly through the maze—Lia, meanwhile, was lost in seconds.

It didn't take more than a few minutes to reach the end of the pipes and engines on the other side of the fortress, where there was a large metal door with STORAGE written across it in pristine white paint.

"It'll be locked," Sydney said.

Lia pulled out her keyring. "Turner already got that covered."

"Of course she did."

The room beyond the metal door was dark. Sydney held up the oil lantern, casting dancing shadows across the walls. It was an enormous storeroom filled with stacked crates of non-perishable foods, casks of wine and beer, shelves of folded uniforms and spare equipment. Lia strode inside, Sydney behind her, and began searching up and down the rows of crates for anything that could be the cargo of the *Red Raven*.

A shadow caught her eye. It moved independently of the patterns from the dancing flame. Lia whirled and crouched low behind a crate—and saw Turner step into the light.

Sydney jumped. Then they saw who it was. "Jupiter's balls."

"Cargo's over here," Turner said as Lia stood. She tossed a rifle towards Lia, who grabbed it out of the air. *Her* rifle, with her badge tied around the butt.

"How'd you get this?" she asked.

"Stole it from the guards. When I saw you head towards the walls, I figured you'd meet up with Sydney and get here eventually."

"Wait," Lia said, "you knew Syd was on board?"

Turner nodded. "Of course I did. I did my research before we came."

Sydney frowned. "Good to see you, too, Turner. Didn't think to come say hi?"

"We were busy—" Turner started to say, then stopped herself. She sighed. "Sorry, Syd. It's been a while. How are you?"

"Helping a criminal, apparently," Sydney said. "You?"

"Being a criminal, apparently. From what I can figure out, all of our records have been erased. Or, at least, McAvoy has letters stating that we're frauds and have no records."

Meanwhile, Lia moved towards the crates Turner stood by. She tried to pry one open—but it was nailed shut. She took the butt of her rifle to it. Wood splintered.

"Where's Brendan?" she asked as she levered the top off.

"Keeping watch upstairs." Turner peered into the crate as Lia opened it. Sydney came over too, holding their lamp above it.

The crate was filled with metal parts—from large sheets of steel to tiny gears and screws, brass pipes and valves.

Lia immediately moved to the next crate as Turner and Sydney looked in.

"Clockwork supplies?" Sydney said. "Steam engines?"

"Remaking supplies, perhaps," Turner said.

"No," Lia said, prying off the next lid and looking in. She reached down and pulled a paper-wrapped package from the inside. It was labelled *Caution: volatile equipment*. "Weapons. Bombs."

The crates were branded with the symbol of the Ottoman Empire.

"So, they apprehended pirates carrying illegally obtained weapon material," Sydney said. "That seems... like exactly what they should be doing."

Lia shook her head. "It was supposedly stolen from the EIC. Why would they have Ottoman explosives? And there was a letter in the senator's quarters. I think this is... payment, maybe. For someone called 'Servius.' The senator is deliberately arming someone."

A door at the far end of the storage room burst open. Lia whirled, hand on her rifle.

"They're coming," Brendan called from the door.

"Let's move," Lia said.

"We have to get off the fortress," Turner said.

"They won't let any ferries leave while they're searching for us."

"They won't stop searching until they find us."

"Then we hide well."

"It won't be enough."

"I have to get out of here," Sydney said.

Lia turned to them. "We could use you."

"What for? A meat shield? I don't think so, Lia."

Turner watched them, but didn't say anything. Sydney glared at Lia.

"They'll find us in the Complex eventually, and we don't want to implicate Syd. Brendan, where were you hiding?"

He'd pulled a pistol from his belt, looking back up the stairs he'd come down. "The *Red Raven*. There's just a couple guards by it, and it's off the fortress itself, I figured—"

"That's perfect!" Lia said. "That's our ticket out of here. Commandeer the impounded ship!"

"Fly a pirate ship. That's very low-key," Sydney said.

"Like you said, we're criminals," Turner said, nodding to Lia.

Lia turned to Sydney. "Syd—there's just three of us, and none of us know engines like you do. We need you if we're going to get out of here."

"What?" they said. "No way, Lia. You're going to get shot out of the sky."

Turner turned to them. "Not with you piloting us," she said. "Syd, you can pilot a cargo ship through a hurricane. You don't think you can escape an ill-prepared skystation in a tiny pirate ship?"

Sydney looked at her, then looked at Lia.

"It'll be like old times," Lia said, the corner of her mouth lifting.

"Do you know how many times I almost got killed in the 'old times'?"

"How long on a skystation before you get bored?"

"They pay well!"

"We don't. But we're more fun."

Sydney scowled. But it was a scowl of resignation.

"Let's move," Brendan said.

"I hate you," Sydney said.

"At least wait until we almost get you killed," Brendan replied, grinning.

"The way up the stairs will be cut off," Lia said. "Syd, can you get us through the Complex and bring us out close to the *Raven*?"

"Of course I can."

The sound of pounding feet came from the staircase leading out of the storage area.

"Now, please," Turner said.

Everyone dashed towards the door to the Complex. The far door burst open again, and Imperial legionaries swarmed into the storage room. Rifles fired, bullets ricocheting off the walls. Sydney ducked and yelped—Lia grabbed them from behind and pushed them through the door while Brendan crouched behind a crate and fired back to cover their retreat.

"I hate you!" Syd called back to him.

Then they were in the Complex and running. Sydney's mind was like a difference engine: they knew every turn through the pipes and steam while the others would be lost in seconds. But that meant whoever was chasing them would be lost too.

"They know we're down here—they'll have the exits guarded," Turner said, jogging up next to Lia.

"I know. Be ready to fight. Brendan, give me your pistol."

Brendan tossed her the pistol; she tossed back her rifle. Then they arrived at the door leading to the upper deck.

"Ready?" Lia asked. The others nodded. Sydney was panting.

They reached the top of the stairs. Then Lia grabbed Sydney from behind, put a gun to their head, and pushed through the door.

"Don't move or the engineer dies," she yelled at the legionaries encircling the door on the deck.

They held their fire, looking to their centurion.

"Lia Song and company, you are under arrest!" the centurion said. "Let Engineer Irons go or we will be forced to fire."

"I'll kill them!" Behind her, Brendan and Turner were slowly moving into position to run.

"Don't do it!" Sydney cried. They sounded convincing; the genuine threat of bodily harm lent them some authenticity.

"We have been authorized to take whatever measures necessary for your apprehension," the centurion said.

"They want me that badly?" Lia said. "I'm touched."

"Dead or alive."

"Less touched. So be it."

Lia pushed Sydney behind her and fired at the guards. Brendan fired from behind her as well, and they ran. Shots rang after them. Lia felt one graze her side, a spray of blood on the inside of her coat.

"They were willing to kill me!" Sydney said, aghast.

"And you wanted to stay?" Lia gasped.

Brendan and Turner leapt up a ladder to the uppermost deck, then pulled Lia and Sydney up behind them. Soldiers were giving chase. A few on the upper deck spotted them, but they were too far away. Cold wind whipped at them, out in the open; the skystation's huge balloon loomed overhead like a storm cloud. The gunshots were muffled by the rushing air.

The *Red Raven* floated nearby, tethered to the side of the skystation on one of the many docking platforms. All its guards were inside the fortress looking for them.

Lia checked her side. Blood matted her clothes and pain pulsed with every heartbeat—but it hadn't hit anything vital. As long as she got it cleaned and bound soon...

"You okay?" Brendan asked at her side, then saw the blood. "By Apollo's pretty face..."

"I'll be fine. Let's go!"

Another volley of shots rang below them as they crouched as low as they could. Staying low, they moved towards Turner, who squatted beside an exterior ladder heading down to the *Raven*. She waved them through, first Lia, then Sydney, then Brendan following close after.

The *Red Raven* was a small ship—only forty feet from bow to stern. Its hull was painted red, worn over time. They leapt onto its deck.

"Brendan, Turner, get her ready," Lia called back to them while she and Sydney headed below decks.

It was a relief to get out of the wind.

The relief was short-lived.

"Lia Song." Centurion Destin Stormcloud stood on the lower deck in front of the helm, arms crossed, fingers of one hand tracing the butt of a pistol in his belt. Two legionaries stood at attention behind him, rifles in hand.

"Centurion," Lia said.

Sydney looked from one to the other, unsure what they should do.

"Go start the engines, Syd," Lia said.

Sydney looked at Destin, but the centurion didn't even acknowledge them. He stared at Lia. Sydney bolted for the stairs down to the engine room.

Lia crossed her arms. "Congratulations, Destin," she said. "You can apprehend the fugitive. That's what you wanted, right?"

"It's over, Lia," Destin said.

"We're going to fly out of here in a minute. With you on board or not. Brendan's fond of throwing people off the edge of airships."

The legionaries shifted their grips on their rifles.

"Yes, threaten me," Destin said. "We don't already have enough reasons to arrest you. Your little crusade is over. I hear you've been stripped of your authority. I guess someone does guard the Guard."

"You think that's what this is?" Lia said, stepping forward. "You think I so overstepped the ethical responsibility of the Guard that someone above kicked me out?"

"I'm sure they've just been looking for an excuse."

Lia snorted. "So, someone sent them a message from this skystation, delivered it to Rome, got me fired, and delivered the message back here. In, what, a day?"

"Must have crossed the line a long time ago, Lia."

"You were the one who delivered the warning, Destin," Lia said. "You said not to look into the senator. Here. Now. And then I'm suddenly a criminal. You've known me awhile, Destin. Have I been lying about being in the Praetorian Guard this entire time? What, forged my badge? Faked my relationships?"

Destin stared at her.

"Vivarius pulled some trigger. Here. Now. Because I got too close to something."

"Because you overstepped your authority—"

"It's my *job to*," Lia said. "I guard the Empire. From whatever threat, whether that's the Ottomans or whether that's the emperor himself. I get close to something involving the senator and suddenly I was never even in the Praetorian Guard. Does that seem right to you? Do you honestly think there's nothing strange going on?"

Destin toyed with the handle of his pistol. Below them, the engine rumbled to life. Outside, propellers began to slowly turn as steam flowed through the pipes of the ship.

"I've never liked you, Song," Destin said.

"My loss."

He pulled out his pistol. Lia tensed. The legionaries brought their rifles up a bit.

Destin glanced at them, then her again.

"I'm not always one to play by the rules," Destin said, looking at his gun. "So I'm sure you don't like me much either. But this?" He looked at her again. Paused. "I like this less. You have far too big a stick up your arse to be the criminal they say you are."

Brendan appeared at the top of the stairs, a question on his lips.

Then, suddenly, Destin levelled the pistol at Lia and fired—and splinters flew from the wall behind her. She gasped, and Brendan stepped forward, ready to charge—but Destin hadn't shot her.

He motioned at her wound. "Unfortunately, you got the ship ready to fly before I could stop you. I didn't have time to get more than a shot off."

He waved to the legionaries, and the three of them walked towards the stairs to the top deck.

Brendan looked at Lia—who nodded to him—and let them pass.

Destin stopped at the top of the stairs and turned back to Lia. Brendan was checking her side. "I don't know who guards the Guard," he said. "But you're going to have to guard yourself now." He took the last step, and added, "Good luck."

And then he and his legionaries were gone.

Sydney emerged from the engine room and looked from Lia to the retreating figures. "What—"

"Get us out of here," Lia said.

They nodded and went to the helm. With a final check to make sure she'd be okay—she waved him away—Brendan ran above deck to cast off.

There was a lurch as the *Red Raven* left berth and floated free of the *Munimentum*, suddenly tethered to gravity once more. The engine roared, thunder accompanied by the cracks of gunshots like rain on a tin roof, half-drowned by the rushing wind.

Lia found some spare cloth and pressed it against her side to stem the bleeding, wincing in pain. She looked out the front window at the grey skies, at the twinkling lights of Londinium far below, as Sydney piloted them away from the skystation, swerving left and right to avoid the fortress's cannons. Millions of people down below them. *Even below our very feet, rumblings of protest and revolt creep through Britannia against Roman rule. The plight of the colonized, they say.* Was that the rot destroying the Empire? Or was it the immune system, instinctively fighting against a corruption rooted deep in the nation? The subconscious guards of survival.

The Empire was broken. It had been for centuries. It was crumbling around them. But it was crumbling from the inside. Rotten.

Was it worth saving?

Lia stood, keeping her weight off her injured side. Sydney glanced at her, but she stood tall, determined. She was a Praetorian Guard. The first and the last line of defense. For the Empire.

No. For the *people* of the Empire.

That's who mattered. This wasn't about some idealized State; ideals were dangerous. Vivarius was a man of ideals.

Lia fought for the people. And as the airship flew above Londinium, she was starting to see that a war was brewing against them.

Chapter 7: Grounded

JULIAN

They walked along the lonely Italian roads in silence for a long time. Julian didn't know what to say. His mind felt empty of thought. All that was left was exhaustion. Still, they walked.

It felt like something had broken in him up in the airship. When Gaius found him. When Gaius had come for him. A dam that he'd built up inside of him over the last year, breached.

But maybe he'd built it long before the last year.

Now he just felt empty.

Finally, Gaius sat down in the shade of a tree. He looked exhausted himself. Julian hadn't noticed how far they'd walked—except now he realized how leaden his legs felt. He sat too, not facing Gaius. He suddenly felt like he could sleep for days.

The hills of the Italian countryside rolled around them, waves of green beneath a grey sky, the colour accentuated beneath the monochrome. It was warm, even a little humid. Birds chirped nearby.

Julian wondered how long it had been since he'd heard any birds other than pigeons.

Suddenly, he felt Gaius's hand on his outstretched leg. He twitched unconsciously—Gaius almost let go at that, but didn't. Julian was glad he didn't.

"...Hi," Gaius said, softly.

It was an absurd thing to say after everything. But then, it was their first *real* greeting in over a year.

Julian couldn't quite bear to look at him.

"I'm sorry," he said. "I don't—" He trailed off. Didn't what? Didn't know what had come over him. Didn't even really know what he'd done. His mind couldn't parse it.

He'd been so angry.

So alone.

Gaius didn't say anything at first. Just kept his hand on Julian's leg.

"I... I don't know if you can tell me what they did to you. Really," Gaius said. He sounded like he was choosing his words with care. "I don't know how long it will be before you can. You're different, Jules, I know that much..."

Was he? He supposed he was. He supposed anyone would be.

"...But you're still my Jules."

Finally, Julian turned to look at him.

Gaius looked tired. Hardened—his shoulders were broader, his skin rougher, his eyes... older. But they were his eyes. The eyes Julian had loved. The eyes he thought had left him forever.

"I missed you," Julian said.

"I never stopped looking for you," Gaius said.

"I thought—" There was a hitch in his throat. "I thought I had nothing left. I thought I'd lost you..."

Gaius shifted closer, and suddenly his arms were around Julian, holding Julian's head to his chest. Julian was buried in his scent, and the tension and worry and anger drained out of him in an instant. He melted into Gaius, and tears sprang to his eyes.

"You're heavier than you used to be," Gaius said, a smile in his voice. Julian suddenly became aware of his metal chest digging into Gaius's body and tried to shift. But Gaius just held him more tightly, and Julian stilled.

"I don't know what I did," Julian said, quietly.

"You tried to change the world," Gaius said. "Like you always said you would."

Julian cried, silently. Sudden images of the terrified airship crew flashed into his mind alongside visions of a Rome devastated by destruction.

What had he almost done?

"I never meant..."

"I know. But you're here now. You're okay."

Julian shook his head, digging it deeper into Gaius's chest.

"Just—no more explosives, okay?"

Julian snorted wetly and softly nodded.

Interlude

Aurelia,

Have you ever planned for something for a long time, worked and worked to make it happen, only to see it crumble at the last moment?

I suppose, in a way, you have.

Where I came from, we were expected to put in the work. That those who deserve it, who work hard, will succeed. That failure to succeed is failure as a person. But sometimes no amount of work can allow for success. No amount of work can make up for things outside of your control. No amount of contingency can plan for everything.

You taught me that, really.

I almost had a good day today.

The Senate had a landmark session. I'm sure you heard. Sweeping new legislation on remaking. It truly will change how the Empire handles industry, how it shapes the economy.

The summit went well. Without a hitch. I was... surprised.

You know how politicians can be. I expected it to be a little more explosive.

Sometimes no matter how many contingencies you lay, you still don't succeed. Sometimes you just have to get back to work.

Another summit is scheduled for a few weeks from now. Everyone should be in attendance to deal with the unrest up north.

I'll visit soon.
— S.

Silence has descended upon a small pub in northern England. Here, news of the new curfew has just reached them. It is taking time to sink in as these pub-goers realize the effect the law will have on their social lives—and their commerce.

But according to Senator Vivarius, these are necessary precautions in a time of uncertainty. The senator, recently appointed Praetor of the Committee on the Imperial Homeland, has returned to the British Province this week to spearhead his new initiative meant to quell rebellious rumblings in the province.

Speaking at a rally of his political supporters in Londinium in response to the factory worker strike in the province, he was quoted as saying, "This is an event quite unlike any we have seen previous. There is no moral justification for a strike of this nature, not when the work of the industrial centres of Britannia are the heart's-blood of this Empire." This statement was met by cheers. He continued, "This act is one against not only the Empire, but also its people who count on the good work of Britannia to feed, clothe, and power them."

The curfew implemented this week is part of a multi-stage plan to ensure the smooth functioning of the industry of the Empire and comes only a month after the Imperial Skystation Munimentum was stationed at Londinium to help uphold peace and prosperity in the city.

You're listening to Imperial Radio, news from the four corners of Rome. Coming up, reports of a victory on the Ottoman front...

PART 2

Chapter 8: Public Affairs

GAIUS

The proprietress of the caffè, Claretta, tuned the large radio to another channel, and Italian music filled the room. Gaius had noticed she tended to switch off the news when it turned to the Ottomans—maybe because of her wife, Omid, who looked like she was from that part of the world. The few patrons who'd been listening to the news report returned to their conversations, a small din to compete with the music. Julian, sitting across from Gaius, remained quiet.

Orvieto was a quiet town, a walled settlement on top of a hill overlooking the countryside. A couple roads wound their way up the hill, but most traffic took the funicular, which brought crops up into the village and people down again. The town centre was dominated by a massive old temple to Mars, a statue of the god out front complete with plumed helm—and naked otherwise. The paint on it was flaking, revealing the white marble beneath.

Gaius kind of preferred that to the garish colours.

Orvieto was several days from Rome, and most traffic along the main highways passed right by it. Vineyards coated the nearby hills and valleys. There was a peace here, only occasionally broken by the news coming over the radio.

Gaius and Julian had found a little place to stay—dank, cramped quarters, but all they could afford with what little money they each had. The landlord had taken pity on them, though they'd been very quiet about where they'd come from or who they were.

Not that either of them was anyone, now.

Other than, perhaps, wanted.

Gaius had gotten bits and pieces of what had happened to Julian this past year. He never pressed it—there was clearly some kind of trauma there, something he didn't want to force out. Something that had driven Julian to that airship. So, he'd taken only what Julian volunteered.

They'd come to this caffè a few times since arriving. They didn't want to draw a lot of attention to themselves, but Claretta had made them feel welcome.

Julian's face had turned sour after the news broadcast. It often did.

"You okay?" Gaius asked, knowing it was a useless question but not wanting to let the silence stretch or let Julian stew.

Julian shrugged. "Vivarius," he said, quietly. "Senators shouldn't have that kind of power. He's just pushed further since..." He trailed off.

Gaius nodded. "Nothing we can do, Jules. Just gotta stay safe, stay quiet..."

Julian didn't respond. Gaius sighed a little.

All he wanted—all he'd ever wanted, really—was to find some peaceful little place where he could live out his life with Julian. Get away from the politics—get Julian away from all the things that made him angry. Leave everyone else to their own problems.

He wasn't sure if Julian would ever settle for that, though. He'd always wanted to change the world—to have the strength to fix the Empire. He had more physical strength, now... But even with that, what could he really do?

His eyes fell on Julian's chest. That metal plate beneath his shirt. The ticking clockwork.

The first time they'd lain together after the airship, naked in bed, he'd been afraid of the prosthesis. Wasn't sure how to handle it. Afraid it would be cold against his skin.

But it wasn't. It was warm, like Julian's body.

No. Not exactly like his body.

But it was part of him. More than that, it kept him alive. That beating pump, the ticking gears. That was Julian now.

He was learning to embrace it. Growing used to the weight of it—as he was sure Julian was, too.

Nothing would be the same as it was when they were young. But at least they had each other again.

They had each other—and in a way they never did before. It was Julian who had brought it up.

"Why did you come after me?" he'd asked.

Gaius had looked at him, bemused. "I promised I would."

Julian had shaken his head, looked away, as if that wasn't the answer he'd wanted. "Gaius, when we were kids, I—you always did as you were asked. Even if you wanted to—it can't—Gaius, *us*, we can't—"

"Jules, I love you," he'd responded.

"I *owned* you," Julian had said, still not looking at him. "Everything we've had, no matter what *you* wanted, if I asked—it's not right—how do I know—"

Gaius had taken his hand in his own, and Julian had glanced at him. "I love you, Jules. I always have, but—Jules, you *never* asked. It was never a... requirement. Not even implicitly."

"You can't know that. Even if you feel that—"

Gaius had nodded, looked down at Julian's hand—so small in his own. "You're right," he'd said. "Maybe we can't just continue on as if nothing changed. Because it has." He'd squeezed Julian's hand, who finally looked at him. "I'm free now. You don't own—well, much at all..." Julian couldn't help but smile. "So let's start over. Fresh. Without... bonds, conscious or not. I didn't come for you because I promised a master. I came because I love you. I came because I wanted you. It was a year, Jules—I came of my own free will."

Julian nodded. "A fresh start."

"I love you."

"I love you, too."

At least they had each other.

Now, Gaius watched as Claretta organized bottles of wine behind the bar of the caffè. Omid came out of the back kitchen with a tray of flatbreads piled high with cured meat.

"Order's up," Omid said.

Claretta planted a quick kiss on her olive-brown cheek and took a raw strand of organ off the tray. She knelt by the bar fireplace, where Gaius had seen her kneel many times to give a quick prayer to Vesta and the genius loci, and tossed the innards into the flames.

Omid watched her do it, then Claretta stood and took the tray from her.

"Hush," she said to Omid.

"I didn't say a word," Omid replied.

"I know."

She brought the tray of flatbreads out to the table beside Gaius and Julian by the foggy window, where a couple of older patrons Gaius had seen here before sat.

"Still keeping the hearth, eh?" the woman asked.

"Italian women only got the right to citizenship in your lifetime, Maria," Claretta said to her. "The least we can do is keep up the res publica."

"Maybe if everyone thought like you, the Empire wouldn't be in this state," said the man, Publius. "You heard what's happening in Britannia? Provincials, I tell you."

"Oh, stop it," Maria scoffed at her husband. "Those people have been pushed around by the Senate for centuries; you can hardly blame them for a little doubt in the Empire."

Claretta nodded. "We must all play our part for a stronger Empire, even the Senate. If they can't keep their own people happy and well-served by the state... well, look what the Ottomans did."

Maria glanced towards the door to the back kitchen where Omid had disappeared once more. "Aye, love. You're not wrong."

"Well, maybe Vivarius can get it all settled down and happy again," Publius grunted.

"Are you kidding?" Maria slapped his arm. "He's going too far, that one. When has stamping your feet and telling the kids to go to their room ever really helped? Harsher rules aren't the way."

Publius shrugged.

"Ah, well," Maria sighed. "At least he's just one senator. The rest will rein him in soon enough. And if not, we can always vote him out, right, Claretta?"

Claretta smiled. "That's right, Maria. Enjoy the food."

Gaius looked at Julian as Claretta moved away. Julian's look had soured further.

"Vivarius wouldn't give up power so easily," he said under his breath.

"What's he going to do?" Gaius asked. "I know he flaunts his power, but come on. He's not Caesar."

"He wants to be."

"Well, what can we do about it?"

Gaius realized his mistake as soon as he said it. It was exactly what had always vexed Julian.

"Stop him!" Julian said. "Expose him, his corruption. Take him down…"

Gaius didn't want to ask what Julian meant by "take him down." After the airship…

"I don't know," Julian said, quiet again, frustrated. "I don't know what I can do. I just—I have to do *something*…"

"The best thing we can do is hide," Gaius said, imploring. "Keep our heads down. People could still be looking for you. We could just find someplace to stay low. Make up for the time we lost…"

Julian nodded along with his words, but Gaius was worried he wasn't really listening.

Chapter 9: Sunflowers

LIA

Thunder cracked overhead, and the wind rocked the ship around Lia and her crew. They'd set down in a field in Gaul, surrounded by sunflowers—the *Red Raven* still a little damaged from their escape and low on fuel. They'd flown all over for a few days, making sure they hadn't been followed, before finally stopping to take stock of things.

Now the yellow of the sunflowers was a sharp contrast to the black clouds above. Even more sharp, though, was the red of the airship.

"We'll be spotted from miles away if they're looking for us," Brendan said.

"They're looking for us," Syd replied. They were half-buried beneath the helm, tinkering with the mechanisms, but Lia could hear the stress in their voice.

"We don't even really know what our situation is," Lia said. She was sitting, checking the bandage wound around her midriff. The wound wasn't bleeding so much now and was slowly starting to heal—but it hurt. Thank Apollo the shot hadn't been much more than a graze. "We don't know the whys or the hows or the extent of it all. Turner?"

They were all on the bridge of the *Red Raven*. Stairs led up to the top deck while a single door led back to a cramped galley and shared bunks beyond. Beneath them were the engine room and cargo hold, currently empty.

Turner was staring out through the bridge window at the lashing rain, deep in thought.

"We know someone has it out for us," she said. "Likely Vivarius, given that, one, we have it out for *him*, and two, he has the power to make something like this happen."

Sydney pulled themselves out from the mechanics, rubbing a sore bicep. "Does he, though? Really? This is pretty fucked up."

"You're not wrong," Lia said. She winced as she shifted position. "But our investigations into his efforts so far suggest that his connections reach very far through the Imperial workings. Old East India favours, other senators he's helped out with influence and money, and supposedly a friendship with Geminius."

Brendan snorted. "Nothing more than a politically advantageous sucking-up, that one."

"Maybe so," Lia said, "but he definitely has the connections. And from what we've seen the last few weeks, he's only just started to really test his limits—pull some of those threads, push the edges of his influence."

"Making a move for emperor, you said," Syd continued.

Lia sighed. "Maybe." She didn't quite believe her own theory. It seemed too... pedestrian for Vivarius.

Turner nodded. "So Vivarius realizes we're onto him and needs to neutralize the threat. Discrediting Lia through the proper channels would be a lot of work; killing us would just cause problems for him, not to mention prove something was going on. So, he pulls some strings, and suddenly—according to anyone important, anyway—Lia isn't a Guard and never has been. His problem is solved—we have no power to do anything about him, and the forces of the Empire are turned against us."

"Meanwhile, Vivarius gets to go about his plans unhindered, and we're back to square one."

"Not to mention out of a job," Brendan said.

"Least of our problems," she said. Lia sighed and hoisted herself to her feet, needing to move. She paced across the length of the bridge, hand held to her side.

"It is? We still need to eat."

"And refuel," Syd said. "And fuel ain't cheap."

"We have enough on us for the short term," Lia said. "And if we get to a city, we can get more out of the banks."

"If they haven't wiped *those* records, too," Turner said.

"Jupiter's greedy little cock, I hadn't thought of that," Lia said. "Would he do that? It seems overkill."

"Won't know until we check," Turner replied.

"We could always *rob* a bank, I guess," Brendan said.

Lia glared at him.

"I'm not entirely kidding!" Brendan said. "Vivarius has forced us outside of the law. If you want to keep investigating him—"

"Of course I do!"

"—which I know you do, *especially* now, we're going to have to do things that are now illegal for us to do, right?"

Lia swore again. "*If* all our records have actually been wiped. There's no way they could've checked official papers while they were up there. Even if he's planned for this for a while, he could've just convinced Stormcloud and the local centurions..."

"How would you find out?" Syd asked.

"Go to Rome and find the archives?" Brendan said.

"That might not go well," Lia said.

Turner crossed her arms. "I can check with some contacts."

"If you still have any," Syd said grimly.

"I do. They can erase papers—they can't erase memories."

Brendan smirked. "Are we sure?"

Lia shot him a look again. "All right. We need more information. Turner, you check with your contacts. Meanwhile, Brendan and I will find the nearest settlement, see if we can't find some fuel—and some paint. This damned *Red Raven* is a little *too* red for my liking. Syd, you stay, watch the ship, and see to those repairs."

"And if someone finds us while you're gone...?" Syd asked.

Lia shrugged. "Pretend you were taken prisoner."

Syd swallowed. "Right."

Lia was lost in thought as she passed the paintbrush back and forth over the hull of the not-so-red *Raven* when she heard the sound of a shotgun cocking. She froze mid-stroke.

"Who the hell are you and what are you doing in my sunflowers?" a gruff voice speaking French barked from off to their right.

Brendan gave her a look, but she made a tiny negation motion with her head. She turned and slowly raised her hands, paintbrush held loosely in one of them.

A man stood among the sunflowers, shotgun pointed at them from the hip. The farmer, she guessed.

"Bonjour," she said. "Nous sommes…" She was never good at French. She switched to Latin. "We're lost. Our airship is damaged. I'm sorry if we damaged any of your flowers."

"What are you doing?" The farmer switched to Latin as well; his accent was strong, but he spoke well.

"We had to make an emergency landing," Lia said. "I'm sorry—"

"What is the paint? Are you pirates?"

Ah. "No, we—" She faltered a bit. There weren't any good excuses for repainting an airship in the middle of someone else's sunflower field.

"We stole it from the Imperial navy," Turner said, suddenly walking into the clearing.

The farmer spun on her—then lowered the shotgun. "Fucking Imperials," he said, spitting on the ground.

Turner nodded sagely.

The farmer looked from her to Lia and back, then said, "You fuck them up some more, we'll call it even on the sunflowers."

"You bet!" Brendan said.

The farmer looked at him, nodded, spat again, and walked back into the sunflowers.

Lia raised her eyebrow at Turner.

"Turns out," Turner said, "not a lot of fans of the Empire in the area."

"Apparently. Good timing. What'd you find?"

Turner's face turned grim. "Nothing good. Where's Syd?"

"Here!" Syd's voice came from the back of the ship. They emerged, covered in grease. "What's up?"

Lia put her brush down.

"I made contact with a local agent. We're in the middle of nowhere so they weren't anyone important. Probably good for us, though their information was incomplete. Nonetheless, it sounds like everyone in the Agentes had gotten the message—we are officially disavowed. No one knows why, but the tone is serious. If I had to guess, this was a trigger Vivarius was ready to pull weeks ago."

"How come this guy helped you, then?"

Turner shrugged. "I have a good reputation. And the Agentes aren't so quick to forget one of our own, whatever the Empire wants."

"That's why I never trusted them," Lia said.

Turner smiled tightly. "And yet."

Lia nodded. "You proved different."

"Anyway, he was willing to give me that much, but not much more. Seemed real cagey the whole time. Wanted to keep it brief."

"So what does this mean?" Syd asked.

"It means it's real," Lia said. "Not just a temporary scare tactic. We're no longer agents of the Empire. And not just me—Turner, too."

"And me!" Brendan said.

Lia nodded.

"We no longer have the law on our side," Turner said.

Lia turned to her. "We have the law on our side—what Vivarius is doing isn't *lawful*. We just don't wield the same *authority*."

"Haven't you been paying attention?" Turner said suddenly. "Vivarius is *making* the laws. It may not be *ethical*, but he does have the law on his side. Which means if we continue—and I know we will," she added, cutting Lia off before she could say anything, "then we're working outside the law."

"Fine," Lia said. "Maybe we won't have the law on our side. But we will have justice."

Syd nodded a little even as Turner rolled her eyes.

"Regardless," Turner said, "our options have become quite limited."

"Doesn't this kind of open doors?" Brendan said. "If we're outside the law anyway, we're not bound by it anymore. We can do whatever we need to."

"We're not about to go completely off the rails," Lia said. "We still serve the *Empire*, if I have anything to say about it. We still serve the people. No harm where we can help it." She picked up her brush and turned her attention back to the ship.

"What now, then?" Syd asked.

Lia painted over a red board, starting to cover up the name *Red Raven* on the side of the ship. Her mind spun, trying to put together where they were, what their angles were. Lay out all the information in her head.

"What did we learn on the *Munimentum?*" she said. "We know Vivarius *is* up to something, something big enough that he'd do whatever it took to take us out of the picture."

"My contact confirmed that, too," Turner said. "He didn't say anything specific, but he was dancing around it. The Agentes have their fingers in some things—and are purposefully overlooking others."

Lia nodded. "We also know Vivarius was showboating on that station—consolidating power, putting some influence over Britannia... But it was a front, too, capturing the *Red Raven* and all. A weapons payment, maybe from the EIC, for someone named Servius..."

"Which could be anyone," Brendan said.

Lia nodded. "There's threads of a lead here, but it's not much."

"We need to find out who Servius is," Turner said. "And what they're doing with the weapons."

"How do we do that?" Syd asked.

Lia slopped grey paint over the word *Raven*. "We talk to someone a little closer to all this."

She looked up as thunder pealed again. A storm cloud approaching.

Chapter 10: Survival

JULIAN

Doing nothing had always been hard.

As a kid, Julian had been shackled by the fears of his caretakers regarding his constitution, forced to avoid doing much for fear of collapse or worse. But the fire had burned in him, the need to do something, anything—watching his parents get walked over, watching the corruption in the Empire grow.

Now Vivarius, who'd sold him and his parents into slavery on fabricated charges, seemed to be making a real grab for power, and Julian finally had the freedom to do something.

Yet here they were, hiding in a little Italian hilltop town, doing nothing. And his mind wouldn't stop showing him what he'd done.

"I have to do something," he said to Gaius one morning.

Gaius looked up as he got dressed. "What?"

"*Anything*," Julian said. "I can't keep just sitting here... I can't—" He shook his head. "When I just sit, when I can't sleep, I just see it all again. The lab where they took me. The blood..." His hand went to his own chest, the metal warm but hard.

Gaius put a hand on his shoulder, concern in his face. Listening, not pushing...

Passive. Like all of this.

"I can't just stay here. I can't just hide. I need to do something. What Servius was doing, what Vivarius is doing... What he did to my parents..."

He drifted off. Gaius pulled him into a hug, but anxiety pulsed in him and he felt claustrophobic, restrained. He escaped Gaius's hold and saw a pained look in his love's face.

"I'm sorry, I just—I need to do something."

Gaius nodded. "It's okay. I understand. I wish there was something you could do, but they're probably looking for you still, Jules. This... Servius guy, wouldn't he want you back?"

Julian nodded a little. "Maybe. But how's he going to find me?"

"If you go out there, try to do something—like you did before..."

"I'm not—I'm not going to... to steal another airship, Gaius." Images of the crew, the terrorized faces, flashed in his head. Then they were replaced by the soldiers raiding his house. The terror on the servants' faces, his parents' faces. And fire burned in him.

He wanted to see the same look in Vivarius. He wanted him to suffer.

But Gaius was right. What could he do?

If he could get close to Vivarius...

He shook his head again. His thoughts had gone to a dark place. He didn't like that place. That wasn't the kind of person he wanted to be.

Political change, that's what he'd always wanted the strength to enact. But he was a disgraced runaway slave—he couldn't exactly enter the political scene, now. And could he even stop Vivarius if he did?

Maybe the dark thoughts were the only way.

He kicked the bed, trying to rouse himself from the thought spiral. He needed something—something to hold onto, something to occupy him, something that could show him a direction to move. Maybe give him answers, insight.

"What happened to my parents?" he asked suddenly. "After I was taken away, what happened to them?"

Gaius's brow raised. "I... don't know. I was gone by then, remember?"

"Thank Apollo, yes," Julian said. "You didn't hear anything after you left? You found me..."

"It was all I could do to find you, Jules. I didn't... I didn't really think to look for your parents. What could they have done for me? Or me for them?"

Julian nodded.

What had Vivarius done with them? What had he *wanted* from them? "How can we find them?"

"Julian, they might not even—" Gaius trailed off.

Julian pushed that thought from his mind. "I know. I just—I have to find out what happened to them. Maybe we can help them—and if not—" He shook his head, the thought spirals threatening to return. "I don't know. It's something. I can't just sit."

Gaius nodded and touched his arm. "Okay. I think that's a good idea, then. How do we find them?"

"I don't know. How did you find me?"

"I... had a friend in Rome keeping an eye on you. I couldn't afford to come until you left for Frankfurt..."

"A friend?" Julian smiled a little. "Since when do you have friends?"

Gaius stuck out his tongue at him, and Julian's smile widened—then fell as he came back to the moment.

"I worked with her in Parisium. Then she went to Rome, working for the EIC."

"If she found me—could she find my parents?"

Gaius shrugged. "I don't know. I don't know where she'd start. I don't know if she'd be willing, but, well, I guess I can ask. I'll send her a letter. It'll take a few days, and no promises..."

Julian smiled and nodded. It was a start.

In the meantime... more sitting, apparently. "Let's get something to eat."

They spent much of the day at the caffè. There wasn't much else to do. Gaius wrote his letter and paid the postage. The day was a little rainy so they didn't want to wander the village or the surrounding countryside as they had a few times before. And Claretta and Omid were good enough company.

It was quiet in the caffè today, which was nice too. The only other patrons were a couple of Ethiopians who lived in town. Crowds had made Julian anxious—and now he felt like people could see through his clothes, see the metal beneath.

They watched Claretta perform a hearth rite as she often did, to keep the caffè's genius happy; not a lot of people in the Empire were still so devoted to the orthopraxy, though the gods still touched their lips and lives. With the caffè so quiet, Omid didn't have much to do in the kitchen and was out cleaning tables and reorganizing wine.

The radio rattled through the news of the day, as it always did—news from the four corners of the Empire and beyond. A Senate summit on educational curricula, tariffs on American helium—which would anger various merchant guilds, though the EIC would probably have exceptions made for them—and rumours of an abolitionist movement amongst the Aztecs.

Julian listened intently to the Roman news. As much as it angered him not to be able to do anything about it, he wanted to hear what transpired in the Empire. He couldn't help but wonder if they were getting the full story. What was happening behind closed doors that the public never got to hear about? Wasn't it the job of the news to keep them informed?

Or just complacent?

When it got to the war with the Ottoman Empire, Claretta switched the channel back to soft music.

Omid passed by to ask if they needed anything. Julian cocked his head to one side.

"...May I ask something?"

"Of course," Omid said. She had a Persian accent, but spoke Latin well. "What do you need?"

"Oh, nothing from the caffè—I wanted to ask something of you. You're from the Ottoman Empire, aren't you?"

Her body language shifted at the question, became a little more reserved, defensive. She crossed her arms—but her face remained friendly.

"...I am," she said after a moment, like she was trying to figure out why he was asking.

"I mean no discomfort," Julian said quickly. He was suddenly glad his heart did not pump the flush of embarrassment into his cheeks; Gaius, meanwhile, was feeling embarrassed enough for the both of them, if his own cheeks were any indication. "I only wanted to ask... Your wife always changes the radio when it comes to speak of Ottoman affairs. Do you... not want to hear of your home?"

Omid's smile faded, though not from unfriendliness; her body even relaxed a little as it did. "Rome is at war with my people. Do you think their reports of the situation would be... kind? Fair, even?"

Julian frowned and nodded. "I guess I can see that. Still, isn't some news better than none? Or do you not care anymore, having come here?"

"I care," Omid said quickly. "I came to Rome out of necessity. Civil war was bringing death to many innocents in Ottoman Turkey. We fled. But not because we did not care about our country. No, I do not want to hear what the Romans say about my people because I know what they think of my people already. I see it every day on your faces."

Julian's eyes widened a little, his mouth opened, but Omid was quick to continue.

"Not *your* faces, no. But many Roman faces. I am a refugee, a foreigner. An enemy, to many..."

She sighed. Claretta had stopped what she was doing and was listening, concern on her face.

Julian nodded. "I guess I can understand that. And—I don't mean to offend..."

"No offense," Omid said, smiling. "It is not... simple. There is never a clear answer, a clear solution for an individual like me, or a whole nation. There is only... surviving. Both as an individual, and as a nation.

"So now tell me, Julian. I have told you why I am here. But you're not from here either, are you?"

Julian suddenly looked away.

"We're just visiting," Gaius said. "Trying to... get away from family for a bit..."

Omid smiled. "I understand. Family does not always understand matters of the heart as they should."

Julian's heart would have skipped a beat if it could. He looked up at Omid with sudden fear and suspicion—but Omid was looking back at Claretta with a soft smile, and Julian realized she hadn't been talking about *his* heart.

Well, not his new one.

He smiled and nodded, a bit too quickly.

Claretta came over to join them—now there was no one else in the caffè, the Ethiopians having made their way home. She smiled and sat at their table. "We're happy you found your way to our caffè, Julian and Gaius," she said.

Julian smiled. "Thanks."

Claretta's gaze drifted to the window—for a moment, all four of them were quiet—then Omid smiled at Claretta. "You're doing it again."

"Hm?" Claretta said. "Oh, I'm sorry. I drift away sometimes."

"Where do you go?" Julian asked.

She looked at him quizzically and smiled. "What a question. I go... out, into the town, into the hills and countryside, the mountains and vineyards and farms, and beyond, the rest of the world... Sometimes I like to think about all the other people out there—how many people there are out there—in the village, the province, the Empire, the world. Unfathomable numbers, and each of them with their own complete lives, trials and dreams, loved ones and needs..."

Julian nodded along. "It's a curious thought. So many people, so many problems, things they need help with..."

"But so many joys, too," Claretta said.

Omid grinned. "Such an optimist. Julian is like me—can't help but see what needs fixing."

"So how do you fix it all?" Julian asked.

"You can't," Omid said. "You just survive. And do as much as you can..."

She drifted off at the end. Julian could imagine where her mind went—home, to war and civil unrest and coups.

His own mind wasn't far off.

Chapter 11: Realignment

GAIUS

Doing nothing had become difficult.

Gaius had been content to hide from the world with Julian, to simply be together again. But he could sense Julian's restlessness. Julian wasn't content to sit, to wait. He was jumpy, still. He had nightmares. He wouldn't let himself relax long enough to simply enjoy the time with Gaius.

That was why Gaius had encouraged Julian to find his parents. Maybe if he found them, there'd be some kind of closure. Julian could rest again. They could just... be together.

But now they were waiting again. Waiting to hear from Alesse. *Hoping* to hear from her—Gaius had no guarantee she'd even received his letter. Days passed. He was starting to worry about Julian. About what he might do if they never heard.

How could he convince Julian to just... leave? They could find work in some little town somewhere nice. Live out their lives and forget Vivarius and Servius and everything. Dis, Julian could even join a town council or something—after they were sure no one was looking for them.

Which was the other problem. Gaius still didn't know much about what Julian had been through. Or who Servius was. Were they in danger? It seemed like Julian had just run away. He couldn't imagine he'd just be let go.

How long could this peace really last?

And then the clockwork messenger arrived. He heard the faint tapping on the door of their tiny apartment—he'd had to tell Alesse where to find them. He opened the door quickly as Julian stirred in bed.

The little thing of brass and gears sat in front of the door. Its internal navigation equipment whirred and clicked. It seemed to look at him.

He idly wondered if it was the same one he'd grabbed out of the air. It seemed peeved.

That felt like years ago now.

He bent down and pulled the little scroll case from its holster. The clockwork thing turned and immediately skittered away.

"What is it?" Julian asked. He was sitting up now and held the sheet over his body. He was still uncomfortable with the metal in his chest. Gaius wouldn't have minded—it was still Julian beneath.

"A letter," he said. He shut the door and sat on the bed as he cracked open the seal on the scroll case and dumped out the rolled paper.

The note was short.

Meet me at the Trattoria Cipresso in Pitigliano on the Kalends.

Alesse was usually terse in her messages, but typically she had a *bit* more to say. A pleasantry or two.

But she was asking to actually meet. He hadn't seen her in almost a year now, and he supposed the pleasantries could wait until seeing each other.

He looked at Julian. "Kalends isn't far off."

"It's not like we have much to pack."

Gaius smiled. With something to do, Julian almost sounded like his old self.

Pitigliano was another hilltop town, a couple of days from Rome and about a day from Orvieto by the main roads. Gaius and Julian walked along smaller country roads instead and camped in a small grove like they had on the way to Orvieto.

Julian had come out of his funk a bit, perhaps renewed from their rest or perhaps because he at last had something to do. They passed the time talking about their shared childhood, the family drama they'd witnessed together, the secrecy of their early relationship when they first discovered it was more than master and servant, more even than friendship. It was nice to remember the past. It kept them both from thinking about present or future.

Then they'd lapse into silence again, but it was a comfortable silence. Like it used to be.

Except then Gaius would think of the present again. Of the future.

He hoped Julian wasn't...

A couple days after leaving Orvieto, they arrived at Pitigliano. The town perched atop its hill like a crown on a king or a hulking eagle surveying its territory. The route from Orvieto wound lazily up along a ridge towards town where it then looked out over the valleys below. The town was full of tight buildings, one large fortress dominating them all.

Julian looked overwhelmed again. It was the people, Gaius had realized. The crowds. The strangers. He clutched at his coat around his shoulders, warm as it was.

Gaius flagged down a passerby and asked directions to the Trattoria Cipresso—it was only a few blocks away. He thanked the woman, and they made their way through the tight, winding streets of the town.

Alesse was waiting for them, sitting on the patio of the restaurant. He spotted her immediately—a larger woman with broad shoulders and short greying hair, endlessly fiddling with her remade hand. She had altered and tinkered with the mechanisms of the hand so much over time that most of the fingers had been replaced with tools of all sorts. He led Julian over to her, and she finally looked up from the hand as they neared.

Her face broke into a smile when she saw him, her skin creasing in hard-worked lines. Gaius couldn't help but grin back.

"Gaius, mon cher!" she said, arms outstretched.

"Don't get up, Alesse," he said, bending low to hug her.

"How are you?" she asked. "And this—this would be Julian, then."

Julian had held back a little. Gaius straightened and nodded. "Thanks to you. Jules, this is Alesse. I worked under her in Parisium."

Julian bowed a little, self-consciously, even as Alesse held out her arms again for a hug. Her smile tightened, but she lowered her arms. "A pleasure. Gaius told me much about you! You must be very happy to see each other again."

"We are," Gaius said, touching Julian reassuringly on the arm.

"Please, sit with me! Have some wine."

They sat as Alesse poured a couple of glasses. Her remade hand rested on the table, bristling with little screwdrivers, wrenches, tweezers, wire cutters, and more. They twitched a little, quivering like spider's legs.

"How's the hand?" Gaius asked.

"Acting up again," Alesse said. "The Company wanted to give me a replacement when I came down here, but I couldn't let them ruin all the hard work I'd put into this thing. Ah well, I get along."

"The thaumaturgical alignment's off," Julian said, quietly.

Gaius and Alesse looked over.

"How'd you know something like that?" Alesse said.

"I—uh—" Julian stuttered. "I worked at..."

"Ah. Of course. The lab where they took you, right?" Alesse said. "I was the one who found you for your dear Gaius, remember."

Julian lapsed into silence and nodded. Gaius put a hand on his knee.

"Well, you're not wrong. Love me some clockwork, but the thaumaturgical side of remaking always escaped me. I'll have to have it looked at."

Julian was watching the twitching tools. "What do you do?"

"Mechanic. Worked the factories with Gaius here."

"May I see?" Julian said, his hand hovering towards hers.

"Be careful—I still need that thing."

Julian nodded. She placed the clockwork hand in the centre of the table, and Julian began carefully examining the mechanisms as he continued to listen.

"Now I ply my craft in Rome," Alesse continued, "while the bulk of my time is spent fighting the gods-damned Senate."

Julian seemed to perk up. "Oh?"

Gaius grinned inwardly.

"The Company—the EIC, you understand—and, well, not just them by any stretch, all the capitalists, all the nobles—no offense—take advantage of the workers. Jobs are scarce so folks will do anything, put up with anything, for a little pay—no matter the danger, the hours, or how little it is."

Julian nodded. "Sure. But if people are willing to do the work..."

"Folks who have always had money cannot understand what it is to not have it. Don't see how stuck we get, no way to pull ourselves out of the hole they forced us in. Again, no offense, little lord."

"I'm... not a lord any more."

"Then you will have to learn what it is not to be, sooner or later. Of course folks are willing to do it, when it is the only option. Anything to keep their loved ones fed, sheltered. But it's not like the companies have no choice. They could pay us a truly livable wage and still make off like bandits. Instead, they just continue to line their coffers—and whatever personal little hobby they might have."

Julian snorted. "You're not wrong about that..."

"It's still better than the alternative," Gaius said. "Isn't it? They could be slaves. Paid nothing instead of something." It had always seemed a strange fight to Gaius, coming from Julian's family household into the labour force. The freedom to work, to make money, to do with it what you wanted...

"Ah, we've had this argument before, mon cher," Alesse said with a smile. "Here's what it boils down to. They both need to be fixed. No more slaves, and no more wage slaves."

"And how do you do that?" Julian asked.

"Unionization. There are more of us than there are of them. If we all get together—we can force them to change or lose their entire workforce."

"And how goes the fight?" Gaius asked.

"Are you still bitter I left you?"

Gaius blushed. Alesse had been like a mother for his first few months of freedom. When she'd left for Rome to pursue her goals, it hadn't been easy.

But she'd found Julian for him.

"No."

She smiled. "I think it goes well. I submitted a report to the Senate a few weeks ago, and I've just been told there's been some movement on it. There may be hope yet."

She twitched suddenly as Julian moved something in her mechanical hand.

"What was that?"

"I realigned the nervespring. It connects the clockwork to the nerves in your arm, lets it talk to your brain... You need some remaker's gel, I think, to lubricate the connection... but that should help in the short term..."

Alesse smiled. "Thank you."

Gaius was watching Julian, eyebrows raised. He'd learned a lot in the last year, he realized.

Then again, Gaius had too.

Alesse looked up from her hand at them once again. "Well, all of that brings me to you. And why we're here."

Julian sat up in his chair as Alesse took a drink.

"I don't know if you really want to hear where your parents were taken..." Alesse said.

"I do," Julian said. "I need—I need to find them if I can."

Alesse nodded. "So Gaius said."

"How did you find them?"

Alesse smiled. "I'm resourceful, remember? So. Senator Vivarius has a lot of friends in the East India Company. When your parents became... indentured to him, they were sent to Aternum. It's a port town, a shipping hub for the Company bringing goods into Rome from the east."

"Are they still there?" Julian asked. "Are they still..."

"I don't know," Alesse said, softer now. "It's not an easy life in Aternum. If they are... it might not be much better than the alternative."

"Of course it's better," Gaius said.

He thought of his own mother, who'd died when they were ten. They'd never been allowed to be that close, but he'd still do a lot if it meant having her back.

Alesse shrugged. "Either way. That's where you'll have to go to find them or learn more. Find Gino. He's one of the workers I know there. He should be able to point you in the right direction."

Julian nodded. Gaius saw a small fire in his eyes once again. "Thank you," Julian said.

Alesse stretched out the tools on her hand. "Thank you, little lord. I hope you find them."

Interlude

*O*ur attention this evening returns to Britannia, where reports are coming in that paint a grim picture. Protests have broken out across the province in response to recent measures intended to help maintain peace in this vital province. Centred in Londinium, Eboracum, and Isca, protesters say that the new laws impinge on their civil liberties, using words like "draconian."

Senator Vivarius, who spearheaded the initiatives, was in Rome this week but released a statement saying that these protests are precisely why his new laws are necessary. "This is a dangerous and volatile rebellious attitude that exists in the undercurrents of the province, and it threatens the safety of friends and family and the very heart of Industrial Rome. It borders on treason, but we hope to find a peaceful solution to these rebellious acts."

So far, these protests have remained largely nonviolent, with marches being heavily monitored by cohortes urbanae. Legate McAvoy, in charge of security efforts from the Munimentum skystation, says that her soldiers have the situation under control and that these protests will not be a danger to, quote, "the majority of locals who understand the importance of peace and order."

However, reports later came in that a protester in Londinium was killed during an altercation with a centurion. McAvoy was unavailable for further comment.

This is Imperial Radio, news from the four corners of Rome.

On the Labour of Romans
A treatise by Alesse Durand

Abstract: Across the Empire, industry and trade are booming like no other time in our history. Millions of new workers have entered the workforce, including women and even children, as demand for labour has met falling wages and increased cost of living. These conditions are unstable at best. Lack of safety, low wages, and increased demands on our time, effort, and even blood result in a workforce that is tired, inefficient, and unsatisfied.

We call for the immediate repeal of the Trade Worker's Act, alteration of the Master and Servant's Act, and the implementation of new guidelines outlined in this treatise, proposed as a new Worker's Rights Act.

Workers must have the right to assembly and organization under Trade Unions to protect their interests from exploitation. This is not only in our interest: it is in the interest of a stronger nation...

Memo:

To Senator Taurinus,

I promised someone I would get this treatise in front of the Senate Committee on Industry. Please, read through it. It's a fascinating read.

Then, feel free to burn it.

Chapter 12: Berlin

LIA

"No part of this seems like a good idea," Brendan said.

"He shot at you," Syd said.

"He shot *past* me," Lia said.

"And he tried to arrest us," Brendan said. "And also, he kind of hates you."

Lia had to concede that. "Nonetheless. He did let us go."

"Once," Turner said.

Lia turned to look at her crew. They were flying through grey skies over eastern Europe. The clouds were low, heavy with the kind of rain that permeates the air, seeming to soak you inside and out; the bridge of the *Raven* was clammy and chilled at this altitude, even with the heat from the engine. But the clouds gave them some cover at least—a rare windfall, as most ships could only fly so high before the thinning atmosphere made buoyancy an issue.

Lia tugged her coat tighter around her. "We're flying with no real heading these days, and we can't follow the procedures we normally would. Vivarius is up to something—a power grab, certainly, but we know there's more to it. Why does he need materials for a bomb? And why does he need them clandestinely?

"Centurion Stormcloud might not be my idea of a good ally, but he seems to be pretty cozy with Vivarius these days. He let us go once because he didn't like what was going on any more than we do—"

"Well, maybe a little more than we do," Brendan said.

Lia nodded. "Fair enough. Still. If we can get anything out of him—" She looked at Turner. "Through persuasion or not..."

Turner nodded.

"It might give us a leg up. Might give us a lead. What is Vivarius planning? How far do his connections go?"

"Okay," Syd said, looking at a map of the Empire spread out on the bridge. "So why in Dis are we going to Berlin?"

Lia smiled. "Destin likes to let off steam on the Empire's time."

The clouds broke as the city came into view.

Berlin was an industrial town, shrouded in smoke and, today, rain. Having been a place of contention for a couple of centuries, warred over by Rome in the west and Russia in the east, it always had a frontier feel even as armies marched through it. More recently, Rome had decided it wasn't worth the effort and effectively handed it over to the Imperial East India Company to govern and manage.

Now it was a centre of industry in the eastern Empire, a trade hub for the EIC, and known for its somewhat lawless nature. Beneath the bustling, smoggy exterior was a thriving industrial entertainment scene unburdened by the oversight of the Empire.

Syd made their approach towards a large raised skydock, burning flares helping guide them in through the smoke and rain. While Lia negotiated docking fees with the EIC agent, Turner broke off for some recon.

"Good instincts," she said upon returning shortly after. "The *Stormrider* docked here yesterday."

"Less 'instinct' and more 'he's literally here once a week if he can be,'" Lia said. "But I still can't believe he practically named his ship after himself."

"Or himself after the ship," Turner said.

"I'm pretty sure he'd have reserved the one with the sexual innuendo for himself," Brendan said.

"Fair point," Turner replied.

"Gross," Syd said.

They disembarked. Syd was tasked with finding a place to stay and some cheap fuel. Turner split off again as soon as they left the ship. Lia and Brendan were heading for Die Molkerei.

The establishment was notorious. Lia had avoided it like the Plague before. It wasn't even worth trying to bust up—and of course, none of it appealed to her personally.

Converted from an old warehouse near the skydock, Die Molkerei was an entertainment club catering to every sexual taste imaginable. Winding through the dark rainy streets, avoiding workers, slaves, beggars, and traders—and keeping a close eye on their coin purses, not that they had much to steal—they made their way towards the club by following the deep percussive beats that reverberated through the neighbourhood. They paid their cover to the bouncer—a man larger than even Brendan—who gave them an appraising look and a shrug and admitted them to the thick heat and noise.

Lia tried to suppress a shudder as she felt the stickiness beneath her boots. The air smelled of sweat and booze and leather and a few other things she didn't want to think about. Dancers writhed against patrons on raised stages to the thumping percussion, clad in scant leather and steel. One woman, utterly naked, wrapped herself around a pole in ways that suggested her spine didn't bend the way most did; a man opposite her waved around a member that made Lia marvel at the advances remaking had made. She turned her gaze to the tables and crowds.

Brendan's eye was drinking it all in, though. "They got boy entertainers, too?" he said as they entered the darkened building.

"Equal opportunity orgies," Lia said. "Just wait till you hear what goes on in the basement."

"How have I not heard of this place?"

"One of the mysteries of the world."

"You think he's here?"

"It's his favourite spot."

"Why do you know that?"

"I wish I didn't."

But she did. And she was right. There he was, sitting sprawled at a table in a corner, three barely-dressed women surrounding him along with empty glasses and probably more illicit substances.

Lia wished she hadn't been right. Then they could have left.

She hated him. Not just for his proclivities towards illicit substances and general lack of decorum—she had bigger fish to fry. No, she mostly hated how he treated the women he surrounded himself with.

Still. A lead was a lead.

"Centurion Stormcloud," she said, approaching the table and pushing past a group of sweaty dancers, their eyes wild on the latest intoxicants.

His eyes wandered up her body until they met her terse glare. He did her the minor courtesy of sitting up a little.

"Lia Song," he said. "Imagine seeing you again. You look good for someone who's not supposed to exist."

"Save it for your admirers," Lia said. "We need to talk."

"Do we? Seems to me, *you* need to talk, and I need to consider arresting you. That being my job and all. You wouldn't want me to neglect my job, would you?"

Lia snorted. "Here," she said, tossing some denarii on the table and looking at the women around him. "Give us a few minutes."

The women were happy to take the money and leave.

"You don't inspire much loyalty, do you, Stormcloud?" Lia asked.

Destin shrugged. "They'll be back. The Empire's paycheque is pretty good—oh, I'm sorry, that's right, you don't have that anymore."

Lia smiled tightly and slid into the booth. She could see Brendan take up position a little ways away, only partly distracted by the two men making out onstage.

"I have some questions after our... last encounter," she said.

Destin snorted. "I'm sure you do."

"Listen. The capture of the *Red Raven* was a cover—"

"Your capture of it? Oh, sorry—theft?"

"No. You know I mean Vivarius's. It was a cover. We found the evidence on the *Munimentum*. Someone wants weapons, and Vivarius wants to keep it off the books—why?"

"Look, *Ms. Song*," Destin said, leaning forward. "Everyone seems pretty content right now with you just disappearing. Like you never existed. You start poking this bear *again*, and they're going to be forced to come after you. *I'm* going to be forced to come after you. And trust me, I'm going to enjoy it."

Lia smiled. "I'm sure you will. But there's something off here. You said yourself you didn't like it."

Destin shrugged. "And what would I know of it?"

"You've been consistently assigned to areas Vivarius shows up at. The *Munimentum*, the rally in Londinium, the Senate hearings in Rome... You his errand boy now?"

Destin sat up a little more. "No. I'm not on his little payroll."

Lia smiled. After his reaction on the skystation, she figured he'd want to distance himself from whatever Vivarius was doing—but he *had* been assigned to Vivarius for a while. She hoped he had some useful information—even if he wouldn't tell her.

"Then tell me, Destin—what happened to the weapons taken from the *Red Raven*? The ones on the *Munimentum*?"

Destin slouched back again. "Transferred. Don't know where."

"Isn't that strange?"

"Sure. But not enough to look into—not enough for this little crusade of yours. These guys do their own thing all the time. I know you can't stand it when not every single thing is by the books and on the books, but that's how things are done. You want me to listen to you, Song, you're going to have to do a *lot* better than that."

"Fine," Lia said, her smile tight again. "I get it. Not willing to risk your cushy ass for anything less than proof."

"My ass is *not* cushy, which you'd know if you ever—"

"Doesn't matter," Lia interrupted. "You've been more than helpful."

Destin frowned.

Lia shrugged. "You may not be his errand boy, but you have been doing his errands when the Empire demands. You know something's up but aren't willing to get your hands dirty. That's fine. By now we've got what we need. Enjoy your evening, Centurion."

She rose from the table, adjusted her coat, and strode away without a backwards glance.

As she did, she heard Destin call a legionary over and demand someone return to his ship to check on security. It wouldn't matter—Turner would be long gone by now.

She smiled at Brendan and pulled him away from the establishment's entertainment to head back to their own ship.

Syd was checking over the exterior propellers of the no-longer-red *Raven* when Lia and Brendan returned to the skydock. They had taken the opportunity to pick up some new supplies, so Turner was already back by the time they arrived.

Syd looked up as Lia came up the gangplank, grease smudged on their thin face. "Well?" they asked.

Lia shrugged and ducked down the hatch to the bridge, and from there to the cramped galley, the closest thing to a common space on the small pirate ship. Turner had some documents spread out on the table there as Lia entered, Brendan and Syd close behind.

Brendan started unpacking the supplies, food going into storage or his mouth in turn.

"No weapons," Turner said as Syd sat at the table. Lia leaned against the door frame, wincing from the lingering pain in her side.

"Didn't think so," Lia said. "Vivarius wouldn't trust Stormcloud enough, I'm sure—and he truly didn't seem to know what happened to them. What *did* you find on his ship?"

"Documents. Looks like orders, memos, mostly en route back to Rome."

"Stormcloud is an airship centurion," Syd said. "Do they really have him... delivering the mail?"

"Punishment for losing us, I'm sure," Brendan said around a mouthful of smoked sausage.

Turner nodded. "I've been going through what I could take that wouldn't be immediately missed. There's not a lot—copies of manifests, fake troop movements—"

"Fake?" Syd asked. "How do you know?"

"If any ship carrying documents like this was to be captured by the Ottomans," Lia said, "they wouldn't want actual intel leaked—but having documents like those amongst the cargo might distract them from gleaning something important from the more mundane-looking papers."

Turner nodded. "Standard Agentes practice for couriers since the war started."

"The Ottoman war?"

"The first one. When they took Constantinople."

Syd's eyebrows raised.

"And they haven't caught on yet?" Brendan asked.

"Sure they have," Lia said. "But sometimes they get lucky, get something real, so they can't just disregard everything."

"And after the coup," Turner added, "a lot of folks who were growing wise were... replaced."

Syd nodded quietly.

"So, speaking of gleaning something important from the more mundane..." Lia said.

Turner nodded. "What do you make of this?" She handed Lia a piece of paper, rolled up like it had been in a scroll tube.

Lia took it and glanced it over. "A letter? Looks like the second half—was there a first page?"

Turner shook her head. "Didn't see one before I had to get out."

Lia skimmed the contents. "Signed M.M.V., probably Marcus Manlius Vivarius. '...ordered their transfer to Barcino for transit to the facility. If she's as good as Fullius like you suggest, she should start as soon as possible. She'll be on the train by...'" She trailed off, reading silently. "A philosopher of some kind? He talks about research..."

Turner nodded. "Based on the date, this philosopher—" She took the page back from Lia. "—Gisela, will be on the train now, headed for whatever this facility is."

"So?" Brendan asked. "A girl's going to Barcino. Sounds fun, but beyond that..."

"If we had the first page we could see where this was going," Lia said. "Still, Vivarius is sending a philosopher to a particular facility. We could probably learn a lot about what he's up to if we could talk to her..."

"Once she arrives, she'll be taken away to wherever this facility is," Turner said, "and we'll lose her. But before she arrives—we can find the train route."

Lia looked at her. "Are you suggesting...?"

Brendan's eye lit up. "Train heist?"

Turner nodded. "Train heist."

Chapter 13: Company Town

JULIAN

Alesse had given them some money before she left. Gaius had wanted to refuse it, but the denarii were sorely needed—especially if they wanted to get to Aternum. The amount was easily enough for Julian and Gaius to afford a train ride the short distance across the Italian peninsula. Gaius had suggested they travel by foot—easier to avoid detection, they could save the money for later needs, and they'd grown used to walking the Italian countryside—but Julian didn't want to let any more time pass than necessary. There was no telling the conditions his parents were in. He needed to find them.

Julian wasn't sure where this need had come from. Obviously, he was worried about them—he missed them. But they'd never really been close. He'd spent far more time with Gaius, and even with Gaius's mother, than his own parents.

But he had to find out what had happened to them. What they'd done since. Maybe it was just a connection back to his past, an instinct towards home. Maybe he needed some new reason to hate Vivarius.

So they took the train despite Gaius's concerns.

As they boarded and found seats side by side in the crowded passenger car, Gaius whispered, "Do you think you're being looked for?

Would anyone have... a description or anything?"

"I don't know," Julian said. He imagined Servius would still want to find him. His test subject, his successful experiment. But how would he look? Would the government know, soldiers or officials? Would there be wanted posters?

Servius didn't seem the type. From what Julian had seen of the man, he seemed more like he always had another plan, another option. But it wouldn't do to be careless.

The train departed, and soon a man was coming up the aisle to check tickets. Julian pulled theirs out, but his palms were sweating. Suddenly, the concern was real. What if he was somehow recognized?

His hand twitched as he imagined a pistol in pieces in front of him, cleaning it, putting it back together. The control he yearned for—trying to ground himself.

His heart ticked steadily along.

The man reached them and looked them both up and down as he took their tickets. "You two have identification?"

Once upon a time, identification papers weren't needed in the Roman Empire. The only people who mattered were citizens, and unless you gained citizenship through special means—such as military service, which would net you a diploma declaring your new status—citizens were part of a social network of tribe, family, and service to the state. Identification was based on reputation, service, notoriety.

As the Empire grew, though, both in size and population, greater means were necessary. Rome didn't want outsiders coming in uninvited, and citizenship was growing to a point that no one could reliably keep track. When Roman women became able to vote and take part in the state as well, new means were necessary, and identification papers became more widely expected.

But many still hewed to the old ways when they felt entitled...

Julian looked at this man. "*No,*" he said, in a tone that asked, *Why in the world would I?* "I am Alexander Spurius Athas, on my way to an important meeting with Company representatives to discuss a land arrangement with my family. *They* know who I am."

The name was from a minor noble he'd known as a child. He hoped the weight of the words would be enough to keep them out of suspicion. He hoped the man didn't have a description of him.

And he was a little surprised at how easily the entitled tone came back to him.

"No private car...?" the man asked. Julian wasn't sure if he was questioning the identity or quietly mocking him.

"*No*," he said, "thanks to an immense oversight, which I assure you I'll be taking up with the district manager."

The man quietly snorted. "Very well. Enjoy your trip, sir."

"I'm sure I will not," Julian huffed.

The man moved on. A few people were staring, but they too quickly returned to their own affairs.

Gaius let out a breath. "Where did that come from?" he whispered.

Julian sighed. "I don't know."

His hand twitched again.

"A man must be able to defend himself, to defend his family," Praefectus Meridianus Graecus Demetrius Leventis said, watching as Julian methodically cleaned each piece of the pistol before him. Demetrius had said as much to him many times over the years, as if Julian wouldn't be capable of doing so—though it was now also weighted with the understanding that defending their family may be increasingly necessary. "You will understand when you have children of your own," his father continued. "Now, practice."

As his father was called away to other duties, Julian exchanged looks with Gaius, watching from nearby. Demetrius had never seemed like the type whose philosophy on life had changed much after having children—and given his and Gaius's last year together, children were not exactly on Julian's mind either.

He began piecing the pistol back together. That morning over breakfast—a rare one for which he'd joined his family—he'd mustered the courage to ask about taking an apprenticeship at the provincial Praetor's office, where his father sometimes worked. It would be a near-necessary step for any career in politics, to begin getting that kind of experience now that he was sixteen. But his mother had refused him.

"And what if something happened to you without your servants and doctors around?" No concern that *she* wouldn't be around. "You can't handle the travel, Julian, never mind the stress of the work."

So he'd come down to the range and cursed himself for getting winded even from such a short walk. But the gun felt good in his hands—its heft, its power something he *could* control. He loaded a bullet, checked it over again, and glanced at Gaius, watching quietly from the sidelines. Gaius was not allowed to touch a weapon.

"You ever feel like you just want to shoot something?" Julian said. He raised the pistol, finger tightening on the trigger.

Gaius shrugged. "I'm just fine watching you, Jules. Besides, there's another gun I'll handle tonight."

Julian snorted, and his shot went wide.

The rest of the ride passed uneventfully. As the sun fell lower in the sky, the train wound around hills and through sparse woods until suddenly the Adriatic Sea burst into view out the window. The train whistled its steam loudly, their destination in sight.

They came down out of the mountains to follow the Aterno river towards the ocean. The lights of homes and businesses flew by them on either side of the valley before slowly coming to a halt as the city sprawled around the train station.

Julian and Gaius disembarked into streets just filling as the day's work shift ended. Julian was endlessly arriving at places engulfed by crowds. He tried to walk as close to Gaius as he could without tripping, Gaius's larger body a shield against the masses. He could feel Gaius's heat—over the heat of his own chest, a heat he was never allowed to forget. He pulled his coat tighter around him despite it.

"Where now?" he asked as they ducked out of the way of the folks streaming out of the train. *Find Gino* seemed like an easy enough goal until he saw all the people, all the workers, the size of the port. He supposed they should ask around, see if anyone knew this person, but where to even start?

"Gino's a dock worker, right?" Gaius said. "There will probably be a worker's bar by the water where they all go after their shifts."

"Wouldn't they want to go home…?" Julian asked.

"Not always," Gaius replied. "Not sober, after a long day's work.

Let's see what we can find."

They started down the street. The train station wasn't too far from the main shipping docks, close enough for easy transport from sea to land, but the passenger terminal was up the hill from the water, further away than where cargo came in and out. Looking around them, Julian guessed that every building in the area was either connected to the trade industry or a public house.

"Which *one*?" Julian asked.

Gaius looked around carefully as they walked, taking in everything. After a moment, he nodded down the street.

"I'd guess that one. The Steampipe. Based on its signage, it's not trying to attract street traffic—it's got its regulars, just far enough from the cargo docks to be separated but convenient... A lot like La Plaque de Cuivre."

"La Plaque de Cuivre?"

"Yeah. Where I went in Parisium after work..."

Julian had forgotten. In all the chaos and uncertainty and re-union, he'd forgotten Gaius had worked for a year in very similar circumstances...

"Right. I guess I'll follow you then."

Gaius smiled at him, touching his arm reassuringly. "Good idea. Probably want to drop the haughty noble act from the train, too. It won't go over well here."

Julian nodded.

The Steampipe was loud and packed full of burly men and women slinging beer and laughing. Julian had never experienced anything like it, and he was struck by panic almost immediately. He felt sweat on his brow, his breathing quickened—he worried suddenly about his health, which only compounded the panic—but there the physiological signs stopped. His heart beat steadily to the tick of the clockwork.

"Hey, you okay?" Gaius asked.

Julian took a shaky breath. He felt claustrophobic, anxious—but the shock of realizing his heart was just ticking along had pulled him for a moment from the spiral.

He nodded tightly. "Yeah. I think so. Let's... just make this fast, okay?"

Gaius nodded. He took Julian's shoulder to help guard and guide him through the crowd as they made their way to the bar.

The bartender, a petite olive-skinned woman who nonetheless looked like she could beat up any of the men in the place, looked them up and down as they pushed their way to the bar.

"What can I get *you*, zuccherino?" she said. Julian realized she'd specifically been looking *Gaius* up and down.

He couldn't blame her, really.

"A couple beers. Whatever's cheap," Gaius said over the noise.

"Wine," Julian tried to loudly whisper to him.

Gaius gave him a look and shook his head slightly.

The bartender nodded. "Anything else, darling?"

"Yeah," Gaius said as he put a couple denarii on the bar—certainly more than enough for the beer. "We're looking for Gino?"

She smiled. "Yeah, he's here. Back table, in the corner. Big beard. Hard to miss."

Gaius took the beers she slid across the bar. "Thanks."

She winked at him and gave Julian an appraising look he couldn't quite interpret.

They pushed their way back through the crowds again towards the back corner of the bar. Julian had had quite enough of crowds like this for a lifetime, but Gaius looked right at home somehow. He moved like he belonged, in a way Julian had never seen him growing up at the villa.

Gino was indeed a large man with an even larger beard. He was in the midst of unbraiding it as Julian and Gaius approached, laughing jovially with a couple other workers.

He looked up at them as they approached, smoothing out the lengths of hair.

"Hullo, who are these fresh faces, eh?" he said.

Gaius smiled at him. "Are you Gino?"

"Of course! I don't recognize you two, though..."

"We're... friends of Alesse," Gaius said. "Gaius and Julian. May we join you?"

"Alesse?" Gino said. "No shit! Please, sit. How is the old metalhead?" He gestured for them to sit, the other two dock workers shifting over to make room.

"I don't know when you saw her last," Gaius said, "but it's metal-*hand*, now."

"Well, shit. Had to be sooner or later she'd have an accident, I guess, eh? Glad she got the remake."

Gaius nodded. "She's doing well. In Rome, fighting her fight."

"I'll drink to that," Gino said, raising a mug of beer. Gaius followed suit, and Julian quickly copied.

The beer was foul-tasting. He'd never understood the appeal. He sipped only a little before putting it down. Gaius drained half of his, to cheers from the others.

Julian wasn't sure he even knew Gaius anymore.

Then again, he'd never known Gaius as anything other than property, even if Julian had never seen him that way. Maybe this was the real Gaius...

He wondered what that would mean.

The look the bartender had given Gaius jumped into his mind. And he wondered suddenly how different things could be. How different they might become... Was the life Gaius would have with him really what Gaius would even want? He'd been so wrapped up in everything that had happened to him—but here was Gaius, following along on his whims, on his needs. He hadn't thought of Gaius's own needs.

The continuing conversation pulled him out of his thoughts as Gaius placed a hand on his leg under the table.

"A friend of Alesse's is a friend of mine and all that," Gino was saying. "What can I help you with, young lads?"

"We're trying to find someone. A worker here, I think," Gaius said. "Maybe you know him." He squeezed Julian's leg, and Julian finally sat up.

"The P—" He stopped himself. He was so used to using his father's full title. "Demetrius Leventis. Do you know him?"

Gino sat back in the bench, his smile fading a little. "Sure. One of the indentured, yeah?"

Julian nodded a little.

"I'm sorry to say you won't find him here anymore."

"Was he taken somewhere?"

Gino sighed. "He died, month or two ago. Working the rigs. Got caught in the ropes of a crane, trying to maneuver a shipping crate."

Tick, tick, went his heart. It couldn't skip a beat. But for a moment, the world seemed to.

"He had a wife." Gaius's voice broke through the silence that had seemed to envelope Julian all of a sudden, and the sound of the world rushed back to Julian. "Nikomache."

Gino nodded, frowning. "Aye, I do remember him speaking of her. She worked up in the magistrate's villa, I think. Housekeeper type. I don't know what happened to her. Could still be there, I guess."

Julian breathed again. His mother could still be here.

Gaius nodded. "Thank you. Appreciate the help."

"Well, Alesse is doing good work for all of us. My pleasure."

Gaius nodded again and stood, Julian following suit.

The cool evening air was a welcome relief. Julian's ears rang with the silence after the din of the bar. Gaius, too, seemed to sigh with relief, then pulled Julian to the side of the building and wrapped him in a hug.

Julian melted into Gaius's strong arms.

"I'm sorry," Gaius said. "That's a bad way to go. He didn't deserve that."

Julian let himself be held for a moment. His father was dead. Killed while working on the docks of Aternum. Hardly given a thought by those who worked with him. Given no thought by Vivarius. Killed *by* Vivarius, really.

And Julian felt... he didn't know. Maybe it hadn't fully sunk in. He was angry at Vivarius, old hatred bubbling up again, but he didn't even know what he felt about his father.

He pushed himself away, putting his weight back on his own feet. "We can still find my mother."

Gaius nodded. He gave Julian a last squeeze, then they faced the street again.

"Glad to get out of that bar, though," Gaius said.

Julian glanced at him. "You, too?"

"I never could quite stand that worker culture... Work all day then piss it all away on drink. No sense of what they're doing it for."

"Survival?" Julian asked.

Gaius shrugged.

Julian squeezed his hand. "I was worried you'd taken to it," he said quietly. "That you'd changed somehow."

"Of course I've changed," Gaius said, and Julian looked up at him.

"But not that much." He smiled. "I love you."

Julian smiled. "I... love you, too."

The magistrate of Aternum had a villa on the cliffs overlooking the port, opposite where the train came into the city. Julian and Gaius climbed the staired road up the hill towards it, despite how late it was getting. Julian certainly wasn't going to be able to sleep yet.

The domus was a sprawling building with a couple of wings off a central hub. The whole thing was a holdover from ancient Roman architectural traditions, still commonly used in the old homes of civil servants. The outer areas of the domus were considered public spaces, where the family would receive guests and hold business meetings, while the inner portions were reserved for the privacy of the family.

On the road to the villa were outer gardens where Julian and Gaius passed by statues of Caesar and Augustus—and a newer one of Lucius Antonius Remus, the first governor of the Imperial East India Company. Past these, they came to a front door that would lead into the central atrium of the villa. They could hear muffled voices coming from inside; lanterns burned, casting their warm light out into the night. Gaius took hold of the heavy knocker and banged on the door while Julian noted a Greek herm just outside it. He passed his hand traditionally over its phallus.

After only a moment, the door opened. An older gentleman in a buttoned-down black suit and cravat stood stiffly before them.

"How may the magistrate be of service?" he asked.

Julian stepped forward, trying to rally himself, trying not to think of the various ways this could play out.

"Hello. I am Alexander Spurius Athas. Am I to assume you're the magistrate's seneschal?"

The voices from inside were a bit clearer now. Julian could hear snatches of the conversation—someone was making some kind of proclamation over the weak protests of someone else.

"I am," the man said.

"We're... looking for someone," Julian said. "Someone who I believe worked for the magistrate. May we speak to him?"

"He is indisposed at the moment," the seneschal said, eyes flicking briefly towards the voices. "But perhaps I can help. Come in."

Julian nodded his thanks, and he and Gaius followed the seneschal into the building. The front hallway led into the large atrium, which was dominated in the middle by a rectangular pond beneath open air above. Around it, covered areas featured couches and tables, a shrine, and doorways to other rooms. As the seneschal guided them towards a pair of couches, Julian caught a glimpse through a doorway to the tablinum, the magistrate's office, where the voices were coming from. An old man sat leaning back in a chair looking frail—a machine beside him whirred, pumping oxygen into a tube he held up to his face. A middle-aged gentleman in a waistcoat and tie stood over him, physically in a position of power the frail old man couldn't escape from, dominating the conversation. Julian heard him say something about taking over another dock.

The seneschal offered Julian and Gaius a seat on one of the couches while he took a seat across from them.

"Thank you for taking the time," Gaius said.

"The office of the magistrate is here at the service of the people," the seneschal responded. There was a hint of strain in his voice. "Now, who are you looking for?"

"A woman by the name of Nikomache," Julian said. "I believe she was in the magistrate's service...? Perhaps she is here?"

The seneschal's eyes softened, and immediately Julian knew what was coming. The floor seemed to fall out from under him.

"Nikomache... is no longer with us," the seneschal said. The way he said it left no question to his meaning.

Julian sat in silence for a beat. Gaius quietly touched his arm.

"What happened?" he asked after a moment. His voice sounded lifeless in his own ears.

But a new voice answered. "She was put down." It was a sneer of a comment.

The waistcoated man from the tablinum stood in the atrium now, nearby. Julian could see the frail old magistrate struggle weakly to stand behind him—to no avail. The seneschal stared daggers at the waistcoated man, who ignored him.

"She caused a disruption to business," he continued. "Screaming to our poor magistrate about some accident..."

"The death of her husband," the seneschal said in an almost chiding voice.

"Whatever. An accident. She disrupted an important business meeting, blamed the whole thing on the Company. What nonsense— the man was careless, and indentured no less. She tried to run from the household. I had her shot. As a favour to the magistrate."

The seneschal continued to stare daggers as the man finally turned to him.

"My business with your dear master is concluded for the evening. You'll be hearing from my people soon. Goodbye." And he turned and let himself out.

Julian sat—stunned, still.

"I'm sorry," the seneschal said. "I must apologize for the... brusqueness of our local district manager, Sir Ignatius. He can be... direct—" He stopped himself as he saw the old magistrate slowly, weakly attempting to cross the atrium towards them and sprang up to help him.

Julian was frozen in shock. He'd seen it coming, and still the news had hit him in a way he couldn't yet even describe.

The seneschal helped the magistrate to sit in a large plush chair. The old man was breathing heavily, rasping.

"Nikomache..." he said, weakly. "She did not deserve it. What Ignatius did. She was a fine servant... A good person, kind. And..." He coughed wetly, trying to catch his breath, and Julian for a moment couldn't help but think of his own mechanical lung, pumping away calmly even as he shook a little. "She wasn't wrong. Could have made a difference if her circumstances were different. Tried to convince me to do something, but... Well, if circumstances were different..."

Gaius nodded quietly, face drawn.

Julian couldn't move.

The seneschal sighed. "I'm sorry to deliver this news, young man. You must have known her well."

Julian could only nod shakily. Then, after another moment, he looked up. "Thank you," he said, only the faintest quiver in his voice. "We should be going."

Gaius looked at him, then nodded and stood. "Thank you for your help."

The seneschal nodded. The magistrate breathed heavily. And they left.

Julian walked. Walked past the statues of Caesar, Augustus, Antonius Remus. Past hedges and gardens, to he didn't know where. He didn't see where he was walking. He only vaguely felt Gaius's presence with him, heard Gaius start to say something vaguely sympathetic before falling silent. Julian walked.

His parents were dead. Both of them, practically sentenced to it when Vivarius took their holdings, their freedom, and sent them here. Into the hands of the East India Company.

They were dead. Let themselves be walked over by the senator, then the Company. Walked over by life.

Julian had pledged never to let that happen to him.

And yet.

His mother had tried, at the end. Rallied, spoken out. Tried to take her life in her hands for once.

And where did it get her?

Where had it gotten Julian? Plotting to murder countless hundreds? Terrorizing innocents?

His face burned. When had he become this? His drive to do something, to fix the Empire, the world—as if one person could fix it all.

His mother had tried. And it got her killed.

Maybe there was nothing that could be done. Maybe he couldn't be that person. Maybe Gaius was right—it was best to hide. To hide from Servius, from Vivarius, from the world. What else could he do?

A voice broke through his thoughts.

"I was told I'd find you here."

And then someone grabbed his bag, pulling hard and throwing him to the ground.

Chapter 14: Bounty

GAIUS

As they left the magistrate's villa, a thousand emotions swirled in Gaius. More than anything, he wanted to be there to support Julian. Nothing else mattered but to make sure he would be okay.

He sensed quickly that Julian wouldn't want to talk, not yet. That he needed time with his thoughts. To come to terms with this in his own time. Gaius would just offer his presence, his silent support—the knowledge that he'd be there when Julian was ready, when he needed him.

In the meantime, he was left with his own thoughts. Demetrius and Nikomache were dead. He wasn't sure how to feel. He'd known them his whole life, lived in their household. But they'd been his masters. His *owners.* They'd been kind enough to him, but—he wasn't exactly sorry. Not for them, anyway—he was sorry for Julian. To him, their absence was just an emptiness, a nothing where once there was something.

Not much different from his own mother. There was something, and then there was nothing.

It was not how he felt when Julian had been taken from him.

But his mind also chewed on something else. The way they'd gone—an accident on the docks, no doubt passed off by the Company as merely a cost of business. And Nikomache, killed while trying to escape, after...

He sighed. After saying exactly what Alesse had been saying for years.

He'd never fully got it—the plight of the workers. It had always seemed infinitely superior to slavery. To earn money for your labour, to have the freedom to live your life outside of work how you wanted. And then to see so many of them piss it all away in the bar. No ambition, no future, any more than he'd had in the Leventis household...

But he'd never imagined that there was much of an alternative. Growing up, he'd always just understood that there were different classes of people. That some had freedom and some didn't. That some people were made to serve, to work, to die.

Alesse had asked him why once. Why did it have to be that way?

Because that was the way of it, he'd said. What other way was there?

But something about Julian's parents. Fallen from noble to slave. And then to death. Nikomache, speaking out against the Company—

—and then killed.

Maybe there wasn't anything that could be done when the Senate, the Company, the Philosophers held all the power.

But maybe there was. Safety, financial freedom, a real life to live. If everyone rose up together—

They killed the workers who did, in India. But they couldn't do that here, could they?

If they *all* rose up?

Julian had always burned with the need to effect change.

Maybe there was change that could be made.

That's when he saw the man in the shadows. They'd wandered far from the magistrate's villa into the hills outside of town. Trees stood sentinel beside the road they walked, and the stars were bright overhead. He stood in the blackness of the trees, a darker form among darkness.

"I was told I'd find you here," he said. And then he leapt out of the shadows.

Gaius didn't know how to react, didn't have time to think. The figure emerged and grabbed at Julian, hand closing on his bag. He used his momentum to swing Julian around, throwing him to the ground as the straps of the bag snapped.

Julian landed with the dull thud of metal against earth.

In the light of the moon, Gaius could see that the man was older, wiry, battle-scarred.

"Julian!" he yelled. The man took a step towards Julian, rummaging with the bag like he was looking to rob them before tossing it aside and drawing a gladius—an old soldier's sword.

Gaius charged at him. He leapt forward, trying to grab the man's arm or neck. He plowed into his body—sturdy as a mountain, the man's shoulder bruising Gaius's chest as he collided. The man crouched and whirled, throwing Gaius to the ground with an aching thud before turning back on Julian.

Gaius had hoped to give Julian time to scramble away, to stand, to run—but Julian hadn't moved. In the dim light, his eyes looked dull. Like he wasn't here.

"Julian!"

"Someone wants you dead, boy," the older man said, advancing towards Julian's prone form. "Looks like you're halfway there already."

Gaius scrabbled for purchase in the dirt. "Jules!"

His hand hit painfully against a rock in the dust—then he grabbed at it, pulling himself up a little so he had swinging room. He threw the rock as hard as he could.

It thumped into the man's back. He groaned and turned back to Gaius, even as Julian still didn't move.

"They said nothing about you," the man said. "But I guess they can have a second kill for free."

Gaius tried to scramble away and stand. "Who are you? What do you want with us?"

The man shrugged. "A paycheque. Not much support for old veterans these days. Thankfully, some folks need the kind of killer the army made me."

Just as Gaius found purchase, the man swung the gladius. Gaius tried to dive out of the way, but he couldn't move fast enough. The sword cut into his upper arm as he went down again, pain lancing through him. He tried not to scream, a noise like a strangled lion escaping his throat.

He had no time to react before the man had grabbed his shirt and yanked him to his feet. He held up the sword ready to skewer Gaius through the gut. Gaius struggled, kicked, but the man was a boulder.

Then hands clapped around the man's sides, and Julian pushed him aside like he was merely shoving through a crowd. Gaius fell to his knees painfully, and the gladius dropped from the man's hand as he tumbled down the path.

Gaius looked at Julian in wonder—and no little gratitude—but Julian still looked only half-there. Gaius jumped to his feet and dove for the sword, extending his left hand while his right arm was kept tucked painfully in.

He managed to hoist it up and point it at the soldier just as the older man struggled to his feet. "Don't move!" Gaius said.

The man stopped, hands raised, wild eyes on Julian, and smirked a little. "Boy's pretty strong for a whelp."

Julian stood at Gaius's back as Gaius held out the heavy sword.

"Who sent you?" Julian asked quietly.

The man shrugged. "I may have left the army, but I still do work for the emperor. Or the Senate. Or whoever pays the bills."

"A... bounty hunter?" Gaius said.

"Whatever you please."

"Who sent you?" Julian asked again. "I can make you tell me."

"Can you?" the man said. "Or is it too late?"

Gaius frowned and made to make a move when he heard a little *click*. Suddenly the man's eyes went dead, blood bubbled on his lips, and he fell to the ground.

Gaius faltered. His grip weakened, and he lowered the gladius to point at the ground as they both stared at the bounty hunter, dead on the path.

"What—" Gaius started. He prodded the man's body with his foot, and it turned. Some kind of metal collar was fastened to the back of his neck. Blood was slowly dribbling out.

Julian blinked. "I..." He fell silent.

Gaius stared. Looked at the sword. Looked at the cut on his arm, the blood starting to drench his sleeve, to drip down his hand.

"We should get out of here," he said. "Now."

Julian only nodded.

❖ ❖ ❖

They didn't return to Aternum. They had no reason to. They weren't going to take the train again—too high a risk of being found, now.

They walked the road away from the coast. They'd quickly agreed to go back to Orvieto—it was the closest thing they had to a place they felt at all safe. They'd figure out what to do next once they'd had a chance to rest.

It was a hundred and fifty miles to Orvieto. A six-day walk. A lot of time to think.

"Are you okay...?" Gaius asked Julian after they'd walked only an hour, most of it in silence.

"I don't know." A pause. "Are you?"

Gaius stopped to adjust the cloth he'd wound around his bicep. The cut hadn't been deep, thank Apollo, but it did hurt as they walked. Not that they had much choice. They'd sleep soon.

"I don't know," he replied. He started walking again, keeping the weight of his bag on his left shoulder—the sheathed gladius stuck through the straps. He wasn't going to be caught unarmed again—not that he knew how to wield it. "Do you think... think that Servius guy sent him? Or... Vivarius?"

Julian raised and dropped his shoulders. He was holding his own bag in his arms, since the straps had snapped. "I guess so. Who else?"

Gaius nodded.

"...Why?" he asked after another moment.

Julian took another few steps. "Maybe Servius wants his heart back. Or Vivarius wants to tie up a loose end?" He lapsed into silence again.

Another hour passed. They heard the rumble of a train passing by behind the hills.

"We should find a place to sleep," Gaius said. His arm burned now. Julian nodded.

By the light of the moon, now low in the sky, they found a hollow in a copse. Farmland stretched around them; it would be safe enough.

Gaius threw a blanket over some underbrush and painfully lowered himself. Julian curled himself nearby in the crotch of two roots. Gaius checked the cloth on his arm—some fresh blood, but mostly dried. He just hoped it wouldn't get infected.

He looked over at Julian. He had his legs tucked up to his body, but his eyes were still open. Staring at nothing.

Gaius reached over to grab Julian's bag, ruffling through the random papers he still had in there to pull out a blanket and drape it over him.

Julian grabbed the edges and pulled them into his chest like a shield.

"Hey," Gaius said softly. "I'm... I'm sorry about your parents. Really. No matter what else, they didn't deserve that."

Julian nodded almost imperceptibly.

"You'll be okay," Gaius said. "Okay?"

Julian didn't move.

"Jules."

Julian looked at him.

"You'll be okay."

The next morning, Gaius's arm still burned. He changed the bandages, happy to see it not start to gush blood again when he removed the old one.

He let Julian sleep longer than he normally would. He had no idea how long it had taken Julian to fall asleep, but now that he was, he should get as much as possible.

When Julian did wake, he lay still for a while. Gaius could imagine it. Crashing back to reality. Trying to reconcile with the fact that it wasn't all a dream.

Gaius was at a loss himself. He'd half-expected that an attempted reunion with Julian's parents wouldn't go as well as hoped—but a *bounty hunter*? Coming after *them*? It seemed so absurd. Someone else's life—the kind of thing you heard rumours about, but only half-believed.

Then again, Julian's very heart fell into the same category. Fiction, dreams, rumours. No one had actually done it.

This was their life now, he thought.

They packed their things in relative silence and headed out on the road once more. The morning passed much the same way, neither saying much, both lost in their thoughts. They found a travelling merchant on their route, traded some denarii for food for the day, and continued on, munching on bread and olives.

Finally, Gaius broke the silence.

"So..." He spat out an olive pit contemplatively. "...What now?"

Julian took a big bite out of the loaf of bread, taking time to chew, avoiding answering as long as he could.

"I don't know..." He chewed an olive. "...Nothing."

"Nothing?"

Julian shrugged. "I don't know, Gaius. What is there to do?"

Gaius frowned. "I don't know, Jules, but we have to do something... Don't we?"

Julian didn't respond.

"Look—you've always tried to tell me about all the things that need changing. We're seeing it. Not just the corruption, the things that happened to your parents—" He didn't finish that thought. "But, I don't know, the whole... The conditions they were put in... And us. Are they going to stop looking for us? I have to admit, a day ago, all I wanted was to find somewhere quiet where you and I could live out our lives. Together. But now? You were right, Jules. Something has to be done. We can't just hide from the world."

"Can't we?" Julian asked quietly.

Gaius looked at him. Julian's face was drawn, dark, staring at the road in front of his feet.

How hard had his parents' deaths hit him?

"Jules, you were always the one with all the ideas, the drive. Tell me what we should do. Tell me how we can change things." He was pleading, suddenly. Somewhere deep inside him, the feelings welled up. The hopelessness, the pain, the need to do *something*.

Julian threw the remains of his olives on the road. "What? What are we supposed to do? We're two runaways with nothing. No power, no hope—gods, nothing has *changed*, Gaius. We're powerless. And even if we tried?" He kicked an olive and got quieter. "Look where it got my mother."

"So, we just do nothing? What, just let them win?"

"What else is there?" Julian spat. "They already won."

He'd never heard Julian this angry, not like this—not at him. Except on the airship.

He sighed.

"I'm sorry, Jules. I don't know what I want... but... I'll support you. No matter what..."

Julian hugged his bag close and continued to walk down the old road. "I just don't know," he said.

Interlude

Aurelia,

In the ancient tradition, the gods were not fans of mankind. They weren't even our creators. That honour goes to the titan Prometheus. He shaped man from clay, and he stole fire from the gods to give it to us—to allow progress, civilization.

The gods punished him for his transgression. You've heard the story. Chained to a rock, having his liver eaten every day by an eagle. The symbol of Zeus.

Also the symbol of Rome, interestingly.

"Prometheus" means "forethought." There is no doubt he would have anticipated punishment. He took the fire all the same, in defiance of the gods. Reached beyond his means to help mankind advance.

I wonder what our punishment will be.

I'm sorry it's been so long since I've written. Rest assured I've read all of your letters, but after my last correspondence, there was much work to do. Arrangements to make, contingencies to plan. And of course, the research continues.

You will have a legacy, Aurelia. And not *his* legacy. I hope you'll be around to see it.

— S.

Last night, an explosion in the underground steamrail in Londinium derailed a train full of passengers. Casualty counts are still being reported, but there are at least twenty dead, and many more injured. The blast took place as continuing protests against the Empire marched overhead and through the nearby station. Local authorities have labelled this an act of a radical faction, as protests turned violent.

These protests have continued throughout the past three months, as local Britons attempt to fight against what they say are attacks on their freedom and autonomy. However, it is they who continue to escalate the conflict despite local authorities' attempts to keep things peaceful. This most recent attack proves the protesters' intentions, endangering otherwise peaceful civilians with their actions.

Early reports from local Legate McAvoy's forces suggest that the bomb causing the explosion may have been of Ottoman make, raising questions as to whether our enemies across the border are working to weaken the Empire from within...

We will bring you more as this story evolves. This report on the safety of the Empire is brought to you by the East India Company—bringing you the fruits of the four corners of Rome and beyond...

Chapter 15: Train Heist

LIA

"An Ottoman-made bomb? You know what that means, right?"
They were gathered around the small radio on the bridge.

"Sounds like those parts Vivarius 'apprehended,'" Lia said.

Turner nodded. "A plant, then. To rile up support."

"You really think he'd do that?" Syd asked. "Innocent people died..."

"I do," Lia said. She sighed. "Okay. Back to it, then."

She brought her knife to Brendan's scalp where she'd left off when the radio broadcast started. Brendan sighed sadly as the last of his green hair fell to the deck.

"Oh, buck up," Lia said, wiping off the knife. "It'll grow back eventually, and in the meantime it's, you know, a touch conspicuous."

"Also, grow a beard," Turner said, coming back in from the galley. She had a harness of sorts strapped around her now, and she held out a hand to Brendan. "Your pistol, please."

"Is that really the best plan?" Brendan said. "I really don't think the response to breaking into a place where there might be guards or soldiers should be 'don't take weapons.'"

"If there are guards or soldiers, they'll most certainly question any civilians with firearms," Lia said. She tossed her rifle to Turner, who snatched it out of the air and strapped it to the back of her harness.

"What happens when a fight breaks out?" Brendan said, morosely handing over his pistol as well. It joined two others and a handful of knives on the front of the harness.

"*If* a fight breaks out," Lia said.

Brendan gave her a look. "Please. 'When.'"

"You're a big boy," Turner said. "Use your fist."

"And bruise these pretty hands?"

"Anyway, I'll be right there behind you if there's trouble," Turner said.

"When," Brendan said again.

"I think I can see it!" Syd called from their place at the helm.

"Scope it out," Lia told Turner. "I'll get changed."

Lia squeezed past Brendan to the stern of the airship where the very cramped bunks were. Turner had acquired some supplies before they left Berlin; Lia hadn't asked how. She opened the trunk under her cot and pulled out the blue dress, holding it up to glare at.

She hated dresses.

But that also made them a pretty good disguise for someone like her. Hide by standing out and not looking anything like Lia Song, Praetorian Guard.

She sighed and threw off her heavy duster, then stripped down, glad the bunks were close to the hot engine. Her side ached a little as she maneuvered the dress onto her body, but it had mostly healed.

When she stepped back on the bridge, Turner and Syd raised their eyebrows. Even Brendan let out a low whistle.

"Oh, Minerva take all five of your eyes and toss them overboard," Lia said.

"Yes ma'am," Brendan said, grinning and turning to look out the bow window.

They were flying through the Pyrenees, green slopes rising close below them. Snaking along the side of one mountain ridge was the train track—and ahead, the telltale cloud of steam marking their target.

"All right," Lia said, trying to adjust the dress around her. "Let's go over it again. Sydney?"

Syd nodded. "I fly in close, try to match speed. We lower you and Brendan when we get to a good stretch so you can get between cars."

"Emphasis on good stretch," Lia said. "We won't have much time to make contact with the train and release the cables before we hit a tunnel, probably, and if this ship makes the acquaintance of the side of a mountain, we're going to have a tough time making any kind of escape."

"Plus, we'd miss you guys if you died," Brendan said.

"Plus we'd miss you," Lia agreed.

Syd nodded. "Roger that."

Lia turned to Brendan. "Then?"

"We get into one of the cars and assess," Brendan said. "Pose as civilian passengers if possible. Do some recon. Find where this philosopher might be."

Lia nodded. "She's being transported to a facility of some kind, sent by Vivarius but presumably off the books. I'd bet it's an EIC operation, so expect private security rather than Imperial soldiers."

Syd nodded. "It looks like an EIC train."

Lia raised an eyebrow. They were still too far away to tell what it looked like.

"Based on the length, speed, and steam output," Syd said. "I'd guess they're using a VulcanMark IV engine. It's pretty high-grade, and not available on civilian trains yet."

Turner nodded. "Makes sense. An EIC operation of some kind, calling in favours from their favourite senator."

Syd frowned. "If it's EIC though, what if they don't have any civilian passengers? Won't your cover be blown?"

"Could be a problem," Lia admitted, "but there's a good chance they'll have a bunch of passengers. They wouldn't transfer a prized philosopher on a train purely for cargo, and it wouldn't be efficient to have passenger cars for just one person."

"And her guards," Brendan said.

"If she has guards, yes. Still." Lia folded her arms. "Anyway, we'll improvise. Brendan and I will recon. Find this philosopher. If all goes well, we find her, talk to her, get what we need to know. If she's under duress, and we decide we need to extract her, or if we run into trouble..."

"I signal Turner," Brendan said. He grabbed a flare launcher from the table on the bridge and stuffed it into the bottom of the small traveller's satchel over his shoulder.

Lia turned to Turner.

"I lower down to whatever car the signal comes from," Turner stepped in, "laden with supplies."

Brendan raised his hand to make air quotes. "'Supplies.'"

"We cover our escape as necessary," Lia said, "and raise ourselves off the train and back to the ship. Again, avoiding the side of the mountain if possible."

"That cable can only reliably hold two people," Syd said.

"If we have to extract the philosopher, she goes back up with Turner if she's still hooked in. Brendan and I can wait for another opportunity. Or, if everything goes smoothly, we just get off the train when it arrives at its destination."

"What part of this plan makes you think it will go smoothly?" Brendan asked.

Lia shrugged. "Who knows? We have no idea what the situation is down there. Could be easy—get on, have a chat, get off in Barcino, get picked up outside of town."

"You really are an optimist," Brendan said.

"Anything goes wrong, I'm in reserve," Turner said. "Extraction, conflict, sabotage..."

"Sabotage?" Syd said.

Turner shrugged. "We can blow up the train if we need to."

Syd blinked. "We... we won't need to, right?"

Turner shrugged again.

Lia smiled tightly. "We'll call that 'Plan B.'"

"Can we call it 'Plan Z?'" Brendan asked. "I'd rather not be blown up. Not my favourite kind of being blown."

Sydney tried not to grin at that and turned back to the helm.

"Point is," Lia said, "we have options. We're just going to have to see how this one plays out."

"I think there's a good stretch coming up, Lia," Syd said.

Lia looked around at everyone. "We ready?"

Nods.

"All right. Let's do this."

"Just like old times, eh?" Brendan said as he and Lia made their way onto the top deck where the cables were. "Remember the Warsaw job?"

"Back when the Empire paid us to keep it safe," Lia said. "Of course, that time we got on the train at, you know, the station."

The wind suddenly hit them as they emerged onto the open deck, and Lia was forcibly reminded that she wasn't wearing her usual heavy duster.

"Sure, but we didn't have Syd at the time. We could've done an airship drop. Like we did on that Greek shipping vessel."

"I wasn't there, remember? I was keeping up appearances in Rome. You and Turner pulled that one."

"Does that mean this is your first moving airship drop?" Brendan asked as he looped the harness around her waist and shoulders.

"Let's just get it over with, hm?" Lia said tightly.

She wasn't particularly worried. Not more than usual when she was working. Politics and action—two things she handled well.

Though she preferred when she had a rifle at her back.

Brendan finished cinching them together as Turner emerged to help them down.

"Syd's making their approach," Turner called over the wind. "You ready?"

Lia gave the thumbs up as Brendan maneuvered them both onto the railing of the deck.

She didn't look down.

"There'll be a short drop before the friction of the winch unravelling slows our descent," Brendan said, his face close to hers. "Then we just hang as Syd takes us down."

Lia nodded. "Remind me how we deal with unpredictable winds."

"Pray?" Brendan suggested.

She smiled. "Let's go."

She left her stomach somewhere around a thousand feet of altitude. She figured she wouldn't need it for a while anyway.

She concentrated on Brendan. His body heat was welcome as cold air whipped around them. She wondered if Syd had taken his metal leg into account when calculating weight limits. She figured it wouldn't matter for very long if not. She wondered what death by sudden impact would feel like—or if it would be instantaneous. She imagined Mercury having a grand old laugh when he came to pick them up.

Dis, at this point she'd probably join in. What in Orcus, Tartarus, and Avernus were they even doing?

And then the descent stopped, the cables cinching into place. A hundred feet above them, the hull of the *Raven* with its balloon blossoming above it. She risked a look down.

The mountains and train were still a ways below them but coming up fast as Syd made their approach. She could see the train better, now, a millipede winding its segmented way along the side of the mountain. She forgot for a moment she was dangling at the end of a cable hundreds of feet in the air.

Then a gust of wind hit them and they swayed wildly off to one side and the cable creaked, and she remembered.

And then the train went through a tunnel below them. And then they were on the other side of the tunnel and descending quickly.

The train came up fast, as it needed to—they had limited time, now. And Lia was looking forward to having something under her feet again.

She'd never been sure how Syd did what they did. Understanding the ship, the engine, the train, the air—all of it well enough to position her and Brendan close *enough* to do what they needed to, all without being able to see them from their vantage point.

Nonetheless. They were getting real close, and Brendan unhooked a grapple launcher from his harness. With a *bang* barely heard over the wind, they were now attached at both ends.

The gun's little engine whirred, and they moved in towards the end of one car as the grappling cable spooled back in. For a moment, there was tension between the two cables, then Syd adjusted and they sped towards the train.

As they approached, Brendan spun his body, grabbing the edge of the roof at the end of the car and swinging them into the space between cars. Quickly, smoothly, he released the clasp of the harness, and they both landed hard on the fenced platform between cars—the harness and cable whipping up into the air as Syd made their quick adjustment to avoid the side of the mountain.

Lia almost buckled, her legs suddenly unused to holding her weight. A lance of pain went through her side from the impact. Brendan grabbed her arm as he tossed the grapple gun over the side of the train—useless now except to arouse suspicion.

"Well," Lia said, trying to make her legs work again. "Now for the hard part, I guess."

Brendan grinned. "After you."

Lia tried briefly to straighten her windswept hair, then tried to yank open one of the car doors.

It budged only enough to suggest it was latched closed. Locked.

Lia frowned.

Brendan reached to try even as Lia opened her mouth to say it was useless. "Must be a cargo car," Lia said. "Got it locked up."

"Hm," Brendan said. He turned to look at the door on their other side. "What do you think the chances are this one is too?"

"If it is, we'll have to climb," Lia said, not relishing the idea. "More importantly, if it's not, then what are a couple of civvies doing coming through this door from a locked cargo car?"

"Hm," Brendan said again. "And you thought this would be smooth."

"We pull a Smiths," Lia said. "Make people uncomfortable, and they'll try not to think about it. Folks are good at assuming everything is normal."

Brendan shrugged. "Sounds good."

Lia put her hand on the handle of the door and hitched up her dress a little. Brendan wrapped himself around her, and she pulled at the door.

It opened. Brendan leaned in to kiss her as they half-fell through the now open door, pretending to stifle giggles as Lia conspicuously smoothed out her dress. As they righted themselves and detached, Lia stole a look around the car.

It was definitely a passenger car, but it was mostly empty. Only two seats were occupied, by a man sleeping lengthwise, a coat thrown over his face.

"Well," Brendan said. "A successful ruse."

Lia snorted softly. "Better safe..."

They started moving up the rows of seats, checking each as they did. All empty until they came to the sleeping man.

Lia motioned for Brendan to watch the door, and he slid towards it while she crouched down by the man. He wore simple worker's clothes, the coat a thick wool. A small bag sat under the seat. She slid it out quietly and opened the clasps.

Clothes and travelling supplies, but one garment had a conspicuous EIC badge stitched into it.

She slid the bag back under the seat and joined Brendan at the door. "EIC," she said.

"Think there are any civvies?"

"I'm working on something. Just play along if it comes to it."

Brendan shrugged and opened the door. Wind hit them again just as the train entered another tunnel. Lia waved them on, and they entered the next car under cover of darkness just before it emerged once more.

This car was a lot fuller. A couple dozen passengers sat in seats up and down the car. A few looked up at them as they entered, and a couple people frowned as she and Brendan stole into a pair of seats.

"Legionaries," Brendan whispered.

Lia frowned and looked up the aisle. Sure enough, two uniformed legionaries flanked the door to the next car.

"What are they doing on an EIC train?" she said.

"Guarding the senator's philosopher?"

"Or his investments in general... Seems like a brazen conflict of interest."

"Maybe they're just hitching a ride with the civvies?"

"Maybe. But I'd bet most of these folks are EIC workers, too..."

They settled into their seats, wanting to give the appearance of belonging and take the opportunity to assess the situation. The noise of the train made it hard to listen in to all the chatter going on around them, but Lia caught snatches of conversation. Based on context clues, it definitely seemed like most of these folks were somehow associated with the EIC. They looked mostly like workers—no executives in a packed car like this.

They sat for about twenty minutes, occasionally talking to each other in low voices. Lia was about ready to give up on recon and try to move on when a couple of people switched seats to join a companion seated right behind them.

"All right," a man said, "we're only a few hours away now. You have to tell us what you know about these new ships."

"I told you before," said the woman who'd already been sitting there. "I'm not supposed to know yet, and I'm not about to lose a cushy job by telling you two."

Lia gave Brendan a look, and they tried to inconspicuously lean in to listen.

"We're going to find out soon enough," said another woman. "What have you heard?"

The first woman seemed to sigh and lower her voice. Lia strained to hear what she said.

"...pioneering new... first tests seem very positive... ships that can fly..." She missed the last part. Luckily the curious parties weren't so discreet.

"Higher than the clouds?" the man said. "There's no way—"

"Shush!" the woman said. "I knew I shouldn't have told you."

"You're making it up."

The other woman cut in. "I don't know. I've been reading some new research out of Oxford. With the right thaumaturgical advancements—"

"Which is why we're being brought in," the woman in the know said. "It's a lot of effort, but..." Her voice was lost to the train again as they entered a tunnel.

Brendan leaned close to Lia. "Ships?"

"Barcino has a huge shipyard," Lia said. "Ships that can get higher than any other—even the clouds... That would be a significant tactical advantage..."

"Why are the EIC interested?" Brendan frowned.

"Military contract, most likely. Might explain the legionaries."

"So, this philosopher is involved in... ship building? Hardly seems *that* noteworthy. Or secretive..."

Lia frowned and shook her head. "I don't think so. The letter—it said something about another facility. It might be something else entirely."

"Hmph," Brendan grunted. "Well, one way to find out."

Lia nodded. "Agreed. We're not going to get much more here, I think. Shall we?"

"What about the legos?"

"I have an idea."

They stood from the seats and walked down the car, holding onto the backs of chairs they passed for balance as the train rocked back and forth. As they approached the far door, one of the legionaries looked up—as anticipated.

"Hey. Where are you going?" she asked.

"Excuse me?" Lia said, all bemused innocence.

"Passengers are meant to stay in these cars until mealtime."

Lia laughed. "Oh, goodness. Hear that, Robert? Passengers. My dear," she looked at the soldier, "we're not passengers. We've donated a *lot* of money to the senator. We're *guests*."

The legionary frowned. "What are you doing back here?"

"Not that it's any of your *business*," Lia said, leaning on the back of the seat in front of the legionary so she loomed over the soldier a little, "but we were checking out the goods. After all, the senator wanted us to see *firsthand* what we were helping make possible..." Lia couldn't tell what the legionary thought of that. Was the possibility of corruption too unsubtle? Was there even anything to inspect? She was just hoping they wouldn't want to risk asking more questions. "So if you'll excuse me," she finished.

The soldier looked like she might protest further, but her companion said, "Just let 'em through," and she acquiesced.

Lia gave her a mirthless smile and pulled the door open.

Wind. The mountainside rushing past. Another door. Then they were inside again. This car, a dining car. A couple servers setting tables. They glanced up then back to their work as Lia walked forward towards the far door like she was just passing through—which she was.

Another door. More wind. A passenger car—but this one was completely empty.

She looked at Brendan.

"Weird," he said. "A buffer between the rabble and the important folks?"

Lia nodded. "Probably. Guess we're close."

The car after that confirmed it: private compartments lined one side, a hallway stretching the length on the other. Right beside the door stood a legionary. At the far end, a security guard in EIC uniform, a pistol and knife at his waist.

"Hey, where are you going?" the legionary asked. The EIC guard was watching them from the other end.

"We have a meeting," Lia said. "Excuse me." She stalked down the hallway and started looking through the windows into the private cars.

The first held a small group of men in dark suits talking intently over a bottle of wine. The next held an older gentleman, sleeping across the bench, mouth hanging open.

Inside the third private compartment sat a lone woman. She looked in her forties, light-skinned, hair in a tight bun. Her hands were clasped together and she stared out the window. She seemed nervous, anxious perhaps.

Lia glanced at Brendan, nodded her head towards her, then slid open the door, and they slipped inside.

The woman jumped a little as they entered.

"Hello," she said, uncertain. "Can—can I help you?"

Brendan slid the compartment door shut as Lia took a seat across from her.

"Are you Gisela?" she asked. She tried to keep her voice calm, conversational.

"Y-yes." The woman sat up a little straighter.

"My name is Lia Song," Lia said, holding up her insignia. "Praetorian Guard." She hoped Gisela wouldn't have heard anything to the contrary. There shouldn't be a reason to have.

The woman sat up completely. "Um. How can I help you...?"

"You're not in trouble," Lia said. "Just hoping you could answer a few questions for me."

Gisela nodded a little. "Of course." She didn't sound certain.

"Do you work for the East India Company?"

She nodded. "Assuming the paperwork has been processed. I signed their contracts yesterday..."

"And you're headed for Barcino now?"

"It's... not my final stop."

"Do you know what is?"

She shook her head. "No one will tell me."

"Who hired you? Who recruited you?"

Gisela seemed a little uncertain. "I don't understand—an EIC representative came to my office at the University..."

"Did they... did they mention Senator Vivarius at all when they spoke to you?"

That caused some recognition. "Yes, he had apparently been interested—" Then guards came up in her eyes and posture. "...Yes," she finished. "Why do you need to know this? What are you investigating?"

Lia glanced at Brendan, who stood at the door, glancing out the window occasionally into the hallway. "We're part of a wide-ranging inquiry," she said evasively. "Just gathering some information. What were you recruited to do? What is your role now?"

"I-I don't know exactly," Gisela responded. "But—well, my research was... bordering on illegal until a week ago."

Lia raised her eyebrows. Something Vivarius pushed through? "What do you research?"

The guards went up again. "They've asked for my... discretion." She paused. "How did—I'm sorry, I didn't think anyone was supposed to know I was here. How did you find me?" She sounded a little cagey now.

Lia frowned. "Like I said, there's an ongoing investigation—"

"We should hurry this up," Brendan cut in. "I think the guards are starting to get suspicious."

Gisela looked at him. "Why would—"

Lia sighed. "Look, we should get you out of here. Whatever the EIC is doing is not going to go well for you, I'm afraid—"

"Get me out of here?" she said. "Are you kidding? They're offering me the chance of a lifetime here."

"I need you to tell me what your research is," Lia said.

"Can I see that badge? Do you have some identification?"

"We don't have time for this," Brendan hissed. "We're not bound by the rules anymore, remember? Do whatever it takes!"

Lia looked at him. She wasn't about to—what, threaten this woman? Just because they weren't operating within the authority of the law anymore didn't mean they could ignore all decorum—never mind morals.

"Please, just tell us—"

"I think you should leave."

"Someone's coming," Brendan said. "Come on, we should just get her out of here."

"I'm not going anywhere—"

"We're not going to *kidnap* her!"

"Kidnap? Guards! Someone—"

"Great," Brendan said.

"By the Lupernal wolf's divine tits," Lia swore. "Move," she said to Brendan.

He nodded, reaching into his bag for the flare gun as he threw open the door to the compartment.

The legionary from one end of the car and the EIC security guard from the other were both moving towards them.

"Hey, what are you doing?" the legionary called out. Brendan was about to move his way, head back to the empty cars and known territory, when the EIC guard drew his pistol.

"Brendan!" Lia said.

Brendan shifted trajectory and leapt towards the guard shoulder first, knocking him back and off balance. Lia shot out of the compartment behind him and gave a swift kick at the legionary's shin as he reached forward to grab her arm. She heard her dress rip. He swore, confusion and anger crossing his face. She took off behind Brendan—that door was closer. Together they shoved the EIC guard against the window, trees and cliffside rushing by them, knocking the gun from his hand, which Lia quickly scooped up as they pushed past.

The wind, now familiar, hit them as Brendan pulled open the door. He slipped through, Lia after him, pulling it closed again as Brendan fired the flare gun into the air above them—

—just as the train entered another tunnel. The flare exploded against the ceiling and then was gone, far behind them as the train continued to rush forward.

"Shit," Brendan said.

"Keep going!" Lia said over the wind.

They moved into the next car just as the door they'd come through was beginning to open again.

Another car of private compartments. An EIC guard was walking down the aisle.

"Who—?" he started, hand drifting towards his holster.

Lia didn't give him a chance to finish. She fired her stolen pistol, clipping the man's gun arm. The man yelled, the *bang* of the gun only half-subsumed by the noise of the train. Someone in a private compartment screamed. There was commotion inside more than a couple.

Lia and Brendan ran forward, pushing past the EIC guard as the door behind them began to open—and they were outside once more.

"Flare!" Lia said, sliding the door shut.

Brendan was fishing in his bag. "I'm looking for it!"

"Look faster!"

"I've only got the one eye!"

Finally, he pulled out a replacement flare and loaded it into the front of the gun. Lia looked up at the scenery rushing past. On one side, the side of the mountain, rocks and trees a blur going by. On the other, a sheer drop to the valley below. She looked up—she had to squint against the bright clouds, but she spotted the dark spot that was their ship.

Then the door wrenched in her grip, and she swore and leaned her weight against it.

Brendan fired the flare into the sky off the side of the train. The *Raven* banked. The door almost ripped itself from Lia's grip.

"Help me!"

Brendan grabbed the door, too, but there was hardly room on the little platform between cars for them to both brace it closed. It shuddered again.

"We have to move on!" Lia said. "Find some cover and wait for Turner!"

"And run into more guards?"

"We can't keep this closed!"

"I hope she brings explosives."

"We're not blowing up the train, Brendan!"

He sighed. "Fine."

Lia maneuvered around him so he could put his full weight into holding the door shut while she grabbed the next one. On her nod, she pulled it open and they both ducked through, leaving the previous door unattended and about to open again.

She took in the next car. A passenger car, she saw to her dismay— rows of seats, filled with people. EIC workers.

Innocents, effectively. Bystanders. Not the best place to make a stand. But maybe the legionaries and guards would be equally concerned with their safety.

She guessed not.

"Everyone get down!" she yelled, raising the pistol in the air. Chaos ensued. She and Brendan dove down behind seats on either side of the aisle.

She heard the door open, the wind rushing in. The legionary pushed his way in first, looking around wildly as passengers scrambled for cover or yelled worried questions to each other.

Lia poked herself up between two seats and fired in the legionary's direction. She missed, but the soldier ducked backward, back out through the door, jostling for position with the EIC guards on the platform outside, taking cover from the door frame.

One of them aimed a gun towards her.

"Get down!" Lia screamed again. The shot hit the seat in front of her. She aimed again, but had no good angle—and limited bullets.

Brendan was rummaging in his bag again. Then, as an EIC guard stepped forward to take aim once more, he emerged from cover with his flare gun.

He'd apparently brought a second spare.

He fired the flare through the door. It exploded in a shower of flame and light. One of the guards screamed and was knocked off the platform as the other two ducked and tried to protect their bodies.

There were more yells from inside the car. Lia cursed herself. The whole point was *not* to endanger innocent bystanders.

But as feared, the guards had no such compunctions. The remaining one rallied and fired three shots wildly into the car. Lia and Brendan ducked, and they heard someone scream.

Then, suddenly, the guard was gone, and Turner landed in his place—apparently tethered to the sky. The legionary turned to her, panicked. Turner grabbed his pistol, twisted it from his hands, and pushed his head into the side of the car. He slumped.

"I saw movement from other cars," she called to them. "More coming. The philosopher?"

"Not coming," Lia said, standing.

Turner tossed over her rifle and Brendan a proper pistol. "Then let's go."

Brendan waved Lia on. "Ladies first."

Then the far door to the car opened. Lia instinctively took cover—but the person who entered was no legionary or EIC guard. They were something far more concerning.

Definitely remade, going by the man's head. His skull was encased in a matte black helmet, skin-tight, with a dark faceplate that seemed opaque from this side. It had to be grafted on. Lia felt bile rise in her throat as she considered that process.

Whoever this soldier was raised a pair of pistols. Lia fired her rifle.

With a shower of sparks, the bullet seemed to bounce right off the man's armour, also a series of matte black plates.

He opened fire in return. Shot after shot down the length of the car. Brendan and Lia ducked, Turner taking cover from the doorway. Turner fired her own pistol back. It deflected off the faceplate.

"Go!" Lia yelled.

They beat a hasty retreat as the man reloaded in one swift motion from clips on his belt.

Brendan got outside. Lia had to duck behind another seat as the man raised the guns once more. "Go!" she yelled again.

Brendan looked to protest, but Turner forcibly swung the harness around him. As the black-suited guard opened fire again, they leapt and flew from the platform outside.

Suddenly, Lia found herself wishing for explosives.

The armoured man stalked down the aisle, reloading again. Lia couldn't tell if any passengers had been hit, blood pounding in her ears. She guessed it likely.

She glanced out the window. On one side, cliff. On the other, empty air.

She didn't have much of a choice. Turner wouldn't be able to come back for her.

As the man raised his pistols again—he was getting close—she ducked around the seats and through the open doorway.

Gunshots fired. She felt something hit just under her shoulder, red-hot pain barely tamped down by adrenaline. She leapt over the fallen legionary, and for a brief moment, saw the land to the side of the train flatten.

She jumped.

The train entered a tunnel. Her momentum threw her into the side of the mountain—just beside the tunnel's entrance.

She fell. Rolled. And the train was gone.

She gave herself to blackness.

She woke as pain shot through her shoulder.

"Hold still. I just have to bind this," Turner said. She leaned over

Lia, winding bandages across and around her chest. "Lost a little blood there. Don't make any sudden moves or we may lose you again—and I don't know if I can carry you."

Lia nodded, moving her head just a little. It pounded like a bad hangover. "Brendan?"

"With Syd and the ship. Didn't want to leave them alone in case anyone came looking. We found a place to set down a little ways from here. It's a bit of a climb, though."

Lia nodded again.

Turner tied off the bandages and helped Lia sit up slowly.

"Was it worth it?" she asked.

Lia sighed.

"Yeah, that's what Brendan said, too. Okay, hold onto me with the uninjured arm, let's get you to your feet."

Lia felt weak, but once she was on her feet, she could manage fairly well. Turner threw her coat over her shoulders, and they started to hike down the side of the mountain.

"They had this... soldier..." Lia said.

"Yeah, I saw. Remade, I'd guess."

Lia nodded. "Nothing like I've ever seen. Full grafted body armour, a material I haven't encountered..."

"We'd been hearing rumours of its development, in the Agentes. Super light, super strong... Didn't know it was in the field."

"EIC is a little ahead of the military, I guess."

Turner nodded. "Better trained, too. Gearing up for a coup?"

Lia shook her head. "Why bother? With Vivarius, they already practically control the Senate."

The remade soldier wasn't what was weighing most on Lia's mind. It was the conversation with the philosopher. Not just that they hadn't gotten any useful information out of her, but also that without her true position, without her authority, Lia had been *unable* to get any useful information out of her.

She stewed in silence until she and Turner got back to the ship, hiding in a thicket of trees. Syd had kept the engines running, though Lia knew they didn't have a ton of fuel to spare.

"You okay?" Syd asked as they climbed aboard.

Lia nodded. "I will be." With time—and some field surgery. She considered that she might have been shot more times since joining the Guard than when she'd been on the front lines.

Brendan helped her into the galley, and they all took seats. "What now?" he asked.

"How'd it go?" Syd asked. "Besides getting shot. And the creepy armoured soldier Brendan mentioned."

"Not great," Lia said.

"We didn't learn anything," Brendan said. "Waste of time."

"Not entirely," Lia said. "The philosopher, Gisela, said her research was verging on illegal until a week ago. Which suggests Vivarius has specifically been putting through legislation to allow that research to go further."

"What does she study?" Turner asked.

Lia shook her head. "We couldn't get it out of her. Nor anything about the facility."

Brendan snorted a little. "It's not like we tried very hard."

Lia shot him a look. "What could we do? She was under no obligation to tell us anything. Not to mention *we* were the criminals in that situation."

"We could've leaned into it!" Brendan said. "I know you're not used to operating outside of the law, but we could've just taken her—brought her back, made her give us more information—"

"Kidnap her, you mean?" Lia snapped. "Intimidate her? Dis, maybe we should have tortured her for information, hm?"

Brendan looked about to respond, but she didn't let him.

"No—look, it's not that I'm unused to working in unconventional ways. Our jobs gave us the authority to do what was necessary. What I'm *not* willing to do is work outside a *moral* standard. We're not going to go around terrorizing innocent folk to get the information we need."

"Well, we're going to have to do *something* different," Brendan said. "Because that? That was a waste of time. Not to mention it almost got me killed..."

Syd whacked his arm. "It almost got *all* of you killed."

"Look, I know," Lia said. She pushed herself to her feet, leaning against the bulkhead. "You're not—you're not *wrong*, Brendan." She shook her head and sighed. "We've been *investigating* for so long, now.

Fact-finding, relying on the rank, and it's gotten us nowhere. Meanwhile Vivarius is making a steady climb in power, and we still don't even know what he's doing—and have no proof of any real involvement with the EIC or whatever *they're* doing. And I'm sick of chasing his crumbs, piecing together the dregs of his plans long after he's moved on." She slammed her fist against the side of the ship.

"So what do we do?" Syd asked.

"I don't know," Lia said. "But I'm not sitting around and letting him get the better of us anymore. I'm going to do whatever it takes to take him down."

She moved towards the cabins so she could get out of the damned dress. She wanted to shoot something.

"What's our destination, Captain?" Syd asked.

She paused. "Rome."

"Can't just fly right into Rome," Brendan protested. "We're wanted—or if we weren't before, we will be now."

"Somewhere close, then," Lia said.

Turner nodded. "A town nearby should be a good staging point. We can do some recon and figure out what's next without drawing too much attention."

Lia nodded. "Fine. Let's do it."

Interlude

CLARETTA

Claretta stood out in the square in front of the caffè, smoking. The American tobacco and the routine helped calm her nerves these days. And from the square, she could see down the street and out over the valleys surrounding the village, the farmland and hills, the setting sun casting purple shadows across them.

A poster was nailed to the building, a print of a Chinese woman's face. "Volens in Lege: Lia Song."

It was emblematic of the feeling that had seemed to settle across the Empire. A sense of unease, of concern, of worried oppression. People were keeping their heads down, except to cast sideways glances at others. Rumours of people being questioned, detained, had spread to Orvieto. The unrest, the worry about the border...

She tore the poster off the wall.

Yesterday, she and Omid had been standing quietly in the warm kitchen after news of another protest turned violent in northern Europe. They had shared a quick kiss and Claretta had sighed.

"There's nothing you can do," Omid had said, reading her mind.

Claretta had sighed again. "People wonder how the citizens of Rome could have sat idly by while Caesar rose to power and betrayed the values of the Republic..."

Omid had nodded. "It was the same back home. It's amazing what people can ignore. Or rationalize."

Claretta had looked at her, and in her saw all of the Empire, all the world beyond.

"But what can we do?"

Then, the sound of shouting and marching feet brought her back to the present. Legionaries had set up camp outside Orvieto yesterday. They didn't sound like they were just here to relax.

Claretta tossed the cigarette and ran back to the caffè. The place was crowded tonight, misery looking for company—and drink and gossip.

Omid was pouring drinks despite the looks she got these days. She wasn't the only one getting looks, though—anyone who didn't look Roman got sideways glances, even regulars who'd lived in the village their whole lives—or generations.

Claretta grabbed Omid's arm. "Legos coming. I want you in the basement. There's that shelf—"

Omid nodded, eyes cast down. Claretta could feel her seethe as she slipped out of the room.

Claretta tried to act as collected as possible when the two legionaries burst into the caffè.

"Proprietaria!" one said loudly as she approached the bar. "A drink for my compatriot and I."

She smiled and began pouring some honeyed wine as the other legionary wandered around the caffè, staring at the now-silent patrons.

The female legionary took a swig of the wine, then said in a mock-hushed voice that carried easily across the room, "There've been rumours of some pro-Ottoman sentiment in these parts. You know anything about it?"

Claretta glanced up and locked eyes for a brief moment with Maria at their regular table across the room. Publius was staring at his food intently. "No, ma'am," Claretta said. "Only patriots in my caffè."

"Hm," the legionary responded, face inside her glass.

The other stopped in front of a table where Tariku and Alemayehu sat. Ethiopian by parentage, though they'd lived in town all their lives.

"You ever been to Britannia?" he grunted.

Alemayehu looked at her drink. "Once on business," she said quietly. "Three years—"

"Ever been to Asia?"

"No, sir—"

"You sure?"

"Please," Tariku said, "we're loyal Romans—"

The legionary barked a laugh. "Come on. We have some questions for you."

"What?" Alemayehu said.

"I said, get up."

The female legionary was watching Claretta, and she raised her eyebrows in a shrug before downing the second glass of wine as she stood. Her compatriot forced Alemayehu to her feet.

Claretta almost said something. But she was afraid.

No one else spoke as Tariku and Alemayehu were marched out of the caffè, their food left cold on their table.

When Claretta performed her sacrifices that night, the hearth flame flickered low and cold as if the gods were upset. She wondered if they'd forgive her.

She wondered if Omid would.

Octavia,

Your analysis in your last letter is spot on concerning the latest changes to the law. Even as they push forward the *philosophy* of remaking, they strip away the protections for those of us who most need it. They experiment, and they plan to use us to do it.

The protests last week in the Forum went well, but we're not getting the attention we need. I'm planning something bigger. We have a few allies here in Rome, even an EIC lady who's organizing some collective action, and we're reaching out across the province. I want to reach out farther. Can you put me in touch with your fellows in Gaul and Britannia? I'm thinking about an *occupation*.

In lighter news, you should see the rig I just finished. Full workshop setup, just like the one Lucia helped me do in the kitchen. Even got a custom mount for my chair. It'll make my work a lot easier. I'll be able to build some more messengers pretty fast now, so we can have more constant contact. Maybe I'll build a transmitter next, if we can find an unused frequency.

Give my love to your sisters. We'll make some change yet.

— Aurelia

Peace has returned to the volatile northern provinces this week after a series of arrests left protests leaderless; without their Ottoman-sympathetic instigators, protesters have returned to home and work to keep the gears of the Empire turning.

The recently elected Consul Vivarius has been hailed for his handling of the protest situation in Britannia. His new bills, passed swiftly through the Senate, gave Legate McAvoy not only the authority to do what had to be done to return peace to the region, but also the means and information. This was, of course, bolstered by a new unit of remade legionaries masterminded by the consul, originally intended for the Ottoman border.

It should be noted that we have received reports of rumours circulating on the mainland of continued protests and unrest throughout the north and east; let us assure our listeners, we have investigated, and these rumours are nothing more than that—falsehoods spread by our enemies to the south, Ottoman sympathizers who wish to see our great Empire and the ideals it represents brought low.

If you hear anything suspicious, you are encouraged to remember your duties to our Empire and report it to local authorities...

PART 3

Chapter 16: Resistance

JULIAN

The news was never-ending: streams from across the Empire about the actions of the Senate, the inherent wrongness of the protests, the unending sense that despite it, the Empire was stronger than ever, especially with Vivarius at the helm.

Everyone knew better, even if they chose to believe it.

Julian knew better. He could see the corruption happening behind closed doors and honeyed words.

But what could he do?

He and Gaius had returned to Orvieto, to their little rented apartment—thanks in part to the small amount of cash Alesse had given them. They spent evenings at the caffè. Every once in a while, Gaius would try to get Julian talking, try to get him thinking about all Vivarius was doing—what they would do about it.

But what could they do?

They had no power against someone like Vivarius. No way to work against him. Even speaking out of turn like his mother—or the protesters across the Empire—could get you killed. Increasingly, Julian was seeing that only real upheaval had any hope of causing change. Part of him—the part that took the airship in Frankfurt—had perhaps always known. Civil war, maybe. But that would certainly result in a lot of death. And given the resources Vivarius had at his disposal, it seemed unlikely to work.

Unless Vivarius or the Senate or the emperor still had any shred of patriotism, of true understanding that unless they were serving the people, they were merely forcing their will on a population that didn't want them.

But Julian doubted that. Not after what he'd seen and heard. They had only their own interests at heart, and they could *convince* much of the population that theirs were the same.

It hadn't escaped him that Imperial Radio was now run by the East India Company.

Despite Gaius's questions, despite the things he saw happening around him, Julian could think of nothing to do.

Nothing but stay here with Gaius. Really, what Gaius had wanted. Find what little happiness they could as the Empire rusted and broke down around them.

And, he thought, maybe he *could* find some happiness. The kind he saw between Claretta and Omid. Love despite the world around them. He'd wanted to be with Gaius for so many years, to live happily together. Now he had that opportunity.

He looked at Gaius—staring quietly out the window of the caffè at the softly lit nighttime streets of the town. He sat statuesque, cheekbones and shoulders and tight muscle and soft eyes. Those eyes shifted back and forth as he stared at the night. Not at peace. Mind darting, tumbling about like Julian's own.

Maybe peace was far away yet.

The rest of the caffè was fairly quiet. Maria and Publius sat at a table nearby, the only regulars who were still here every night. A lot of the townsfolk stayed in for evenings now. And Claretta had quietly implied what had happened to Tariku and Alemayehu while they were gone. The couple hadn't been seen in several days.

The only other patrons were a strange crew Julian hadn't seen around before, visitors from out of town. They wore heavy cloaks despite the summer evening heat and talked amongst themselves in low voices.

In the otherwise quiet caffè, Julian could hear snatches of their conversation. Claretta had just delivered them wine and coffee and their voices rose for a moment after the interruption.

"We can still stop this," one of the women was saying, a Chinese woman. There was some desperation in her voice. A lot of folks were desperate these days. "If we can get some solid evidence, there are still enough people in Rome who would listen..."

The other woman spoke up. "If we could figure out who this Servius character is... But all my sources are dry."

Julian sat up. The sentence had barely registered except for the name—then the rest clicked into place.

It was a common enough praenomen, but he had to check. He turned his head a little, tried to listen to what they said next. But they'd lowered their voices again.

Then Gaius sat up. He hadn't been listening, but something outside had caught his attention. He'd stiffened when Maria's voice called from the other table by the windows, a hand touching Julian's leg.

"Claretta—the legionaries are coming back."

Rushing wind seemed to fill Julian's head, every fibre tensing even as his heart ticked on. He saw Claretta look at Omid, and the crew at the far table turn.

All he could do was stare at Gaius and say, "They're here for us."

Claretta looked at him. He didn't know how she'd react. But he knew they needed to hide—to run.

"Or us," the Chinese woman said, quietly. She, too, was looking at him.

Omid snorted softly, looking at Claretta. "Or me."

It was one thing not to know what to do when time seemed long and the time to think and ponder and rethink stretched out to fill the days. It was another when there was no time. But Julian did not know what to do.

Tick.

He saw Claretta turn to Omid. "Go hide. You know where."

Tick.

"What about them, Claretta?" Omid asked.

"We'll only bring them down on us!" Claretta said—but then she stopped.

She looked at Julian and then the other crew. Maria and Publius sat silent, staring wide-eyed at it all.

Tick.

Julian didn't know what to do. Could they run?

Gaius looked at Claretta, pleading perhaps in his eyes.

The other table looked ready to spring into action.

"What about Tariku and Alemayehu?" Omid said. "What about the others? The others you're always imagining, the townsfolk, the farmland beyond. All the provinces out there. If this is happening *here*—"

"It's happening there," Claretta said quietly. "Thousands of people in danger, the Empire coming down on anything they can blame. All their lives, their trials and dreams, loved ones and needs..."

Tick.

"Vivarius doesn't see them," Claretta said, looking at Omid, then out the window. "Not as real people. With real lives and struggles."

The Chinese woman stood up. "You can't help all of them. Maybe no one can. But you can help some..."

Tick.

"What did people do when Caesar rose to power?" Claretta said quietly. "When the Ottoman coup happened? Some sat by and watched.

"Some resisted."

Julian's heart ticked again, but he could feel a shift in air pressure in the room.

Claretta stepped to the Chinese woman's table. "Lia, right? There's a room downstairs, an old wine cellar from some past structure here, hidden behind a shelf. It opens into these old labyrinthine tunnels below the city. Go. Follow Omid." She turned to Julian and Gaius. "You, too."

Gaius nodded, standing. Julian moved close beside him as they started to head towards the kitchen where Omid stood.

Tick.

Claretta looked around. Maria was smiling gently at her; Publius was staring at his food. Claretta frowned as Lia and her crew gathered their things.

"Wait. You, bearded one."

Julian looked over at the big man with the shaved head, beard, and eyepatch.

"Brendan."

"You stay here with me. Ditch the patch."

Brendan looked at Lia, who nodded.

Julian, Gaius, Omid, and Lia and her remaining crew all crowded into the small kitchen. Omid was pulling at a shelf of cookware; Gaius pushed forward to help her.

Then they heard the legionaries come through the caffè door.

"Proprietaria," one called. "Where's the Persian?"

"The kitchen help?" they heard Claretta ask, bemused. "My husband here fired her weeks ago. Didn't want any sympathizers *here*."

Julian peeked through the crack in the kitchen door as Omid slipped behind the shelf, followed closely by Lia and the others. He saw Brendan smile and give a noncommittal shrug.

Then Gaius took Julian's arm and helped him behind the shelf as well.

"Search the kitchen," the legionary told her compatriot.

Julian and Gaius pulled the shelf over the tunnel entrance together, and they were plunged into tense darkness.

The space was not large. Julian could feel the body heat of these other people around him in the dark. Pressed against Gaius, he could feel Gaius's heart pounding.

His own ticked away steadily.

Tick.

Tick.

Tick.

They could hear the legionary in the kitchen, pots being moved, the jangle of the legionary's rifle strapped to his back.

Tick.

Then the legionary seemed to leave the kitchen.

Omid breathed, "Come," and Julian could feel the line of people move farther into the darkness.

He stretched out a hand to touch the wall of the tunnel, then moved it to hold onto Gaius's back. The other hand clutched his bag to him, never far from reach—still full of random notes, clothes, and denarii.

Tick.

Tick.

After a few more minutes, they heard the kitchen shelf move. They held their breath.

Tick.

"Blast, it's dark in here," Brendan's voice muttered. "Lia?"

A collective release of air. The strike of a match and a small oil lantern glowed to life in Omid's hands.

Julian looked around as the man named Brendan made his way towards them, pulling his eyepatch back over his head, his metal leg clumping against the stone. The tunnel was ancient, carved through the soft volcanic rock of the butte.

"That was close," one of Lia's crew said, the pale-skinned one.

"Should've heard the lady," Brendan said. "After the legos left, she turned to one of the patrons and said, 'Publius, you ever tell the legionaries about us again, and you'll need to question what I put in your food every day.' Ha!"

"Publius?" Gaius said.

"Should've seen that coming," Omid said quietly.

"His wife sure looked shook," Brendan said.

"Where's Claretta?" Omid asked.

"Still up there. Said we should get out of town."

Omid nodded. "It's a bit of a journey through these tunnels, but you can get past the walls."

"What about you?" Julian asked.

She sighed. "I'll have to stay hidden, I think. But I know Claretta. We'll do what we can now. There are others that need protecting. Maybe we can get some folks out of Italy."

Julian nodded. Something to do.

"Where next?" Lia asked, turning to her Ethiopian companion.

Julian looked at them. "Did I hear you say you were looking for someone named Servius?"

Lia looked at him.

"My name's Julian. I think I might be able to help."

Chapter 17: Light in the Tunnel

GAIUS

Gaius instinctively took a step towards Julian, standing now at his side. The group—seemingly fugitives, all of them—stood in the cramped darkness of the carved rock tunnel, in the glow of Omid's single oil lamp.

"Lia Song," the Chinese woman said, stepping to the front of her group. "Brendan. Turner. Syd."

"Gaius," Gaius introduced himself.

Lia nodded greeting to both of them. "We used to be Praetorian Guards," she said. "I've worked against corruption in the Empire for years. Until, I believe, Vivarius took that away from me."

"Is this wise?" Turner asked quietly. "We don't know these two..."

"Vivarius took everything from me, too," Julian said. "From both of us. If you think you can do something..."

"I think there's a connection between Vivarius and someone called 'Servius,'" Lia said. "Something that could help. But we don't know anything about him."

"I do," Julian said. "I... worked for him. Until I ran away..."

Lia's eyebrows rose. Gaius put a hand on Julian's shoulder.

"We should move on," Lia said. "In case those legionaries come back or can hear us. Clearly they have reason to be after all of us."

Omid nodded. "There are some larger chambers deeper within. We can hole up there for a while."

Julian nodded in agreement, and the group of them began moving through the tunnels once more, following the flickering of Omid's lantern. Lia and Turner spoke quietly to each other, Syd trailing along behind. Brendan brought up the rear behind Julian and Gaius.

"Hey, are you two..." Brendan trailed off a little.

Gaius glanced back, but the man's face in the dim light didn't show any potential hostility—far from it, in fact.

But he still wasn't sure how to answer. "We're... together."

Julian slipped his hand into Gaius's. "Partners," he said.

Brendan's face broke into a grin. "Called it when I saw you together in the caffè. Very cute." He punched Gaius lightly on the shoulder. "You remind me of me when I was your age. All protective and stuff. That was before the mohawk. And the eye. And the leg. And when I realized I could get myself killed any day and started shagging any guy that would have me."

Gaius's eyes widened a little. He was unsure if this was meant as a compliment, warning, or solicitation.

"Um," he said.

"Will be nice to have some other men of the town around, is all. And some real love! Turner and Syd used to be like that, you know? But it didn't work out. And Lia's not really into any of that stuff. We're all just real good friends now. Which is great! But you know. I miss seeing folks like you."

Julian gave Gaius a bemused look, but it was mixed with a little amusement, too. Gaius let out a quiet laugh and smiled at Brendan.

"There was always this assumption I'd have to get married someday," Julian said, looking ahead. "I guess it's nice to know someone that shows it doesn't have to be the case."

"Nope!" Brendan said. "Lifelong bachelor, as they euphemize. Even when you have someone like that." He lightly punched Gaius again, and Gaius squeezed Julian's hand.

They'd never really talked about their relationship outside of their love—what it might mean, where it might go. Gaius had never really wanted to think about it back when he was a slave—it was an impossible thing, then, both because of who he was, and who Julian was. Like they'd talked about more recently, it was impossible to have any kind of equal partnership before. Any real consensual relationship. And Julian was, as he'd mentioned, expected to marry.

Since their reunion, he hadn't put much thought into it either, other than that one conversation—no thought to the future. He was just happy they were together again. That they loved one another.

It made his heart thrill to hear Julian use the word "partner." He supposed that's what they were. What they *could* be, now.

And certainly, there were no longer any expectations put on Julian.

He smiled at Brendan again.

And then the tunnel opened up. It wasn't a huge chamber—the size of a small root cellar perhaps—but it gave them the space to spread out a little, have some breathing room.

Omid sat the lantern on a small ledge while Brendan moved to rejoin Lia, Turner, and Syd. Julian and Gaius stuck together, holding hands now, and turned to face the others.

"We should be safe here for a while," Omid said. "There are no supplies or anything down here, but these tunnels are a secret the people of Orvieto have kept for centuries. They say they're from pre-Roman times, even."

"Enough time to get our bearings, at least," Lia said.

"Where do the tunnels lead?" Syd asked.

"Out of the city. Into the countryside surrounding the butte," Omid replied. "Escape routes in case of siege."

Syd nodded. "We should be able to get to the *Raven*, then."

"The *Raven*?" Gaius asked.

"We have an airship," Lia said. "But first—we've got some talking to do."

Julian nodded.

"Senator—sorry, *Consul* Vivarius, needs to be stopped," Lia said. "His rise to power is motivated solely by personal ambition and has led to increasing unrest, xenophobia, and the removal of freedoms."

"Not to mention, he's an ass," Gaius said.

Brendan nodded in concurrence.

"But how?" Julian asked. "What can you do?"

"Well, it sounds more like what can *we* do," Lia said. "We've found some connections between him and this 'Servius,' and while we don't know much, it certainly seems like understanding Servius and this connection could help reveal that corruption. And if we can find some real evidence of wrongdoing, there's still a chance we can bring him down. And you, Julian, know Servius."

"Kind of," Julian said. "I know him, but I don't—I don't *really* know who he is. But I was indentured to Vivarius's estate after he black-mailed my parents, and ended up in Servius's service. So, I know they are connected..." He trailed off a little.

"What kind of things do you know Vivarius has done?" Gaius asked. "What do you know that connects them?" He'd never really gotten much from Julian about this Servius person, not wanting to bring up bad memories or push Julian over the edge again. But now it seemed like something could maybe be done.

Lia turned to Turner.

"Vivarius seems to have provided Servius with the materials to make bombs," Turner said. "Bombs that could appear to be of Otto-man make."

Omid's eyebrows furrowed. "Like the attacks in Londinium?"

Turner nodded. "Good excuses to ramp up security and impose the beginnings of martial law. It seemed maybe in payment for some-thing—organizing a shipment of other weapons or something to Italy..."

Gaius glanced at Julian, but his face had become carefully stoic.

"Servius also found and arranged transport of a philosopher to some secret research facility Vivarius was funding. We're unsure of its purpose.

"But as for Servius himself, his identity and importance have es-caped us."

Lia turned back to Julian.

"Vivarius's extortion of my family—once the Praefectus Graecus Meridianus—resulted in all of us becoming indentured to him," Julian said. "I was sent to work for the man called Servius, acting as an... as-sistant to a remaker. I only saw him sometimes after that.

"When I did see him, he often talked about changing the Empire. He seemed to think for the better. Some of his ideas were pretty radi-cal—dismantling a lot of the government, removing regulations, even starting a war. I'm not surprised he and Vivarius are connected, seeing what Vivarius has done since. And yet... they definitely had different ideas, different plans for Rome..."

"If we can find him, we can ask him," Lia said. "Find his home or office, and we can find evidence of what's really been going on, whatever it is."

Julian looked away. "I never knew where he came from, where he lived. Even who he worked for, really. Himself, it seemed."

"Then we're no closer," Brendan said.

Julian pondered a moment. Gaius watched him. He hadn't told Gaius much, but he had mentioned the lab he'd worked in. Wouldn't that be a good start?

Then Julian's eyebrows raised. "Maybe—I grabbed some notes and documents of his when I ran." He held up his bag—the straps tied together in a knot where they had snapped before. "Maybe there's something in here."

Lia nodded. "It's as good a lead as any. Better take a look now. Do you want a hand? We scan documents for evidence like that all the—"

Julian frowned. "No, I-I'll know what's just—notes and things... I can do it."

Lia nodded, and Julian found a little corner of the room near the lantern and sat on the hard ground, then opened the bag and began to sift through its contents.

Meanwhile, Lia and her crew talked in low voices together. Gaius was left to stand and wonder what would come next.

There would be no safe escape for him and Julian now.

Maybe that was for the best.

He'd originally hoped closure with Julian's parents would help him be willing to settle down, to leave the problems of the Empire behind. But after seeing what had happened to them—how the Empire had broken them—he was beginning to see what Julian had always said, what Alesse had always argued. Gaius had changed. Now he saw that Julian *shouldn't* give it all up. That there was important work to do.

As he stood there a little uncomfortably, he noticed Omid doing much the same. A little ways from the others, looking around at the chamber and tunnels around them with a strange expression on her face—a mixture of sadness and determination.

He stepped over to her quietly.

"I don't think anyone's thanked you, yet," he said.

She looked at him and smiled a bit. "It was the only thing to do. I'm glad Claretta agreed."

"Could easily have turned us in."

"They would've just taken me, too. If not today, then tomorrow or next week. I've seen it before." She returned her gaze to the tunnels around them. "...I was just thinking how similar these are to some of the routes we took to get out of Turkey."

"Why did you leave?" Gaius said. "If I may ask."

She looked at him. "What have you heard about the Ottoman Empire, Gaius?"

He looked down. "I wouldn't presume to know what's happening there, Omid. Sometimes I think I barely know what's happening here."

"That's because all we hear is lies and half-truths," Turner said, joining them. "Even before Vivarius's rise, Rome never wanted its citizens to think of the Ottomans as anything other than the enemy."

"So what's the truth?" Gaius asked.

Omid snorted softly. "Some of us *are* the enemy." She paused. "Most of us are not. Ottomans are as diverse as Romans, from across Turkey, Arabia, Africa, Persia, to the borders of India, China, and Russia. Most just wanting to live out their lives in peace like anyone. And most do! It's a vibrant place. We have cities and markets and farmland and universities and everything else. Poverty and riches. Happiness and sorrow. But you wouldn't know it from the reports. You wouldn't know it from our leaders.

"Sultan Osman, 'the Liberator', took control years ago. They say it was a bloodless coup, that our Ministers surrendered. They may have surrendered; it was not bloodless. The sultan's control over the Empire now is seemingly absolute. He and his government are the boogeymen Rome warns its people of. Murderers, torturers, their secret police sweeping through neighbourhoods at night for dissenters..."

"That's true?" Gaius asked, aghast.

Omid nodded. "But it is not all of what Ottomans are. There are those among the leadership that want change, that want peace and prosperity for everyone. Serdar Khalid was one of them. Have you heard of him?"

Gaius frowned. "No."

"I have," Turner said. "The official report, for a while, was that he was a dangerous nationalist, a very capable military leader, and a threat. Then we thought he could be a tool when we realized he was a dissident, too, and the support he had—he could bring civil war to the Ottomans, split their forces."

Omid snorted. "Dissident, indeed. He was hated by the military leadership, but he was too much of an asset to remove. Things were getting tense. A tipping point was coming. Because, of course, Ottomans hate our leaders as much as Romans do. Or at least, many of us. The army has its supporters, of course. Mostly those who benefit from its power.

"But many of us chafe under them. And with Serdar Khalid, we might have a chance at change. Rumours of civil war *were* starting. Rebel groups were already fighting in Damascus and back home in Tehran. Khalid was poised to make a move. So we all thought. I'm sure the leaders were ready to remove him even if it might cause an uprising—better an uprising without its most capable leader."

She sighed. "Then, he fell ill. Badly ill. No longer a threat to them, and no murder, no martyrdom to spark a rebellion."

"And is that true...?" Gaius asked. "I mean—isn't it possible he *is* dead, that the leaders lied?"

"It is," Omid replied. "Of course it is. But word of his survival spread through the rebel circles, through the streets, from supposedly reputable sources. Word that he was still out there.

"That's when I felt the change coming. The coup was bad enough. True civil war would have been bad enough. But this, this leaderlessness, this uncertainty... it was messy. Rebellions increased, bombings and raids and fights. But never united. And the leaders began to stamp down on any and all of it. Any hint of dissent and you would be hunted and made to disappear."

"Gods," Gaius said. "I had no idea it was so... complicated."

"It's an empire of millions of people, hundreds of cities," Omid said. "Of course it's complicated."

"At least it's not so bad here," Gaius said.

"Of course it is," Turner said. "Haven't you been listening to the news? Haven't you seen what happened in this town alone? It may not look exactly the same. But it is exactly as bad. And Vivarius will make it worse."

Gaius went silent. The protests in Britannia—the worker deaths in Aternum and elsewhere—the mass murders in India. And even those came from news filtered through rose-tinged radio waves.

His mind went to Alesse. Someone fighting, struggling against the powers that be, to make life better for the common worker. For a long time, he hadn't thought her fight so important. Suddenly, he couldn't imagine her succeeding. Certainly not with Vivarius taking power. Not when the EIC had their fist around the throat of the Senate.

"What if Serdar Khalid was alive?" Gaius asked Omid. She'd been staring into the middle distance, lost for the moment. Back home, perhaps. But she returned at his words. "What if he recovered?"

She shrugged and sighed. "I don't know, Gaius. Maybe real civil war. Maybe change. Maybe just more death."

He nodded.

Then he heard Julian's voice from across the small chamber.

"Huh. I think I found something?"

Everyone immediately turned their attention to him, crowding around. Gaius squeezed past Turner to be at Julian's side, helping him to his feet—he knew how much Julian disliked tight crowds.

"What did you find?" Lia asked.

Julian was holding a few pieces of mostly crumpled paper, though he was trying to smooth them out. "I'm not fully sure. I never noticed these pages before. They must have been stuck at the bottom of the bag or something... It looks like—there's a legal document or ledger of some sort, as well as architectural sketches? As far as I can tell, Servius and Vivarius were partnered on some new facility they were building. There might be something here to connect them financially, maybe find Servius..." He trailed off at that last, and Gaius gave him a look he hoped was a mixture of question and support.

"May I?" Lia asked.

Julian nodded and handed over the pages. Lia took them, glanced through them, and handed a couple to Turner while Syd looked over her shoulder.

"This numerical designation suggests it's in Greece," Lia said. "Sounds like an entertainment venture. Gambling, dice... fights."

"Highly secure, it looks like," Syd said. "There's lots of information in these diagrams on vaults, locks... They're anticipating a lot of denarii going through this place."

"Laundering money, maybe," Turner agreed.

"Okay, but how does this help us?" Gaius asked.

Julian pointed at the bottom of the page Lia was scanning.

"The building is complete," Lia said. "The final paperwork was to be signed and filed onsite. And there were apparently special arrangements made to hold some... personal effects and documentation for the controlling partners outside of Italy." Her eyebrows raised.

"Yep, I can see it there," Syd said, pointing at one of the diagrams. "Private offices and vaults for the partners."

"Is it just me—" Brendan started.

"Too good to be true," Lia agreed. "Still. We have to check it out. If there's something there that tells us who Servius really is... If there's anything there that shows the nasty stuff Vivarius is into or evidence of laundering—and it sounds like it very well may—then we need to get our hands on it."

"Okay, but how?" Gaius asked.

Syd shrugged. "We have the building plans. We can probably find a way in."

"What about all that security?"

Lia smiled. "I'm sure we can figure something out."

Gaius frowned and looked at Julian. He was toying idly with his bag.

"Well," Julian said. "Good luck, I guess."

"Jules," Gaius said. "We have to go. We have to help them."

"What help can we be?"

Lia shrugged. "You know Servius. You may be exactly what we need to make this happen. And you'd be more than welcome to join us."

Julian looked unsure.

"We can't stay here," Gaius said. "We'd just be putting Claretta and Omid in danger. And we have to do something, Jules. You've said it yourself."

Julian nodded a little.

"Then it's settled," Lia said. "Both of you can come. We'll hit up this gambling house and see what we can't shake out of its pockets. Dis, bring it crashing down if we have to. We're going to find Vivarius and we're going to stop him."

Her crew nodded. Gaius nodded. Something had to be done—even if he was unsure about... What even were they going to do? Break in...?

Whatever it was, he would be with Julian. Jules seemed to have lost all his drive, ever since Aternum. Gaius would help him get it back.

He looked at Omid. "You?"

"Staying here with Claretta. Even if I have to do it in secret. Good luck, though." She smiled. "It's good to know there are folks here in Rome with as much fire as the folks back home."

The group bade their goodbyes as Omid instructed Lia how to get through the tunnels and out of the city. They would find Lia's airship and head towards Greece—making a plan along the way.

As the group prepared to depart, Gaius pulled Julian aside.

"Hey. Are you okay? Are you all right with this?"

Julian nodded, quietly. Gaius knew the look, knew Julian was all up in his own head.

"Jules," he said. Julian looked at him. "What about the lab? The place you... worked."

Julian looked away again.

It seemed like the obvious answer. Someplace they could find Servius—or find how to find him.

"I can't go back there," Julian said. "I don't want to remember."

Gaius just nodded and pulled Julian close to him.

They hugged. Gaius was getting used to the hard metal in Julian's chest. The mechanical warmth of it.

He smiled, gave Julian a last squeeze, and prepared to leave Orvieto.

Chapter 18: Plans

LIA

They had a target. A destination. A goal. Lia was starting to feel a little hope again, to see a path forward.

Gather evidence. Put together a case against Vivarius—and Servius. Do the job—even if it wasn't her job anymore.

No—it wasn't her career. It was still her job.

Protect the Empire. Protect the *people* of the Empire. The people like Julian and Gaius and Claretta and Omid.

The tunnels beneath Orvieto were extensive. They made their way by the light of Omid's lamp; she had turned back towards the caffè, feeling her way through the familiar darkness. A tentative plan made, they walked mostly in silence. Their footsteps were marked by the *clump, clump* of Brendan's leg and the occasional soft ticking that must be someone's pocket watch.

Omid had given them rough directions—markings on the walls where the tunnels branched pointed the way to the exit. At first, the tunnels sloped downward—at times quite steeply, winding their way down from the top of the butte before eventually levelling off. Then they went straight for a while, one long tunnel disappearing into blackness at the edge of their light.

Then it began to rise once more—and soon, a door. Hewn wood, covered in dust and moss—the barest hint of fresh air beyond.

Lia held up a hand as the group came to a halt, wincing at the pain in her shoulder as she did. Her side had been healing just in time to get shot again.

"Turner?" she said quietly.

Turner nodded and came up to the door with her. Lia loosed her rifle as Turner quickly pushed the door open.

Dust fell as air rushed in. Lia aimed the rifle out, doing a quick sweep of the brightness beyond; she couldn't see much as her eyes adjusted.

Turner slipped out the door and pulled it closed once more.

Eyes half-adjusted, Lia was plunged into darkness.

"Gonna scout out the area, just in case," she heard Brendan say to the boys.

Lia's eyes readjusted to the dark just in time for the door to open once more as Turner returned.

"All clear. Looks like the legos have an airship docked at the town though. Takeoff will be tricky."

"All right," Lia said. "Let's get to the ship."

This time, she led as they pushed the door open once more, rifle still out, just in case. The tunnels opened into a thicket surrounded by underbrush that fairly effectively hid the entrance—whether on purpose or just through the passage of time, she wasn't sure.

She crouched amongst the plants as everyone filtered out, letting her eyes readjust once more, trying to look for trouble. By the time the door was closed behind them, she could finally see.

"Any idea where we came out?" Lia asked Turner.

"Vaguely."

"I think we're close, actually," Syd said. They could see the butte through the trees from here. "Looks like we're south of the town. Follow me."

"Stay low," Lia said. "They could still be looking for us."

They nodded, and the group set off.

The engines rumbled to life even as Brendan and Lia pulled away the branches that had been trying to camouflage the *Raven*—they had no time to waste. Turner led Julian and Gaius up the gangplank, then climbed up the ropes wrapped around the balloon to remove some of the brush there. They'd found a large enough copse to hide a camouflaged airship in while in town—it made for a slower escape, though.

Lia followed the boys inside after a moment as Brendan and Turner finished the deforestation. She came down into the bridge where Gaius and Julian were standing uncomfortably as Syd prepped the ship for takeoff.

"Grab a seat," she said, moving towards the galley and bunks beyond. "Might be a rough takeoff." She returned a moment later, spyglass and goggles in hand—the boys were still standing awkwardly in the bridge—and went back up to the deck.

"How are we looking?" she called to Brendan and Turner.

"Commanding yet ravishing as always, Captain," Brendan said.

She rolled her eyes.

"Haven't drawn any attention yet," Turner said, sliding down a line to the deck. "As far as I can see. We may be able to get away before they have a chance to rally."

Lia went to the north side of the ship and snapped open the spyglass. The Imperial ship was still docked at Orvieto—there was a little movement around it, but not much.

"All right, let's get her in the air before they notice."

Brendan clambered up the gangplank and inside, calling, "Take 'er up!"

Turner stood beside Lia as propellers revved to life and the balloon above them swayed.

"What do you think of the boys?" she asked.

Lia shrugged. "Hard to know. Gaius seems to have a fire in him, even if he's unsure how to direct it. Julian... He comes from a political background and definitely has reason to have it out for Vivarius. He could be an asset. But whatever his connection with Servius or Vivarius, he's been through something. Trauma of some sort, I'd wager."

Turner nodded. "Something to keep an eye on."

"Of course. On the other hand, this is our first real lead in a while. This could be what we've been looking for."

There was a lurch as the *Raven* lifted off the ground. Lia smiled and turned to go back inside.

"You're not usually one to take on strays," Turner said.

"I took on you," Lia said over her shoulder.

The waters of the Adriatic were deep blue below them as the airship raced beneath the clouds. They hadn't been followed out of Orvieto—whether because they hadn't been noticed, or the legion had more important things to do than follow a random airship, no one was sure. With their direction set, Syd joined everyone in the galley. Lia had the structural diagrams spread on the galley table while everyone sat or stood around in the cramped room.

"So," she said. "Our goal is evidence. Something that identifies Servius, something that tells us what Vivarius is really doing or ties him to illegal activity... At the very least, documents showing their partnership in this gambling house, if we can get anything tying it to money laundering. So the private vaults seem like our best opportunity, right? Which means we need to find a way into Vivarius's office and through the locks. A way that doesn't get us arrested or killed, ideally."

"Ideally," Syd said.

"Turner?" Lia asked.

"Definitely too much security for me to simply break in. And those vaults are likely to be far beyond my ability to unlock. If we were going for the main vault, we could get someone who works there to open it for us, but I doubt anyone but Vivarius will know how to get into his."

Syd pulled the vault diagrams over to them. "With some study, I may be able to figure out how the mechanism works... But it looks like a combination lock of some kind, and brute-forcing that's going to be impossible."

"Could it be automated?" Lia asked.

Syd shrugged. "With the right resources and time, maybe."

"We'd still have to get to the offices unnoticed *and* get out again," Brendan said.

"We'll need a distraction," Turner agreed.

"Or two," Lia said.

Julian nodded slowly. "We need access to the offices, or at least the area near the vault... a distraction while we get in... and a way to get out again, ideally without anyone noticing there's been a break-in..."

Lia looked at him. "You sound like you have an idea."

Julian bent over the plans. "Gambling house, offices... and of course there's a coliseum attached. Vivarius does like his remade gladiators..." He looked up at Brendan, who smiled cheekily. Then he turned to Lia. "Can any of you... act?"

Lia looked at Turner, at Brendan—deep cover stuff had never really been their forte.

Syd slowly raised their hand. "I used to do community theatre as a teenager?" they said, uncertain.

Julian smiled. "I think we can work with that."

They spent the next hour going over Julian's idea. There were some holes in it, some of which they tried to patch. They wouldn't know enough to fix the rest until they could do some recon. This would be a long game—a multi-day operation at least. Lia hoped not much longer than that. The longer they waited, the harder Vivarius would be to stop, at the rate he was going.

"We should be coming up on the coast soon," Syd said. "I'm going to check our heading."

Lia nodded. "Let's get out of this cramped galley. We have some work to do."

She began to roll up the diagrams. Turner went to join Syd on the bridge while Brendan climbed up to the deck for fresh air. Gaius and Julian stayed in the galley.

Lia was going to join Syd and Turner on the bridge when she heard them talking.

"We haven't had much chance to talk," Turner said.

Syd glanced at her. "Is-is there something you need to talk about?"

Turner turned away. "I just thought, maybe you'd—"

"Don't tell me after all this time, you still—"

"No! I just thought you—"

Syd laughed, but kindly. "You always were such a worrier under that tough exterior. Turner, I'm good. I am. Yeah, I hurt for a while, but—Venus's tits, we were *never* right for each other."

Turner tried to hide a small smile by looking at the floor. "No, we weren't."

Syd turned, and took her hands. "I love you, Lane. But we're so much better as friends."

Lia smiled, turned away from the bridge, and went back to the bunks to rearrange some things for the boys.

A few minutes later, she heard Julian's voice from the bridge.

"Son of a bull."

She quickly ran back onto the bridge. "What's wrong?" she said.

The coast of Greece was ahead of them. Cliffs rose from the Adriatic over white beaches, and a brand-new stone building sat resplendent atop them overlooking a small village down by the water.

"That's where I grew up," Julian said, quietly. "Vivarius built his gods-damned gambling house over my home."

Chapter 19: The Domus Helii Auri

JULIAN

Julian hadn't anticipated the crowds. The gambling house, the Domus Helii Auri, had only been open for a few weeks, but apparently it had already managed to attract a sizeable patronage.

Given how dark and stuffy it was inside, Julian wondered if some of the patrons had even left the building since its opening. Like a bottle of sweet water set to trap flies, it was easy to get in—and easy to get lost inside once you were. It had taken Julian almost half an hour to find the doors to the outdoor atrium, where he was now trying to get some fresh air and a break from the crowds—and even the atrium didn't have a true exit to the outside world.

He wished Gaius was here to offer a comforting shoulder. The crowds still made him anxious. More so now that he was pretending to be someone he wasn't.

But Gaius had his own role to play. At least his heart gave him the physical strength he needed without a shoulder to lean on.

They'd needed to plan, to set up the pieces of their play before they could get what they needed, but Lia hadn't wanted to wait too long. The longer they waited, the further from their reach Vivarius would get. So, though they'd felt rushed and could have done with weeks or even months to prepare, they'd taken only a week. And today was when those preparations would start to be tested.

Julian's heart was steady, but adrenaline still made him shake a little. He breathed in the fresh outdoor air, trying to calm himself.

The air smelled so familiar here. He'd been trying not to think about it this whole time, tried not to get distracted, but it was impossible.

He grew up here. These were the hills he'd played in as a child—as much as he'd been able to play. This very cliffside was where his home had stood, the villa of the Praefectus Meridianus Graecus. Now it was gone. A gambling house in its place.

That seemed like Vivarius's true evil. He corrupted everything he touched.

Julian shivered and shook his head. Time to go back inside.

Syd would be arriving soon.

He composed himself, smoothing down the prim waistcoat they'd obtained for him. He hadn't asked how, exactly. Had to look the part. Then he turned from the all-too-familiar view of the Adriatic and pushed past the other patrons outside, several sporting the latest in fashionable remade parts—acting for all the world like he expected them to move for him—and re-entered the Domus.

The smell hit him first as his eyes adjusted to the dimmer light—there were no windows in here. The ceilings were high, but the sheer number of people invariably caused a stench. The various perfumes of patrons and staff alike mingled in a way that only augmented the odour.

The sound hit him next. Yards of curtains covering the walls and ceiling could only do so much against the din of voices, cries, yells of triumph. And if that wasn't enough, it was punctuated by the endless ringing of the gambling machines.

He'd observed these things over the last few days, even tried one. There were rows and rows of them, clockwork contraptions one slipped a denarius into, wound, and released, making a series of wheels spin until it ran out of energy, leaving a set of images facing you. Match the images and the machine paid out. Otherwise, you lost your denarius.

Julian had lost his denarius.

From his observations, there seemed no skill in it. No matter how you wound it, how long or how fast, it didn't seem to affect your odds of winning. It was purely luck—not interesting to him at all. And yet, rows of machines were occupied, seemingly constantly, by rich and almost-rich alike.

There were no commoners in this establishment. The dress code assured it.

This had surprised Julian. He'd figured Vivarius would jump at the opportunity to deprive folks of what little money they had. Maybe he had other facilities for that purpose.

Suddenly, a steam whistle sounded out over the crowd, and a distant wave of cheers broke through the noise of the place. A fight in the coliseum had finished—the fighting rings were connected to the main gambling hall so patrons could seamlessly flow from one to the other as whims dictated.

He hoped Brendan was doing well. He wasn't nearly as heavily remade as many in those rings, but he'd proven his skills pretty quickly. Julian had watched one of his early fights.

The muscular, sweaty men had intrigued him at first, but Julian lost all interest when they started fighting.

He brought himself back to the present task and moved towards where he thought the main entrance was. He'd scoped it out enough times by this point, but it was still too easy to get turned around. He took a glass of honeyed wine from the tray of a server as he passed, and only as he was walking away again realized it had been Gaius.

He glanced back to try to catch his eye, but Gaius had moved on with the tray. Probably for the best.

He spotted a table of viginti unus not far from the entrance to the gambling house, put some tokens on the table, and settled in.

He hadn't played viginti unus since he was a kid—playing for shells from the beach—but had found he was quite good at it. Today, though, he wasn't paying enough attention to win. The denarii didn't matter.

It was twenty minutes before Syd arrived. Julian kept glancing over his shoulder looking for them until one of the other players at his table said, "Trying to avoid someone, m'lord?"

Not for the first time, he was glad his heart couldn't skip a beat.

"N-no," he said, quickly trying to recover his composure—and act. "Merely waiting for an acquaintance. Late, as usual. As expected from a Gaul, am I right?"

This got a snort of approval. He turned his attention back to the game at hand, hating how easily the noble prejudices came to him.

And then they arrived. He heard them from a couple tables away, the American accent they'd been practicing all week carrying over the noise of the gambling.

"I will *not* let you search my bag," they said loudly, turning a few heads. "It will go directly to your exchange for the appropriate tokens, and no one else will touch it."

"Sir—"

Julian could *hear* the glare.

"—uh, ma'am—"

The glare intensified.

"We can't simply allow—"

"I will speak to your superior."

"Uh—she'll say the same—"

"I'm done speaking with you."

Julian tried not to grin. This role seemed to suit quiet, well-mannered Syd. He made sure to wait a couple minutes, finishing the round of viginti unus as the hapless host found his superior, then conspicuously looked over his shoulder again to spot Syd.

They looked good. Syd was dressed in a spectacular blue suit and cloak, a grey top hat perched on their head at a forward angle. They held a case in front of them in both hands.

He made a show of half-recognizing them, and hurriedly collected his tokens.

"Who's that, then?" his table-mate asked.

"Brook Thompson?" Julian said. "You haven't heard of Brook Thompson? Absolutely masterful latrunculi player. Legendary. I've got to meet them. Excuse me!"

The tablemate raised an eyebrow, and the dealer shrugged, but Julian made his escape.

A manager of some kind was approaching Syd.

"Excuse me," she said, "I'm told there's an... issue?"

Syd drew themselves up. "Your man was insisting on taking my bag. As if I would allow anyone but the exchange to touch it."

"Master...?"

"Thompson."

"Master Thompson, it is the policy of the Domus Helii Auri to search any bags before they can fully enter the premises. As a security precaution. You understand."

"I most certainly do not," Syd said. "Accuse *me* of being a security threat? I may very well take my business elsewhere."

That was Julian's cue.

"Brook Thompson?" he said, suddenly approaching. "By all the gods, you're Brook Thompson! I suspected this place was the real deal, and surely it is if *you're* here. It is such an honour to meet you. I heard of your legendary match against Ivan Ivanov when I was abroad, and it's just an absolute honour!"

Syd looked down the bridge of their nose at him. "No closer, please. And you are?"

Julian bowed very low. "Lord Alexander Spurius Athas, at your absolute service." He looked at the manager. "This establishment is truly lucky to have someone like Brook Thompson appearing, and so soon after you opened! Blessed by Fortuna, that's for sure. Excuse me, I don't mean to be a bother. Please, enjoy your gaming, Master Thompson."

With that, he backed away, bowing again, and turned away just as he confirmed the look of confused yet eager concern on the manager's face.

"Please, Master," he heard the manager say. "Right this way to the exchange…" Julian smiled. Step one, complete.

He trusted that the pull he just helped Syd establish would get them through step two. And he hoped Gaius was making good progress on step three…

Chapter 20: Ante

GAIUS

Gaius wove through the crowd of gamblers with his tray of drinks. He hadn't had to dote on the wealthy and powerful since the last time he was on this land, but it wasn't something easily forgotten after a lifetime of service.

And it was strange, being here again. Every time he saw the acreage around the gambling house, a tumult of mixed feelings ran in him.

At least now as he served the Greek wealthy, he was getting paid—paltry as that pay was. Not that there weren't slaves serving here, too—of course there were. They were relegated to the back of house, though—preparing food and drink, laundering uniforms, cleaning. They weren't trusted to actually serve the clientele, not with that much money flowing. Instead, servants like Gaius were the front-facing labour. At least he'd only be doing it for a few more days.

The job had been easy enough to get. Still being fairly new, the Domus Helii Auri needed cheap labour. All it took was a demonstration of his skills and a faked reference that Lia and Turner orchestrated. And now they had an "inside man," as Turner put it.

Speaking of, she'd be getting into position soon.

While he wasn't on a strict timeline—they hadn't been sure when he'd be available to do his part, especially if his managers had kept him busy—he didn't want Turner to have to wait around too long. Good as she was, *any* delay increased the chance they were caught.

But first, he had to find his target. They were intended not to be noticed, and he'd been surprised to find just how hard it could be to spot a giant metal spider crawling around the gambling house.

He'd spent the last few days of work learning their telltale signs. The clockwork contraptions—"enhanced security drones" they were technically called, though all the servers called them "spyders"—were about two feet across, which was mostly legs. The centre held a clockwork motor, a series of lenses, and a small radio transmitter.

He'd asked how exactly they worked on his first day.

"No one's sure," one of the other servers had said. Castor—they were on a lot of shifts together. "And we're highly disincentivized to ask."

"I guess that makes sense," Gaius had replied, "if they are part of the security system..."

"Some of us think that's a big if. After all, there's still human security. I don't think a clock could really tell if someone's cheating, do you?"

"Then what?"

"Don't know. Spying on particular patrons, maybe. Following their movements. Or maybe those radio bits are transmitting, you know? I've heard the Philosophers think human brains have similar—what do they call them, waves?—as radios. Maybe they're, like, influencing our thoughts."

It sounded far-fetched to Gaius. But then again, a year ago, so would a remade heart.

The spyders tended to stay up high. People don't normally look up, and it would supposedly be easy for them to keep an eye—or lens—on the people and proceedings below. That could make it hard for Gaius to do what he needed to—except that they did, on occasion, descend.

In fact, it was possible there were always several prowling the floor of the place. They tended to move under tables, through rows of gambling machines, still out of sight. Every once in a while, though, they'd have to move through the open, through the crowds. When they did, they caused a telltale parting of people, like water in the wake of a duck.

Most people still didn't even notice them. Consumed by their gambling, their conversations, or their drinks, people would shift to let

them pass like they would Gaius with a tray of drinks, not even ac-
knowledging what was moving past. At least, after the initial shock of
noticing the clockwork contraptions in the first place.

And so, Gaius turned his gaze to the crowds. Half his attention
looked for empty glasses, empty hands—he was to keep the patrons
lubricated to more easily extract their denarii from their fingers. The
rest of his attention looked for that wake.

It took a bit of time. He moved around the floor of the gambling
house. The bulk of the space was taken up by the rows of gambling
machines. Surrounding them were tables of latrunculi, viginti unus,
and other games Gaius didn't know. On one side of the large room
were a series of doors leading to the coliseum, the fighting pits. He
could hear the cries of the crowd over the din of the gambling machines when he walked past. At the end of the Domus opposite the
entrance were the doors to the back of house, and above that a large
staircase led to a second-floor balcony where managers could watch
the activity on the floor—and beyond the balcony: meeting rooms,
offices, and the vault.

At one point he risked walking past the exchange counter where
Syd had gone—near the doors to the coliseum. Syd had asked to speak
to a manager again after receiving their tokens—they weren't going to
spend many of them today, as the money was borrowed from an old
acquaintance of Turner who owed her a favour—and stood now in
conversation with him.

"Yes, in two days," he heard them say. "Of course I'll be back. Unless,
of course, everything I've heard of this place is a complete fabrication..."

"No, Master, of course not. We will be happy to host—"

"Yes, yes. More importantly, I will have a package with me of immense value. I will not wish to keep it on my person—"

"We have a private safe for our guests' valuables—"

"And I will *not* have it in the same common safe with men's pocket
watches and ladies' handbags. You have a proper vault here, I assume?"

"Of-of course—"

Gaius tried not to smile as he moved on. Syd was doing well. He'd
never have thought it of them, reserved as they usually were.

Then, he saw the crowds part for nothing a row of tables away.
Target acquired. He pushed his own way through the throng, trying

to keep an eye on the path of the spyder. He lost it for a moment as it passed under a table, then spotted again the parting of people nearby.

It moved quickly, but he maneuvered in front of its path. As the spindly metal legs appeared out of the crowd, he pounced—planting his foot squarely into one of the legs.

The spyder stumbled, tried to struggle free. Gaius made a small show of noticing his "mistake" as he snapped another leg. Now incapacitated, he quickly scooped it up into his arms—squirming as it was.

Now people made room for him as he made his way towards the back of the facility, giving him looks of mixed annoyance and horror.

He was almost at the door that led to the back of house—where the various workers kept their things, or worked the kitchen—when a floor manager stopped him.

"Where are you going with that?"

He turned. "Sir! It looks like someone stepped on it. Its—what is it called?—navigator must be faulty. I was just taking it to the back to get it out of the way of the guests. Maybe get it repaired—"

The manager frowned. "Very well. Hand it over. I'll get it dealt with. You have guests to attend to."

Gaius frowned, heart and mind racing. "Sir—"

"Excuse me! Excuse me, I need a manager."

Relief flooded Gaius as he heard Julian's irate voice over the crowd. He must have been tailing Gaius in the throng.

The manager turned to address this new issue, and Gaius ducked quickly into the back room.

The workers had a small antechamber here—ostensibly a sitting room or break room, but they didn't get any breaks. It was more of a staging area for folks moving to or from the house floor. A door led into the busy kitchen and bar, and a hallway led to worker change rooms and a back servants' entrance.

Holding the struggling spyder, it was there he headed.

"Gaius, everything good?" Castor called to him from the kitchen.

"Yeah, just meeting someone to have this taken care of," Gaius replied, hoping they wouldn't question him.

"Aw, poor little bugger get hurt? Serves 'em right," Castor said.

Gaius grinned an affirmative and moved off down the hallway.

Servers had access to a key to the back door, the servant's entrance, in case of emergencies. Gaius grabbed it off its hook, struggled to open the door while holding the spyder, and pushed it open.

Out back was a walled courtyard with its own locked gate and spikes lining the top of the wall. They couldn't have servants and slaves in charge of an entrance to the building after all.

Luckily, Turner was more of an escape artist than the average worker. She was waiting in the shadows of the courtyard by the door, having made her way past guards and over walls, presumably.

"How'd Syd do?" was the first thing she asked.

"Real well," Gaius said. "Here." He pushed the spyder towards her, its remaining legs clawing at the air.

She reached into the tangle of metal and turned a dial of some kind. It died, the legs curling up around it like a real spider.

Gaius blinked. "Well, if I'd known it had an off switch…"

Turner smiled. "Hang around Syd long enough and you pick up a thing or two about machines. Everything has an off switch. Here—" She took the mass of metal in her arms and slipped it into a bag she unfolded from her belt.

"You going to be able to get that thing out of here?"

"You worry about your job," Turner said, but she said it with a smile in her voice. "We'll see you tonight."

Gaius nodded, and before anyone saw them, slipped back into the gambling house.

A few hours later, he was packing up for the night. It was late by now—after midnight. The gambling was still going strong and would for a couple more hours, but he'd finished his shift for the day—he'd started at noon. After so long on the run with Julian, working a regular job was jarring. Half-falling asleep already, he was beginning to really see what Alesse was fighting for in Rome, what she'd been fighting for her entire career.

Gaius needed this job for their secret operation—but afterwards, whenever this was over, he'd still need to work somewhere. Work was hard to find, and the people who ran this place could get away with asking their workers to do far more than they signed on for. After all, there were a dozen others looking for a job to replace you with. Sometimes it seemed like it was that or join the army and get yourself killed.

But it was hard. He'd barely get enough sleep at this rate, never mind be able to enjoy what money he earned.

As he prepared to leave, he cast a glance back towards the kitchens. The slaves there would be working another couple of hours for the guests, then a couple more to clean up. Then they'd be allowed to sleep—on the premises—before starting all over tomorrow.

He frowned.

They had to do something, he'd told Julian.

He slung his bag over his shoulder and left the Domus Helii Auri.

Chapter 21: Pocket Ace

LIA

Lia waited on the airship, hidden once more in a copse. She'd spent the day they landed cutting branches and camouflaging the airship—favouring her still-injured shoulder as she did. There were benefits to a mobile base of operations; stealth wasn't one of them.

The days following, she'd been holed up here, mostly just waiting. Sometimes she'd help Syd practice their role or go over the plans again, but there was a lot of waiting. Brendan was getting involved in the fighting pits; Gaius was getting a job; and Julian was establishing his own part.

And Lia—she couldn't be seen anywhere near the Domus. She was wanted and an easily recognizable face. They couldn't risk it.

So, she was here. Waiting.

She hated it.

Today, especially. The pieces had been set up and opening moves were being made. While she waited here.

She heard a noise outside and started. Voices followed.

"Shit... Where is it?"

"That's it, there."

"Gods, yeah. And I only had one drink after the fights!"

"How many did you have before?"

"I don't know how that's relevant."

Brendan and Gaius, back already. Was it that late? All the sitting had made it hard to keep track of time.

They clambered aboard, Brendan's metal leg clumping against the deck overhead next to Gaius's tired, dragging steps, then descended to the bridge where Lia awaited.

"Damn, Lia," Brendan said. "You really did do a good job of hiding this thing."

Lia smiled tightly. "Oh good. My one role."

"Hey now, that's not true," Brendan protested.

"Wouldn't have been able to coordinate all this without you, I imagine," Gaius said. He looked exhausted.

Lia's smile warmed a little. "I just wish I could be more useful, is all, Gaius. I'm not used to sitting around, not being the one to take action."

"Well, your presence, even back here, certainly helps," Gaius said, collapsing against the bulkhead.

"Yeah," Brendan nodded, "plus you're our wild card."

Lia rolled her eyes. "I told you, it's less 'wild card' and more 'last resort.' How'd everything go today?"

"Won two fights!" Brendan said, smiling. She noticed he was missing a tooth. "Also, I got stabbed." He pointed to his side where she now saw a reddened poultice.

"Apollo's breath," she said, "you okay?"

He nodded. "Won't be too bad. They made me take tomorrow off. They want me in good form for a fight against 'The Beheader,' which suits our timeline just fine."

Lia raised her eyebrows at "The Beheader," then sighed and nodded. "Gaius?"

"Everything looked good from my end. Syd played their role pretty flawlessly from what I saw. And I got the package. Hasn't Turner returned?"

Lia shook her head. "She had some other things to take care of. I expect her soon. Gaius, you don't have to wait up. Get some sleep."

Gaius shook his head. "No, it's okay. I'll wait a bit."

Another twenty minutes passed before Julian and Syd showed up. Gaius almost nodded off a couple of times while Brendan changed his bandages.

Julian had left the gambling house hours ago but had taken a very circuitous route back to the *Raven*. None of them wanted to be seen heading in the same direction as the others after leaving. Lia figured he might want some alone time around his former home, too...

Syd had stayed late, playing sparingly, not wanting to lose too much money—both for their funds and to not reveal their actual ineptness at gambling. Rather, they played at testing the workers, enjoying the offerings of the servants and making plans to return.

The two had joined up, out of costume, away from the Domus Helii Auri before returning to the airship. Gaius forced himself to his feet to greet Julian with a hug.

"All good?" Lia asked.

Syd nodded. "It is not easy to decline that many free drinks. I think I may have overindulged in food to compensate."

Lia smiled.

"Everything seemed to go well," Julian said, leaning against Gaius's chest. The bigger boy swayed under the weight, fighting sleep.

"This one's a better actor than he let on," Syd said, thumbing Julian.

"Good," Lia said. "We'll need that in two days. Just one more step, then."

"Got the goods right here," Turner said, appearing at the top of the stairs with a large sack. She descended and sat it on the floor with a heavy clunk.

Syd eagerly pounced, pulling the sack open.

"Beauty," they said as the spyder was revealed. "A few minor repairs, some tweaks to the internal workings... Did you have to break that many legs?"

"Sorry," Gaius yawned. "I didn't know it had an off switch."

"Everything has an off switch."

"Now I know."

"All right," Lia said. "Everyone's back safe. Let's get some rest. Lots to do tomorrow, still."

The group collectively nodded and began filtering towards the bunks.

Turner stayed behind a moment.

"All good?" Lia asked.

Turner nodded. "All good."

Lia nodded back. It was Turner who taught her always to have a contingency—or two.

Chapter 22: The Bluff

JULIAN

"Welcome back, sir. How can I help you?"

Julian looked around the gambling house like this middle-manager didn't quite merit his full attention.

"I have a meeting here with Sir Reginald Cancillius, District Outreach Officer for the Company," he said. "I was told there was a meeting room in the back waiting for us."

The manager tilted his head to the side ever so slightly. "I had not heard of such an arrangement, my lord, nor that Sir Cancillius would be joining us tonight..."

"That sounds like either your problem or your boss's problem," Julian said, now turning his attention to the poor man. "Certainly not mine. I was informed that Servius had made special arrangements..."

"Of course, my lord," the man said. "My apologies. Let me look into this—"

"And leave us standing here?"

"You may avail yourself of our full facilities while—"

Julian glanced back at Turner very briefly; dressed as a servant, she stood an appropriate distance behind him and didn't raise her gaze to meet his. He was on his own.

"I will wait in the meeting room," he said, turning back again to the floor, trying to put a look on his face like he detested both the thought of staying on the floor to wait and of speaking any more to this man.

He forced himself to channel Vivarius to do so. He'd witnessed that derision from the man before. It made him feel like he'd just dipped his hands in a fetid pond, but he needed this to work given the lack of an actual impending meeting.

A pause. He glanced at the man and saw a swirl of mixed emotions. He turned his full glare on him.

"Y-yes, m'lord. Right this way."

Julian nodded.

The manager led Julian and Turner down the central aisle of the gambling house floor, past the tables and rows of gambling machines whirring and clicking away. At the far end of the large room, a staircase—flanked by security guards—led to the upper-level balcony that overlooked the floor. The manager led them up, and Julian garnered only glances from the guards.

At the top, he got a look around. The balcony looked out across the whole floor. A doorway led to a similar balcony that overlooked the fighting pits in the coliseum next door. Hallways led to meeting rooms, security stations, private offices, and, of course, the vault.

The head floor manager stood at the edge of the balcony overlooking it all. She gave Julian a quizzical look but was quickly distracted by someone delivering a report. Slaves and servants scurried around as well—more actively than Julian would have expected. They were preparing for something of note. Julian hoped it wouldn't cause them too many problems—the extra chaos might even be beneficial.

They were led down one of the hallways. As they left the balcony, he suddenly realized they'd passed right by Syd. He'd been so focused on his own task that he hadn't seen them. Now he strained to overhear their conversation before he got too far away.

"...Yes, I've been well-assured of the safe's efficacy, but as I mentioned, only the full vault will satisfy my concerns..."

Not going as smoothly as hoped, then. Too late to turn back now, though. He trusted Syd would find a way to make it work.

Then they were ushered into a meeting room. A long table and plush chairs, red velvet on the walls, and windows looking out at the balcony.

Julian turned to the manager. "We'll await Cancillius here. Thank you for your accommodations."

"Yes, m'lord. I-I'll let him know when he arrives—"

"Yes, yes. Please, we have much to prepare."

The man bowed a little, frowning, and backed out of the room.

As soon as the door closed, Julian sighed as Turner began to circle the room, closing the curtains hanging over the windows—it would do no good to be seen now.

"Hopefully, he's not about to go ask too many questions about this impending meeting," Julian said.

"Looked like he might be too busy to get into it," Turner replied. "Folks look a little flustered."

"Think it will be a problem?"

"Undoubtedly. Still, we do the job."

Julian sighed again and nodded. Now the hardest part—waiting.

Chapter 23: The Cards You're Dealt

GAIUS

Gaius watched Julian and Turner head up into the balcony. So far so good. He made his way to the back of house where servants and slaves were scrambling about their duties.

The back of house was underneath the upper level, beneath the offices and meeting rooms. One staircase allowed servants access to the upper level—it was one of the possible escape routes for the crew.

Meanwhile, his actual job here had kept him busy. The Domus Helii Auri was apparently hosting some kind of functionary tonight, probably to watch the fights. If so, the functionary was in for disappointment. Nonetheless, the back of house was in a little more chaos than normal.

This morning, when the news had arrived, one of the kitchen slaves had cut himself in nervousness. He'd been flogged on the spot while Gaius watched. He'd shaken his head at the time, and all day the sight of it had stuck with him.

He didn't have much to do during the day besides work his job. His role was primarily just to be eyes and ears on the floor, now—and he'd been thinking back to conversations with Julian when they were teenagers, with Alesse in Parisium, and with Lia and her drive to do something about the injustices she saw.

He'd never seen himself like them. They were great people doing great things—fighting for a better future. He was just Gaius. Julian's ward, bodyguard, slave. A worker. Just trying to survive, really. He'd only ever just wanted to survive—and to be with Julian.

But here they were, about to cause chaos in this gambling house. Julian and Lia, about to be heroes, maybe—in a strange, illegal, anarchic kind of way.

Maybe he could be a hero, too.

But then he was out the door, back onto the floor surrounded by patrons and gamblers, a fresh tray of drinks in hand, just waiting for the plans of the rest of the crew to come together.

He heard the hush go through the crowd, a wave of whispers. And then, partially covered by the susurrus, the announcement.

"Presenting His Excellency, Consul of Rome. All hail, Consul Vivarius."

Saluting guards. Cheers from the gamblers—whether for his work of state or for providing their current entertainment wasn't clear. Legionaries began filing down the aisle.

"Shit," Gaius said.

The house was hosting a functionary, they'd been told. He hadn't bothered to ask who.

Gaius began weaving through the crowd—tray of drinks penduluming back and forth as he endeavoured not to spill anything—and headed for the back of house again. He had to get up the stairs to warn Julian before Vivarius saw them.

He realized he wouldn't get up in time that way and redirected to the main staircase. He was just ahead of the legionaries. He hoped the tray of drinks would be excuse enough to be allowed up.

The security guards at the stairs barely acknowledged him as they kept patrons back, anticipating the soldiers. Gaius took the stairs as quickly as he dared.

He hadn't even seen the consul yet, through the crowd. Didn't bother turning to look.

Hoped Vivarius wouldn't recognize him.

But why would he? Last time they met, Gaius was a mere slave. Vivarius wouldn't have given him a second glance.

He made the balcony, saw the curtains drawn over the windows of one of the meeting rooms, and beelined towards it. He heard the manager call for him, but he didn't dare stop.

Julian and Turner were alone in the room, Turner standing quietly in the corner while Julian paced. They both looked up suddenly at Gaius's arrival.

"Vivarius," he said, panting and kicking the door closed behind him. "He's here."

Julian gaped. "What?"

Turner's eyebrows rose a half-inch.

Gaius put the tray of drinks on the table. "He just arrived. We were told someone would be coming to be looked after—Dis, I thought they might have meant Syd after all we set up—but it's him. He just got here. He's on his way up to the balcony."

"Shit," Julian said. "Shit. Shit. Brendan—"

"There's no delaying," Turner said. "Syd is in position, Brendan will be acting soon."

"He's going to *use his office*," Julian said.

Turner nodded. "No problem. We go for Servius's instead."

"Lia—"

Turner just nodded again. "We've gotten through worse. Just keep nimble. Gaius, you've been here long enough. Leave the drinks."

Gaius nodded. He was just a servant. He wouldn't get made—better to get out of the way.

"Good luck," he said.

Turner nodded.

He caught Julian's eye. *I love you.*

Then he was out on the balcony once more—just as Vivarius himself crested the stairs. Pristine black suit under the purple consular toga. Imperious and imposing.

Then he heard the commotion—this one expected. Shouts, the sound of something large breaking from the direction of the fighting pits. Then the yelling started to spread through the audience until it could even be heard by the patrons on the floor. People started to take notice. Guards started to move in that direction—including a couple of Vivarius's legionaries.

That was the signal. It was go time.

In the sudden commotion, Gaius ducked away, not making eye

contact with Vivarius, and moved down the hallway towards the back staircase—and the private offices.

He passed Syd—hardly noticing, so preoccupied. They met eyes. Syd raised their brow in a brief expression of uncertainty but resignation—they all knew there was no going back now.

But there wasn't much else for Gaius to do. When he got back down to the back of house, the commotion from above was dulled—the commotion here more mundane. Servants and slaves doing their work.

And all Gaius had to do was wait and be ready to help if it was needed.

He frowned.

Maybe there was a way he could help...

Chapter 24: Rolling the Dice

JULIAN

Julian was staring at the curtained door of the meeting room. The drinks Gaius had brought sat untouched on the table.

Vivarius was here.

Tonight, of all nights.

He was here. Because of course he'd be here. It was his establishment. And Julian was here. And it was Julian's home. So, of course Vivarius would be here just to remind Julian of his utter powerlessness.

For a moment, Julian thought it might be an opportunity. Face him down. Stop him, here and now.

But what would he do?

What could he do?

Then they heard the shouting, the commotion. Brendan, doing his part. The plan had been to lose a fight and be particularly unhappy about it. Enough to cause a brawl. Hopefully, not enough to get himself shot.

With Vivarius here, though—there would be increased security. Julian hoped he'd be okay.

"That's the cue," Turner said. She had moved to the door and peeked out through the curtains. "Vivarius is being surrounded by guards. Now's our chance."

Julian nodded, still wondering for a moment if there was a chance to do something else. Something more final. But there wouldn't be.

He joined Turner at the door. "Ready?"

She looked out the window again through a crack in the curtains. "Wait—and—yes."

Julian gathered himself, opened the door, and swept out into the hallway.

The commotion was about as planned—if not bigger. The noise was the biggest draw—security guards and managers were struggling to get through to the coliseum as patrons crowded them, gawking. The legionaries—not part of the plan—were just making things worse, pushing their way into crowds in an attempt to take control of the situation. Vivarius was nowhere to be seen—a crowd of legionaries suggested he was being kept away from the commotion, constrained to one end of the balcony.

Julian was a little glad for that. He didn't know how he'd react to *seeing* the man.

They moved down the hallway, Julian in the lead. He could see the doors to Vivarius's office—already guarded by an additional pair of legionaries—and opposite it, what would be Servius's. At the far end of the hall, not much past the offices, the main vault's antechamber.

Syd was already waiting there, patiently arguing with a manager as a security guard stood nearby.

The legionaries in front of Vivarius's office would be a problem, but it was too late now. Hopefully, Turner was as good as Syd had assured him she was.

The legionaries watched them approach warily, but Julian's gaze went right past them. "Excuse me," he called towards the manager, summoning any ounce of privileged annoyance he could.

The security guard turned and stepped out into the hall. The manager, busy with Syd, turned, attention split. "Sir, if you could wait just a moment—you can't be back here—"

"Excuse me?" Julian said. "*They're* here—" he started to protest as the security guard approached him, hand out—then he grabbed the guard's arm like Turner had shown him, used the momentum and the strength borne him by his heart, and slammed the guard backward into the wall—head first.

He saw Syd's eyes widen. He'd maybe used a little too much unexpected strength.

"What—" the manager started. He also heard the legionaries move up behind him, but quickly there was a scuffle and a couple of thuds courtesy of Turner, and Julian swept past the security guard's body into the vault antechamber.

"Help!" the manager started to scream. Julian wasn't quite close enough, quite fast enough—

Then Syd clocked him across the back of the head with their package—a package Julian knew for a fact was particularly heavy. The manager fell to the ground.

He let out a breath. "All good?" he asked.

Syd nodded. "He was insisting on examining the package. At least it allowed me to delay him while I waited for you."

"Yeah, there's been a wrinkle."

"Vivarius?"

He nodded.

Turner appeared at the doorway. "Clock's ticking now. Servius's office. Go."

Syd moved to the office door. It was locked, but they bent quickly, picks in hand, and soon it clicked open. Julian grabbed the manager and security guard by their coats and dragged them away from the vault and to the office door. Turner already had the legionaries across the hallway.

Once the door was open, they all shuffled the bodies in with them and closed the door.

Servius's office was extraordinarily well-appointed—dark-stained wood-panelled walls, a huge desk, plush kline—the dining couch—by a low table, thick Ottoman carpet on the floor. Against one wall—adjacent to the gambling house's main vault—was a thick steel door with an obviously-complex clockwork mechanism on its surface.

Despite its richness, it was otherwise sparse. No paintings on the walls, no papers on the desk, not even a liquor cabinet. Nothing to suggest a hint of personality. Nothing that suggested Servius had ever actually used it.

Julian was, momentarily, glad for that. He wasn't sure how he would feel to be confronted by something that actually reminded him of the man.

"We going to find anything here?" Syd said, suddenly unsure. They had walked right over to the desk and started opening drawers.

"If there's anything, it'll be in his vault," Turner said.

"And the documents we found suggested there should be," Julian said.

"Let's put the package to work," Turner said.

Syd stood up from the empty desk and nodded, returning to the bundle and moving over to the steel door.

Julian glanced at the unconscious guards.

"You hit pretty hard," Turner said. Her voice seemed a mix of admiration and suspicion. Julian adjusted his coat. "But they'll be fine. Relatively."

He nodded.

Syd meanwhile had removed the bag from around their package—the spyder Gaius had stolen. They and Julian had spent all yesterday reprogramming it, and now as Syd switched its activation switch, it got to its legs and started crawling up the vault door. There, it settled—intricate clockwork interfacing with the locking mechanism. It began to whir, and gears started turning all up and down the door, this way and that—looking for the weakness, the right combinations.

"Think it'll work?" Julian asked.

"Of course it will," Syd said.

They waited in tense silence punctuated only by the ticking of the spyder—and the quieter ticking of Julian's heart.

Tick. Tick.

The wait was excruciating. Turner stayed by the door, an ear pressed against it, listening to the chaos outside that Brendan was causing. Listening for guards.

Then after five solid minutes, the loud *clunk* of a heavy metal bolt being withdrawn from the wall.

The spyder fell to the ground and curled upon itself. The vault door slowly opened an inch.

"We're in," Syd said, the barest hint of surprise in their voice.

No time to waste. Julian pulled the door open.

Lamplight swathed the vault interior as the door swung wide.

Inside was about ten square feet of space, lined with shelving—almost all of it utterly empty.

But one box sat on the floor with a single envelope sitting on top of it.

Julian slowly knelt beside the box. He passed the envelope up to Syd, then removed the lid of the box.

It was full of folders, envelopes, documents.

If his heart could beat faster...

He started thumbing through them, pulling some out to take a look. Syd, meanwhile, had opened the envelope.

"It's the signed deed," they said. "Showing joint ownership. And some accounting documents... At the very least, it proves Servius and Vivarius are in business together... If we comb through the financials, maybe we'll find something else."

Julian nodded absently. He was looking at all the documents in the box. Some seemed to be letters, correspondence. Some were definitely financial in nature—invoices to or from the EIC, ledgers of expenses, accounting records. Shipment manifests. Even what looked like drafts of legislation, requests submitted to the Senate...

It would take hours to really figure out what it all was, but...

Julian smiled. "I think we've got it."

Turner stepped over to him and took a few of the documents, giving them a quick scan. She nodded. "I think we do."

"You never can just smile about something, can you?" Syd asked.

"We're not out of this yet," Turner said, handing the documents back to Julian. He grabbed all the ones that looked potentially relevant and packed them into Syd's bag—along with the curled-up spyder—before hoisting it over his shoulder. "They've noticed the guards are missing," Turner continued. "I think they're coming to investigate. I've locked the door again so we may have a few minutes. They probably won't suspect us in here right away—but there won't be an easy exit."

"Well," Syd said, sobering, "we have contingencies."

Turner nodded.

"But Vivarius is here," Julian said. "He'll recognize Lia."

Turner nodded again. "We might not be able to count on her."

Syd blinked. "Do... do we have other contingencies?"

"Yes," Julian said, clutching the bag. But he'd started to tremble.

Chapter 25: The Gamble

LIA

Lia was waiting nearby. The Domus Helii Auri's grounds, being the former grounds of a praefectus's family, were filled with gardens and statues and fountains. It was easy enough to hide—and wait.

More waiting. She hated it.

There was a chance she wouldn't be needed at all. There was a chance Turner and Julian and Syd would simply walk out before anyone knew anything was wrong.

But given how everything had gone for them so far, what were really the chances of that? Only Fortuna knew.

She'd be able to hear the commotion caused by Brendan's distraction from out here. Then she was to give them fifteen minutes—get in, open the vault, find what they needed, and get out through the chaos.

If they didn't make it, she'd go in and arrest them. And pray to all the gods she wasn't recognized.

A solid enough plan. And they had contingencies if they needed them. Which, given their luck so far...

And then the legionaries arrived.

And then Vivarius arrived.

And suddenly Lia wondered if they had enough contingencies. All bets were off now. If anyone at this gambling house had known of their scheme, there'd be some very large piles of denarii being stacked against them right now.

And then, just as suddenly, she wondered if the theft was even necessary. If the documents, the evidence, were really necessary.

As she watched Vivarius enter the Domus, she suddenly wondered if any of it was.

Vivarius was here. Now. Under guard, sure. But she had the element of surprise.

And not a lot left to lose.

She heard the beginnings of the fight from inside spilling into the gambling house floor. As she waited for fifteen minutes to pass, she unslung the rifle from her back and began to check it over.

The others hadn't emerged. She didn't know if she'd be any help getting them out. But either way, she was going in.

The gambling house was about as she expected it. There was commotion at one side of the room as the brawl from the fighting pits continued—but still, folks gambled, denarii flew. There were more legionaries than they'd originally planned on, but most were on the balcony or trying to contain the fight.

She stalked inside.

Someone tried to stop her almost immediately.

"Ma'am, you can't bring—"

She held up her insignia. Her paperwork might have disappeared, but no one had physically taken this from her—yet.

"Praetorian Guard. You're being robbed. I've been tracking these thieves for weeks. Let me through."

The man's eyes widened in fear and confusion and concern. Even if he'd wanted to stop her, he didn't get the chance as she pushed past him.

The crowds were easier to navigate. Not many even noticed her, so focused on their games.

Up on the balcony that overlooked the floor, she saw him. Vivarius in his purple consul's toga over a fine black suit. A handful of legionaries around him, trying at turns to keep people away from him and perhaps move him away from Brendan's brawl.

"Vivarius!" she yelled.

He didn't hear over the din of the gambling. A few people nearby looked at her, some with concern, but she kept pushing forward. Too far away, still. She couldn't afford a mistake.

She neared the stairs and stopped—she couldn't lose the angle. She unslung her rifle.

The crowd almost instinctively cleared around her.

"Vivarius!" she shouted again.

This time, he heard, even dimly over the din. He glanced towards her. She levelled her rifle.

She expected his eyes to widen. They narrowed instead, and he pointed at her. His mouth moved. "Shoot her."

Legionaries turned.

And Lia pulled her trigger.

Bodies moved. Sparks flew. Vivarius stepped backward—hit? Screams from the crowd. The legionaries levelled their own guns. Shots fired, and Lia ducked down. More screams, people clearing away from her. She was an easy target now.

She didn't care. She aimed another shot, but Vivarius had moved back—she'd lost the angle. And the legionaries were aiming again.

And then, suddenly, the doors to the back of house opened—and kitchen staff started swarming out. They were running—it looked like they were gunning for the front entrance to the gambling house. Some of them even turned to tackle security guards as the swarm moved past onto the floor. And Lia was surrounded by bodies.

There were cries of confusion and anger around her. She heard legionaries yelling—"What in Dis?" "We can't get a clean shot!"

And Vivarius's shouted response: "I don't care. Put them down if you must."

Gunshots. Lia ducked down and cast around for cover. What were the staff doing? And where was Gaius? He was meant to be their lookout.

Her eyes landed on the open doors to the back of house. Which seemed like it could be conveniently empty now. She leapt in that direction, pushing through the running slaves like a salmon pushing upriver. She got under the balcony—out of the legionaries' sight—and then through the doors.

Chapter 26: Raise

GAIUS

Gaius heard the gunshots just as the kitchen slaves were gathering. "Now's your chance. Go, go!" he said. They began swarming towards the doors to the floor. Some had kitchen knives in hand.

Gaius had never been one for words. That was always Julian's domain. Or Alesse. He hadn't known if his rhetoric could motivate the way he thought it would need to, despite their inspiration. So he'd decided to coat his rhetoric in a few small lies. *That* he knew how to do. He'd needed to in order to survive as a slave, a worker, a fugitive.

He'd stoked a flame that burned in most slaves, no matter how small or dim. He'd told them he was here to free them. He'd told them to stage a revolt.

Now, as the slaves pushed their way out, he saw Lia pushing her way in. He waved her over.

"What in Dis is going on?" Lia said.

"Did you *shoot* Vivarius?" Gaius said.

"Well, I *tried* to. It didn't seem to take. And he was going to recognize me anyway—I couldn't follow the plan. Where are the others?"

"As far as I know, still upstairs."

"Okay. Also, what in Dis is going on?"

"I, uh, organized a little slave revolt," Gaius said. "I thought, while we had this distraction—and it could help provide more cover—and I had to do *something*, we know what conditions people working for Vivarius live in—"

"What do you expect is going to happen to them?" Lia asked.

"The back door is walled and guarded," Gaius said. His plan, which he'd been fairly proud of, started to seem a little flimsier under Lia's glare. "I thought in the chaos they could make a break for the front—"

"There are a dozen armed legionaries out there!" Lia said. "You're going to get them killed, Gaius."

Gaius blinked. They wouldn't just kill them, would they? If they got caught, they'd be punished, but—then again, what did Vivarius care? He'd almost certainly have replacements—or be able to come up with them.

But some might escape. Wouldn't that be worth it? Worth... a life? He frowned.

"It doesn't matter now," Lia said. "We have to get the team out, and it won't be as simple as walking out the front door like we hoped."

"It's wild out there," Gaius said. "We can't make a run for it?"

"Did I not mention the legionaries? Even if we don't get shot, it'll be easy enough for them to follow us."

"Right," Gaius said. He started to think through the options. "But—all of our contingencies involved getting out in the chaos... With Vivarius here—"

"Still got some tricks up our sleeves," Lia said. "Once Brendan gets out onto the floor—"

Suddenly, the sounds of chaos outside grew exponentially. Brendan had taken the brawl into the stands and past them, breaking out onto the gambling floor. Chaos, indeed.

"Let's wait and see if Turner and the others can get out."

"If not? There will be tons of guards up there now—"

"Tricks, remember?"

Chapter 27: Fold

JULIAN

"Why are there gunshots?" Syd said, eyes wide as Turner crouched by the locked office door.

"Our dear captain may have been recognized," Turner said.

"Did you see how many legionaries are out there?"

Turner didn't respond.

Julian clutched the bag to his chest. He tried not to let the hard shell of the spyder clunk against his metal plate. He didn't know why he cared if Lia's crew knew about it—but he did. He'd concealed it from them so far, half out of instinct, half out of he didn't know what. Shame? Or just... uncertainty as to how they'd react?

"At the very least, it's delayed any investigation in our direction," Turner said, "but for how long, I don't know. Time to make our own distraction. Julian?"

Julian clutched the bag tighter to him. He was trying not to think about the airship, about the... blood. And it was suddenly hard not to. "W-what if she's still on her way?"

"We can't wait. We have to move," Turner said.

"I don't know—" Julian said.

"What's going on?" Syd asked.

"The contingency," Turner said. "Julian, we don't have time for this."

"For what?" Syd suddenly demanded.

Julian looked at them. He was shaking. "The spyder. After you re-programmed it, Lia and Turner added explosives. Just in case."

Their eyebrows raised, alarmed. "What are we going to do with explosives?"

"Distraction," Turner said, sighing. "Lob it towards the balcony, and everyone will be far too busy to stop us going out the back."

"What?!" Syd said. "We can't just—Lia could still be out there—and all those people—"

Turner sighed. "And this is why we didn't tell you. We don't have many options here. Julian, let's go—Dis, we have the added benefit of ruining Vivarius's enterprise and maybe getting rid of some of his soldiers. Maybe even him, if Lia didn't already. Let's go."

Julian was trembling. Didn't move.

He'd been avoiding thinking about this possibility since Turner and Lia had told him about it. It surely wouldn't be needed, not when the rest of their plan worked out. And even when he was forced to con-sider the possibility, he always imagined the blast area to be... empty. Abandoned. People away from the target, pushed back by Brendan or evacuating the facility or—he didn't know.

And at some point, he might've even considered these acceptable losses. A fair price to escape with the evidence they needed to bring down Vivarius. To bring down the pillar of the Empire.

But there were so many people out there. He saw the airship crew again. He saw the blood.

He shook his head. He felt like he was going to throw up. Or pass out. He wished Gaius could be there with him. Supporting him. Giv-ing him strength...

His new heart made him physically strong in a way he'd never been before—but all that had led to was the travesty on the airship. He didn't *want* to be capable of that.

But then... physical strength hadn't been what *motivated* him to do that. That wasn't from his new heart. That was the fire that had always burned in him. The strength Gaius had always said he had, no matter what his heart had done.

The strength of his new heart wasn't what mattered. It wasn't what drove him. It wasn't what would make the difference between doing what *should* be done or not.

"I-I can't."

Turner sighed and stood. "Fine. Give me the spyder. I'll do it."

He clutched the bag tighter, shaking his head. He did wish Gaius was there, support at his back—but just because he loved him. Not because he *needed* him. He could stand on his own. Stand for his beliefs.

He'd always been able to.

"No Turner—Syd is right. *We* can't. There are too many people."

"We don't have time for this," Turner said. "It's them or us, Julian. We talked about this. You seemed to understand."

"Turner!" Syd said.

Julian shook his head. "I'm not doing it."

Turner sighed and drew a pistol. For a moment, Julian thought she was going to aim it at him, but she just turned back to the door.

"Then I guess we're fighting our way out," she said, "and hoping *one* of us makes it."

Chapter 28: Full House

LIA

By the sound of things, the chaos on the floor was about as planned. Maybe worse. Fighters from the pits pushing into a crowded gambling house, legionaries desperately trying to keep order, slaves running for the entrance along with evacuating patrons. There were occasional gunshots. Lia tried not to think of the ramifications.

But despite all the noise—

"No explosion," she said.

"What?" Gaius said.

They had moved back from the doors towards the servants' change rooms and back door in case anyone came in looking. Lia's rifle was still out, reloaded.

"The spyder had explosives in it. Julian was supposed to set them off as a last resort, give them the distraction they needed to escape."

Gaius gaped at her. "You gave Julian *explosives*?"

She nodded.

"That's—I can't—that was really bad."

She frowned. "It was a last resort."

"You don't understand—he's—gods, I hope he's okay—"

"Well, he hasn't used them, so either they're already compromised or something else happened. Either way, I need to get up there and rescue the evidence, if they found any. Where are the back stairs from here?"

Gaius pointed. "D-down that way. They bring you up a ways down from the offices and vault."

Lia nodded.

"What should I do?" he asked.

"Stay here. We'll probably need these stairs to get back down. Can't have them compromised." She pulled a spare pistol from her belt and tossed it to him.

Gaius caught it and nodded. Lia checked her gun one last time—reloaded, ready to go.

"Oh!" Gaius suddenly said. "They won't be in Vivarius's office. With him here, they were going to go for Servius's."

Lia nodded. "Thanks." Then she took off towards the stairs.

The upper levels were in chaos. The whole facility seemed to be. The stairs deposited her down a hallway from the balcony and down another from the vault. She could see the crowds on the balcony, legionaries and management scrambling. Some of the soldiers were even firing rounds towards the floor. A few servants ran past her but didn't stop to question her presence.

The same wouldn't be said of security. She had to move quickly.

She dashed down the hall towards the offices, trying to bring up the map of the place in her mind.

Two house workers were coming down the office hall towards the vault. Behind them, she saw a couple legionaries. As they looked away, she dodged past the workers—sparing them only a glance—and came to Servius's office door—

—just as it opened, Turner pushing out with a pistol raised.

"Lia!"

The workers were at the vault now, looking around. One of them looked their way.

"Let's go. Back stairs. You got something?"

"Hey!" The shout of a legionary. She looked up the hall.

Vivarius was coming their way, surrounded by soldiers.

"Yep," Turner said. "Time to go!"

She pushed by Lia, heading towards the stairs. Julian and Syd came after, clutching their own things and ducking past. Lia turned her rifle on the guards, firing a shot to cover their retreat, and then she turned and followed as legionaries levelled their own guns.

As she passed the vault again, she looked in to see the workers piling denarii into bags. Right on cue.

"Stop! Thieves!" Lia yelled—then ran right on.

"Hey!" one of them called after her. But she was gone.

She heard the legionaries behind her. Heard Vivarius shouting orders. Heard the confusion—

Because they *were* being robbed. And she was sure Vivarius was *not* prepared to lose that much money.

The legionaries hesitated and split up. It gave Lia enough time to follow the others down the back stairs.

Chapter 29: All In

JULIAN

They reached the downstairs back of house just as Brendan burst through the doors from the house floor. Julian ran into Gaius's arms as everyone gathered.

"It's a bloody mess out there," Brendan panted. One eyebrow was split, as was his lower lip; red marks from blows covered his face and arms, and he bled from a dozen minor cuts. "What's the plan?"

Julian looked at Lia. "Who were those—are there actually thieves here? Right now?"

Lia nodded. "We hired them. Contingencies, Julian."

He gaped. "They're going to get arrested! Killed, maybe!"

"And we'd be dead if it weren't for them, since you didn't use the spyder."

Julian frowned.

"I did what I had to do," Lia said.

"Like fire on Vivarius?" Julian asked.

"Hey, we don't have time for this!" Syd shouted. They could hear legionaries above them. "And we seem to be out of contingencies."

They were right. Men were running down the stairs. A gunshot fired, and everyone dove for cover behind couches and corners.

"We could fight our way out?" Brendan said.

"We won't get far," Lia said. "Back gate?"

"We'd be sitting ducks in that courtyard," Gaius said.

Julian shook his head. He felt overwhelmed. Gunshots fired around them. They'd come so close, maybe even found what they needed—they'd been right next to Vivarius all over again...

And now they were about to die here.

It was appropriate, he thought. To die back on his family's land.

Lia and Turner returned fire at the legionaries. Gaius tossed his pistol to Brendan.

Julian always thought he'd die here. He was amazed he'd lived so long with his heart. He'd always imagined dying, playing in the yard or down in the tunnels. Buried here.

He blinked.

The tunnels.

"Wait," he said.

Brendan and Lia fired towards the legionaries. "What?" Lia yelled.

Julian closed his eyes, tried to place himself on the grounds. Tried to remember where the house had been, the outbuildings.

"Outside!" he called.

"We'll do no better there—" Turner started.

"Gaius, the tunnels," Julian said.

Understanding spread across Gaius's face. "Outside!" he agreed. "Out back!"

Turner and Lia looked at each other, ducking down as gunshots fired and a lantern exploded from a stray bullet, sending flaming oil across the wall.

"Let's move!" Lia said.

Turner went first, Brendan shortly behind. They burst through the back door, weapons raised. Julian and Gaius followed, Syd behind them, as Lia covered their retreat.

The courtyard was mostly empty, practically quiet after the chaos inside. A couple guards at the far gate turned, confused, raising guns. Above them, guards in the watchtower turned as well.

Julian pulled the curled-up spyder from his bag and threw it with all his strength into the courtyard. It flew far, the strength of that heart sending it deep.

"Shoot it!" he yelled.

Turner, Lia, and Brendan levelled their weapons.

The guards in the tower emerged from cover and levelled theirs.

Gunshots filled the air.

Then a thunderous explosion overtook them. Rock and dust blasted into the air. Julian covered his face. A moment later, the dust and rock still falling, he looked back.

A hole was blasted in the ground. A hole that opened onto tunnels below.

His victory was short-lived as the door behind them burst open, legionaries pouring out.

"Go!" Lia yelled.

And they ran, and they dove, and they rolled into cool darkness. Darkness that Julian knew. Darkness that he'd hid in many times as a child.

Waiting to be buried. Waiting to die.

Chapter 30: Take the House

GAIUS

The run through the tunnels—tunnels Gaius knew, tunnels he'd never thought he'd see again—was quiet. At first, distant shouts followed them, but the turns and branches soon left those behind. Just panting, footfalls.

These tunnels had been built decades ago, maybe centuries. Not as old as Orvieto's, certainly, but with similar purpose. The architects of the villa or whatever had stood there before had discovered natural water-carved tunnels in the cliff beneath the structure. They'd expanded them, forming root cellars, claiming water sources, and, of course, building a secret escape route should they come under attack.

In Gaius and Julian's childhood, they'd been marvellous hiding spots. Now, they had, for the moment, saved their lives.

They eventually reached an exit—the darkness of the night so much brighter than the black of the tunnels, lit only by what ambient light could filter in. Stone underfoot gave way to sandy beach. The crash of waves from the Adriatic punctuated their gasping for breath.

Gaius instinctively sought Julian's hand as Lia took stock.

"Okay," she said after a moment. "Split up. Get back to the airship. They'll still be looking for us."

They paired off, Gaius with Julian, Syd with Brendan—he was injured, but still strong enough to run or fight if needed—and almost without another word, started on the move again.

Everyone clearly had a lot they wanted to say. Everyone knew it was not yet the time.

"Who were those people?" Syd demanded. "At the vault, as we left?"

They stood on the bridge of the *Raven*, still hidden under foliage, all of them. Tired, hurt, and angry.

"Thieves, looked like," Lia said.

"And they just happened to be burgling the place while we were there? Causing all the distractions for them?"

"Lia and I hired them," Turner said. "Gave them the tip, the map. Another distraction, another contingency."

"So, you hired dupes to take the fall for you while you escaped," Syd stated.

"We did what we had to do," Lia responded. "And guess what? If we hadn't, we'd be dead."

"We'll circle back to leaving them to die later," Syd started.

"Can't wait," Lia said.

"What really galls me is that you didn't tell us. That you didn't trust us with that information."

"If I had, we'd just be having this argument two days ago, and I needed everyone focused," Lia responded.

"Plans within plans," Brendan shrugged.

"No," Syd said, "you don't just get to brush this off. You didn't tell us anything. Explosives? In the spyder?"

"Yeah, what was that about?" Brendan said.

"It *should* have been an earlier exit for Julian's group," Lia said.

Gaius felt his face flush with anger suddenly. "Do you not realize what you could have done?"

"What happened?" Lia turned to Julian.

"I—" Julian started. "I just—couldn't do it. *Wouldn't* do it. Not with that many people out there. It was too high a price." He was standing tall, Gaius noticed. Not as hunched in on himself like he'd been for weeks now.

Gaius shook his head. "How could you even expect something like that—?" He didn't want to add what he was really thinking. How much those explosives could have brought back for Julian. How much it could have hurt him. Those memories made fresh.

Lia turned on him. "Well, it would've been less of a problem if not for the *slave revolt*. What in the gaping hole of Avernus were you even thinking?"

Gaius flushed deeper. "I told you—I thought it was an opportunity, a chance to hurt Vivarius, help those people—"

"Well, I'm sure they're all thanking you as they get rounded up," Lia said angrily.

"No, hold up," Syd interrupted. "You do *not* get to be self-righteous about that. You knew your role was compromised, but you came in anyway and took a *shot* at Vivarius!"

"Hey, what now?" Brendan said.

"I had an opportunity," Lia said. "If we could just take Vivarius down right here and now, that would be it. So I took it."

"Yeah, that would be 'it,'" Syd said. "It for *us*. We'd have never gotten out of there."

"Not to mention, 'it' for the Empire," Julian said, quietly. "Kill him now in cold blood, who knows what would happen. He'd be a martyr, wouldn't he? There'd be a huge uproar."

"War, maybe," Turner mused.

"Well, maybe it's time to burn it all down and start over," Lia said.

Gaius frowned. He'd heard that before.

"This is just so not like you," Syd said.

"They're right, Lia," Brendan said. "You never take the shortcut."

"And look where it's gotten us," Lia said.

"And by the way," Syd said, suddenly turning to Julian. Gaius instinctively stepped closer to him. "Where do you even get off being so goddamn strong? I mean, not exactly my top priority right now, but you're built like a goddamn twig."

"How strong is he?" Brendan asked, curious.

"Threw a guard across the hall," Turner said.

Gaius looked at Julian. He was shrinking once more under their questioning.

"Hey, leave him—" Gaius started.

Then Julian set his jaw, stepped forward, and tore open his shirt. Shiny metal glinted in the dim light of the lanterns. Everyone stared.

Chapter 31: Cashing Out

JULIAN

The endless arguing. It reminded Julian of his parents.

The stares, the questions. It reminded him of his childhood bullies.

Until he couldn't take it anymore. What was he even hiding?

He stepped forward and tore open his shirt, revealing the metal beneath, the pressure gauge, the endless *tick, tick, tick.*

They stared.

"Glory of the gods," Syd breathed.

"Are you—remade?" Brendan said.

"A heart," Turner said quietly.

"Yes," Julian said. "*This* is what Servius did to me."

"*To* you?" Syd asked. "If that works—that's miraculous."

"So miraculous," Julian agreed acidly, "to watch the doctor try over and over again, on slaves, on soldiers, on *children*, each one dying a bloody death until he turned those hands on *me*."

"Is *that* what Servius is working on?" Brendan said.

"If Vivarius has access to technology like that..." Turner started.

"If that's what he's working towards," Lia said, "this secret facility, he could heal himself of any ailment—"

"So, your gunshot wouldn't have done much good anyway."

Gaius took Julian's hand as they all started talking again, talking over each other, talking about the gambling house and arguing once more until Lia's voice lifted above the rest.

"*Enough*," she shouted. Silence fell instantly. "It is what it is. We got some documents, hopefully enough to connect Servius and Vivarius to illegal activity. We got out, however it happened. They'll be looking for us. We can't take to the air again until the turmoil dies down. So we wait here. And we rest. Got it?"

Nobody spoke. Syd was looking at the ground. Brendan gingerly prodded at his swollen face. Gaius squeezed Julian's shoulders, who tried to pull his shirt back over his chest.

"All right," Lia said. She sounded suddenly very tired. She looked like she was going to say something more—then she just sighed, shook her head, and turned towards the bunks.

Everyone avoided one another's gaze. Julian shivered, then pushed past them all towards the stairs. He needed some air.

Gaius followed him. Outside was starting to get cool. The stars shone above them, crisp. Julian breathed in the familiar air.

"You okay?" Gaius asked him quietly. The only sound around them was the chirping of crickets, a chorus of innocence. "You didn't have to... show them."

Julian sighed and adjusted his shirt. He'd ripped it, and it wasn't staying closed properly. "I don't know why I was even hiding it in the first place," he said. "From them, anyway. Just—the questions, you know? There are always the questions. Questions I don't want to think about. Things I don't want to remember."

Gaius put his hands on Julian's shoulders and kissed his forehead, tracing a finger over the skin and metal of his chest alike. Julian laid his forehead against Gaius's chest—solid, comforting.

They stood like that in silence for a moment, just listening to their own breathing, the crickets, the soft ticking that always accompanied him. These days, Julian only noticed it in moments like these. It had become so much a part of the soundscape of his life that it usually didn't even register.

"So," he said after another moment. "What's this about a slave revolt?"

He felt Gaius do something between a cough and a chuckle. "Um. Yeah. I may have... stoked some anger among the kitchen staff..."

Julian looked up at him with a bemused smile. "I had no idea you cared so much."

Gaius looked out at the night. "I don't know," he said after a moment. "I don't think I used to. Being a... slave, it was always just... how it was. Being angry about it was like being angry at the tides. Uncontrollable, natural." He looked down at Julian. "But then... I've been thinking a lot about Alesse. She was always talking about ways to make life... better. For workers, for the common folk. And thinking about you and how you always talked about wanting change...

"And then I just—I thought maybe I could make a difference, you know? Like she always talked about. ...Like you used to talk about."

Julian smiled at him and leaned back into his arms, hugging him tightly.

But then Julian's smile faded a little.

Used to talk about.

What had changed?

Interlude

*L*ong thought ineffective as a body, mired in debate and deadlock, the Imperial Senate today passed sweeping legal reforms set to drastically improve life and political functioning in the Empire. Spearheaded by Consul Vivarius, this massive bill amends hundreds of previous laws and restructures whole branches of government, promising more efficiency, commerce, and freedom throughout the Empire.

Emperor Geminius, a long-time supporter of Consul Vivarius, has praised these changes, saying they align Rome with the vision of the Empire's golden age and holy Caesar himself. Vivarius's supporters have started calling for him to be named Geminius's successor.

Among those organizations being restructured is the controversial Praetorian Guard, long considered an artifact of an older time and a potential danger to the stability of the Empire. No longer servants of the emperor, the Guard will now be managed by the security councils of the Senate—led, of course, by the consul—to be true protectors of the Empire as a whole.

Along with this restructuring, the Praetorian Guard will be remade with the latest in elite equipment pioneered by the funding Vivarius secured for the Imperial Philosopher's Council. This massive project was granted to an outside contractor, the East India Company, whose work in remaking has helped revolutionize the Empire...

Aurelia,

Thank you for your latest letters. I'm sorry I have not visited in recent weeks.

I miss our games of latrunculi. Your mind is sharp; you always kept me on my toes, forced me to think steps ahead, to see the whole board. Training that served me well in life, too.

I've been busy. I'm sure you've been following the news, though I have been less involved in all that these past months. I've had other projects. Other plans.

My board is set. The pieces falling into place. Moves ahead, playing out as planned.

I have another trip to take out of Rome. But perhaps I shall visit soon.

I've been practicing.

— S.

Chapter 32: Leads

LIA

They were airborne once more.

Lia always felt better in the air. Untethered from gravity, from natural barriers and borders, the landscape open below them. One continuous earth, unconcerned with politics, national boundaries, divisions. She felt safe—and free.

She was neither, anymore. They'd left Greece behind and had avoided being noticed by any Imperial vessels, but that could change at any time. And she had a duty to do, a job she could not escape.

Too many lives were at stake. A whole empire. A whole world.

Somewhere in the last few weeks, she wondered if she'd forgotten that. When had it become so personal?

When had she become so willing to make sacrifices?

The atmosphere outside the ship was thin. Inside, it was thick with unspoken words. Tensions had calmed since the gambling house, but it felt like it was only a matter of time before another cog slipped. Nothing had really been resolved. Everyone had done what they'd done, and there was no going back and changing it. Lia wasn't sure what she'd change if she could.

Nothing, maybe.

Everything.

She turned her attention back to the matter at hand. She, Turner, and Julian were poring over the documents stolen from Servius's vault—though each of them seemed equally lost in their own thoughts as they did.

The box in Servius's vault had been filled with files, folios bound together by subject, by intent, by document. Records of payments and incomes going back years—personal files, properties and reports. Some of them were from the East India Company; they were older, from a time when it seemed Servius worked for them. Some were independent. Some were relevant; many were not.

As the three of them worked through the papers, they were divided into piles—those that were of no help, by far the larger pile, and those that might be.

"What exactly are we looking for?" Julian had asked.

"Vivarius is the one we want, and Servius is the gateway to him," Lia had said. "So, anything that might be evidence of Vivarius's corruption. We're talking payments made for passing laws or indications that votes were bought to get him to the position he has now."

"There's unlikely to be a smoking gun," Turner had added. "We're not going to find a letter saying, 'Hey, thanks for blackmailing thirty senators into voting my way, I've sent along payment.'"

Julian snorted.

"But," Turner continued, "any evidence, any hint that something untoward is happening, can be useful. Build a case."

Lia nodded. "And beyond that, anything that might help us understand what Vivarius and Servius are up to. The research, the remaking. The rise to power. Is it all just ambition? My gut has always said there's something more."

"So what about Servius?" Gaius had asked. "It's *his* papers we got."

"They're working together in some way," Julian said. "Maybe some communication between them. Or a problem Servius 'handled' for Vivarius..."

Lia nodded. "More likely still, anything that indicates *Servius* is involved in something illegal or corrupt. Even just shady. If we can build a case against *him*..."

"We can use him to get to Vivarius?" Syd asked.

Lia nodded.

"Hold on," Brendan said. "What are we even building a case for? We're not the law any more. What are we going to do?"

Lia had smiled thinly. "We find someone who *can* help."

Since then, they'd just worked through the files, one at a time. Mostly the three of them while Syd flew. Gaius and Brendan helped occasionally but never really knew what would be useful or not. Even the rest of them had to check when they found something.

"What about this?" Julian asked, holding up a small folio. "It's like a record of expenses, addressed to the EIC...?"

"Expense report," Lia said, looking over his shoulder. "What kind of expenses?"

"It looks like... meals, transportation—here, remaking supplies. Books..." He fell silent.

"Not immediately damning," Turner said, "but if we can cross-reference those materials with something that indicates their use..."

Lia nodded, and Julian put it on the "maybe" pile, then picked up the next folio. Lia turned back to her own stack, reading through some mundane correspondence before noticing that Julian hadn't moved since he'd picked up the next document.

She glanced over. He was staring at the paper, eyes darting as he read it. His face was otherwise utterly still.

"Did you find something?" Lia asked, glancing at the document.

For a moment, Julian didn't respond. Then, "I—"

Gaius, who'd been lightly dozing against the bulkhead, sat up. "Jules?"

Julian blinked. "He—he arranged a shipment in Frankfurt. Weapons and explosives. It... it didn't have a stated destination. It was on orders to wait. And... there were orders to leave it unguarded."

Lia frowned. "What do you mean?"

Julian swallowed. "He wanted me to find it..."

Gaius put a hand on his shoulder. "Jules, he couldn't have—"

"'I've ensured that documentation of the shipment will be available to interested parties,'" he read. "'Should things not go according to plan, you will be notified and instructed to leave the ship unguarded...' Gaius, I watched the guards leave their post."

Lia frowned, unsure what Julian was talking about.

Julian put that document down and picked up the next. "A copy of a contract... a bounty hunter." He looked at Gaius, then back at the document. "'...deliver the attached documents. Ensure the target does not know they came from you...'"

Lia looked over his shoulder again. "It lists the attached documents. It's... it's the architectural drawings. The documents about the gambling house..."

Julian put the paper down. "He's been... using me. This whole time. He *wanted* us to find the gambling house. He wanted us to find *these*." He waved over the documents in front of them.

Lia frowned. "Wait, you're saying you were the 'target?'"

Julian didn't even nod. "A bounty hunter came after us. Grabbed my bag... He's been manipulating me this whole time..."

"Why?" Gaius said.

"If he wanted us to find these," Turner said, "can we trust them?"

Lia set her jaw. "If these documents are enough to bring Servius in, even if they are faked somehow—then we can ask him himself."

She looked at Julian, who still looked shocked, stunned.

"We're going to get answers, Julian."

"Are you really going to ask who I think you're going to ask?" Brendan said, walking into the crew quarters.

Lia looked up from her bunk where she'd been lying, staring up at the ceiling. "For what?"

"To help. With Servius. We can't exactly arrest him."

Lia looked back up at the ceiling. "He may be an ass..."

"The biggest ass."

"But remember what he was like when we talked to him? He could tell something was up, and he didn't like being used. He wouldn't go so far as to risk his cushy position by *doing* anything about it. But if we brought him the evidence? If we showed beyond a reasonable doubt not only that something *was* up, but also that we had what we needed to *do* something about it?"

"In other words, if we do his job for him."

Lia grinned. "Exactly."

"Need I remind you, *again*, that he almost shot you?"

"And I'd love to shoot him right back. Maybe someday I'll get the chance. In the meantime, this is more important."

Brendan was silent a moment.

"He's a dick, Lia."

"Yes, he is."

The trip back to Italy wasn't long—just six hours across the Adriatic and southern Italy. Soon, the hills and farmland stretched out below them. And they had a growing pile of evidence.

No smoking gun. But enough to bring Servius in for questioning. Enough to threaten him. Maybe—if they played their cards right—enough to get him to turn on Vivarius.

They just had one problem remaining.

"We have one last thing to solve," Lia said, entering the bridge where the rest of the crew were quietly hanging out, watching first fields and then mountains go slowly by below them.

Lia had been trying to figure this one out for a couple hours. The problem was that all of her solutions involved asking for help from people who might not be willing to help her (or might try to arrest her on sight) or using authority she no longer had.

"We have enough, I think, to have Servius brought in for questioning. Maybe put on trial. We're going to head to Rome itself where the highest courts may still listen, and bring our evidence to someone who can make it happen."

"Rome's going to be incredibly dangerous for us," Syd said.

Lia shrugged. "Likely. There are also a million people to blend in with. If we're careful, we should be able to keep a low profile. Regardless, the evidence won't help us if we can't find Servius himself."

The crew exchanged glances.

"He's evaded us so far. A single praenomen, unidentifiable, a ghost in the Empire. Only one of us even knows what he looks like."

She glanced at Julian, who only nodded quietly.

"Rome seems like the best place to start looking, at least," Lia finished.

"We can put some feelers out," Turner said, "with whoever will still talk to us. Someone's got to have heard of him if he's had this many dealings with the EIC and Vivarius."

"I'm not confident anyone *will* speak to us at this point," Lia said. "After the Domus Helii Auri, we'll be more than wanted. We'll be blacklisted. But it's a start. Otherwise—I don't know. Stake out the Curia Julia, Vivarius's villa... We'll have to get a full description of the man," she said to Julian.

Julian nodded quietly again, then sighed.

"There's an easier way, I think," he said.

They looked at him.

He took a deep breath. "The lab. Where I—where he had me working... It's in the city. He used to make regular visits. Used it as his office sometimes—watching me, and Fullius..."

"Fullius?" Turner asked.

"The... remaker."

"Ah."

Lia pursed her lips. Julian was having a hard time with this, and she could understand why.

"You sure?" she asked.

Julian nodded.

"Well, that's the best lead we have. We can stake it out, see if he returns, track him back to his home..." She put a gentle hand on Julian's shoulder. "You don't have to come. You can stay here or find some place to hide..."

Julian shook his head. "No... No. I may not want to revisit that place, but... we have to. I have to."

Lia nodded. "Then it's settled. We'll land outside Rome in another hour and head into the city on foot with the local traffic. Then we'll find this lab."

Chapter 33: All Roads

GAIUS

Rome.

The beating heart of the Empire. The coiled spring that made the whole thing tick.

A spring that was rusted, perhaps. Breaking. Trying desperately to turn gears that were coming loose, losing teeth. But a spring that had endured for over two thousand years.

Gaius had never been to Rome.

With Julian's heart, he'd only ever accompanied his father on one trip there, and Gaius had been left behind. Gaius had only heard the stories. The Forum, the Colosseum, the massive palaces and legendary tram, connecting all seven hills and beyond. A city sacred to Mars but these days falling far more into Vulcan's domain.

Machines, trains, remakers. Steam and gears, sweat and perfume.

The first thing Gaius noticed as the city came into view was the smog. Great billowing clouds of smoke and steam from all corners of the city—industry at work to blot out the sky.

The second thing he noticed, after they landed miles outside of the city and trudged along the road towards the gates, were the people. Hundreds of them, thousands, streaming down all the roads to the legendary city. Up from Ostia and the Mediterranean beyond. Down from Italy and Europe past that.

All converging on one place.

How did it hold so many people?

Then sprawling out from the city limits: makeshift carts and stalls and tents and huts giving way to sturdier buildings, the homes of those who didn't fit in the city anymore. All along the road, merchants were selling food and water and clothes and perfumes and more to the crowds streaming daily towards the city or out again.

It took an hour or more just to get through the crowds into what might be considered the city proper. But suddenly, they were there.

The buildings were huge—that was the first thing he noticed. Some towered four, five, six stories above the street, massive islands in the sea of people. And the people—people of all colours, clothing, classes, many remade in a hundred different ways. He heard a whistle, and suddenly a train was rumbling past them—the tram, intracity transportation. People drank from fountains on the street, clockwork contraptions pulled carts past, priests chanted prayers or curses over the noise. Above them, dozens of airships flew here and there.

He'd simply never seen anything like it.

They split up as they got into the city. Turner went off to see what contacts she could make. Brendan and Syd separated from the group as well but planned to stay close. Better to avoid detection.

Lia stayed with him and Julian, as Jules guided them through the city towards the lab he once worked at. The lab that remade him. The lab he escaped.

Julian hadn't spoken a lot this whole time. Gaius couldn't imagine how he was feeling. He just tried to stay close, supportive, as much as he could.

As they wound through the city, though, Julian began to show signs of greater distress. He kept looking around like he thought someone was watching him, jumping like he was startled. His breathing quickened, and Gaius saw sweat on his brow.

Then suddenly, Julian ducked into an alley, out of the crowds. Gaius followed—Lia didn't even notice at first and kept walking.

Julian was bent over, hands on his knees, breathing hard.

"Hey," Gaius said, reaching out a hand. "You okay?"

Julian was shaking now, sinking to the ground. He shook his head. Tears were in his eyes.

Lia appeared at the opening to the alley as Gaius stepped closer, knelt down and wrapped his arms around Julian.

"Hey, hey, it's okay," Gaius said. He pulled Julian closer, tight. "Hey, shh, it's okay. It's okay, Jules..."

Julian was shaking his head over and over. "I-I can't—I can't—" He sounded like he was choking.

"Breathe, Jules. It's okay."

"What's wrong?" Lia asked. Gaius gave her a bewildered look.

"I just—I can't—I can't unsee it all," Julian said, choking back sobs. "All the blood. All the blood. I shouldn't—I can't let him have this... this kind of power over me..."

He was shaking, rocking in Gaius's arms.

"I know," Gaius said, "I know, Jules. It should never have happened..." He didn't know what to say. He didn't know what to do. All he could offer was his presence.

Lia crouched down in front of Julian.

"Hey. Julian. Look at me." Her voice was surprisingly soft. Julian looked up, slowly, still breathing hard. "I get it. I do. It's all coming back, all the things you don't want to remember. You can't control it. You can't control your own thoughts. Your own emotions. You're back there.

"You can't change what happened. You have to understand—everything you're feeling right now? It's valid. It's real. You're not weak for feeling it.

"Just breathe. Breathe through it. You're here now. You're loved. You survived. And we will get through it. You don't have to come. You don't need to go back. Tell us where it is, and we can go. You can stay with Gaius and Brendan. You don't have to go back."

Julian's quaking had lessened. Gaius was looking at Lia with some wonder. But Julian was shaking his head a little even as he was trying to catch his breath.

"I... I have to go back. If I don't see it... If I don't face it..."

Lia shook her head. "That's bullshit. You don't need to face it to get over it. It's traumatic. You're allowed to move on without revisiting the trauma. You're allowed to move forward with a new life."

Julian nodded. His shaking had stopped.

"I know," he said quietly. "But I won't let Servius control me. I want to bring him down."

Lia nodded, patted his arm, then stood.

Julian leaned into Gaius's arms, breathing heavily, but steady. Lia watched the road while Julian calmed. Gaius just held him.

Finally, Julian got shakily to his feet and gave Gaius a small smile.

"You sure?" Gaius asked him quietly.

Julian nodded.

Gaius looked to Lia. His questions must have been plain on his face, because Lia answered them.

"A panic attack. Probably related to the trauma. They call it Post-Combat Shock in the military. I had it for years. After I fought on the front lines."

Gaius raised his eyebrows.

"You ready?" Lia asked.

Julian nodded.

The grinding of metal, the whistle of steam, and the crashing of stone heralded their arrival at the lab Julian was once imprisoned in. Some huge machine, steam pouring out of it, roared as a clawed arm crashed into the building. Tearing it down.

The three of them had stopped dead.

"Is that—" Lia started.

"Yes," Julian said. His voice sounded far away.

For a moment they could only stare.

"No," Julian said. "No no no no no no..." He stumbled back a little, hitting the wall of a shop beside them, sliding to the ground once again. "No no no no..."

Gaius looked at him and back at the machine. Demolishing the building, the very building they were here to find. Destroying what they needed to find Servius.

Lia was staring at it quietly, then looked up at the sky and closed her eyes.

Julian covered his face with his arms. "I failed. I failed again. I could've—if I'd said something before, we could've come straight here. Before this. Could've made it. I should have said something earlier—"

"Jupiter's fat fucking cock," Lia said. "They must have known we'd come. Everything we needed was going to be in there. They must have—I took a shot. He saw me, he knew I was coming. If I hadn't taken the shot—"

"Could've come earlier, before they knew—" Julian was saying. "If I'd just been stronger, braver, if I'd just come back earlier—"

"I gave us away. He wouldn't have seen us. He wouldn't have recognized us—the timing is too good. If I hadn't taken the goddamned shot—"

Gaius stood by, looking at them, watching dumbstruck as the building was torn down by this massive machine.

He'd never felt so helpless.

He wanted to help, to do something, to say something. He'd always been able to before, to face down the bullies or whatever it took. But now—what could he do? What could he say or do that would help Julian now? That would help Lia?

Were they done now? Were they sunk? This was their one lead to actually find Servius. Short of staking out the Domus Helii Auri again hoping Servius would show up eventually—but they'd surely be seen, and even if they weren't, by the time they found him, would it be too late? Would Vivarius's grab for power be absolute?

What else did they have?

Julian and Lia were still talking to themselves, despairing. Gaius frowned. There must be something else here. Would the person running the machine know anything? Was there anything left they could salvage? Stop the demolition before it was *all* gone?

He ran towards the building. He was frantic, looking at the machine wreathed in steam, looking for any indication that there was still anything in the lab, papers flying around in the turmoil of demolition, anything that could help, anything that could give them anything.

But there was nothing. No papers. Nothing left in the lab. He could see through one window before it came down—emptied out. Even if there was something, it was under tons of rock and wood now.

And then his eye did catch something. Not something he was looking for—but movement. Familiar movement. Movement he'd trained his eyes to catch back in Parisium so that he never missed word from Alesse, word from Rome.

The telltale insectile movement of a clockwork messenger.

He watched, still for the moment. The clockwork messenger had approached the lab, landing on the building next door. It acted unsure. Its destination was... gone.

It sat. And Gaius knew if no one collected it, it would fly away once more. Return to sender.

For an instant, his instincts carried him in its direction. He'd have to climb the building—hope no one really noticed or stopped him, he'd cross that bridge when it came—and grab this thing before it flew away. He couldn't afford to lose it, to miss word of Julian—no, not Julian—any message for Servius?—

And then he stopped himself as his mind raced.

What good was a letter going to be to them? Even if it was for Servius, what could it possibly say that would help them find him? When the sender clearly didn't know he wouldn't be here?

No. This messenger would provide much better information than that.

He turned and ran back up the street to Julian and Lia, both now lapsed into silence. Lia was watching him, frowning. Julian had his head in his arms still.

"Jules!"

He looked up blearily.

"Servius worked here at the lab sometimes, right? Would he get stuff... delivered? Letters? To him? At your lab?"

Julian blinked. "Yeah? Sometimes."

Behind them, the clockwork messenger took to the air as Gaius glanced back. He looked around frantically. "Get up—get up, we have to—" He saw Brendan down the street looking out from an alleyway, wondering what was happening. Gaius caught his eye, waved, pointed to the flying clockwork.

"Follow it!" he yelled. He didn't care who heard. This was their chance.

Brendan looked confused, followed Gaius's finger. Gaius turned back to Julian. "Get up, we have to go—the messenger—it will return to whoever sent it—if we follow it—"

"Whoever sent it might know something," Lia said quietly.

"However little they know, they knew to send a messenger here. Maybe they know Servius. Maybe they know how to find him."

Lia nodded and took off down the street. Brendan had already disappeared.

Gaius held out his hand to Julian. "We still have a chance."

Julian sniffed, took his hand, and pulled himself to his feet.

Chapter 34: Remade, Remade

JULIAN

They ran through the streets of Rome.

The clockwork messenger flew just above the roofs of the buildings around them, at first mostly warehouses, small apartments, and the like. Not confined to the haphazard grid of streets, it was easy to lose for moments at a time. Under instruction of a few hand symbols and waves, the group fanned out, following different streets and alleyways, coming out into a new street to see someone else pointing the direction the thing had flown, turning to chase it down, get it in sight, and direct the next person closest to it which way it flew.

Julian quickly outpaced them all. His heart, like the flying messenger itself, did not succumb to fatigue. He ran, heedless of the people around him, taking turns into alleyways and onto broader streets. He was gaining on the messenger. He had it in his sight.

Then a turn, and it was gone. He stopped, looked around, but the others weren't close yet—he'd left them behind. He couldn't have lost it. He couldn't have—

Then he saw it.

It had landed. It crawled along the railing of a balcony, which served as the entrance to a small apartment up a flight of stairs from the street. Innocuous. Plain.

Who lived here?

Suddenly Lia and Gaius were behind him, panting. Brendan was coming up the street, Syd a ways behind them.

Julian pointed.

"What now?" Gaius said, after a beat.

"We knock?" Brendan said, panting.

"We don't know what's waiting for us," Syd said.

"Brendan, set up watch. Keep an eye on the street in case trouble comes looking. I'll secure the inside once we get up there. Julian—whoever we find, you going to be okay to talk?"

Julian nodded. He didn't even have to think about it. He didn't know if he *was* ready, but he would do it.

So as Brendan suggested, they knocked.

There was a pause.

Then, he heard "A moment!" faintly from inside.

Another pause, and then the door slowly swung open. The movement was smooth, measured. Automated. Julian could hear the whir of mechanisms, the turning of gears.

"Lucia, is that you?" The voice, feminine, came from inside in another room. "You forgot your coat again."

As the door opened, the clockwork messenger suddenly buzzed past them and inside.

Julian looked at Lia, a question on his face. Did they enter?

"We're not—Lucia," Lia called into the door.

"Oh!" A pause. "Please, one moment."

They heard shuffling, the sound of another mechanism, metal on metal. Then after a moment, someone came out of a back room and into sight of the door.

It was a young woman—maybe around Julian's age. She was heavily remade. She *rolled* into sight—it looked at first like she sat in a wheeled chair before Julian realized that her entire lower body had been replaced by the wheeled contraption. One arm had been replaced as well, and Julian could also see metal plates on that side of her chest. There was even a little metal on her head surrounded by short-cut dark hair. Julian had never seen such extensive remaking.

She frowned at seeing strangers at her door. "Can... I help you...? I don't get a lot of visitors."

"Do you... know Servius?" Julian asked.

The woman cocked her head to the side a little. "Sure."

Julian looked at Lia, then said, "We're... acquaintances of his. We're hoping maybe you can help us with something."

She frowned. "Are you... government? EIC?"

Julian shook his head, then frowned himself. What were they? "No... I-I used to work with him in the lab." He hesitated, then pulled his shirt aside a little. "He remade me."

The woman's eyes widened. "You're the apprentice."

He frowned. "Slave, more like."

"Yeah," she said. "Well, complain after you've been *experimented on* as much as me. I'm Aurelia."

"Julian. This is Lia Song and Gaius."

She nodded to each in turn, then considered them silently for a moment. Then she said, "Well, why don't you come in."

And she turned around, the wheels of her lower body moving with a jerking motion, and rolled towards the back room once more.

Lia and Julian and Gaius all looked at each other, then Julian led the way inside. The door began to close automatically behind them.

Aurelia led them into a sitting room. All along the hallway and the room they entered, they could see dozens of machines and contraptions. A clockwork device to open the door connected to pulleys leading into the back. Other pulleys and gears led to other rooms. Pipes carried steam. Things higher on the walls, on shelves, were accessible with extending poles.

The sitting room was really part lounge, part workshop. A couch sat below a window beside a small bookshelf stacked with volumes, while the opposite wall featured a massive workbench, low enough to be accessible at Aurelia's height. Clockwork contraptions were everywhere, the whole workbench outfitted with dozens of tools rigged up to be easily reachable, extendable, and maybe even connectable to Aurelia's arm. A large claw extending from the base looked like she might be able to latch herself onto it, a swivel mount that would give her uninhibited freedom of movement while she worked at the bench. Pieces of partially completed clockwork messengers lay strewn over it beside what could be a broken-down radio transmitter.

"So." Aurelia had situated herself near the workbench across the open floor from the couch. The clockwork messenger sat on the workbench beside her. She motioned for them to sit. Julian and Gaius did. Lia remained standing. "I guess he wasn't at the lab."

"The lab was being torn down," Lia said.

She raised her eyebrows. "Oh. Then he definitely wasn't at the lab. How'd you find me, by the way?"

"Followed the messenger," Julian said. At this point, he saw no reason to lie to this woman. "How did *you* know Servius? Are you a slave, too? An... experiment?"

She laughed, which was not what Julian expected.

"Slave? No. Captive, maybe, though not his. Experiment?" She laughed again. "Takes one to know one, I suppose."

Julian felt himself flush a little—not that she was wrong. "Who are you?" he asked.

"No, you're in my home, such as it is. You first. What do you want?"

"We're trying to find Servius," Lia said. "We thought he might be at the lab, and when he wasn't... we thought you might be able to help."

"I might. Why are you looking for him? Last I heard, your friend Julian was trying to get away from him. You going to bring him trouble?"

Julian sighed and shrugged. "I can't say I wouldn't want to. But he's not really who we're after. We think he can help us."

"Who are you after?"

Julian looked at Lia, who also seemed not to know how to play this. Aurelia was being cagey—to her credit. He sighed. The truth had worked out okay so far.

"Vivarius's rise to power has been built on fear and corruption—" he started. But he was interrupted by Aurelia's laugh.

"Vivarius? You're 'after' Vivarius?"

Julian and Gaius and Lia looked at each other again. "Yeah," Julian said. "He... he destroyed my family, he—"

"You do *not* have to tell me the many ways Vivarius has fucked people over. What in Dis do you think *you* can do about it?"

"I am—*was* a Praetorian Guard," Lia said. "I still have some connections. It might not be too late to stop him."

"It's not what we can do," Julian said. "It's what Servius can do. He knows Vivarius's secrets, his crimes... If we can get him to talk..."

"If we can get Servius to help..."

"And what makes you think he'd want to help?"

Julian looked at Lia. "We... have some information that we think can convince Servius—"

"Ah. You're going to blackmail him."

"Incentivise," Lia said.

Aurelia snorted.

"Look," Julian said. "We've told you the truth. We're just trying to stop a man from hurting a lot of people. A lot *more* people. From making this Empire something—well, something a lot worse than it already is. You said you know Servius. Can you help us find him?" He paused. "How *do* you know him? If you were a subject of his work... why were you sending him a letter?"

Aurelia looked away. "He... helped me. After my father gave up on me."

Julian frowned. "Who's your father? How did he help?"

Aurelia turned around and absently busied herself with some contraption on the workbench. "I said I was no stranger to the ways Vivarius has fucked people over, didn't I?"

Julian's mouth dropped open.

Lia finally sat down. "You're... Vivarius's daughter?"

"Bastard daughter. In the flesh," Aurelia said, turning back with a humourless smile. "What flesh there is left."

"Did he... do that to you? Did he *okay* that?"

"Oh good, is it life story time? Sure, he okayed it. My mother was one of his remade fuck gladiators. She tried to blackmail him to get me taken care of as a kid. He was probably just going to have us both killed when I got into a bad accident, broke my legs, damaged my spine a little. He didn't care about me, but suddenly he had a reason to keep me around. See if he could '*fix*' me." She scoffed.

"Has anyone... remade a spinal injury before?" Lia asked.

"Had anyone remade—what did you get, Julian? A heart? Lung?"

Julian nodded.

"No one *had*. Then again, no one really did on me for a while, either. They fucked me up a *lot* before they got anything right. I guess it wasn't enough that my *existence* was a failure to him. I had to be a failed experiment, too."

Julian looked down. Part of him felt like he knew what Aurelia had gone through, what she was feeling.

But he didn't. His experience was so different.

"You look... mobile, healthy, now," Lia said.

"That wasn't his doing. He assumed I would die, set me up in this little place, gave me servants to help me feed and piss until the inevitable. Even as his technology improved, even as Servius made his breakthroughs—hearts, for instance—" she looked pointedly at Julian, "—I was ignored by him.

"Servius, on the other hand..." She sighed. "He's a complicated man. Maybe he just wanted to keep experimenting. But he eventually got it working—*this*, working." She motioned to herself. "Well enough, anyway. He would still visit sometimes. Write."

She absently stroked the back of the messenger, still sitting, now still, on the table.

"So, yeah," she said, looking back up at them. "I'm an experiment. The forsaken bastard daughter of our glorious leader-in-the-making." She snorted at that as if she'd made a joke. "But you get that, Julian. You're an experiment, too. Just... a later version. Version one. I'm version zero-point-one."

Julian sighed, looking at her.

He did see something of himself in her, she was right. Used, experimented on, for technology that surely paved the way to Martin Fullius's work. His work. His heart.

But he was a living embodiment of the finished product. Aurelia was the prototype. He was the success story. She had been discarded.

Then again, how did he know he wouldn't have been discarded, too? What had the goal been once he'd been remade? He hadn't stuck around long enough to find out.

"Look, there's no point comparing," Aurelia said, sighing and rolling towards them a little. "We're all in the same boat at the end of the day. People *used* so that Vivarius and those like him can figure out how to '*make people better*.' I don't truck with that."

Julian nodded. Servius had said something about that. Remaking to "fix" people. He didn't truck with that either. As he'd finally started to see clearly at the gambling house, he'd been just as strong before his new heart. Just as worthy. Not something that needed "fixing."

But then something Aurelia had said circled back to him. "If Vivarius is supposedly trying to make people better... if I was just another experiment, if my heart was version one... What's version two?"

Aurelia sighed, was silent, then nodded. "What indeed. ...I could probably tell you where to find Servius. I don't even know if I care what happens to him. But what do you think you're going to do?"

Julian shrugged. "If we can get Servius to turn on Vivarius," he said, "if he can give us... real proof of the corruption, the *evil* Vivarius has done—to you, to me, to the *Empire*..."

"There might still be those who would listen," Lia said. "Depose him. Stop him before it's too late."

Aurelia snorted. "Yeah. It's already too late. You're going to get yourselves killed, you know that, right? Or get someone you love killed."

"He already killed my parents," Julian said.

"Yeah. He's killed a lot of us," Aurelia said with a sudden softness in her voice.

Julian simply nodded in response. "We can stop him. With Servius's testimony. With your help."

She just shook her head slowly.

"Yeah. All right. I'll tell you where Servius lives, at least. He's not there a lot, but you'll find him eventually. If you don't get yourself killed, Julian, there's some folks I think you should meet. But... if you really think you can take down Vivarius..." She shook her head again. "Yeah. Fuck him up for me."

Interlude

*T*onight, we bring you breaking news. After days of debate and rumour and after dozens of victories for the Empire both at home and abroad, Consul Vivarius has been elected Dictator by the Imperial Senate. Given sweeping authority to ensure the Empire stays on this glorious path he has set for us, Vivarius will remain in this position for life unless first made Emperor by Geminius's passing.

This victory has been duly met with great celebration across the Empire. Crowds filled the streets of Rome for the announcement and inauguration, the likes of which haven't been seen in centuries. Reports are saying that the Senate's vote was nearly unanimous.

The few dissenters were heard to say that this victory is a threat to Rome's civil liberties, spreading lies about unrest across the Empire. Whatever information they think they have is greatly exaggerated; we here at Imperial Radio have our finger on the pulse of the Empire, and it is jubilant today...

PART 4

Chapter 35: Prometheus

SERVIUS

The lamb died screaming.

"May Justitia and all the gods watch over these proceedings," the priest said in the uncomfortable silence that followed. He wiped blood from his cheek and prepared the innards for the fire while the magistrate took his place.

Servius watched the routine unfold calmly, chained to his chair. His too-blond hair was slicked back neatly, his high-collared coat in immaculate condition. The manacles around his wrists didn't bother him; he was where he was meant to be.

He hoped Justitia and all the gods *were* watching.

"May the trial of Servius, agent of the East India Company, come to order."

He hoped they knew the show to come was for their benefit.

"You see these new regulations Geminius is bringing in?" His father slapped the newssheet. "New taxes, new restrictions on what I do with *my* land." He spat on the floor. "Well, he better hope the publicanus doesn't come round to *my* property, or I'll show him what a free market thinks about his new regulations." He waved a hand at the row of firearms that lined the wall under his hunting trophies.

"You know what the free market is, boy?"

Servius said nothing. He didn't have to; his father would keep going until something distracted him—usually drink.

"Silence, of course. Your mother died screaming when you came into the world, and you were silent as a lamb. Unnatural, it was. Forsaken by the gods. Ah, Dis, we're all forsaken by the gods anyway, aren't we?

"A free market means no emperor telling you how to live your life. If you find a way to make money, you make money. If you can't, you don't. Survival of the fittest. Makes us all stronger."

Servius cocked his head to one side. "What about people who can't help themselves, pater? If they're sick or poor? Isn't that what the emperor is doing? Helping his people?"

His father cuffed him upside the head, though not hard. "Think, boy. What did I just say? People have to take care of *themselves*, pull themselves up, put in the work. If they can't? Well, then society is stronger without them."

Servius's eight-year-old mind couldn't understand. Why wouldn't you help people if you could? Why wouldn't you be nice if you could?

But then he thought of the gods. Didn't they have the power to help those in need?

Why didn't they?

"I am no longer an agent of the East India Company," Servius said, addressing the magistrate.

"No? It shall be struck from the record, if true. The records show you are no longer an employee, but do you not still serve them in... other capacities?"

Servius didn't react. Instead, he said, "What are the charges, Magistrate? What evidence do you have against me?"

The magistrate raised an eyebrow, then lifted a sheet of paper to read from. "Murder. Conspiracy to commit murder. Treason. Conspiracy

against the Empire. Blackmail. Smuggling. Bribing Imperial officials."
The list went on. Servius smiled to himself.

"To present evidence against you, the court calls upon Praefectus
Destin Stormcloud, agent of the Empire."

Servius raised his eyebrows as the praefectus entered, his normal
swagger replaced by hesitation, suspicion, even uncertainty. Interesting. Not who Servius would have expected to try to bring him down.
From what he knew of Stormcloud, the man wasn't always one to play
by the rules, never mind stringently uphold them.

Was this Vivarius's doing, perhaps? No, he wouldn't risk what Servius knew.

Which meant the Praetorian had found an unlikely ally.

His father was finally arrested when Servius was ten for shooting at
the publicanus. Servius thought it pathetic. For all his talk of freedom,
his father had failed to see that those handing down their laws and
regulations had similar ideas about taking power, but they had the
resources to hold onto it.

Servius went to one boarding school, then another, then another,
each time testing the limits of his *own* power, his own ability to control his life like any unruly teen. When he was sixteen and an adult,
he'd tired of simply acting out. He wanted to find something more. He
travelled to Delphi.

The Pythian oracle was popular, rich citizens willing to offer anything to the gods for some glimpse of their future. He convinced one
patrician to sponsor him, offering him greater glory for getting an
extra vision of the future and a promise of servitude he had no intention of keeping.

He wanted to see for himself what the gods thought of him. If they
had an answer to his childhood questions.

The Pythia sat in a chamber in the temple over the fabled chasm
Apollo threw the python into. Servius sniffed the air, watched as
the oracle entered an ecstatic state, the fumes wafting up from
the chasm making her high like the herbs the students smoked in
school. They said the gods found it easier to speak through such

a vessel, though he wondered if her visions were merely the fever dreams of an addict.

"I see the highest of mountains, and you astride it. You are destined for great things, young one... Danger and glory coupled in a future that will burn bright and fast. You will challenge the gods themselves."

Servius snorted. Platitudes, as expected. He didn't need the ramblings of hallucination to tell him that. Destiny was a lie. If people were unable to escape some fate, it was because all of society was set up to ensure it.

His father was right that everyone was out for themselves. He was wrong to think *anyone* had power.

He cocked his head to one side as the Pythia subsided. He considered that one could still break the system. A touch of chaos, the truly unexpected, and you break free at least momentarily.

He decided to test this new theory. He stepped forward, and snapped the oracle's neck.

Adrenaline rushed through him. He smiled and looked up towards the gods.

"What do you think of that?" he asked.

Stormcloud loomed over him.

"Ms. Song has you doing her dirty work?" Servius asked.

"I was presented with some compelling evidence by an anonymous source," the praefectus said. "So, yes, I sent for your arrest."

"And here you are, mopping up her mess."

"I just don't like the way you smell," Stormcloud said, this time quietly enough that only Servius heard.

Servius snorted. He supposed he could call an objection of some kind for that remark, but he had no need.

Stormcloud turned to the magistrate and pulled a sheaf from a satchel. "I present to the court these documents."

"What am I looking at, Praefectus?"

"These letters are evidence that Servius was conducting illegal experiments at the behest of the East India Company."

Servius shrugged. "Easily falsified."

"I would call a witness to corroborate this evidence," Stormcloud said. The magistrate nodded.

"I call Dr. Martin Fullius, free-lance remaker in the employ of Servius." Servius raised an eyebrow.

There was a pause of silence in the near-empty courtroom. The bailiff approached Stormcloud and whispered something to the praefectus.

Stormcloud frowned. "Apologies to the court. It seems Dr. Fullius is unable to participate as a witness. He seems to have... committed suicide this morning."

"Such a wasted mind," Servius said. He'd had to tie up loose ends. "Still, his work opened many doors..."

Stormcloud waved his hand towards Servius. "He admits a relationship with the doctor. I would posit that the trauma that led to this tragic event was brought about by his very work for the accused."

"Conjecture," Servius said.

"So noted," the magistrate said. "Nonetheless, these documents seem quite damning. There is attached analysis here suggesting the signatures are authentic, even if they lack official EIC seals..."

Servius shrugged. "They will deny any recent dealings with me, never mind whatever charges you hope to level against them."

"That's fine," Stormcloud said. "We don't want them. Not today."

"Then you have nothing on me."

"Quite the contrary. I call Julian Leventis, son of Demetrius, ex-Praefectus Meridianus Graecus, as my next witness."

Servius found some purpose in the Imperial East India Company. For all his father's many failings, his rants about free markets taught Servius a lot about business—or at least what business *could* accomplish given the right decisions. It made him valuable for a time.

And he found others with shared ideas.

"Marcus Manlius Vivarius," the director said. "Meet Servius, our newest member of the strategies team."

"Just Servius?" Vivarius asked, shaking his hand.

"My family names mean nothing to me anymore," Servius responded.

"I prefer just Servius."

"Just Servius it is. Welcome to the team. Have you seen our latest?"

"I was told you wanted the pleasure."

Vivarius smiled. "Come with me." He began to lead Servius down the hallway towards the research offices. "Our people have been studying the thaumaturgy of the East. Some remarkable things they're achieving."

Servius nodded, noting some of the project names on various doors they passed.

"But we believe the true potential of their work is being missed. You've heard of *Thaumaturgy: Technology, Biology, and the Forces of Nature*? *Philosophy of Steam*?"

Servius nodded. Seminal philosophical and technological works.

Vivarius opened a door. Surgeons laboured over bodies, blood covering gloved arms. Servius held a scented cloth to his nose; Vivarius seemed to revel in it.

"Remaking?" Servius asked, behind the cloth.

Vivarius smiled. "We believe there's potential here for so much more..."

Julian's testimony was damning. Servius listened with interest to the boy's description of the carnage Martin Fullius wrought at Servius's demands. And of course, Stormcloud had records of a few of the victims, showing Servius's hand in their untimely deaths.

Some of it was, of course, circumstantial. Servius had attempted to remain mostly above the actual crimes committed. But there was enough to be convicted, especially if the magistrate *wanted* to convict him.

Of more interest to him right now was Julian. He spoke of his experiences with horror and barely contained hatred. But he was stronger than he used to be. The heart that Servius knew powered him had worked. And he still had the fervour that Servius had recognized those years ago. The anger at the world.

Good.

As Julian was escorted out once more, casting one glance back at him, Servius looked to the magistrate.

"Fine," he said calmly. "It looks like you have me."

"Are you pleading guilty, then?" Stormcloud asked.

Servius ignored him. "Why don't you tell me what you really want here."

Stormcloud and the magistrate exchanged looks.

"Conspiracy," Stormcloud said. "We know you've worked with Dictator Vivarius. We know you helped him orchestrate his rise."

Servius smiled noncommittally. "And where's your evidence that there was any orchestration at all?"

"You're going to give it to us. For a deal."

Servius looked at him. "But you have nothing I want."

Vivarius lounged on a couch overlooking the warehouse floor where a makeshift caged arena had been built. Servius stood nearby, watching Vivarius more than the fight between the two remade women.

Vivarius sipped a glass of uncut wine. "The final paperwork goes through the Senate today. The Imperial East India Company will soon be the independent East India Company."

Servius nodded. "Good. After you make your senatorial run, you can claim ignorance about the doings of the corporation."

"I hear you're leaving, too."

"I'm more useful to them as a free agent. A deniable asset."

"Your idea?"

Servius nodded.

Vivarius pumped a fist as one of the women drew blood. "You have a chance to look over the latest research?" he asked, turning his attention briefly to Servius. There was a gleam in his eyes.

Servius nodded again. "It's promising. It will take a lot of work to realize. This is years ahead of current remaking standards."

"Of course it will. But can you imagine it? The kind of power we'd have?"

Servius raised an eyebrow. "Philosophers have written about immortality since Greece and Egypt. Its potentials and its potential failings."

"Is that pessimism I sense?" Vivarius asked. He turned his attention back to the fight as if Servius bored him now. "If we can remake any part of the body, then there will be no more bodily failures. No more cancers or disease, no more aging. No end to rule. Remake these flawed vessels. Create the fountain of youth. *Control* the fountain of youth!"

"We will be gods," Servius said dully.

"Ruling over those lesser than us," Vivarius agreed.

Then he jumped from his seat excitedly as one of the remade gladiators fell to a hidden blade, blood splashing over her foe.

He waved to a servant. "Have the winner taken to my chambers. Directly. For a celebration."

Servius turned to watch the floor of the warehouse. Vivarius's arousal was obvious.

Vivarius turned to him as he prepared to leave. "You'll handle the next steps?"

Servius nodded. "Experiments will begin soon. I know of a freelancer in Londinium—"

"Fine. Good. Make it so." Vivarius hurried out of the room.

Servius watched as the bloody warrior was escorted out of the cage. She wouldn't be allowed to clean herself; Vivarius liked the scent of death in his bed.

"Like gods," Servius said to himself. No, he would be more than the gods; he would defy the gods, who had always defied him.

Servius leaned back in his seat, chains clinking lightly. He glanced at the magistrate, then returned his gaze to Stormcloud.

"So, I turn on the dictator. I give you some evidence that his power is less than lawful, yes? Or some other crimes?"

"I know you can," Stormcloud said.

"Fine. Then you use this to bring Vivarius down, is that it? If you can. He already has the power to hold onto what he has."

"There are still laws that apply to him. And he's not emperor yet."

"So you bring him down. Then what happens?"

"The Empire is returned to normalcy."

Servius snorted. "Normalcy. Is 'normal' what you want for the Empire? What is 'normal'? And regardless, you think toppling a widely popular dictator will return it to so-called normalcy? You'll create chaos. There will be open rebellion. Is that what you want?"

Stormcloud was stone-faced.

Servius leaned forward intently. "What if it's what I want?"

Debts are dangerous things, even when manufactured. The Praefectus Meridianus Graecus had been arrested, his assets taken by one of the newer senators exercising his newfound power. The praefectus's son had been brought to Rome, an indentured servant now.

"Julian, right?"

The boy looked up at Servius, sitting in a Senate antechamber awaiting his fate.

"Who are you?" the boy asked. His voice was weak; he looked like he hadn't slept in days, and it was taking a high toll.

"Call me Servius. I'm a friend."

"Where are my parents?" Julian asked.

"If they cooperate, they'll find comfortable arrangements."

"They'll cooperate," Julian spat. Then he was overcome in a fit of coughing.

"Will you?" Servius asked.

"Does it look like I'm strong enough to do anything else?"

Servius smiled. "I think you might have a lot of strength, Julian."

The magistrate rubbed his eyes. "Let's take a twenty-minute recess."

Stormcloud stared at Servius as a guard unchained him from the chair and escorted him out of the room. Servius went calmly.

He was shown to a small waiting chamber and shoved in unceremoniously, the door locked behind him. But he wasn't alone.

"Lia Song, I presume," he said, greeting the ex-Praetorian Guard who sat at the single small table in the middle of the room. He catalogued the others with her—her companions, ex-Agentes in Rebus Turner Lane, her muscle Brendan, her pilot Sydney. He'd kept tabs on all of them since Vivarius had their identities destroyed.

And behind them was Julian—standing tall. He was so glad to see the heart still working well. Beside Julian, a youth he didn't know.

Gaius, probably, the way he stood protectively beside Julian; the boy had spoken of his former slave often.

"Did I miss an invitation to a party?" Servius asked, sitting across from Lia. "It's nice to finally meet you all. Julian, you're looking well."

Gaius moved to stand in front of Julian, but the boy didn't shrink from Servius's gaze.

Lia put her feet up on the table. "Servius. About as greasy as I was expecting."

"Flattery will get you nowhere."

Lia smiled humourlessly.

"How did you get in here, anyway?" Servius asked idly. "I heard you were having some trouble with your papers."

"Stormcloud jumped at the opportunity to make a name for himself, so we made a deal," Turner said. "Like you're about to."

"Am I?"

"We can put in a good word with the magistrate," Lia said. "Make life real comfortable for you. If you cooperate."

"Afraid Stormcloud won't get me to flip? Wish you could be the one out there putting the pressure on me? Oh, to be a Praetorian Guard again—though I suppose you'd pretty much be working for Vivarius now if you were. I hear he's made some changes."

Lia shrugged. "You know the benefit of not being official anymore? I don't need to go through official channels. You tell Stormcloud what he wants, maybe he does the right thing for once and maybe he can do something about Vivarius."

"You tell *me*, and I know I can."

Servius snorted. "Of course. Ever the crusader. And what exactly would you want to know?"

Julian stepped forward, unable to contain himself any longer. "Whose orders were you under?"

"When?"

"When you put me on that airship."

Servius smiled. "You did that all by yourself, Julian. Your own anger, your own self-righteousness. The Senate would have deserved it, no?"

"I know you manipulated me. I know you made sure I'd get there. Vivarius wouldn't have been in Rome. Did he hope to rise to power faster if the Senate weren't in his way?"

Servius smiled. "Oh, Vivarius would have benefited, I'm sure. He can find a way to benefit from any situation. But no, there were no orders. Just an angry boy and a conveniently unguarded shipment of explosives."

"Why?" Julian shouted. Gaius put a hand on his arm.

Servius leaned back in his chair and turned to Lia. "I'll tell Storm-cloud what he wants. I've no love for Vivarius anymore."

"Just like that?" Lia asked. "What's the catch?"

"No catch."

It was weeks since Julian had fled the lab. Servius put down the pen, pausing in his letter writing as a radio broadcast interrupted the music he'd been listening to.

Vivarius had just enacted a curfew in the British Province to try to curtail unrest. It wouldn't work, of course, and Servius knew Vivarius knew it.

Servius turned to look out the window of his study. It was raining in Rome today. The water streamed down the thick glass, making the world outside blurry and warped.

He hadn't spoken directly to Vivarius in some weeks. Not that he missed the man—no, he was happiest when he didn't have to see the senator's face. Their plans moved forward nonetheless—the political moves, the gambling house they'd both invested in as a neutral ground away from Rome, the research...

But Vivarius had lost sight of the vision. Like the world blurring beyond the rain, his priorities had shifted, warped. He'd had a taste of power. He didn't want to lose that.

As Servius listened to the man give a speech about power and stability in the Empire, he realized that their paths were diverging. Vivarius's usefulness was coming to an end. Because he'd shown Servius just where his vision was lacking.

He would have the research finished. But why should only Vivarius have it?

Business. Free markets. Power consolidated in the hands of those at the top of the pyramid, everyone else placated by the false hope of someday ascending.

Servius's own childhood words came back to him. "What about people who can't help themselves, pater?" And the words of the Pythia and the dispassionate feeling of her neck breaking. Breaking the system that the gods had set up.

After all, the gods were only human.

Their current plans were not enough. It needed to all come down. Vivarius with it.

And Servius had just the tool.

He'd been disappointed weeks ago when the Senate had convened. He'd hoped Julian would have been angry enough after all the time Servius had spent with him, stoking his feelings of injustice—leaving the manifest out on his desk. He had to stoke that anger again.

His spies had tracked Julian to Orvieto along with Gaius. The slave. Gaius must have a weakness, a contact Servius could exploit. Show Julian just what happened to his parents...

Then—Servius's mind whirred, turning like the gears of a clock, clicking into place. He had to give Julian information, evidence he could use and track down, make sure he felt like he was in control, like he had the power to make a difference...

Get him to the gambling house, maybe. Leave evidence there. He could hire someone, orchestrate an encounter, slip the information about the Domus Helii Auri into his bag...

Have it all lead back to Vivarius. To him. To... the research. To the facility.

Give him the gun. Show him the trigger.

Then watch as the world fell apart, the gears bursting from their settings, the springs flying away into oblivion. Watch as the gods fell.

"What changed?" Lia demanded.

"I've never been particularly fond of the man," Servius said. "His tastes are... disturbing, his ambitions... pedestrian. Once we thought to topple the standing order of the Empire, the corruption we saw. Now, he's simply become part of it."

He shrugged, and then he turned to look at Julian again, locking eyes with the boy. "There's an island. It doesn't appear on any map. The Company found it years ago." He listed off latitude and longitude, watched as Sydney scrambled for paper.

"What's there?" Brendan asked.

"Fire."

Lia raised an eyebrow, but Servius was looking at Julian. "Release it to the world."

He stood up as the door opened, the guard there to escort him back to the courtroom.

Servius surveyed the equipment splayed out across the room. A marvel of engineering and thaumaturgy, to be sure. Vivarius would be pleased. Though perhaps not for long.

He turned to a servant. "Radio the senator—I'm sorry, the dictator. Tell him it's ready for him."

An airship was waiting for him to take him back to Rome. He had an appointment to keep: he figured the Praetorian would be closing in.

Everything was in motion. He'd see Julian again soon. Then, his job would be done.

He hoped the gods were watching.

"Come to a decision?" Stormcloud asked him as court was brought back to order.

Servius shrugged. "I'll tell you what you want. Everything you want on Vivarius. Just know that it's small fish you're after. Taking down a mere mortal."

"What do you mean?" Stormcloud asked.

Servius looked up to where a balcony overlooked the proceedings. He saw the man there, cloaked in shadows, matte black metal covering his face, his arms. One of Vivarius's new remade Praetorian Guards loading a crossbow.

Vivarius thought he could be silenced. It wouldn't matter. His job was done.

Why should only the powerful have power? Why should the gods rule man?

"Everything is going to change," Servius said. "I am a modern-day Prometheus. Bringing low the gods." The crossbow was aimed towards him.

"Let them fall with me."

Interlude

Alesse emerged from the factory onto a street near the edge of the city. The air was warm, but it felt cool compared to inside where machinery clanked and hummed and burned.

She stretched and massaged the skin around her mechanical hand. The talks had gone well. There had been no movement in the Senate weeks ago, despite what she'd been promised, so she'd had to move forward without it. She'd brought together an EIC labourer from India, shipwrights from Barcino—folks who were ready to act, ready to rise up, if they had to. If they could—they had to be careful. The foreman who had hosted them was busy now making sure the owner of the factory remained ignorant of the proceedings.

They'd have to wait for the right moment. A moment that seemed further every time a news report came across the radio waves.

Alesse took a deep breath of the smoggy industrial air. Her hand twitched, and she whacked it a couple times absentmindedly. There was a shift in the breeze. She could feel change coming. Hope in the air. The calm before a storm.

The magistrate of Aternum looked out the window of his study, his breathing laboured. The last few weeks had been hard, a chest cold leaving him even more exhausted than normal. Outside, the valley rolled away towards the sea, buildings clustered around a river that once sparkled and now ran brown. Cranes maneuvered huge crates off of ships in the harbour, each emblazoned with the EIC logo.

He'd been appointed here years ago at a time when his health was already failing—appointed to be walked over. As the years had ticked by, he'd lost more and more of his city to the Company, in all but name.

When he'd been a young man, a young politician full of vim and vigour, he'd had great hopes for what he could do for his people. When he was a young man...

But, alas, no more. No sense wishing. As he aged, his body had done what all bodies do. He was old and tired now; he could barely speak above a tortured whisper without coughing.

He sighed and coughed into a handkerchief again. The world was changing, moving long past him.

Distant gunshots echoed across the moors. Ainslie stumbled up the rise before collapsing against a stone.

"Beira's eye," she swore, wincing. She risked a look at her thigh. The cloth of her pants was ripped, soaked in blood.

"How bad is it?" Glenn panted, coming up behind her.

"Just a graze, I think," she said. "I told those fools it was a doomed effort."

"You can't blame the lads for trying. We can't just sit idle, Ains, not when the keg's ready to blow."

Ainslie rolled up her pantleg so it tightened around her thigh in lieu of a bandage and looked out over the moors. The sky was grey above, but she could still see the looming shape of the Munimentum skystation, summoned north from Londinium by the local insurrection.

"Look at that thing, Glenn. You can't fight something like that, can't fight the Empire with bullets and powder. We're hopelessly outgunned, and nothing's going to change that."

"We can't just sit!"

"Then fight and die, but there's no winning. Not when apathy and lies fill the air. You hear what they say? They deny our little war is even happening."

"So you can be sure it's happening elsewhere, too! If we're not the only ones—"

"'Twon't work, Glenn. They'll put us down."

"There's got to be something we can do."

Ainslie sighed and carefully got to her feet again. They'd have to get home soon, warn the townsfolk that trouble might follow—though the skystation above would be warning enough.

She looked out again over the grey landscape, and something caught her eye. A ways away, on one of the taller hills: a radio tower. A broadcast relay, maybe, bringing the word of Rome north—but with the right equipment...

"Maybe there is, Glenn. Maybe there is."

The ringing bells of the gambling machines chimed over the din of voices. The Domus Helii Auri had reopened after only a short period of repairs. Rumours swirled about what had happened—an attempted but failed robbery being the most prominent—but the denarii must flow, and so the doors were open once more.

The procurator leaned over to the man playing beside him, who seemed to be having as poor luck as him. "So, you hear the latest? Our glorious new Caesar?"

The man grunted. He wore a fine suit, though the procurator hadn't seen him around before—perhaps a Roman on vacation. "Hardly new," he said. "Vivarius has had the position in all but name a while now. Was only a matter of time."

"Suppose you're right," the procurator said, feeding another coin into the machine. "Every new title just gets me thinking, is all."

"Thinking?" the other man said.

"Sure, just thinking. Seems like he's going too far sometimes, you know? Is all that pomp really necessary?"

"'Course not. He just likes the show, the little ego boost."

The procurator nodded sagely. His conversation partner wasn't a diehard supporter, then. "I don't know that everything he's doing is in the best interest of the Empire, either," he said, cautiously. "The poor folks are going to have a hard time."

The other man shrugged. "Would hate to be them. But I don't know. It's not too late. He's not the emperor, you know? I think Geminius will put a stop to things before they get too out of hand."

"Of course," the procurator agreed. "He's always done right by us." He fed another coin into the machine and pulled the lever.

Claretta smiled and bid goodnight to the legionaries as she collected their plates and cups. She locked up after them, cleaned up the bar, and closed the curtains around the caffè before heading back into the kitchen.

"We're clear," she called softly.

With a scraping of stone, the back shelf pushed open. Omid ushered their guests out into the warm kitchen. These ones were a mother, her sister, and four young children. From Egypt originally, though most of the children had been born in the city of Rome.

"Let's get you some food," Omid said, "then we'll make up some beds for you in the tunnels."

"You can stay there for a couple of days while you wait for your husband," Claretta said. "But then you'll have to move on. It'll be safer. We'll send him after you if he shows up."

The mother put her hand to her mouth at the thought that he might not, while the sister bowed a little.

"Thank you. You don't know what this means to us."

"Of course we do," Omid said, handing some warm bread to the children.

It had only gotten worse since Julian and Lia and the others had escaped. Since Claretta and Omid had been shaken out of their routines. The Italian countryside was a hotbed of support for Vivarius and his measures. Xenophobia had taken a sharp rise. Even the cosmopolitan cities like Rome and Neapolis were giving people undue trouble.

And so Claretta and Omid had found something they could do to help.

"Where will we go?" the mother asked.

"North," Claretta said. "There are a few other places like this on the way—all the way to Berlin. You'll be safer there. The Empire doesn't have the same presence. There are others like you."

She nodded even as her eyes widened at the distance.

Omid put a hand on her shoulder. "The first step is the hardest. You will be safe. We will all find peace, eventually."

She nodded again, silently. Her youngest, a boy, clung to her leg as he munched on the crusty bread.

Claretta looked out towards the front of the caffè. The curtains were closed, but she could see the town beyond in her mind—the hills and valleys, Rome and Berlin and everything beyond.

She hoped Julian had made it out all right. She hoped they were out there still. She listened to the news every day, but of course it was all the same.

She could feel change coming.

She hoped it would come soon.

"Caeso! Get the engines going, he's coming!"

"Who's coming?"

"The emperor. It is his ship."

"Wants an inaugural flight on the new hardware? Took him long enough. Where are we going?"

"The facility."

"...What?"

"The facility. He wants to see it."

"Are—are we allowed to take him there?"

"It's the emperor, Caeso."

"Okay. Yeah, okay. But I'm not the one who's going to tell Vivarius."

"Just get the engines going!"

"Yeah. Jupiter help us."

Chapter 36: The Facility

JULIAN

The steam engines hummed, warming the cramped bridge. Julian felt the vibrations in his chest, the resonant frequency of his own machinery. It always felt a little strange, but the metal in his chest was part of him now; he liked being reminded that it was there.

Though it also reminded him of who put it there.

"It doesn't make sense," Sydney said, coming onto the bridge with Lia, maps clutched in their hand and flapping through the air. "It's not just that the charts don't show this supposed island. It's that the currents wouldn't even flow the way they do if there was an island there!"

"I don't think Servius was lying to us," Lia said. "And I doubt he was *mistaken*—the whole thing seemed very planned."

"Just like everything he's done," Julian said.

"Yeah, that was intense," Brendan said, entering behind Lia and scratching the beard he'd still not grown used to. "You okay?"

Julian shrugged.

"Maybe it's a skystation," Lia said, looking at Syd's maps.

They shrugged. "Maybe. But then it could move from that location..."

"Well, let's get this boat in the air and see what we can find," Lia said.

Syd nodded and started getting the *Raven* ready for flight.

Not wanting to be in the way, Julian left the bridge as the airship lifted, going back into the cramped galley.

Gaius sat at the mess table, quietly—he straightened up immediately when Julian entered. Julian sat beside him, leaning his head on Gaius's shoulder, tired. Gaius put an arm around him.

"So," Gaius said. "He's dead."

"Hm?" Julian said. His thoughts were aswirl; he'd barely heard Gaius.

"Servius," Gaius said. "Before he could turn on Vivarius... You okay?"

"No." It wasn't just that it would be harder to depose the would-be emperor, now.

Servius was still hanging heavily on him.

"Why do I feel like everything is going exactly as Servius planned?" he said. "My family, this," he gestured to his own chest, "Frankfurt, Aternum, the bounty hunter, the gambling house, finding Servius again... And now this island, or whatever it is."

He felt Gaius's breathing, and it calmed him somewhat, though his thoughts churned like the clouds in the wake of an airship.

Gaius nodded. "He did seem unusually confident for a man about to die."

"You think he knew that was coming?" Brendan asked, entering the mess from the bridge.

"Absolutely." That from Turner, sitting in the corner of the room by some crates of supplies. Julian hadn't even noticed her. "Or at least he suspected it. He spoke like a man who knew his fate was sealed. Which makes me all the more curious about what's at this island he's sending us to."

"Sending *me* to," Julian said. "He seemed very clear about that..." He lapsed into silence.

Brendan sat beside him, putting a large hand on his shoulder. "We'll figure this out. Lia and Turner, they always do."

"He was all ready to turn on Vivarius," Gaius said. "Think he really would have?"

"Whatever Servius wanted, whatever he wanted from Julian, it's divorced from Vivarius's goals," Turner said, standing. "I imagine Vivarius was just another tool in Servius's plan."

"Well, he's dead now, and the assassin kill-switched with him," Brendan said. "Just like that bloke on the *Munimentum*. Vivarius is the key now, right? What this has all been about?"

"We'll see," Turner responded before heading to the bridge.

Julian sighed. None of it made sense. Everything seemed like it had been in service of Vivarius's rise to power, but if Servius had been willing to turn on him, what did he really want?

What did he want with me?

"Hey," Brendan said. "Whatever happens, we'll get through this, yeah? You got each other. There's a lot of strength there. Real strength, not like me." He flexed a little, but his joking smile had true warmth in it.

Julian felt Gaius's arm go around him. Brendan was right; their love was a strength beyond what his clockwork heart gave him. He looked at the older man.

"You have anyone like that?" he asked. In all their time together, he'd never really asked. Never really gotten to know this crew. These friends.

Brendan leaned back on the bench, putting his back against the hull of the ship. "Eh. Never had it in me to commit. Too many birds in the sky, you know? But there is one guy, I guess. I've seen him a few times. Lives in Vienna, we used to go there for work. Always liked him. Maybe after all this is over, I'll look him up."

"It's worth it," Julian said.

"Ah, you're young, what do you know?" He winked. "And in the meantime, I'll just enjoy the eye candy on this ship."

Julian and Gaius both blushed deeply. Brendan let out a laugh and stood. "Ah, you two. To be young and in love. I'm going to catch a nap before this all goes down." He slapped Julian gently on the shoulder, then headed to the bunks.

Julian sank back into Gaius's arms.

"It'll all be over soon," he said, quietly.

Gaius pulled him closer.

"We don't even know what we're going to find," Julian said.

"If anything," Syd added.

They were all standing on the bridge as the *Raven* approached the coordinates Servius had given them.

"Given the way Servius was talking, I have to imagine it's some way to bring down Vivarius," Lia replied. "Some evidence of his wrongdoing."

"I don't know," Julian said. "He didn't even seem to care about Vivarius that much. What if it's nothing to do with that? We've lost the one person whose testimony could stop him."

"Vivarius can't be allowed to stay in power," Lia said. "People have already died because of him. I have to do something."

Julian looked out the glass window at the bow, out at the edge of land giving way to grey ocean, clouds heavy with unshed rain above them.

"We could off him after all," Brendan suggested.

"We can't assassinate the dictator," Syd said, aghast.

"Why not? Brutus did."

"He would be far too heavily guarded, for one," Turner replied matter-of-factly.

"It would make him a martyr," Julian said. "He has supporters out there; they would rise up, united. There could be civil war."

Lia nodded. "Julian's right. There's got to be some other way to stop Vivarius…"

"I guess we'll see what we find at this island," Gaius said.

Julian glanced at him, his rock. Back when they'd first found each other again, Gaius hadn't wanted to do it. To do any of this. He'd wanted to find somewhere quiet and live out their lives together after so long apart.

Julian couldn't blame him. He wanted that, too. But nowhere would be quiet while Vivarius ruled. Not inside the Empire or out.

"I'm telling you, this doesn't make any sense," Syd said, turning back to their charts. "Look, it's supposed to be in sight by now. There's nothing."

Julian looked out the window again. Nothing but grey now—the ocean and sky with only a darker horizon to separate them. The land left behind. Nothing in sight.

Servius had been so sure. So confident. Was he just trying to get rid of Julian? No—the way he'd said it… that Julian would find fire there. To spread it to the world.

There was no fire here. Just the shadow of Servius that had loomed over him for years. He'd been used.

He looked up at the clouds, putting a hand on the cold glass while Sydney shuffled through chart after chart. A shadow over the ocean.

...Shadow...

"Wait," he said. "Look."

A shadow amongst the clouds. A darker smudge, but unmistakably solid.

"A skystation, then," Lia said. "Like I thought."

Julian shook his head as the ship flew slowly closer. It was not a skystation. It didn't have the shape of it, the ordered lines of Roman architecture. Then—

"It *is* an island," he breathed.

A chunk of rock. Not rising from the sea—but floating among the clouds.

The crew looked at it, agape.

"How?" Gaius said.

Lia raised her eyebrows, stunned.

"Um," Syd said. "I mean. The thaumaturgical energies that are used to augment standard flight mechanisms are known to occur naturally in various forms, which could contribute to—but not—I've never heard of *anything* like that..." They trailed off, falling speechless.

"That would explain the charts," Turner said. "And the secrecy. Can we reach it?"

Syd shook themselves out of their thoughts. "It's above us, and we're just about at our max altitude. Most ships can't reach that height with the atmospheric pressures... Or at least, they're not designed to. I can try."

Lia nodded. "Tell us where you need us."

As Syd started ordering the crew to various positions to kick the engines into high gear, Julian stared out the window.

A floating island. An impossibility as far as he was concerned. Even the old gods lived on a mountain firmly rooted to the ground. His whole life felt like that island—untethered, yet locked in place, defying reason or self-control.

He saw the silhouettes of birds gliding around the island. They didn't care that it shouldn't exist; it was a haven above the sea. They were free to come and go.

Julian blinked. They were large birds.

They weren't birds.

As the engines began to roar and the propellers strained, pushing the *Raven* higher into the sky, closer to the island, Julian called for Lia, then pointed silently when she approached.

"Turner, Gaius, help Syd. Brendan, with me, on deck. We're going to have company!"

The unsure but determined atmosphere on the bridge quickly turned frenetic. Lia and Brendan grabbed their rifles while Syd ordered Turner and Gaius around the bridge, checking gauges and cranking valves.

Julian stood at the bow window. His pulse didn't rise with the adrenaline. He was growing used to the meticulous indifference of his clockwork heart.

He watched the birdlike forms that weren't birds. They were people. He started to see dim light glint off metal as Lia and Brendan went up to the top deck. People remade, given wings large and powerful enough for flight.

He'd known Servius and Vivarius had been experimenting with remaking. He hadn't anticipated this.

Gunshots punctuated the engine's roar, fired from both sides as the winged soldiers soared closer. Above them, the island loomed nearer—but still above them.

"We're going to need some extra torque," Syd called. "Gaius, grab that lever. Pull it as hard as you can. It'll fight you, be careful!"

Gaius did as he was told. He'd always been the strong one. Julian watched the island above them.

The ship rose excruciatingly.

Then Lia's voice called down as gunshots continued. "We need more gun hands!"

"Gaius!" Turner called and tossed a pistol towards him.

Julian acted without needing thought, jumping towards Gaius to grab the lever as Gaius released a hand to grab the gun. The ship lurched a little, then held.

"Let's go!" Turner said. "Gotta be alive to make that island." She ran up to the deck.

Gaius looked at Julian.

"Go!" Julian said.

His hands were wrapped around the lever. His heart pumped. He was strong now, too.

Gaius turned and disappeared.

"Keep pulling!" Syd yelled.

Pressure built in his chest. Adrenaline hardly affected him, but the mechanisms could sense effort. Blood pumped, and it made him strong in ways he'd never fully understood.

He pulled.

Gunshots rang.

The *Raven* propelled itself forward and up, past the winged remade, towards the rock looming above.

"It's going to be close!" Syd yelled.

Julian threw his weight onto the lever. He could feel the pistons in his chest strain in a way he'd never felt before.

Then impact. Julian's whole body rattled and shook, and he was thrown from the lever. There was a grinding and yells from above. Then stillness.

They'd landed—in a sense.

Could they even consider themselves land-bound?

Julian slowly picked himself up. Syd panted at the helm, their knuckles still white as they clutched it. The front window was cracked, but it was clear—the *Raven* had made it high enough, hitting rock and scraping along it until it finally came to rest.

"We're sitting ducks," Lia called urgently from above. "Let's move, now!"

No thought as to how they might ever get home. No thought but whatever came next. Julian grabbed his bag and followed Syd out onto the top deck.

It was cold. That made sense. His heart was warm, but his limbs were still chilled. Gaius was on deck and tossed him a heavy coat, which he accepted graciously. Then he saw the blood on Gaius's arm.

"Are you okay?" The cold was forgotten.

Gaius's face was a little white, but he nodded. "I'll be fine."

Julian felt something pressed into his hand—Lia handing him a pistol. "Come on," she said.

Julian clutched the gun in both hands, once again taking the strange sense of comfort and control from its heft, and looked out from the deck. The *Raven* had landed on an outcropping of rock, poking out from the bulk of the floating island like a promontory. Unlike a promontory, of course, it wasn't supported from below; Julian wondered how much weight it could hold, then quickly turned his mind elsewhere. Ahead of the *Raven*, the rock of the island rose like an iceberg through the air, a mountain in the sky. And perched on that black rock were buildings ranging over crags and ridges, rising a handful of stories.

The facility looked more factory than fortress. A couple of windows flickered with electric light, but it seemed largely... abandoned. Whole wings looked like they had been left to ruin. Corrugated roofs rusted in the mist-shrouded air.

What was this place?

On the other side of the island, they could see a sleek grey Imperial ship docked.

"How did *they* get up this high?" Syd said as they scrambled up the deck.

Clouds hemmed the island in on all sides, some flowing closer; moisture in the air clung to Julian's clothes, damp cold penetrating the jacket Gaius had given him. The weather was only going to get worse.

"They're coming around!" Brendan called, looking out into the empty sky. Not so empty: the dark forms like birds whirled. Brendan pointed his rifle and fired into the grey.

"Come on," Lia said.

They all slid off the tilted deck onto the hard rocks below, moss-covered and slick, and ran towards the facility ahead. There was an entrance close by. No fences blocked their path—who would need them up here?—but the short run was treacherous. Gaius helped Julian over the rock, wincing occasionally at the pain in his own arm while Brendan brought up the rear, firing his rifle again.

Cold rain began to fall on them as they approached the door, obscuring the view of the flying remade behind them—but a muffled shot said they weren't far behind.

Lia slammed her good shoulder into the door, bursting it open and holding it for everyone to scramble inside. As soon as they were, she and Brendan swung it shut again.

They were in darkness, only a little bit of grey light getting in through a barred window on the door. It showed a hallway disappearing into shadow. Some scrap metal lay against one wall, which Lia and Brendan quickly maneuvered against the door.

Syd found a large electrical lever on the wall and pushed it up with a *clunk*. Pale light filled the hallway, revealing it pushing forward into the rock of the island and stairs heading up. A few doors led off to either side.

Everyone paused to catch their breath.

"Dis is this?" Brendan gasped.

"Meant never to be found, whatever it is," Turner said.

There was a bang against the door.

"Okay, run," Lia said.

They ran down the empty hallway. It *felt* abandoned, but there were signs of recent life—papers scattered on the ground, lockers hanging open with uniforms inside. The doors they passed first led into small storage rooms, then quickly turned to working facilities of some kind— workbenches and machinery, metalworking and something else...

Passing these rooms, glancing through open doors, Julian began to recognize what they were. He recognized them from the workshops of Martin Fullius. He had a sudden flashback of blood and stumbled on a set of stairs. The group stopped.

These were labs. Remaking equipment. Some kind of research facility? Factory?

Or both?

"Catch your breath," Lia said. Her rifle was in her hands, and she was peering down the hall ahead. "We're heading deeper in. Looks like this wing connects to the main facility."

"What is this place?" Brendan asked.

"More importantly, what are we looking for?" Gaius said.

"Information," Julian said. "Evidence. ...Anything."

"Those labs looked pretty cleared out," Syd said. "Like they'd finished whatever work they were doing. Maybe the results will be in the main facility...?"

Lia nodded. "There are guards, as we've discovered, and a ship, so this whole place isn't abandoned. Let's move."

Nothing else to do. Julian drew a breath, his clockwork heart pumping away, and they moved.

The place they had entered must have been an abandoned research wing; as they moved further in, they found what would be the main facility. It, too, was quiet, but showed more signs of life. The hallway they followed branched down to other labs and offices, but nothing looked prominent enough to really have the answers they needed, and they didn't want to dawdle. The way they were going felt like it must come to some central area.

And it did. Ahead, a doorway opened onto what looked from here like a large atrium. And then they heard voices.

"My dear Emperor. What brings you to my humble facility?" The voice was Dictator Vivarius.

Lia held up a hand for stillness and silence. Another voice answered Vivarius.

"I think it's time you told me all about this operation, Marcus."

Geminius, Lia mouthed, shock in her eyes. The emperor himself was *here*. She crept towards the door—Julian was close behind her. They looked out into the large atrium. Statues of past emperors and remade soldiers flanked a wide entranceway, lined with low beds that might have been intended for gardens but sat empty. Halls stretched away, and stairs climbed to a second level balcony and more rooms beyond.

There, standing on the balcony, was Dictator Vivarius. He was flanked by two of the matte black metal-covered soldiers that made up his new Praetorian Guard. Below him, with his own black-metal Praetorians, was Emperor Geminius.

Vivarius clicked his tongue. "Your timing is unfortunate, Geminius. I can't have interruptions. Not now." He sighed. "You could have lived a long and ineffectual life, old friend."

Julian saw him raise a finger. And one of the Guard—standing right behind the emperor—raised a gun.

"No!" Lia shouted. Then a *bang* echoed through the hallway.

Lia leapt into the room, the rest of them instinctively following. Seeing them, the Praetorian Guards whirled, raising pistols and rifles as the emperor's retinue moved to join Vivarius. Everyone quickly dove for cover amid the statues and garden beds.

Julian was pulled behind a statue of a remade soldier by Gaius.

Lia had dived behind a garden bed near the body of Emperor Geminius. Blood gushed from his neck—the Praetorian had been startled out of his headshot by Lia's yell. She pulled him behind the low barrier with her, pressed her hands to the wound as the emperor coughed blood.

"So," Vivarius said. His voice carried down to them easily. He sounded tired of all this. "Servius finally betrayed me."

"He was never working for you," Julian called out. Was he defending Servius?

"I know. He served his purpose."

"Dictator Vivarius!" Lia said, still holding her hands against the emperor's neck, blood welling between her fingers. "You can't get away with this. We're here to put an end to your corrupt rule."

One of the guards trained his rifle in Lia's direction.

"Are you?" Vivarius said. "And how do you plan to do that?"

"You shot the emperor!"

"A tragic accident. Heart failure, you know. Tsk. And who to deny it?"

"Us," Julian said. "We'll find the evidence we need to bring you down. We'll get justice for all those you hurt. For the emperor. For my parents."

Vivarius laughed. "How cliché. Is that Julian down there? I remember the Praefectus Meridianus Graecus. Insolent man. But hardly worthy of my time—a stepping stone, no more."

Julian's face flushed with anger.

"But *you*. You were so much more. A prototype. I want to personally thank you for what you've given me."

Julian turned to peek out from behind the statue, gun clenched in his hands. Vivarius was looking directly at him.

What did he mean?

"Such power in you. But not enough. Not what I'll have."

"We'll stop you!" Julian said.

"Yes, so you said. With 'evidence.' You really think *evidence* will bring me down? Everyone who could be convinced by *evidence* already wants me gone. The point is, it's too late."

Brendan trained his rifle on Vivarius and the guards while Turner crouched beside Lia.

"He's not wrong," Turner said, quietly.

"So let's kill him after all," Brendan called.

Julian's grip on the pistol tightened.

"Ha!" Vivarius barked. "Soon it will even be too late for that. You were the key, Julian. The key to what remaking *could* be. Farewell, Julian. Lia Song. This has been fun."

Vivarius turned away, and the Praetorian Guards opened fire.

Everything happened in an instant. Vivarius fled. Bullets ricocheted around them as Julian ducked back behind the statue. Brendan and Gaius both opened fire in return. Julian looked at his own gun—but he knew it was useless. That sense of control it gave him, it was about the skill, the practised movement, almost a meditation. Not a weapon. Not something he could use against someone. That wasn't him.

Then Julian saw Brendan pull something from his belt and heard a little *ting!*

"Heads up!" Brendan yelled.

And something went flying through the air towards the stairs. Julian crouched down, closed his eyes, and covered his ears. The *bang* was still deafening. The flash still visible behind closed eyes.

There was a moment of ringing silence.

Slowly, Julian opened his eyes and peeked around the statue once more.

Turner Lane stood at the top of the stairs, a bloody knife in her hand. All four remade guards lay dead at her feet.

"Brendan!" Lia called.

Brendan leapt in her direction, crouching down beside the emperor's body and helping to try to stop the bleeding. Julian was close behind.

Geminius's breathing was fast, ragged. Blood spread across the floor, Lia's efforts unable to contain it.

"He's getting away!" Turner called.

"He's not going to make it," Brendan said quietly.

"M-Marcus—" the emperor sputtered.

"We'll stop him," Lia said.

"He's—" A cough, a splatter of blood. "—a good—man..."

Lia's face hardened into steel.

Geminius's face fell slack.

Lia stood and wiped bloody hands on her coat.

"Let's move," Lia called before anyone could do more than stare.

Vivarius couldn't have gotten far. Julian gave the emperor's body one last glance, unable to keep the same contempt Lia had shown from his own gaze. Then they leapt from cover and ran up the stairs after Turner.

At the top, a grand hallway made its way deeper into the facility—always deeper. They sprinted down it, Julian's breath coming evenly—he could feel the little gauge on his chest move a little higher.

They could hear the retreating footsteps ahead. They turned a corner and saw a heavy door close.

Then two guards appeared at the end of the hallway and opened fire.

"In here!" Lia yelled, bursting through a nearby door. Julian hesitated as everyone dove through. Vivarius was so close.

He staggered back as he felt something ping against his chest and looked down, stunned.

Chapter 37: Fire

GAIUS

"Jules!" Gaius shouted.

Julian had stopped dead in the hallway, looking down at his chest. There was a hole in his coat.

Gaius grabbed his arm and pulled him through the door as bullets flew down the hallway.

Lia slammed the door shut, and Brendan barred it.

Gaius pulled Julian aside, quickly pulling open his coat, feeling for warm blood, for any signs of injury.

His fingers brushed over the metal of his chest. There was a dent in the brass. It was warm.

"You okay?" Gaius said.

Julian looked stunned, but nodded slowly. "Yeah."

"Thank Apollo," Gaius said, pulling Julian into his arms. Gaius's own heart was racing. For an instant, he'd thought he'd lost Julian. Thank the gods for the strength of that metal.

Slowly, he let Julian go, and they turned and looked around.

The room they were in was large, stretching away across the building. Tall windows along one wall looked out at the dark grey sky and the floating island facility stretching out below them, rain pounding against the glass. But the light coming through was only enough to shroud the expansive chamber in gloom.

"We need a plan," Lia said. "We can't take many more of those guards."

"He's, like, *right there!*" Brendan shouted.

Lia shook her head. "Hold on. Let's regroup. Everyone in one piece?"

Gaius nodded as Syd found the large electrical switch by the door and heaved it up. With a series of *ka-chunks*, bank after bank of lights came to life, illuminating the room before them. Rows of desks and electrical equipment. Cords coiling across the floor. Blinking lights coming to life. In the centre, a huge conference table covered in large sheets of paper—plans, diagrams.

"Radio equipment?" Syd said.

They and Turner began ranging out into the room, investigating. Gaius slowly walked in amongst the banks of equipment, approaching the central table, Julian close behind him.

"I know those plans," Julian said.

Gaius looked down at them as they reached the table, sifted a few around to uncover others. They were diagrams of machinery, of human bodies. Remaking plans. Notes and calculations were scrawled across them.

He recognized the writing.

It was Julian's writing.

"This is radio equipment," Turner said. "Look, it's set to broadcast at the official Imperial frequency. But also—a few others. Specific closed frequencies, ones used by the Ottomans, and Americans... These are top secret."

Syd was examining the equipment. "There's a message that's... ready to be broadcast. Some kind of data stream?" They turned and looked at the diagrams, joining Gaius and Julian at the table. "Remaking..."

"Remaking unlike any the world has seen," Julian said. His hand drifted to his chest, fingering the dent there. "This is what he wanted me to find."

"What do you mean?" Gaius asked.

"These are my notes. Fullius's work. Continued in secret, here..."

"And ready to be broadcast across the world?" Turner said.

Lia and Brendan joined them.

"Fire," Lia said. "Ready to be given to humanity."

"*This* is what Servius wanted?" Gaius asked. "Why?"

Lia shrugged. "Maybe he felt regret. Some good he could do, not letting all this be kept secret."

Julian laughed suddenly as he tossed his pistol onto the table—a bark that emerged with a wave of cynicism. "No. Servius wanted chaos, to bring the whole system down. Put this out into the world instead of letting Vivarius keep it for himself. This knowledge, what Martin was working on—not just *this*—" He touched his chest. "So much more. Look—remaking organs, healing wounds, diseases..." He moved some of the sheets of paper, revealing others piled beneath.

Syd looked over them. "Would this work?"

"That was the theory."

Suddenly, what Vivarius had said to Julian made sense. *A prototype. I want to personally thank you for what you've given me. Such power in you. But not enough. Not what I'll have.*

Version two.

Then a noise filled the room, a mechanical hum. Gaius turned and looked at the wall opposite the window where it seemed to come from: the wall was covered in vertical metal slats. He hadn't paid attention before, but saw now what it was. He stepped towards the wall and pulled a lever beside the slats while Julian turned to watch him, expression blank.

They clicked back one at a time from the centre of the wall, folding in on themselves and revealing a thick glass window beneath. An observation window. Looking into an operating room.

There were no doctors, no surgeons, no remakers. Just giant metal arms moving mechanically above an operating table.

Vivarius lay on the table, body uncovered. Blood trickled down his side as the metal arms worked, smoothly cutting, parting, inserting, welding—removing a metal plate from his chest, a plate with a dent in it—Julian touched his own, absently—and then—

"They're giving him a clockwork heart," Gaius breathed.

Julian had stepped up beside him. "And after that, a clockwork everything else," he said.

Gaius took his hand, then pulled him closer, holding Julian to his chest, both of them staring as the others joined them.

Vivarius was replacing his aging body. Vivarius was remaking anything that in his mind could become diseased, sick, or dying.

Vivarius was Dictator for Life, like Caesar before him. And he planned for that life to never end. The reality was dawning on all of them.

Gaius watched in despair as Vivarius's heart came to life. It pumped in unison with Julian's, ticking away beneath his touch.

They stared. They couldn't move.

Suddenly, Brendan slammed the butt of his rifle against the glass. It barely scratched it, but it pulled everyone from their stunned reveries.

Syd looked back towards the table in the centre of the room. "Well, let's do it then," they said.

"What?" Brendan asked.

"Broadcast this. Servius has given us what we need, right? We broadcast this out to the world, and everyone has access to this technology. No more secrets. Vivarius doesn't get it all to himself. He gets real opposition, right? And people can be helped, can be healed—"

"But it *won't* help," Julian suddenly yelled, pulling away from Gaius, who felt Julian tense and released his embrace. Julian turned his back on the operating room. "Even if we broadcast this data, this research, like Servius *wants*, who gets it? The Ottomans. The Americans. Right? Top secret military frequencies. Sure, maybe Vivarius gets some opposition—he won't rule the *world* uncontested—but it's all just more war. And the Empire, and the people—we'll all still get walked over, caught in the crossfire. The rich and powerful will make themselves immortal and just bring themselves more riches and power. You and I? We're just as fucked as ever. More so. And all this, as if it's *people* that need fixing and not this fucked-up world, this fucked-up Empire." He grabbed a microphone off a nearby desk and threw it across the room.

Gaius flinched, stepped towards Julian, but Julian was having none of it. His eyes were wild, darting around the room like he wasn't even here.

"I've been *used*. This whole time. My whole *life*. Used by Vivarius and used by Servius. To develop this technology. To try to bring chaos to the world and power to a few. And even this—led here to serve *Servius's* goals, and no one else's. This won't even create anarchy. This isn't freedom.

"This isn't what *I* want."

"So, what do we do?" Gaius asked, quietly.

He saw tears prick Julian's eyes. He turned back to the window and slammed the lever, forcing the metal slats back into place, hiding Vivarius once more.

"I don't know," he said as the operating room disappeared. He sounded angry, he sounded broken, but mostly he just sounded empty.

The room fell into silence for a moment, save for the whir of machines, the hum of electricity.

Outside, ships rose in the grey sky. The same sleek Imperial ships as the one they saw docked earlier, climbing to the level of the island, coming closer.

Gaius frowned. This technology—it would make Vivarius nigh-immortal. It could make his enemies immortal. But what about everyone else?

"What are we going to do?" he asked again.

Julian shook his head, uncertain.

"What can we do?" Syd said.

Lia was quiet. She and Julian looked at each other. Both so close to an answer, and yet without one.

"In spite of all that, we *could* broadcast this," Lia said. "It's not perfect, but it's something. Better than leaving it only in Vivarius's hands."

"And do exactly what Servius wanted?" Julian asked. He shook his head. Something pounded against the door.

"We destroy it, maybe," Brendan said. "Bring this place down. No one gets it."

"But there's so much good, here!" Syd said. "This knowledge, think how many people this could help, how much pain could be lessened!"

Gaius stepped forward and put a hand on Julian's shoulder. "What if we *do* broadcast it?" he said. Julian looked at him, about to protest, but Gaius kept talking. "Just—not how Servius wanted." He looked at Syd, at Turner. "It's set to broadcast, what, only to military leaders? Could we *expand* that?"

Syd nodded. "Sure. To what?"

"Everyone."

They raised their brow. "I'd have to adjust some settings at the tower, probably..."

Julian looked at him. Gaius looked back. "Broadcast it to everyone.

Not just the rich and powerful. Not just military or EIC or whatever. Everyone. Put it in *everyone's* hands."

Julian shook his head, getting angry again. "But that won't help! Even if you sent this data to everyone in the world—remaking takes *resources*. It takes *power*. You think if Claretta and Omid hear this on the radio, all their problems are solved? They won't be able to do anything about it. Only the *powerful* will."

Gaius nodded. "I know—but it can help *some* others. It could help Alesse, and she *has* resources. It could help that old magistrate in Aternum, help him stand up to the EIC. You're right, it can't immediately help *everyone*, but it can help some people. Help people who not only can stand up to Vivarius, but also people who can help *others*."

Julian sighed and shook his head. "Sure, that's better, I guess. But it's not enough. The problems aren't with *people*, they're with society and culture and government. You can't create equality with something like this when there are power structures that already exist! It's not *enough*."

"Of course not," Gaius said. His thoughts charged forward like a train, no slowing them down now. "Of course it's not enough, all on its own. Jules, you always told me how all the problems of the Empire were so ingrained, so systemic, that no one thing could fix them all. There's no sword to cut this Gordian knot. It's one step of many. And if you want to change the world, you're going to have to *work at it*."

Julian frowned, looking at him. Gaius stepped forward and put his hands on Julian's shoulders.

"You can change the world, though, Jules. Slowly. With effort. But... I'll be there beside you. I'll always be there to support you."

He looked in Julian's eyes, and slowly, slowly, he saw Julian's old look come back. The determination.

The hope.

Finally, Julian slowly nodded. "I think... I think maybe there are some things we can do."

The others gathered around. "What are you thinking?" Lia asked.

"We do what Gaius suggested. Expand the broadcast. Send it out to everyone, across all the bands we can."

"I can get the tower ready if I can get up there," Syd said.

Lia nodded. "I'll go with you in case there are more guards."

"Good," Julian said. "Thank you. And at the same time... Brendan suggested we bring this place down. Make sure Vivarius can't use it again. A setback, at least. Brendan?"

Brendan nodded. "I can rig something up downstairs?"

"Be careful."

Turner began moving towards the door.

"Turner?" Lia said.

"We can do one more thing," Turner said. "This is our only chance—if Vivarius dies *now*, then it's a mechanical failure. An accident befalling a man who reached too far. No martyrdom. No uprising."

"The guards are still out there," Syd said, worry clear in their voice.

"Brendan can cover me on his way down."

"Be careful."

Lia didn't object. She couldn't. Julian nodded.

"And you?" Lia asked Julian.

"I have a message to broadcast along with the data," he said. His eyes were darting around as his mind raced. "Maybe we can change some minds. I don't know."

Lia nodded.

Gaius looked at Julian. Saw the familiar determination. He couldn't see the future. But for the first time in a long time, he saw hope.

Chapter 38: The Coming Storm

LIA

Lia and Syd left the room across from where they'd come in. Syd had spotted some cables heading into the walls in this direction and thought they remembered seeing a tower. They hoped it was accessible.

The hallways were dark, this side of the building apparently unnecessary for Vivarius's operation. They moved quietly just in case, but as fast as their attempted stealth would let them.

At one point, not too long ago, Lia had stopped caring what happened to the Empire. It was broken. Vivarius was corrupt, and it all needed to stop. She wasn't a Praetorian Guard any longer—what was stopping her?

But then, just now, she'd seen the look in Julian's eyes. It was a look that reminded her of herself many years ago. It was a look that reminded her what she once fought for.

And suddenly, title or not, she felt like a Praetorian Guard again. Running a dangerous mission with her team, but this time not to stop a dangerous spy or terrorist cell, corruption or injustice. This time, to stop a would-be despot. To keep her Empire alive—

No. To keep the *people* of the Empire alive. The structure didn't matter, the title, the power. What mattered were the people.

Could they stop Vivarius? She didn't know.

Could they help someone, anyone, to survive the world Vivarius was creating?

She thought, maybe, yes.

"Here," Syd said. They'd been throwing open doors as they moved and now stood at the foot of a tight, twisting staircase.

Lia nodded. "Go!"

Syd started up the stairs—just as a dark shape appeared at the far end of the dim hallway and a gunshot rang out, echoing loudly in the mostly empty hall.

Lia dove towards the door Syd had disappeared through, levelling her own rifle and returning fire to give them cover before slamming the door shut and taking the steps two at a time up behind Syd.

"Those guys are creepy," Lia panted as she caught up.

"I much prefer the old model Praetorian," Syd responded. They were fiddling with their own bag as they ran—and almost fell, tripping up the stairs. Lia caught their arm, then they pushed through a door at the top together—just as they heard the door below them crash open.

They found themselves in an observation room, small, at the top of the radio tower. Windows looked out at the rain and the dark and sleek Imperial ships floating towards them. Radio equipment abandoned. A single door exited to the outside, to a tiny platform and ladder up to the radio dishes above.

Syd pushed something into Lia's hand.

"What is this?" Lia asked. It was a long strip of whitish metal.

"Magnesium," Syd said. "Put it in the door seal and ignite it. It'll fuse the door shut."

Lia looked up at them. "There's no going back through there—"

"Do it, Lia. If it gives us the time to give Julian what he needs—if we can make that happen—gods, Lia, I don't know what else we can do. And we won't be able to do any of it if they get in here while I'm working."

"Sydney," Lia said. "This was never your gig. You should've stayed on that skystation—"

"I would have died of boredom. Lia, you didn't force me to join you—not this time, not last. I choose this."

They could hear feet running up the metal stairs below them.

Lia nodded.

She turned to the door, pressing the strip of metal between the door and jamb. Just as the sound of feet outside was reaching the top of the stairs, she struck a match. The metal suddenly flared a blinding white, and Lia turned away. Moments later, something pushed against the door—but it held, fused shut.

She turned around, surveying the radio equipment in front of them. "Now what?" she asked.

Syd had been looking over the equipment and grimaced. "Yeah. We're going to have to go outside."

"What?"

"This place isn't set up for, you know, mass communication. It's a secret base. They're set up to access very specific bands, and that's about it. Even what's set up now—the bands Servius presumably prepared—is a little beyond what they expected here. I'm going to have to manually adjust some things, and that means accessing the dishes."

Lia looked outside. The rain was hard now, blown by a strong wind against the windows. Then she looked around the room. "Any cables in here that aren't needed?"

Syd frowned. "Why?"

"We're not going out there without tying ourselves down, Syd. We may not survive the day, but we've got to survive the next few minutes."

There was another bang against the door.

Syd nodded. "I'm sure there are."

They moved quickly, opening panels on pieces of equipment and pulling out loops of wire and cable. Lia went where Syd pointed, sparks flying around her. Soon they had enough. Lia tied a loop around her own waist and one around Syd's, then, holding the loose ends, nodded towards the door to the outside.

The air was bracingly cold as the wind blew the door from their hands. The rain hit them like hailstones. Lia pulled up her collar, and Syd gasped—but they pushed forward into the wind.

The door opened onto a tiny platform next to a ladder that climbed up the remainder of the tower. At the top, a tiny walkway circled the massive radio dishes. Lia tied the end of Syd's cord to the ladder, then her own, and Syd began to climb.

The metal of the ladder was freezing and slippery with wet. Syd wrapped their hands in their coat sleeves and ascended slowly. Lia kept her hand on their back as long as she could, then watched tensely. Once they'd scrambled over the top, Lia followed.

Syd was already getting to work as Lia tied additional holds to the top of the ladder. The platform was slick and small—she almost slipped as soon as she got onto it. As Syd tried to pry open small boxes at the bases of the dishes, eyes darting around as they did calculations in their head, Lia looked out at the dark sky around them.

Below, the facility stretched out, several wings climbing over the rocks of this impossible island—and beyond them, dark clouds and a ten-thousand-foot drop to the ocean. In that dark sky, those sleek Imperial airships were moving towards them.

"How *do* those things fly?" Syd panted, trying to push one of the dishes. Lia turned to help—it was stiff, but together they could move it slowly.

"You're the one that understands the physics," Lia grunted.

"I don't, though. We barely made it up this high. They must have some new thaumaturgical augmentation technology…"

"The research," Lia said, suddenly remembering. "The people on the train were talking about new ship technology, the ability to fly above the clouds."

"Guess it worked."

One of the ships was turning towards them now, and moving quickly in their direction.

"How long?" Lia said.

"A few more minutes?"

"Don't know if we have that long, Syd. I think we've been seen."

"I'm moving!"

Then Lia saw a more imminent threat.

She'd forgotten about the winged soldiers.

"Hurry, Syd!" She slung her rifle off her back as her coat whipped around her. She fired towards the flying forms, which dipped and banked in response. She heard the distant crack of their guns—something showered sparks on her. She fired back again, hoping to keep them too busy dodging to shoot at them.

The Imperial ship flew closer.

"Syd!"

"I need another minute!"

The winged soldiers soared close, splitting off to flank them, circling the tower. Lia fired impotently. The soldiers raised guns as they flew into sight.

Then—gunshots.

And one of the soldiers dropped out of the sky.

The other banked quickly, pulling in its wings to roll to the side as another volley of shots rang out—from the Imperial airship.

Lia frowned, then saw her shot and fired at the remaining soldier. They fell.

She reloaded, numb fingers fumbling the ammunition, turning to face the Imperial ship, unsure what would come next.

She could see a figure now on the deck. She aimed her rifle.

And then she recognized him.

"Stormcloud?"

She saw the praefectus wave as the ship approached, slowing.

"Captain Lia Song. In a spot of trouble, as usual?"

"What in Mars's armpits are you doing here?" Lia called over the wind.

"We followed you. Figured that East India asshole told you something before he got offed. Didn't expect to find you trapped at the top of a radio tower."

"You shot one of those soldiers!"

"I'm hoping they were, uh, private security. Otherwise, that may have been *slightly* treasonous. Regardless, something to deal with another time. What are you doing, Song?"

The airship had slowed to a hover only twenty feet away from the tower and was slowly turning its broadside to them.

"Almost got it," Syd said, just loud enough for Lia to hear over the rain.

"Trying to make a difference," Lia called. "You?"

"Saving your ass again, apparently."

"Again?"

"What's the plan, Song? Where's your crew?"

"Downstairs. Waiting for us. We're going to stop him, Destin, or at least slow him down. Vivarius, he—he had Geminius shot. He has secret research here, he's trying to make himself... well, immortal. I won't let him keep it secret. We're going to send a message to the whole Empire. Maybe change things."

Destin watched her with arms crossed.

"Got it!" Syd hissed.

Then an explosion rocked the tower, coming from below. Lia slipped, grabbed onto a dish for stability. The guards had found a way through the door.

"His guards are coming, Stormcloud. What's it going to be?"

Destin cocked his head to the side. Lia heard the outside door open at the base of the ladder. Then Destin drew a pistol and pointed it—down. He fired, and a few of his own legionaries ran up beside him, forcing the Praetorian back inside for cover.

"What was that about treason?" Lia yelled.

"I'll deal with that later."

"Doing the right thing, Stormcloud?" Lia said. "I'm amazed."

"I *just* started to like you, Song. Don't fuck that up. Men, take the tower."

His soldiers grabbed lines off the side of the ship and began swinging down towards the door and the Praetorian. Then he threw a couple lines over to Lia, who grabbed them out of the air.

"Get on the ship, Song."

Lia looked back to Syd, who'd pulled a radio microphone out of one of the boxes by the radio dishes. "Julian, we're a go," they said. Then they nodded to Lia.

As gunshots rang out below them, they climbed aboard Destin Stormcloud's ship.

"Can *you* tell me how this is even flying up here?" Syd panted, trying to warm their hands as their feet landed on the top deck.

"New experimental ships," Stormcloud said, shrugging. "At least, I thought they were new—looks like Vivarius has a few of his own already.

"Now—let's go get your people."

Chapter 39: Catalyst

JULIAN

A strange quiet had fallen over the room. Rain lashed against the windows. Julian and Gaius stood in the centre by the large tables, listening to distant muffled gunshots. Julian fiddled with a microphone hooked up to the equipment in the room while Gaius adjusted his grip on a pistol, watching the doors.

Julian could feel the heat of Gaius's body.

"What are you going to do?" Gaius said, quietly.

Julian shook his head. His thoughts were a jumble, ideas and arguments and questions tumbling over each other. He thought of everything Servius had done—manipulating him, manipulating Vivarius, all to cause chaos and attempt to bring down the whole system, clog up the gears, break the mechanisms that made it tick. Vivarius, who was using the system, rising up the counterweight as the Empire ticked away.

Then he thought of his parents and what they had done. Their own careers, rises to power, the good they'd tried to do and the harm they'd allowed to continue. Cogs in the machine.

The machine Julian had always hated. The one he'd always wanted to bring down, himself.

But not Servius's way.

Because he thought of how his parents had died. He thought of Claretta, and of Omid. The old magistrate in Aternum. The pilot he'd terrified in Frankfurt. Aurelia.

And Gaius. From slave to worker to... the only thing that had kept Julian grounded at all, these last weeks and months.

He looked at Gaius. Julian's new heart had given him strength, but it wasn't what had made him truly strong. He'd always had that strength inside of him. Of course he had. He'd realized that in the gambling house.

And Gaius... Gaius had always been the "strong" one. Standing tall, worried for Julian, but willing to do whatever it took. His rock, his protector. His love.

He didn't *need* Gaius to be strong. But Gaius made him *stronger*. Together.

People were stronger together.

"I don't know," he said, finally. "Not exactly. I think... I think it will come to me. It's all in there. Waiting. You were right. There's no... one solution. Can't just bring it all down. Can't just give this technology to everyone. There are many steps we'll have to take."

Gaius nodded. "We'll take them together."

"It's going to change things. No disappearing into obscurity, now."

"I always knew you'd never be happy with that. I'll go wherever you go, Jules. You know that."

Julian looked at him. "It might be hard. It *will* be hard."

"I love you."

Julian smiled. "I love you, too."

Gaius gathered him up and kissed him. Warmth spread through him despite the cold outside. His thoughts calmed in an instant.

Then a brief bit of feedback came through a speaker, followed by Sydney's voice. "Julian, we're a go."

Gaius broke away, but held Julian's hand. Julian took a deep breath, pressed a button, and raised the microphone to his mouth.

"Hello, all who are listening across the Empire—across the world if you're out there. Emperor Geminius is dead. Dictator Vivarius had him killed, the last thing between him and absolute rule." He could hear his words echoed throughout the facility intercom. He could imagine them echoing through radios around the world. He took a deep breath, and lifted his chin.

"My name is Julian Leventis, son of Demetrius. My father was the Praefectus Meridianus Graecus; my family was extorted by Senator Vivarius in his early days. His ambitions have been long and always ruthless. When he wasn't orchestrating his rise to power, he was experimenting with remaking, far beyond the limits of ethical standards. Hurting people along the way.

"And now, hands bloodied by his work, he thinks he has achieved immortality, bested the gods themselves. Endless rule. The evidence accompanies this broadcast. He hoped to keep it for himself, or for the privileged few, the corporations or his conspirators. But I won't allow that. This technology must be shared with all citizens—no, all people who live in the Empire and abroad. And Dictator Vivarius must be removed.

"The Empire is broken. It allows corrupt men like Vivarius to rise to power. It kills those it deems unnecessary. Subjugates those who object. Lets corporations control the direction of policy.

"It could all be changed, but not with platitudes and half-measures.

"It needs to be remade.

"Rome must become a republic once more. Must release its hold on the provinces, make amends for the horrors wrought upon them. The emperor is dead; the Empire should die with him.

"I intend to do everything I can to help make this change. Please, let us rise up together and restore decency to this world. Celebrate our differences, celebrate each other. Let us forge a new age."

Then he flipped the switch Syd had shown him. Reels turned, and data was sent out along the waves.

The room fell to near-silence once more.

Julian wasn't sure what he'd just done. What would result. Maybe he'd just caused more chaos than Servius could ever have hoped for.

But maybe it *could* be the start of something better. No growth without growing pains. No remaking without blood.

Then the door blew open in a gout of flames.

Gaius raised his gun, but it was Turner and Brendan who ran inside. Turner's side bled. Brendan reloaded his gun, panting.

Julian looked at Turner, but she shook her head.

"He's gone. Unfinished, it looked like. The guards are in chaos out there, unsure—sounds like they don't know the ships approaching."

Julian looked out the window. One ship was flying straight towards the facility.

And Vivarius had escaped.

If his heart could sink, it would.

"Good words, though," Brendan said. He trained the rifle at the door. "We did *something* at least. Right?"

Julian didn't know. He didn't think it was enough. He wasn't ready to give up yet.

But then the sleek Imperial ship fell into sight, right at the level of the window.

Brendan whirled to point his rifle towards it. The window shattered.

Cold wind and rain blew into the room. Turner lifted her weapons as well.

But it was Destin Stormcloud who emerged onto the deck and jumped down into the room—with Lia and Syd behind him.

"Having a party?" he asked.

"Lia!" Julian said.

She smiled.

Destin looked at Julian. "That was you on the radio?"

Julian nodded.

"You're not wrong, kid. You could do some good for this old Empire. Come on, get on the ship—let's get you all out of here."

"Guards are coming!" called Turner, retreating from the door.

Brendan cocked his rifle. "You all go! I'll hold 'em off. Cover your escape and make sure the charges blow."

Julian looked at him. "You can't. You have to come! What about the guy in Vienna?"

Brendan smiled. "Tell him I was a hero. As long as you two get out of here—"

"Oh, cut the bullshit," Destin said. He waved a hand and armed legionaries emerged from his ship. "Get on the damned ship, Brendan. We'll cover the guards and make sure this place goes up in flames."

Lia gave Destin a nod of respect.

Destin shrugged it off. "Fuck Vivarius if he thinks he can pull this shit out of the public eye. Now get out of here."

They scrambled aboard Destin's ship and soared away from the facility as explosions shook the island.

"Quite the speech," Lia said. "Running for Senate?"

"I don't know," Julian said, arm around Gaius. "Something like that."

"Think you can handle this?"

"I have to try. And I won't be alone, right?"

Lia smiled and nodded. "There will still be war, I fear. You're asking for full dissolution of an empire that's lasted millennia. Vivarius will still have his followers—and with Geminius dead, he holds all the power. Folks won't give up that power voluntarily."

"We can do whatever we can to mitigate the death it will cause," Julian said. "Whatever we can to get this technology to everyone. Support those who cannot support themselves. Make something better."

Syd aimed them away from the floating island, back towards land—back to the Empire, back to home and the future.

"No easy answers," Gaius said.

Julian shook his head. "No. But right ones."

Interlude

Aurelia,

The lab is quiet. Far quieter than it's been in a long time. The research, the manufacturing, it's all moved to the other facility now. The final preparations being made. Though the work is not yet done, it is very close.

All my work is very close, now.

Your father wanted me to pass on his thanks. For everything you've done to help him. But we both know he lacks sincerity. Nonetheless— we *have* done great things. I hope you can see that.

I cannot see the future. My "forethought" is limited in that way. But I can predict.

I may not be able to write you again, at least for a while. I've made arrangements to ensure you are taken care of.

The future of our world is uncertain. I hope you find a place in it.

— S.

Julian,

We're in day six of the sit-in, now. I didn't think we'd last more than two or three. But what are the senators going to do? Have a hundred remade civilians carted out of the Curia Julia by force? I'm sure my *father* would like nothing more, but with the eyes of the world on the Senate right now, they won't dare.

A lot of us aren't in great shape. We're a ragtag bunch, a lot of folks with prosthetics that haven't gotten the attention they need in years. But we've got heart. No one wants to leave. Not until we get some change. Not until they pay attention.

Heart. Ha. Turns out heart can get you far, eh?

Alesse has been a great help. She and her crews have been bringing us food, bedding, whatever supplies we need that we can't get without leaving. The Ottoman Refugee Alliance, too.

I hope you're helping everyone else get the same support. We've got allies, Julian. All across the Empire. We *will* make change.

— Aurelia

One, two. Is this on? We're broadcasting?

Hello across the Empire, and to our friends beyond. This is Real News Radio, uh, the real news from the four corners of Rome. Bringing you the truth that they won't tell us.

We've gotten reports that a protest in Barcino has shut down shipyard production for several days. Authorities responded with a legion in full battle gear— what we here at Real News Radio would call a "disproportionate response."

We're hearing rumours that some of the protesters have actually commandeered one of the Empire's new high-altitude ships in retaliation. No news on what has happened to that ship—nor would we report it, in case they're listening!

Uh, what else? A handful of senators have quietly spoken out against Vivarius, though simultaneously cautioning against radical action, hoping to keep the mechanisms of the Empire running smoothly. All we can say is, check your voting records, Senators. We know you're just trying to keep your voters appeased. Let me tell you, centrist platitudes aren't going to get it done.

Julian Leventis, if you're out there—stay safe, my friend.

That's it for this broadcast of Real News Radio. Forging a new age!

And, cut there. Are we off? Yeah, hit the—

Chapter 40: Clockwork Heart

JULIAN

"Remaker, Remaker, make me a nation..."

"What was that?" Gaius came up beside him.

Julian half-smiled and shook his head. "Nothing." He took Gaius's hand.

He'd grown used to airship travel. Grown to love it. The freedom it represented, allowed—Lia had worn off on him.

Now they flew over the sunflower fields of Gaul, heading north to take meetings in Londinium. Syd was piloting; Turner had gone ahead to help set things up; Brendan was absent, having decided to take a little vacation to Vienna before things got even more intense.

Lia was standing up on the top deck, staring off into the horizon, cold wind notwithstanding.

The emperor was dead; long live the emperor. They weren't exactly heroes of Rome. Officially, they were treasonous enemies of the state. Officially, they had been accused of regicide—not that everyone believed it. Vivarius, when he'd surfaced again in Rome, had issued proclamation after proclamation against them, and the state propaganda machine was in full swing. With Geminius gone, there was no buffer anymore. Vivarius was unopposed as ruler. It had forced things to a head. Forced folks to think about taking a side.

But Julian's words had been heard all across the Empire. In some places, revolutions erupted with renewed vigour. In others, it was quieter—whispers starting, secret meetings convening as people began to work towards... something. Change.

And they had allies. All over the Empire. Not just folks they knew, but hundreds, thousands they didn't. They'd started to build a network. An alliance.

The effort would be multifaceted, Julian had realized. Working both within the system and without. Within the Empire and without. Change would not come quickly.

But it could come.

Elections fuelled by dissatisfaction and coordinated effort, pushing back against propaganda and entrenched interests. Protests in the street. Aurelia's sit-in for remade rights and remaking regulations. An Empire-wide general strike that Alesse was organizing. Even a shift in foreign interests—Turner had made contact with friends in Asia, and it seemed even the Ottoman's despotic hold was being challenged now that news was spreading that Serdar Khalid was recovering—thanks also to Julian.

And to Servius.

The last thing Servius had perhaps succeeded in. But he was not in control anymore.

Julian had found his own strength. And it wasn't just his heart, or even his hopes, his convictions.

It was the people around him.

Lia, who had heart, too, who had the belief in a just world.

And Gaius, who had the belief in Julian, the strength to support him when he needed it.

His friends. His *family. Community.* They made him stronger. They made them all stronger, together.

He squeezed Gaius's hand as the engines of the *Stormrider* hummed around them, occasionally dipping into a register that resonated with the metal of his own heart—he felt the vibrations throughout his body.

If Rome was a machine, at times rusted, broken, at times moving endlessly on, it was not without heart. No matter that it was a clockwork heart.

A clockwork heart beat just as strong.

Acknowledgements

If I've learned anything from game development it's that you need a good team for any creative endeavour, no matter how seemingly solitary—and this novel is certainly no exception.

Thanks first to my parents, who were always supportive even as they warned me that writers make no money. (I have yet to prove them wrong.) And to my husband Ken, whom I love dearly, who is a shoulder to lean on through disappointment and a champion of every success.

Thanks to my Creative Writing professors, especially Linda Svendsen, who over a decade ago read early drafts of a couple of the short stories that became this novel, and who encouraged my weird genres and my ambitions. To my history and classical studies and Latin professors too, who each in some way inspired this world; I hope I didn't mess up the Latin too badly.

Thanks to Shaun Duke and Lillian Boyd for wrangling my commas, and Julian Stuart for really getting what I was going for. To Guy-Pascal Vallez for the gorgeous cover art. To Rekka at CreativeJay and Frank Cvetkovic for making this all so pretty. To Chelle Parker and L.D. Lewis at Fireside for helping take this over the finish line.

And a huge thank you to Ace Tilton Ratcliff, who helped me understand what kind of story I was telling, and how to tell it right—I've learned so much from you, and gained a friend to boot.

But mostly thank you to Brian White, who bought one of my very first stories for Fireside Magazine's very first open call, who took a gamble on me as a partial stretch goal for one of Fireside's early Kickstarters, and who looked at those stories and years later said to me, "we were wondering if you might be interested in fleshing this out into a novel." What a thing to get in my inbox one day, and what a support you've been through the whole process since. Thank you for putting your faith in me and in this story.

About the Author

Lucas J.W. Johnson (he/him) is a writer, game designer, and entrepreneur. He is the author of several published short stories, and the Founder and Studio Director of Silverstring Media Inc., a narrative design studio working primarily in videogames.

Lucas has experimented with interactive narratives, game design, and emergent storytelling for his whole life, writing stories and running tabletop roleplaying games since he was young. With Silverstring Media, he creates queer and feminist work that explores deep narratives, pushes the boundaries of what interactive experiences can be, and constructs vast and meaningful storyworlds. Diverse and queer stories are core to all of his writing.

He has written several critically-acclaimed and award-winning games including *Glitchhikers* (finalist for Best Indie Game of 2014 at the Canadian Videogame Awards), *Extrasolar* (Indiecade finalist), and *Timespinner*. He's spoken at conferences across North America about game and transmedia design, education, and business practices.

Lucas lives with his husband and cats in Vancouver, BC.

CPSIA information can be obtained
at www.ICGtesting.com
Printed in the USA
BVHW041755080622
639178BV00001B/1